SUITS and SPARK PLUGS

ASPEN HADLEY

SWEETWATER BOOKS
AN IMPRINT OF CEDAR FORT, INC.
SPRINGVILLE, UTAH

This is a work of fiction. The characters, names, incidents, places, and dialogue are products of the author's imagination and are not to be construed as real. The views expressed within this work are the sole responsibility of the author and do not necessarily reflect the position of Cedar Fort, Inc., or any other entity.

ISBN 13: 978-1-4621-3818-0

Published by Sweetwater Books, an imprint of Cedar Fort, Inc.
2373 W. 700 S., Springville, UT, 84663
Distributed by Cedar Fort, Inc., www.cedarfort.com

LIBRARY OF CONGRESS CONTROL NUMBER: 2020945615

Cover design by Shawnda T. Craig

Printed in the United States of America

10 9 8 7 6 5 4 3 2 1

Printed on acid-free paper

For Joel and Jasec, my two sons.

You were named for men who are

dependable, loving, selfless, and honorable.

You have those same qualities.

Which is all that really matters.

ADDITIONAL BOOKS BY ASPEN HADLEY

Simply Starstruck

Blind Dates, Bridesmaids,
and Other Disasters

ACKNOWLEDGMENTS

My husband, Steve, whose name I try to work into every novel. He's my biggest support, my number-one fan, and the one whose wisdom I constantly seek. He's my drink run driver, my back scratcher, and the soother of my hurts. He's the guy who keeps the freezer stocked with ice and reminds me that our people need to eat. He's the guy I tease the most and always come home to. Love you, Goose.

My four kids. You've grown into some of my best buddies—so hooray for my clay molding abilities. Oh, wait, this isn't about my parenting skills. I love watching you all develop your own talents, interests, and opinions. I love that you seek knowledge, that you have wicked awesome senses of humor, that your taste in music is improving daily, and that we've survived COVID-19 together with zero near-death experiences. I'm so grateful to be your "Mom-O."

A special shout out goes to my dad. My father is an auto mechanic by trade. He's the go-to fix-it master for me and pretty much everyone in his circle—a true magician! I've spent hours and hours of my life in shops around tools and engines. (I still love the smell of grease and gasoline.) It was so fun to write some of that into this novel. The kissing scenes, however, were from my own imagination. Otherwise, eww.

My mom, my husband's parents, our siblings and their spouses. I just love you guys and can't begin to express how little fun my life would be without all of you. Thanks for letting me think I'm funny, keeping me in the will, and only busting my chops like 28 percent of the time.

My friends who always ask how my writing is going, ask how I'm juggling it all, and provide me with great material for writing awesome friendships. You buy me Cokes, drop off chocolate, go with me to lunch, commiserate about the junk, and basically make me feel like the most special girl in town. You're too many to name, but you all make my life brighter. Thank you for your examples of stellar womanhood.

The lovely people at Cedar Fort Publishing, for endlessly and kindly answering my questions and continuing to teach me so much. One time they even let me hang a hand-drawn stick figure picture of me on their wall of glory. It was really fun to show off at the family reunion. Thank you for giving me this chance . . . a third time!

And last, but in no way least, I'd like to thank my beta readers B.B. and B.F. (Wow! That's a lot of Bs.) As always, your input is invaluable.

CHAPTER ONE

Scientifically speaking, the human mind is a beautiful and mysterious machine. Take, for example, its ability to multitask. It came in very handy on days like today, when my body needed to work but my brain wanted to obsess over much more interesting facts. Jake's Diner—my home away from home—was in full swing with dishes clanking, silverware tinkling across plates, orders being called out, and conversations happening all around me. I darted around refilling drinks, taking orders, clearing plates, and cheerfully conversing with customers. But the entire time my mind was chugging happily over the unexpected twist my life had taken. I, Liv Phelps, was dating someone.

His name was Blaine. Blaine Harris. Even his name oozed class. My love life had always been like a car on cinder blocks, and I'd preferred it that way. My neighbors and friends saw it as an eyesore, but I had zero plans to fix it up. However, Blaine had walked into Jake's Diner a few weeks ago, and for the first time I'd decided to put the key in the ignition and see if the old junk pile had a chance of running.

I'd been wiping down the bar countertop when he bypassed the hostess station and came straight to sit on a stool directly in front of me. My head had popped up in surprise, my hazel eyes had met his ice-baby blues, and something inside me had taken notice. It would have been hard not to. I'd lived my entire twenty-four years in the small mountain town of Oak Hills, and I knew all the guys there were to know. This guy was definitely not from around here.

"What do you recommend?" he'd asked. His voice was smooth and somehow cultured, as though he'd been specifically taught how to speak correctly. It set him worlds apart from the usual stool sitters.

"Meatloaf," I'd finally stammered right as one of my troublesome black curls fell from my forehead and across my line of sight.

His eyebrows had dropped, and his head had tilted to the side. "Your recommendation is meatloaf?"

I'd blinked a few times, flicked the curl back into place, and slid over a step to start wiping the bar top again, my eyes fixated on imaginary crumbs as I pulled my thoughts back into order. Just because he was the first guy I'd noticed in a while didn't mean I was prepared to have a conversation. I didn't know the first thing about being flirty or graceful. "Uh, no, not really. Not unless you enjoy taking chances."

"Not usually, no. However, today might be a good day to be daring."

I could hear the smile in his voice, and when I'd looked up I had felt that smile tickle my stomach. "How about a club sandwich?"

He had ordered the club, with a side of my phone number, and I had happily served up both.

Blaine lived thirty minutes down the mountain in the bustling city of Springfield, known for its fast-paced and cut-throat corporate life. To be honest, I hadn't really expected to hear from him. He wasn't the first guy to make a pass at one of the waitresses of Jake's Diner. But he'd called, and even scarier, I'd said yes.

After a slightly awkward first date—okay, three incredibly awkward dates—he'd continued to call. Blaine was the first person to actively pursue me. I was equal parts terrified and excited as I tried to understand the intricacies of a dating relationship when I'd never had a chance to experience it before. Sure, I'd watched my best friend, Kelly, date around, so I knew a few things about pick-up lines and over-the-top reactions, but I'd never wanted that type of drama in my life.

Blaine's cool confidence and assertive air drew me to him. Everything about him screamed dependable and decisive. I lived with a teenager sister who was an emotional wrecking ball, and a mother who seemed to have checked out of life. So to me, he was a breath of much needed fresh air. His habit of wearing pressed suits in varying shades of blue added to his mystique. I'd never encountered a man like him and felt like I was constantly playing catchup, but I was enjoying the game, a lot.

I knew very little about his personal life in Springfield, but I got the impression I was as far out of left field for him, as he was for me. I often wondered what it was about me that he'd found interesting enough to ask out and then keep asking out. I was driven and independent, yes, but I wasn't nearly as polished as he was. In fact, if we'd written a list of our attributes down on paper, we'd have been a mismatch for sure. Yet here we were, starting into our second month of sporadic dates and still plugging along. We were too new to have spent any of the holidays together, but he'd surprised me by calling from his party on New Year's Eve and celebrating the ball drop with me over the phone.

Today was January first, and the memories of the previous night were making it hard to concentrate. This, of course, was a detail my fellow waitress and previously mentioned lifelong best friend, Kelly, had noticed.

"Did he call you, or did he throw you down a flight of stairs?" Kelly asked as she brushed past me on her way to the kitchen. The scent of lavender trailed after her, bringing me back to reality.

"What's that supposed to mean?" I responded, following her to pick up an order of my own.

She flashed her blue eyes in my direction, letting me know that she knew that I knew exactly what she was trying to say. "I swear every customer in this place has been asking me if you're okay. Your neighbor, Mr. Matthews, used to be a doctor and says you're showing warning signs of a stroke."

I looked out to the dining area to see that all eyes did seem to be trained on me. I dropped my eyes quickly and mumbled, "They're only looking because you talk so loud."

Kelly pierced me with a look as she picked up the heavy tray and slid past me. "I'm not that bad."

She tossed her long, curly, bright red ponytail behind her, barely missing whipping me across the face as she walked away with it swinging behind her. I looked to the kitchen window to see the owner, Jake, and two of the cooks looking at me also. I threw my hands up.

"What?" I asked.

"Didn't think I'd ever hear about you dating somebody. You finally changed your mind?"

Neither of us said anything while he lazily moved a toothpick from one side of his mouth to the other, as though it was easier to speak that way. Then he wiggled his nose while he sniffed. It was very mafia, although that little toothpick move was the only thing even remotely cool about the fifty-six-year-old, gray-haired, heavyset, and frumpy-dressing man I called my boss. "Yes, but you didn't need to add the *finally* part," I replied tight-lipped.

"Good for you. Your order's up." He slid three plates heaped with food toward me and turned away.

Kelly was back before I was done loading my tray, and she gave me yet another look as she zigged past me. "I swear I said nothing to Jake about you dating."

"Stop reading my face," I retorted, annoyed for the zillionth time with her ability to always know what was on my mind. She called it the Best Buddies Broadcasting System, BBBS for short. I called it irritating and refused to use that ridiculous acronym.

"Then stop broadcasting your thoughts," she replied, also for the zillionth time.

I lifted my tray onto my arm. "Remember last month when you were dating that Tyler kid?"

"Not relevant."

"Completely relevant." I pressed past her and looked over my shoulder as I turned the bar corner. "I didn't bug you about it, and I'll thank you to do the same."

Nothing more was said for a while as we went about our duties, which was fine by me. It gave me more time to daydream about Blaine's glacier blue eyes and how much I enjoyed looking into them. He was only a few inches taller than my five feet, four inches, which made it so much easier to soak up the beauty of his eyes.

While I took more orders I imagined what oil paint colors I'd need to mix on my pallet to get just the right blend of blue and gray to match his eyes. It would be tricky because I'd noticed some almost white flecks when I'd seen him last.

When I returned to the drink station, Kelly was there too. "I'm in a dry spell, Liv," she said to me. "I need a man."

I pulled a face. Kelly had been searching for a man with the same amount of effort that you'd put into plucking unwanted chin hairs. Although I'd known her since we were in elementary school, I'd never fully understood her desperation to be in a relationship. Kelly came from a solid family, had a quick-witted intelligence that had been our bonding force, and was attractive. But there seemed to be a loneliness in her that she couldn't quite fill. I hated that she thought she needed a man to plug into that place.

I repeated the same thing I'd been saying since we'd graduated high school six years ago. "Your life is fine without a man." Then, in case she tried to accuse me of not validating her feelings, I added this helpful tidbit. "Statistically speaking, something like sixty-three percent of adults have never been married. They seem to be getting along just fine."

"Says the girl with a boyfriend." Kelly hip bumped me.

"I'm not sure I'd call him my boyfriend," I replied.

"I'll bet a solid eighty percent of your statistical people wish they could find love."

I shook my head. "I doubt that. Choosing to stay single can be very fulfilling."

"Your science is bunk," Kelly replied as she lifted her drink tray and walked away.

"He's definitely not my boyfriend yet," I called as softly as I could manage. The wiggle of her head told me she heard.

Like I said, Kelly had been in love with the idea of love for as long as I'd known her. She'd never listened to me when I'd told her she should pour that energy and focus into something more productive. She simply liked men too much and was holding on until she found "the one."

As for me, I hadn't been looking at all. I'll admit that for one brief moment, years ago, I'd gotten starry-eyed over someone, but I'd quickly learned that he wasn't worth my time. After that, well, time had flown, and now I was busy enough working at the diner full-time, going to school online, and doing the bulk of caring for my family's needs. I'd gone from not interested to having no time for romance. Obviously that's when it had come calling.

Kelly returned with her empty drink tray at the same time I was passing an order through to the kitchen. "Maybe the guy destined for me is eating in the dining room right now." She made an overly cheery face while clapping her hands silently under her chin.

"Doubtful."

"Ah, there's the glass-half-full Liv I love so well."

I grinned. "You've already dated all the decent options, and flirted with the rest. But, as your best friend, I'll do a subtle sweep while I take these orders out. Maybe someone new has wandered in."

I did a quick perusal while hefting orders, hoping I could point someone out to Kelly and get her to stop analyzing my new situation. No dice. It was all the regulars today, which meant Kelly truly had already dated any of them who were under forty.

"Sorry, pal, no fresh meat today," I said to Kelly when we were back together, filling drinks. "Maybe you should consider an older man. Scientifically speaking, men live shorter lives than women, so you could at least get some rich widow time out of the deal."

"How dare you. I'm in my prime and I'm not settling for anything less." She playfully pouted. "More important, no one in this town is rich." We shoulder bumped, which was what we did when we couldn't laugh out loud but wanted to. After a second of amusement, she stopped and chewed her lip while her eyes went dreamy. The minute she glazed out on me I braced myself for what I knew she would say. She didn't disappoint. "I haven't dated Connor, and he's here, in the corner booth."

I filled a cup with ice and started some cola running into it. "You do not want to date Connor Hunt." I said the same thing every time.

"Yes, I do."

"Kelly, you do not. You know exactly why. He's got a terrible reputation. Breaking hearts, flirting, toying with people. Who knows what else he does that no one sees?" I placed the filled cup on a tray and started another.

"All while twisting his waxed mustache and watching old ladies try to cross the road alone. I know, I know." Kelly slid in next to me and got a mug to fill. My lip raised slightly on the side she couldn't see. I really did love her comebacks.

"You joke, but we've been hearing about the awful things he does for years," I stated.

"I know, Liv. I'm the one who told you half of the gossip. Still, he's actually good-looking and has a steady job. I'm not picky."

"Those two things may be true, but they don't undo all the other stuff. Be pickier."

"I've been flirting my socks off for at least two months, and I think he's finally ready for me to play my cards."

I scoffed as I filled the final cup and picked up the tray. "You've been flirting with him ever since we graduated from high school."

"True, but these past two months I've really stepped it up. Did you notice he's been coming in almost every day since Halloween?"

"I can honestly say I haven't."

I took my drinks to the waiting customers, cleared a few tables, and totally stole a glance at Connor out of the corner of my eye as I made my deliveries. A few years older than Kelly and me, and admittedly good-looking, his unusually colored auburn hair and way of moving had caught our attention on the first day of our freshman year of high school. It had definitely helped that he was a senior and seemed impossibly grown up. We'd learned all about him as fast as we could, and none of it was good. He had his uses as a mechanic, and that was about all I had to say about him. I'd steered clear for years and wasn't about to let my best friend get herself attached to that runaway train.

When our shift was over, Kelly and I met up in the employee lounge. It felt good to untie my apron and kick off my sensible work shoes. Kelly stood next to me, shaking her hair out of its ponytail and rubbing her scalp.

"Maybe Blaine has a cousin, or a college buddy, or a co-worker or something?" I said as I bent to retrieve my snow boots from my locker.

"Don't take offense, Liv, but I don't think anyone in Blaine's world would be interested in dating me." I gave her a startled look, which made her laugh. "I know what you're thinking, and I'm so lucky to have a friend who thinks I'm awesome. The truth is that I'm a small town girl working in a diner. I'm not going to school and looking to the future like you are. I don't want to leave this town the way you do."

"You never know, Kelly. There might be something bigger and better out there."

"There might be, yes. Or, I might have everything I need here." She closed her locker and gave me a pat on the shoulder. "See you tomorrow?"

"Yep. Early shift."

The drive home was so short that my car didn't have a chance to heat up before I pulled into the cracked driveway. In the soft twilight glow the house looked warm and inviting, and rather than rush right in I turned off the car and sat for a moment, my artist eye catching the variations of whites and yellows glowing out of the front window. In this light the normally rough-looking exterior could hide its faults and appeared less run down, more how it had looked before Dad had . . . well . . . just before.

The cold eventually stole the moment and forced me to hustle across the crunchy snow and into the heat of the entryway. From there I could see into the front room, which looked the way it usually did when I returned from a shift.

Sadie, my seventeen-year-old sister, was sitting on the brown couch with the TV blaring, painting her fingernails a shocking lime green color. A few yellow and orange candy wrappers were scattered on the cushion next to her, but her face was hidden behind the waterfall of black hair draped over her shoulder.

For a moment I was struck by how much she'd grown up in the past year. We were seven years apart in age, which often meant I still struggled to see Sadie as the young woman she was. I wondered if I'd ever think of her as anything other than my baby sister.

My eyes took her in, thinking about how often people were surprised to find out we were sisters and not cousins. We had enough similar features to mark us as family but not quite enough to be sister-level related. Our hair was the same midnight black color, our eyes were the same hazel, and our noses were an exact match. That's about where it ended, though. Sadie's hair cascaded in perfect beach waves down her back. I, on the other hand, had chin-length ringlets that dashed all around my head like Medusa's snakes. When I'd turned eighteen I'd decided to stop fighting the curls and let them be. Since then I'd grown to love my funky style, even if my side of the bathroom had double the hair products of Sadie's. Curls are nothing if not finicky.

Sadie was also a full four inches taller than me, standing at five-foot-eight, which she liked to remind me of often. I definitely took after our mom's side of the family, with less height and more curves. Sadie was a dead ringer for our father. Sometimes I could see a flash of him in her expression or the way she moved through a room, and it pinched a little. I tried my hardest to not let it affect the way I treated her, but I knew I failed on occasion.

"Hey, what's for dinner?" Sadie asked when she spotted me.

"Never a, 'Hi, Liv, how was work?'" I teased as I took off my coat and set my things on the front entrance table.

"Hi, Liv. Anyone choke to death today?" Sadie turned back to her nails.

"Nice." I pursed my lips, instantly annoyed. "Did you do any cleaning or cooking today?"

"I'm on winter break," she replied, just another in a long line of excuses about her unwillingness to pitch in. I made a noise as I headed into the kitchen, which had her look up to me again. "Even if I wanted to, I don't know how to cook."

I said nothing in return, just entered the kitchen, which was separate from the front room living area. Sadly, it was probably true that Sadie didn't know how to cook. Sadie and I were being raised by the same mother but in two very different ways. A couple of years ago, Dad had left his job in Oak Hills and gone to work for an oil operation in North Dakota. It was supposed to be a big opportunity for our family, but instead it had become a big opportunity for him to start a new life.

The abandonment hadn't been immediate, but over time he came home less, sent less money home, and called less and less. Mom eventually ended up taking a second job on nights and weekends to make ends meet. Gone was the home with two parents who'd been home every evening, working together, cooking, cleaning, talking, and supporting their daughters. It had been about six months now since I'd actually spoken to my father. I doubted Mom had spoken to him either in that time. It wasn't something we talked about.

"Have you seen Mom?" I called to Sadie from the kitchen.

"She popped in about an hour ago, but she had to leave. She ate a sandwich, I think."

I nodded even though Sadie couldn't see me. Of course, Sadie had opted to wait for me to come home and cook her something rather than eating a sandwich with Mom.

I whipped up a salad and spaghetti, which we ate silently while watching *Jeopardy*—the curse of people who had to rely on antenna TV and reruns. Afterward I made my way up to my room. Entering my bedroom was my favorite part of the day. It was my own private oasis. I'd decorated it in whites and creams and then accented it with colors. It always felt peaceful and inviting, a place of refuge in my crazy life. I went upstairs with the intention to study, but the sight of a fresh canvas waiting for me near the window proved to be more of a pull than I could resist.

I'd discovered oil painting in middle school, and it was my secret passion. I walked across the room to where the canvas was sitting to the side of my north facing window and ran light fingertips over it, allowing my mind to run free, pondering what I could bring to life with brushes and a free spot of time.

When I'd been picking up groceries a few days before, I'd noticed the way icicles were hanging from the light pole out front. It had captured my imagination, and I'd taken a photo on my phone. Now I reached into my back pocket, intent on looking at the picture, but my shoulders drooped in defeat when I unlocked it and saw the time. Already after 8:00 PM. The painting would have to wait. It was study time.

As my family had begun to show the cracks, I'd resolved to make a brighter future for myself and had started online schooling to work toward a nursing degree. Nursing, I believed, would provide some flexibility as a career. I'd be able to work just about anywhere and would make enough money that I would never need to depend on another person for my well-being. I was determined that my life would never look like my mother's.

Painting dreams took a back seat to textbooks, and the hours rushed by as I read the assignments and planned out my week in scrupulous detail. There was no room for failure if I stuck to the plan, no matter how rigid.

CHAPTER TWO

I was surprised to find my mom in the kitchen the next morning when I came down bleary-eyed and wishing for more sleep. She was standing at the sink holding a mug, steam rising out of it while she stared out the window. Her dark hair, the color of a cocoa bean, was becoming streaked with gray, and her face drooped from the same lack of sleep I was experiencing. Always curvy, she'd lost weight and seemed too thin in her skirt and button-up shirt.

"You going in late today?" I asked with forced cheer as I entered the small room.

Her head popped up and she managed a smile, although it didn't reach her brown eyes. Mom used to wear makeup and dress stylishly. It was one way she and Sadie were alike. She took a lot of joy in getting dolled up and making the most of her large eyes and curvy figure. Now her outfits were more about functionality, and her eyes had lost some sparkle. Only a small amount of mascara marked her efforts in preparing for the day.

"Morning, Liv. Mr. Lawson had meetings out of the office this morning and I'm taking advantage." Guilt made her cheeks pink, and without forethought I went to her and wrapped her in a hug. The scent of her peach herbal tea drifted up, comforting and familiar.

"Don't feel guilty for being a little bit late to work. I'm sure Mr. Lawson won't mind." Mom had worked for the Lawson Insurance Firm for as long as I could remember. She was a solid employee and kept things running smoothly for them.

Mom hugged me back, briefly letting our foreheads press together, but I felt the tension in her body, the way she held herself slightly away from me. It hurt. There was a time when I'd had more hugs than I'd wanted.

"You're sweet, honey. Would you like some breakfast? I'm making toast, but I could fry up an egg or two." Mom set down her mug and went to open the fridge.

"No, I'm good." I wasn't much of a breakfast person these days.

"Sadie will be up soon. I could make her something." Her voice was muffled by the fridge door she was standing behind.

"Sadie leaves for school at 7:15. She's been gone for a while," I replied in a gentle voice. "She usually just grabs a granola bar or something."

"Oh, of course." Mom stood and shut the door quickly just as her toast popped up. "Where's my head?"

"Probably in a million different places." I smiled kindly.

"How's this Blaine you've been dating?"

Mom's slender fingers pulled the toast out by the tips, careful not to get burnt. I watched as she spread the butter, sparking memories as the silly poem she used to sing to me flooded my mind.

I don't mean to brag
I don't mean to boast
But I love lots of butter
On my hot, fresh toast.

A nostalgic smile tugged at my lips. "Blaine is great. I'm going down to Springfield tonight. He's taking me to see a show."

"What kind of show?"

"The theatre with an R-E kind. He said to dress nice." I knew my voice had risen with my excitement. I didn't get down to Springfield often, and I was thrilled that Blaine had invited me. So far any time we'd spent together had been in and around Oak Hills. Even more exciting was the face that I'd never attended the theatre before. I couldn't wait to experience something new.

Mom looked at me with raised eyebrows and a hint of the teasing smile she used to have. "Well, that sounds fun. What are you going to wear?"

I looked down at my staunchly functional pajamas and back up to Mom, happy to see her smile had warmed into something more natural. "I suppose this won't do?"

She chuckled. "No. But I might have something that will."

My smile grew. My mom's closet was a treasure trove that I'd long wished to dive into. "Really?"

"Yes. What time are you going?"

"I need to leave here around six."

Mom's brows lowered as she glanced at the clock on the microwave. "That's before I get home from work. I have ten minutes before I need to leave if I want to beat Mr. Lawson into the office. Let's make this happen." She shoved her toast into her mouth and led the way out of the kitchen and up to her room. "What's your plan for hair and makeup?" she asked, forgoing manners and speaking around the crunchy, buttery bread.

"The usual," I replied, having given it little thought.

"Hmm." Mom's tone sounded unimpressed enough that I decided I'd need to Google some fancy makeup and hairstyle tips.

She flung open her closet doors and reached to the back where her dresses were hung in plastic covers. She handed a few to me, which I laid on the bed with hungry eyes. In the end there were three to choose from. All of them were worthy of a night at the theatre. Mom quickly pulled the plastic covers off and set them to the side.

"They might be a little dated. I haven't dressed up for quite a while." Her tone and expression were apologetic, and I hurried to soothe her worries.

"These are classics, Mom. They don't go out of style. Which should I wear?" I fingered the hem of a blood red dress with some tasteful beading on the bodice.

"With your black hair and fair skin, I think something bold would be a good choice. I'd go with that red you've got your hand on, or maybe this emerald green." Mom held up a second choice. "Of course, you can never go wrong with a black cocktail dress." She pointed to one lying across the head of the bed.

"What would you wear?"

Mom's lips pursed as she looked over each choice, occasionally darting a glance back at me. "Go with the emerald," she said at last. "It'll pull out the green in your eyes and make them pop."

I picked up the long emerald dress and held it up to see how it fell. It had a wrap style top that tied at the waist and draped down to my ankles. It would be elegant without being gaudy, and I loved it.

"I have to go now, honey. Will you put the others back in my closet? And make sure to take a picture of yourself before you go. I wish I could . . . " Mom trailed off, the sadness returning to her eyes. It seemed like the look was becoming more and more permanent every day.

"Don't worry about it. I'll take a picture, and I'll have a wonderful time." I made the dress do a little dance in front of me. "Thank you so much. Now go sneak into work before your boss gets there. It's fun living on the edge, but only until you get caught." I smiled and was glad when she returned the look.

"Love you, Olivia."

"Love you too, Mom."

Mom left the room, and I quietly went about the work of storing her dresses in their plastic and gently hanging them in her closet again. I heard her car start up and pull away. The house was quiet. In the stillness I noticed the comforting smell of Mom's perfume and the more subtle scent of her hand lotion. I remembered sitting as a little girl with my legs tucked under me on the bathroom counter, watching her get ready. Dad would come in and kiss her neck and tell her she was the most beautiful woman in the world. Those were happier times, but to me she still was the most beautiful woman in the world, even if she'd somehow forgotten.

* * * * *

I was in absolute heaven. Incredible music swirled around me in the darkness as an actress sang her dramatic solo in the single spotlight on the stage. I leaned forward in my seat, taking in the oranges of her dress, the way the light sparkled off her jewels, the blacks and purples behind her. My hands clenched in the folds of Mom's emerald gown as I imagined how silky soft the fabric of the performer's dress must be, hoping to use my paintbrushes to replicate the way it folded down to the floor. I wanted to capture it all in my mind.

She reached a crescendo, and the small hairs on the back of my neck stood at attention. My heart pounded and I had to swallow hard.

I'd never heard anything like this. In the darkness of the theatre it seemed as though her voice filled every corner. Sure, I'd heard music, but there was something about being there in person that doubled the experience. Unfamiliar, and long repressed, pure emotion rose, making the back of my throat tickle.

Blaine's light sound of amusement, followed by his hand taking mine, pulled me out of the trance. I looked to see his bright eyes shining at me. "You're darling," he said.

He may as well have drizzled a melting ice cube down the back of my dress. Oddly embarrassed to have been caught in that unguarded moment of bliss, I sat back in my seat. "What's that supposed to mean?" I asked.

"If I'd have known how much you'd like your first time at the theatre, I'd have taken you weeks ago."

"What makes you think this is my first time?" I asked.

"Don't be insulted, Olivia. You're incredibly adorable over there, soaking it all in." He squeezed my hand in his.

I had a lot of thoughts about that comment, but the main one was that I didn't love being called adorable or darling in this context. It felt insulting.

My posture tightened. "Would you rather I pretended to be bored?"

His eyes were questioning even as his smile remained perfectly in place. "No, no. I want you to enjoy yourself."

"Then don't be condescending about it," I mumbled. It occurred to me that he'd never seen me cross before, and he was probably as surprised about that as I was to discover that he could be patronizing.

"I'm not trying to be. It's just that it's fun to watch you take pleasure in something new."

I took a breath and smiled back at him. I was probably overreacting. The fact was, I was a little embarrassed to find out he'd been watching me while I let myself sink into the performance. My reaction to it had practically been a spiritual thing, and for someone as habitually private as me, it felt unnerving to share that with someone else, even if that person was someone I was forming a relationship with.

I continued to hold his hand but crossed my ankles and did my best to keep my expression neutral as the actress finished her song. Some of the magic had been lost, but the picture would stay in my mind. I hoped to transfer it to canvas before I forgot the small details.

When the show was over, Blaine escorted me a few blocks down to a nice restaurant where he held out my chair. His warm hands skimmed over my shoulders lightly before he sat next to me.

"I ruined things for you with my thoughtless remark," he said after we'd ordered. "I apologize."

I didn't answer immediately, taking a moment to gaze at him as soft background music played. As usual, he was dressed in a blue suit that would have been at home on a fashion runway. His black-rimmed glasses never seemed to slide down his nose, and his army-short blond hair was in perfect order. Blaine was completely in his essence tonight and most likely had no idea that I was experiencing something totally foreign and new. I sighed, willing to let it go.

"I shouldn't have gotten upset over it," I replied at last.

"No, you should have. You were right, it did come off rudely. I only meant to tell you how happy it made me to see you love it."

I let the last feelings of annoyance wash off and offered him a small smile. "It was incredible."

"Now that I know how much you like theatre, I'll have to make sure we go more often."

My stomach flipped at the idea of him not only wanting to keep seeing me but also offering to take me back there. "I'd like that."

He leaned close and took one of my curls between his fingers. I resisted pulling away. Some of it was out of years of habit. People without curly hair don't understand how temperamental curls can be. There's an assumption that I'm simply letting my hair do whatever it's going to do, but nothing could be further from the truth. Curls have a mind of their own. They only behave if they want to, they never curl the same direction twice, and they get frizzy at the slightest touch.

Fickle curly hair aside, I'd never really been one to casually accept people touching my hair because it felt intimate and suggested closeness. For me, the hair was a hands-off situation.

After a few moments I leaned to the side under the pretense of adjusting the ankle strap on my high heels, forcing him to let go. When I sat back up I said, "Tell me about work."

That was all it took to get him going. Blaine co-owned a marketing company with his father. While the company was quite successful, his stories of working with his dad often made me grateful for the freedom my family gave me. He'd made it clear that his parents were kind but had high expectations of their only son. From what I could see, he was living up to them.

" . . . Mother, of course, wants grandbabies as soon as possible. When I told her that finding the right person, getting married, and having children takes a while, she suggested I come up with a marketing campaign. Can you believe that?" Blaine was saying as I fully tuned back in.

I forced a laugh, despite the nerves I suddenly felt, and gave him a smile. "Hilarious."

"Marketing for a wife and mother. What would those ads look like, I wonder?" Blaine's eyes danced as his mind focused. After a few moments he looked warmly my way. "Don't worry, I'm not going to ask you to meet them yet. I wouldn't give Mother the hope, or you the pressure."

"Thank you." I grinned. "I'll do you the same favor."

We finished dinner, and Blaine helped me put on my coat. We walked slowly back toward the theatre, chatting about small things until we arrived where my little beat-up car was parked.

As we approached, I watched his face closely, knowing he'd never seen what I drove. I was rewarded with a look of pure horror flashing across his face before he could mask it. The tiny two-door car had once been maroon but was now more of a brown color. It was functional in the most stripped down terms, and I tried to not notice people around us giving it a double take as they walked to their own vehicles.

Blaine had always driven us in his shiny luxury auto, but his car was in the shop having some routine maintenance. He'd been working nearby and had a friend drop him at the theatre to meet me. I'd insisted on taking him home afterward, rather than having him call a cab.

It was blazingly clear that he wasn't excited about being chauffeured in my rattle-trap, but he graciously forced a smile and held the driver's door for me while I got in. He walked around to the passenger side while I buckled. I turned the key and nothing happened. Shoot! Blaine got in and I pretended that I'd been waiting for him before starting the engine.

"Let's hit the road," he said with forced cheer.

I turned the key, and luckily this time it caught, although the engine chugged a few times before actually starting, which obviously drew some looks from people passing on the street. I appreciated that Blaine didn't try to duck and hide his face.

"That didn't sound good," he said.

I shrugged and looked over my shoulder to see if traffic was clear. "No big deal. It's a cold night and she's particular."

"She?"

"Yes, this car is a woman."

"Does she always groan and knock like this?" he asked.

I listened for a minute, trying to pretend I didn't know what he was talking about, when in reality I knew very well that my car sounded like it was dragging a sheet of metal down the street underneath it while someone knocked on the trunk.

"She's tired, but she always comes through."

He used his forefinger to push his glasses unnecessarily closer to his face, landing them exactly where they'd already been. "I'm not feeling confident about you making it back to Oak Hills tonight."

"Psh." I made a noise and shrugged casually. "Her name is actually Old Reliable. That's what I call her."

"Uh-huh."

"I'm hoping she'll be inspired by her name."

"I'm feeling very uninspired right now." Blaine shook his head, his expression serious. "Seriously, Olivia, you need to get this car looked at. Maybe even consider scrapping it and getting a new one."

There it was, the reminder that we lived in two very different worlds. I hated it when I had to be reminded of that, rather than floating along in la-la-land. I shrugged casually. "I work at a diner and I'm going to school. This is my life right now. Old Reliable will get me where I need to go." I pulled up in front of his apartment but left the engine running. I didn't want to take any risks of not getting the car started back up. "Thank you so much for a lovely evening. I really did like the theatre, and dinner, and being with you."

He leaned over and took my face between his two warm hands. "You were the prettiest girl in the city tonight." He pressed his lips to mine, and I felt soft warmth flow through me. Kissing someone regularly was a new experience, and in my mind I compared kissing Blaine to putting on a pair of comfy socks and wrapping up in a blanket. It felt dang good. "Drive safely. Please call me when you get home. I'm going to be worried until then."

"Nothing to worry about. Now get out of my car." I pushed at his chest playfully.

He gave me one more quick kiss before stepping out onto the snowy street. At the doorway to his apartment building he turned and gave me a wave. I waited until he was inside before I pulled away from the curb, grinding and knocking the entire way.

* * * * *

I was lost in my own thoughts the next night as Kelly and I sat in the back corner booth of Jake's, rolling silverware. The diner was closed and all the lights were off except for where we sat prepping the fork and knife sets for the following day. The background music was still playing softly, and I'd kicked off my work shoes and tucked my feet up under me.

Silverware rolling was one of my favorite jobs. I loved the stillness of the closed diner, the mindless task, and the chance to chat with Kelly. Although tonight I wasn't saying much because my mind kept seeing the swirls of color and hearing the soaring music of the night before. I knew it would be something I'd think of often over the next little while.

The squeaking of the vinyl broke the silence as Kelly shifted her weight back and forth. Then she tapped her feet a few times. I looked up in time to see her chew her lower lip.

"Out with it," I demanded.

"Well, I did a thing last night while you were off at the theatre with Mr. Rich Dreamboat Pressed Suit . . . "

"That's a long name," I interrupted.

Kelly quirked an eyebrow. "As I was saying, while you were on your super classy date last night, I maybe did a thing."

"What kind of thing are we talking about here?" I couldn't help the smile that tugged at my lips. Kelly and I had been having conversations about her escapades since the third grade when she'd told off a substitute teacher and then left class and walked home alone. The entire school had been sent out to search for her, but it was her mom who'd found her coloring in her room.

One brightly manicured hand reached up to her throat where she rubbed unconsciously. "Well, this is sort of your fault. I mean, I would have called you to chat about it first, but you weren't available, so . . . "

My smile died as immediate understanding flowed through me. "You did not."

"I stopped by Mainstreet Mechanic and had a little chat with Connor Hunt."

I stopped wrapping silverware and looked with big eyes across the booth at Kelly. Silly, naive, never-listens Kelly. "Why?"

"Stop looking at me like that and get back to rolling." Her hand fell away from her throat, and she tossed a napkin at me.

I threw the napkin back at her. "I hope my look says you're insane," I grumbled as I refocused on my job.

"Well, I'm not. I'll have you know that when I told him I was interested in going out sometime, he was very kind and let me down easy."

My gaze shot back up to hers, shock making my mouth go slack. "He turned you down?"

She nodded. "He did. Thanks for being so surprised by that. I was starting to wonder if I'm losing my touch, although . . . "

"You're not losing your touch," I jumped in. It was true. It would be impossible for Kelly to lose her touch. To me, at least, she was the whole package. Beautiful, funny, kind, intelligent, loyal, and up for adventure. She was one of those women that men loved and women didn't get jealous of. She made everyone happy.

"Yeah, Connor told me that I've still got it."

"What?" I set down the silverware and gaped. "Who says that after . . . Never mind, just start at the top and tell me everything."

She held tightly to the silverware in her hands and leaned forward, happy to finally share everything. "Okay. I got all cleaned up after my shift and strolled into the garage bay where he was working. I told him I'd been noticing him coming into the diner for a while and said I thought maybe I was the reason for that. He didn't say anything, so I asked him if he'd like to go out."

"So you just brazenly walked in there, dressed to kill, and told him you were interested in dating him?"

"Pretty much, except for the dressed to kill part."

"You said you got cleaned up."

"Right. As in I changed into clothes that didn't smell like fries and ran my fingers through my hair."

I shook my head, still baffled by both her bravery and his rejection. "And he told you he wasn't interested?"

"Yep. But he was really nice about it."

"So you aren't going out with him?"

"Nope." She sighed and went back to her work.

I picked my silverware back up too, although I wasn't really focused on it. "I'm not sure what I'm more surprised about. The way you just marched right in there, or the fact he didn't take you up on your offer."

"He's not the first guy I've chased down. I hardly even get nervous anymore. Although, you're starting to make me wonder if *I'm* the first woman he's ever turned down." Kelly's lips pinched.

I wasn't about to hurt her by telling her that to my knowledge, she *was* the first woman playboy Connor Hunt had ever turned down. "He must have a girlfriend we don't know about."

"He doesn't. I asked."

You could have shoved my entire fist in my mouth, it opened so widely. "You asked?"

"Well, sure. I mean if a guy's going to turn me down when I went to the effort of combing my hair, then I want a reason."

She had a point. Kelly's naturally bright red hair was just as curly as mine. While I chose to leave mine short, she let hers grow long. It practically had a life it its own, but it so perfectly suited her that I couldn't imagine it any other way.

"Did he give you one?"

"Yep. He said he had a feeling we'd make great friends, but not a great couple. He asked me if I wanted to get lunch sometime. I said yes."

"Lunch?" I was struggling to keep up. "After he turned you down for a date, he asked you to lunch?"

"Yes, lunch. Lunch is for friends. Dinner is for couples. Everyone knows this. So, we're going out to lunch together tomorrow."

My mouth opened and closed twice before I could come up with a response. "You're going to have lunch with Connor tomorrow, because friends have lunch together and he thinks you two would be good friends?"

"Yep."

"I . . . wow."

"Think of it this way—lunch or dinner, I still get to look at him across the table, and even friends can look if they don't touch."

I laughed out loud at that, shoulders shaking. "Oh my gosh, Kelly. I can't believe you."

"Hey, I'm just trying to live my best, most authentic life."

She joined me in laughing until our sides were sore and Jake had to come tell us to get back to work. When Jake went back to the kitchen I made her reenact the scene for me, which involved her hamming it up by walking down the aisle between booths shaking her hips and puffing up her lips as she begged an imaginary Connor to take her out. This, of course, resulted in more laughter and another rebuke from our boss. It was worth it.

CHAPTER THREE

I groaned as the sound of my cell phone ringing pulled me out of my head the next morning. It sat chirping away on my bed, and for a moment I debated just not answering. I was standing in front of a paint canvas that I'd finished the background on only moments before. Swirls of blue, purple, and black created the backdrop of the theatre stage that I was recreating. I was getting ready to mix in some white and yellow streams of light to filter in from the top. My mind was filled with the colors I remembered from that magical performance.

The phone chirped again, and I let out a deep breath. I didn't get phone calls often, so it usually meant it was something important. I set down the palette, keeping it carefully balanced so the brush wouldn't roll off, and padded across the room to my bed while I wiped paint off my fingertips onto the stained apron I was wearing.

"Hi," I answered.

"Hello," Blaine's voice greeted. "I hope I'm not interrupting anything?"

I couldn't tell him that he had, because the truth was that Blaine had no idea I painted. No one outside of my family and Kelly knew. It was something I kept to myself. I put a smile into my voice and told him I was free to chat, even if my eyes did wander longingly toward the canvas. Another thirty minutes would have been amazing.

"Great," he said. "I wanted to see how your car is doing."

"My car?"

"Yeah. I've been worrying about it ever since we went out the other night. It sounded truly terrible. I don't think it's safe for you to keep driving in its current state."

This was unexpected. Were we to the point in our relationship where he suggested things like this? Who knew, but as kind as it was, I did not want to talk to Blaine about my beater car situation. "You're so sweet to worry," I replied as genuinely as possible, "but it's not anything to be anxious over. I've been driving this same car for years now and it's never let me down."

"Yes, you mentioned you named it Old Reliable." His tone was as dry as the Sahara.

"Right, I did. For good reason. She's never failed me."

"Listen, I really think you should take it into a shop and get the problems diagnosed. Maybe there's nothing major wrong, and it's just some creaks and groans from old age. I'd feel a lot better at least knowing that."

Only someone living Blaine's life would call my car old. It wasn't that old. Nine years was not a big deal. People drove cars like mine all the time—sort of. They were probably running better, to be totally fair.

"Again, I appreciate your concern, but I'm sure it'll be fine. No reason to spend money at a shop for them to tell me it's something I can DIY."

"I didn't know you knew basic car repair." To his credit, he did not say that sarcastically.

"We haven't known each other that long, I'm still a woman of mystery," I teased. I knew a few things. For example, I knew how to use a wrench to hit the engine in various places while wiggling wires until it started, how to jump it when the wrench technique didn't work, and how to walk to work when all else failed.

"Well, aren't you full of surprises."

I laughed. "What are you up to today?" Redirection was a favorite move of mine.

"I've got a few meetings this afternoon and a lot of catch up planning to do tonight. I was hoping to get up to see you the day after tomorrow. What's your work schedule?"

"Day after tomorrow? I work breakfast, six to two."

"Hmm. Sounds like it'll have to be a breakfast date at the diner then. Save me a plate of hotcakes."

"I definitely will."

"Oh, and Olivia?"

"Yeah."

"Nice try, but we're not done talking about your car." His voice sounded amused, and I could picture him smiling at me.

I smiled back, even though he couldn't see. "We'll see," I replied. The last thing I heard before he hung up was his laughter.

I put the phone down on my bed and went back to my canvas, but some of the magic had been lost with the topic of my car. It really did fine around town, and before Blaine had come into my life I hadn't had much reason to travel more than the six-mile radius that made up our little community.

Obviously, I'd noticed problems with the car. It hadn't been starting well, there was a grinding noise that was only getting worse, and it was anybody's guess why there would be a knocking noise coming from my trunk. There was nothing to do for it but to drive the thing and pray for mercy from the car angels. No matter how I played it, I didn't have the extra money to pour into automotive repairs. Blaine and I definitely were not at a point where I was going to tell him all of this. Heck, I still didn't call him my boyfriend. I hadn't even mentioned my car struggles to my mom or Kelly. It was my problem, and I'd figure it out.

Rather than continue painting, I cleaned and packed up my brushes. There was some peace in the mindless routine, and I appreciated it. When that was done I did a little tidying of my room and then made my way to the bathroom to get ready for work.

My eyes looked a little tight around the sides when I glanced in the mirror. I knew it was stress, but I didn't linger over it. I wetted my hair and did the work of resetting my curls into some sort of order. After applying some light makeup and a good dose of deodorant, I was as ready as I could be for my work shift.

I was happy to see Kelly bustling around in the back when I entered the employee lounge area to put away my things and get an apron on. I always liked it when we worked the same shift. There was a reason we'd been friends for so long. Our personalities complemented each other. Kelly was outgoing and unconquerable, a total bright spot, while I tended to be more cautious and slower to warm up. Despite those differences we spoke the same language, and I often felt like she was the only one who truly understood me.

"What's making your eyes all squingy this morning?" she asked as she tied on her apron.

"That's not even a word."

"When it comes to how your eyes look when you're annoyed, then yes, it's a word," she stated.

"Blaine called and told me my car is a pile of junk and I should have it fixed."

She walked over to the sink area and used the mirror to start French braiding her hair. "I can't believe he's not a fan of Old Reliable."

"That car is going to run forever."

"I assume you told Blaine your theory about the immortality of your metal heap?"

"Not exactly."

"Oh, so you went with the 'we haven't known each other long enough for me to let you in on my business' option."

"Sometimes it stinks having a best friend," I mumbled as I hung my coat on a hook.

She laughed. "He's not wrong about your car, even though you want him to stay out of your business."

"Can you blame me?"

"For driving a beater, or for wanting him to butt out?" She met my eyes in the mirror and raised a brow. My look was answer enough. "I shouldn't have to be the one to tell you this, but boyfriends are not good at staying out of your business."

I pursed my lips and gave her a look of my own as I tied on my apron. "He isn't my boyfriend. He's a guy I've gone out with a couple of times."

Her shoulders lifted carelessly. "You hate being told the hard truth, and you always have. Your car is on its last legs. You really should take it to Mainstreet Mechanic and have Connor give it a once over."

"Pass." I moved to stand next to her at the sink and pulled some bobby pins out of my pocket.

She finished her braid and used a rubber band to tie it off. "I know you don't like his reputation, but he knows what he's doing with cars."

"That's probably a good thing for the guy who owns the only auto shop in town." I pinned curls this way and that, attempting to meet health code standards by having my hair pulled back. "How did lunch with him go the other day?"

"Really good. He's . . . " She let the sentence hang.

At her unusual hesitation I turned to face her directly. "He's what?" Her cheeks pinked up and I took a step back, my mouth dropping open. "What happened?"

"I want to tell you something, but I know you're not going to believe me."

"Oh my gosh, Kelly, you genuinely like him." My heart sank as her face confirmed the truth. "How did this happen? We've always watched him saunter around town like a conceited Casanova and been appalled."

Her nose wrinkled. "And a little intrigued too, if we're being honest."

I ignored that, even if it was the tiniest bit true. We had giggled a whole lot over the years when talking about him. "Did he slip something into your Coke at lunch? Did you hallucinate?"

Apparently she realized I wasn't going to murder her, so she relaxed and gave me a big smile. "You're being a dork. I haven't hallucinated since you gave me a ride home and the exhaust fumes made me see ponies prancing on the dash board."

I rolled my eyes. "Be serious, Kell. What's up?"

"Lunch was great. Did you know he went to school and has a business degree? The shop is doing good. Talking to him was really comfortable and nice. He actually got all my jokes and kept up with me, even though you and I always thought we were the only two in town who can understand each other. He's not at all what we thought he was. So yes, I do like him."

I hadn't known those things about him, but they certainly weren't going to sway what I knew to be true. "So he can talk fast and he looks good on paper, but still, he's Connor Hunt. How can you be falling under his spell? You do not want your name added to his list of conquests."

"Conquests?" Kelly laughed and turned to scrub her hands before heading out to the dining room. "I'm talking about friendship, not going to see him in the medieval jousting tournament this weekend."

I turned back to the mirror and finished pressing in the last of the pins to secure my hair. In my frustration I wasn't gentle, and I winced a few times. "Okay, let's say for one minute that I believed you. What's the point of being his friend? I thought you were looking for the next Mr. Right."

"I am." Kelly stepped aside for me as I washed my hands too. "But until he comes along, there's nothing wrong with spending a little time with Mr. Delicious."

I couldn't stop the immediate amusement that pushed up, making me shake my head and grin. "Your plan is to spend time chumming around with him, using him as eye candy until you find love?"

She laughed. "You make me sound terrible. Honestly, Liv, I like him a lot. I even went by the shop again and visited with him for a bit, and it was good. It wasn't just a fluke at lunch. He's really clever and funny. The way I see it, I'm done judging him by who we thought he was."

"Who we *saw* he was," I retorted.

"Fine, who he used to be. I don't think he's the same person anymore. There's something really great about him."

I dried my hands, and we walked together toward the exit. "Are you trying to replace me with him?" I teased.

She hooked her arm through mine. "No. He's nicer than you, and I'd miss your snark." At my expression she grinned. "Just take your car in. I'm sure he'd be happy to look it over. It would get Blaine off your back and give you a chance to make your own judgments about Connor."

"I'll think about it." I bumped my shoulder against hers.

"Good. Oh, and dibs on the bar seating tonight." She let go of my arm and wiggled her eyebrows as she hurried out to claim her area.

I didn't bother reminding her that Jake scheduled us where he wanted us to work. It was pointless. Kelly worked the sections she was in the mood for, and I worked the other. It was life with Kelly, and I'd long ago accepted it with good grace the same way she accepted my quirks. I watched her chat with a customer and promised myself I'd be there to catch her when this newfound friendship of hers broke her heart.

CHAPTER FOUR

As promised, two days later Blaine came for breakfast while I was working the morning shift. His eyes were bright and his smile warm as he sat down on a stool at the bar where I was working. He was dressed in his signature blue hues, but this time he'd added a trendy bow tie, and, honestly, he looked pretty great.

Also as promised, we were not done discussing my car. While he told me what a junk pile he thought my car was, I zoned out completely. I hadn't meant to do it, but I was working and uninterested. Sadly, I was seriously busted when he interrupted my daydreams about an afternoon nap by clearing his throat. I looked to him and saw his expression shift into one of annoyance. Oops. My face warmed.

"I can see what you're thinking," he said.

"More juice?" I replied, hefting the carafe I was holding in my hands.

"I'm being serous here." The barstool squeaked under him as he shifted. He put his utensils down and shook his head as I once again wiggled the orange liquid his way. "Your car needs help."

"Be right back," I tossed over my shoulder as I turned and walked down the long counter to replace the carafe and pick up the next order.

The diner was hopping. It was seven-thirty in the morning, our first pre-work rush, and much too early to be receiving a lecture about my car. In fact, never o'clock would have been my preference.

I glided by with another customer's order, avoiding Blaine's eyes, and smiled at them as I set their food down before making my way back past Blaine again. "I'm happy living in denial," I said to him. "Getting told my car is barely cheating death is not my idea of fun."

He pulled a face, but I'd walked away before he could reply. There were some definite bonuses to having him attempt this conversation while I was distracted. I doubted he'd be patient for long. I got the feeling that Blaine Harris was not a man used to being put off.

"Olivia," he called after I'd delivered the next plate.

Before I could answer, Kelly walked by and mouthed "Olivia?" at me. No one called me Olivia, except occasionally my mom. I'd gone by Liv since kindergarten when I'd introduced myself to my teacher that way. My teacher had looked to my mom who had shrugged, and that was that. However, Jake had gone with my legal name on my name tag. I'd never bothered to correct Blaine, who had met me when I was wearing it.

Kelly turned to him before I could. "She's working. Be patient." She walked out from behind the counter to attend to the booths and gave me what we liked to called the solidarity smile when Blaine looked away from her and back to me.

"Look," he said, "I know you're working right now, but we seriously need to have your car looked at. I wasn't sure you'd make it back home the other night. I worry about you."

"The risk is all part of the excitement," I replied with a grin.

"Worry isn't exciting," he stated.

I raised my eyebrows but said nothing as I walked down the bar to take an order. I watched him go back to eating his breakfast out of the corner of my eye. His shoulders were tense. I felt a little bad. I wasn't trying to be difficult. Still, I had a very full plate in life and no interest in addressing what I saw as a non-problem.

After a few more minutes I stopped in front of Blaine again with an apologetic smile. "Let's go on pretending my car is fine by making sure we always take your car," I said. "Win-win."

"If your car breaks down, you won't be able to get to work." He reached out and snagged my hand before I could dart off again. "Please, babe. I hear there's a local guy who is magic with cars. We can take it to him."

Babe? Another step I wasn't aware we'd progressed to. First automotive repairs and now pet names. The thought distracted me enough that I had to replay the entire sentence in my mind. When I did, the thought that he'd been asking around about local mechanics didn't make me feel looked after, which was probably what he'd been going for. I was completely capable of handling automotive issues when, and if, I felt like it. Heck, half the time I drove with the fuel light on for two days just to see how far I could go. I hadn't run out yet. A couple of times when my car wouldn't start, I'd just banged on things until it had worked again. I trusted that the car would do its thing. And when it stopped doing it, I'd figure that out.

"I can walk to work. It's a small town, things are close," I replied, tugging at my hand.

He held me firm and stroked the back of my hand with his thumb. "It's January. It's cold and sometimes you work early mornings or late nights. Walking in the dark isn't safe. Besides, is it honestly that big of an issue to have this man take a look?"

It was a big deal. I was about as broke as I could be, and I knew exactly who the mechanic was that he was talking about. He *was* a magician, but instead of getting balloon animals and a laugh, I'd end up with a debt I couldn't pay back. Once again, my face betrayed me as it heated. Having to occasionally remind Blaine that I was perpetually short of money was embarrassing. I looked away and shook my head.

"Is it the money?" he whispered.

"No," I lied.

I tugged my hand free at the sound of the kitchen bell signaling an order up. Hopefully he'd pick up his check and go.

When I finished delivering three more plates of food I glanced to where Blaine had been sitting. He was still there, but now he was holding a piece of paper and waving it at me. I sighed and went to see what it was.

"Here's the information for the mechanic I was telling you about. It's quite close. Promise me you'll at least drop by and talk to him."

I shook my head. "Blaine, I'm not worried about my car. I'll handle it when it's time."

"I'm happy to help cover the repairs."

"No way," I stated flatly.

His jaw tensed and I knew his teeth were pressed tightly together. Our eyes locked in stalemate. It was obvious that he wanted to look after me, yet my instinct was to fight for independence. It wasn't necessarily on principle, and it wasn't against Blaine personally. I wasn't against a man caring for his woman any more than I was against a woman caring for her man. In fact, some days I'd have given anything to have someone care for me the way Blaine wanted to. Yet we'd only known each other for two months, and there were still boundaries up and conversations we hadn't had. We should still be in the sending flowers and chocolates phase, not discussing car repair and money issues.

"You two okay?" Kelly asked as she came to stand next to me. "You're going to scare customers away with those glares."

"Her car is going to explode the next time she tries to drive it anywhere. I'm trying to get her in to see a mechanic," Blaine replied.

"My car is fine." I turned to Kelly, still stone faced.

Her pretty blue eyes lit up with amusement. "You know Connor would take a look at that for you."

"Connor, yes. That's the name of the man I was just telling her about." Blaine's expression cleared into one of hope. "Over at Mainstreet Mechanic?"

"I know who Connor is, and he doesn't need to be bothered," I replied. "He's running a business, not a charity organization."

Kelly patted my back and looked around. "I just saw him here. Let me see . . . " I nearly jumped out of my skin when Kelly hollered out and waved to a man I hadn't noticed before, sitting in the back corner booth. "Yep, I knew it. He's coming over."

"Probably thinks the place is burning down, the way you screamed for him," I said.

Connor Hunt, magic mechanic and town bad boy, arrived in front of us before I had time to decide how I was going to get this to stop. I trusted him completely with my car. I just didn't trust him with anything else. At all. And maybe I was an eensy-weensy bit jealous over finding out there was another person out there that Kelly really clicked with.

For a brief moment, when he came to stand next to the counter, I was struck by how rough he looked standing next to Blaine's scissor-like polish. Blaine was all cool blues in his pressed suit, while Connor was all warm honey brown in a T-shirt and jeans, with a leather jacket draped over his arm. The contrast was fascinating to my art-obsessed soul. Auburn hair clashed against pale blond. It was . . . well, it was nothing, really.

Connor raised his eyebrows toward Kelly, asking without words what she needed. Oh great, now they could communicate without words. If he got in on the BBBS (Best Buds Broadcasting System) I'd be ticked. I still didn't understand what they saw in each other, despite Kelly's attempts to explain.

"Liv is having car trouble, and her boyfriend wants her to get it checked out. She's being stubborn. I said you'd take a look." Kelly pared it all down while Connor silently listened, giving away nothing. I admired his poker face.

His amber eyes turned to meet mine for the first time I could recall, which made me unaccountably jittery. I folded my arms defensively across my chest. "I'm not looking for charity and I can't afford to pay for repairs right now, so there's no point in having this discussion." At the end of my speech, a curl fell into my face, and rather than reach up to fix it, I blew it back into place.

Blaine acted like I'd said nothing and turned his glacier-blue eyes in Connor's direction. "The car needs to be looked at. Perhaps it's a smaller repair that won't cost much."

I shook my head and opened my mouth to argue back, but Connor, who'd never broken eye contact with me, beat me to it. "I don't mind taking a look. What time do you get off?" he asked.

I swallowed hard on a lump of mortification. How many times did I have to say it out loud? "I can't pay you."

"Diagnosis is free," Connor replied easily, finally turning his gaze from me as he slid his arms into his jacket.

"Great. She's off at two." Kelly gave Connor a big smile.

He nodded and left before I had a chance to say anything else, or at least before I could think up anything else to say.

Blaine, happily the winner of that exchange, smiled and leaned over the counter to press a quick kiss to my cheek while I remained frozen in place. "Have a good shift, babe. I'll call you later."

Kelly and I watched both men get into their cars—Connor's a shiny, full-size truck, and Blaine's a sleek black BMW sedan, slung low to the ground—and drive away.

"He calls you babe?" she said to me with a giggle. "When did that happen?"

"I've been shanghaied," I said in response.

"Take the offer, appease your man friend, and move on," she stated and went to the kitchen to get her orders.

When I went to start my car after my shift several hours later, I had to admit that Blaine may have had a point. It took several attempts to finally get the engine running, and as I pulled onto the street I cringed at that suspicious grinding noise. I'd barely paid attention to it until it had been discussed publicly, and now it was as subtle as a fog horn. I'd had every intention of going straight home. I had classes I needed to study for, a few papers to write, some instructional videos to watch for school, and most likely some cleaning to do. I didn't have an hour to take out of my day. The universe, as usual, had different plans. Biting my lip, I changed direction and drove a couple of blocks to the small gray building where automotive voodoo happened in our little town.

The three big bay doors were closed against the January snow, and even though I could see movement in the shop area there was no one in the foyer when I entered. The smell of lemon cleaner and some sort of vanilla scent reached my nose as I walked to where a small bell stood on the counter. I gave it a cheerful little ding and took off my mittens so I could rub my hands together. One price of small-town living was that the car never had time to warm up between stops.

Connor came through the glass side door that was connected to the shop. He was wearing full coveralls and wiping his hands on a rag. "Didn't think you'd actually come," he said, catching me off guard with his bluntness.

"I wasn't planning on it," I replied, returning honesty with honesty.

He nodded. "Your boyfriend must have realized that."

"What do you mean?" I asked. He gestured and I turned to look behind me. Blaine was parking his shiny BMW next to my compact car. We watched in silence as he got out, straightened his bow tie, and buttoned his suit jacket. "You've got to be kidding me," I said under my breath.

"I wouldn't have though you needed babysitters anymore," Connor said in a lightly teasing tone.

"Shut up," I retorted. Then I was forced to blush because the only words I'd ever spoken to Connor in my life had been "I don't have any money" and "shut up." I was supposed to be a grown up. "Why is he here?" It was a rhetorical question, but Connor answered anyhow.

"I'd guess he's making sure his girl does what she's supposed to do."

I spun back around, knowing full well that my irritation would show in my expression, and gave him a look. "I am not his girl and he doesn't give me instructions to follow."

"Someone should probably tell him that."

The door opened on a rush of cold air before I could reply, carrying my well-groomed love interest through the door. He smiled as he came to stand next to me, but then glanced to Connor and went into business mode. I groaned inwardly as I watched Blaine straighten his posture. That kind of stuff probably worked on other guys, but it wasn't going to work on Connor—especially in Connor's domain.

"Afternoon." Blaine took off his brown leather glove and extended a hand to Connor. Rather than shaking it, Connor held up his own hand to show Blaine that it was stained black from his work. Blaine gave him a polite nod in acceptance and tucked his hand back into the glove. "Are we ready?"

"For what?" I asked.

Blaine finally turned to me. "For Connor to diagnose your car."

"I thought you were working with a client today," I said.

"I was. We finished early and I wanted to make sure everything went well here." He put his arm around me and gave me a light squeeze.

"That's a hour round-trip just to check up on me," I said out of the side of my mouth.

"Worth every mile," he replied in a similar manner.

"I'm ready. Are you ready, Liv?" Connor looked to me. His expression was one of polite interest even though based on the light in his eyes I could almost guarantee he was loving this little interaction between Blaine and me. I nodded tightly. "Great, I just need your keys and I'll pull your car into one of the bays." I dangled the keys from my fingers and dropped them in his hand when he held it out palm up. "Give me about fifteen minutes to look things over. I'll come out and tell you what I find."

I nodded, and a little perverse moment of satisfaction hit when I realized that my seat would be much too far forward for someone of Connor's height. Imagining him banging his knees on the steering wheel after having teased me about being Blaine's compliant little girlfriend wasn't kind, but it made the situation slightly more tolerable.

"Thank you," Blaine said as Connor walked back into the shop to open one of the bay doors. He turned to me. "I know you're frustrated, but you shouldn't take it out on Mr. Hunt. He's doing you a favor, diagnosing it for free. Most shops charge for that."

I let out a deep breath and nodded. He was right about the fee, but I wasn't about to go into my reasonings for being frosty to Connor. There was history there that he'd never understand.

We sat on two hard plastic waiting room chairs, and I listened politely while Blaine told me about his latest client and the ongoing politics of his office life. I usually found of lot of what he did really interesting—plus I cared about Blaine even if he was being heavy-handed—but my mind was chewing over what Connor was going to report back. He'd pulled the car into a bay and had it lifted in the air. Whatever was wrong, I knew it wasn't something a five-dollar roll of duct tape would fix.

True to his word, Connor spent the next ten minutes poking all around my car before lowering it back to earth and using the last five to look under the hood. He emerged from the shop, once again wiping his hands as Blaine stood, but I stayed sitting. After my eight-hour shift at the diner, sitting felt wonderful.

"Have you been having a hard time getting your car started?" Connor asked me.

"Recently, yes," I replied.

"You have?" Blaine frowned. I shrugged.

"When is the last time you had to have someone jump start you?" Connor asked.

"A couple of days ago."

"Oh, Olivia." Blaine said my name in a very disappointed tone, which I chose to ignore.

"It looks like your alternator is dying," Connor said. "Your brakes are junk too. You haven't noticed that constant grinding noise while you drive?"

"I was hoping I'd picked up a rock or something." I smiled innocently.

"What about that knocking noise?" Blaine asked.

"I didn't notice anything. I'd need to actually drive it around the block. Where's it coming from?"

"The trunk," Blaine replied.

"The trunk?" Connor's brows dropped.

I pasted on a sardonic grin. "I keep a guy I kidnapped in there. He pumps my gas and gives me piggy back rides when the snow is too deep." Connor raised his eyebrows, and Blaine blinked a few times. It was oddly satisfying. In the silence, I stood. "Okay, well the diagnosis was free, right?" I asked.

"Yes," Connor replied.

I walked to where Connor was standing and held out my hand. "Great. So I'll just need my keys back so I can head home."

"You can't be serious." Blaine turned to me. "You just heard what he said. You're lucky your car started today. Tomorrow it might not. You're lucky your brakes didn't fail on the way back here from the city after our date."

"Yes. I am lucky. The universe loves me." I dimpled at Blaine and wiggled my fingers at Connor. "Keys, please."

Connor shook his head. "You can't keep driving it like that."

"I'm not planning to. I'll take it home, park it, and walk. I have two perfectly capable legs and no money. Problem solved."

"Plus the guy giving you piggy back rides," Connor added deadpan.

Blaine looked to Connor, who shrugged while I tamped down on an unexpected grin. Kelly had said he was quick.

Blaine cleared his throat. "I can cover the repairs, and Olivia can pay me back. A little at a time is fine with me."

"Nope." I stood my ground.

"Babe, I can't let you walk around in the winter like this. Not when I can help you. Really, I don't mind."

Sigh. He was being hard-headed, which meant my subtle clues weren't working. It was unfortunately time to use a bigger weapon. "What if we break up before I can pay you back?" I cocked my head to the side and looked at him.

His mouth opened a moment before words actually came out. I understood, the big weapons could be jarring. "You don't think we'll last?"

"I don't know. We're still pretty new. I'd hate to owe you money and then break your heart on top of that," I replied.

Connor made an unidentifiable noise, looking away and clearing his throat when we both glanced at him.

Blaine sighed and removed his glasses, rubbing a hand over his closed eyes while he thought. After a few seconds he replaced his glasses and smiled at me. "I don't think I understood until now how independent you are. It's a good quality, but I just want you to be safe."

He reached out and gathered me into a hug. I relaxed against him, enjoying his expensive cologne and the feel of my cheek against his soft suit coat. He really was such a nice guy. I needed to relax. I holstered my weapon of harsh truth and snuggled closer.

"I'm not comfortable borrowing money from you," I whispered.

"How much would those repairs cost?" Blaine asked Connor.

"The car needs full brakes and rotors, and an alternator. It will be about nine hundred dollars for everything. That includes labor."

I closed my eyes as my stomach tightened into a knot. "Pocket change," I tried to joke, but it came out wobbly.

Blaine's arms tightened around me, and he leaned his head close to my ear. "It sounds like a lot, but I can cover it."

"I can't imagine how I'd pay that back," I replied quietly. "Let me think about it. I'll take the car home for now and figure it out." I raised my head and gave him a half-hearted smile before stepping out of his embrace. I turned to Connor, who had been trying not to watch it all play out. "Keys, please."

"You sure?" he asked.

"Yep."

"I have to back it out of the bay. You can meet me in the parking lot," Connor replied. He exited the small lobby area again, and I tried not to make a face when I heard the sputtering of the engine echoing around the bay. It didn't sound good, or right, or normal, and it definitely wasn't starting.

"Say nothing." I held up a hand when I heard Blaine take a breath. "It's not that bad."

"It's that bad," he said, but at least there was a smile tugging at his lips.

Thankfully, he was finally seeing the humor in the situation, which only grew as we saw Connor climb out of my car, still in the bay, and come walking toward us. I smiled when Blaine started laughing. He was so attractive when he laughed. I watched his face, enjoying his expression, wishing he could laugh more.

"It won't start," Connor said plainly.

"This is a car shop. You have jumper cables, yes?" I asked.

"I don't want to have to tow you home tomorrow because I let you take the car today," he replied. "Let's just get it fixed. We'll figure out a payment plan or something."

"That's an excellent solution. I didn't think to ask if you do payment plans." Blaine brightened up considerably.

"I don't," Connor replied.

"But you just said . . . " Blaine stammered, confused.

"She's a local girl. We'll get her sorted." Connor looked at me for an answer, which I appreciated, because it was my car, after all, and my money we were talking about.

I needed a minute to think, so I held up a hand and looked at the floor. After doing some quick calculations in my head I looked back up. "The most I can pay you is fifty dollars a month. So it would take me a year and a half to pay off. Who knows if the car will still be running then?" I gulped.

"We'll figure it out. Have your boyfriend take you home. I'll get the parts ordered and the repairs done. Come back in three days," Connor said.

I simply nodded as Blaine effusively thanked Connor and shook his hand, this time careless of the grease. He kept chatting about what a nice guy Connor was the whole way to his car and on the short drive to my home. I knew the truth, but kept my mouth shut for once.

"Thanks, Blaine," I said when he pulled up in front of my parents' house.

"I'm glad it's all worked out."

He leaned over and gave me a light kiss. He apologized for having to run, but I was secretly relieved as I waved goodbye, then made my way inside and up to my bedroom. Worry was my companion as I got dressed in comfortable clothes and settled in to study before it was time to make dinner.

What was Connor going to demand for payback? Could I trust him? How much was this actually going to cost me?

CHAPTER FIVE

The soft sounds of oil paint sliding across canvas soothed me into a dreamlike state as the mountain scene I was painting took shape. Gentle strokes to make snow drifts, harder strokes to create the depth needed for pine needles to jump off the page, purple and blue mountain peaks in the background. The sharp tang of paint thinner filled the air, and I could feel a wet spot on my jeans where I'd dripped some below where my apron covered. My mind forgot my worries as I tapped and swirled the brushes. This was my escape, my happy place.

It was a precious Saturday off, and I didn't have time to be painting. The kitchen needed a major clean up, our food supplies were at critical level, and I needed to pick up my car from Mainstreet Mechanic this afternoon. Still . . .

I dabbed a fresh brush into pastel pink, deciding to paint the underside of the clouds and make it look like sunset. My tongue stuck out between my lips as I concentrated, a habit I'd had since childhood. I tasted the hint of strawberry in my Chapstick.

"Hello? Earth to Liv," Sadie's voice interrupted me. I startled briefly but managed to keep from swooping the paint through a cloud and ruining what I was doing.

"What?" I grumped, not bothering to turn and look at her.

"You left your phone downstairs and it's been ringing for the past ten minutes. If you're too preoccupied with your hobby here, I'd be happy to talk to this Blaine of yours."

"Don't be silly." I snapped back to reality and set my brush down. "He's thirty and you're seventeen. He isn't interested." This time I did look at her.

She was still wearing pajama pants and a T-shirt, her uncombed hair high on her head in a messy bun. She did a funny little shake of her hips and smiled at me. "He could be."

Entertained by the picture she made, I grinned. "You're a dork."

She tossed my phone onto my bed and shrugged as she left. Almost immediately the phone started ringing again. I hurried to wipe off a hand in order to answer.

"Hello?" I knew I sounded a little breathless.

"Olivia, there you are. I've been trying to reach you." He didn't sound annoyed, which made me relax.

"I'm so sorry," I said cheerfully. "I left my phone downstairs and got caught up in my school work. My sister finally brought the phone up and told me to open my ears."

"What were you working on this morning?" he asked.

"Physiology. Cells, tissues, organ systems, that kind of stuff," I replied in an awkward voice as the lie made my cheeks warm.

"That sounds interesting."

"Hmm. Very. How was your morning?" I turned to talk to him and was grateful when he picked right up and told me all about breakfast with his parents and errands he'd run that morning.

While he was talking I tried really hard to not worry about the fact that I should be doing my own errands, grocery shopping, thinking about what to make for dinner, and how I was going to pay Connor for the car repairs. I'd really wanted to relax and have a nice few hours off. It wasn't easy.

"Hey, listen, I'd be happy to come with you to pick up your car. We can chat with the owner about your payment plan and make sure everything was done properly," he said eventually.

My first reaction wasn't polite, so I cleared my throat and tried for a nonchalant tone. "Oh, uh, that's okay. I can take care of it."

"Do you think there's going to be any problem with the payment plan idea?" he asked after a brief pause.

"No. I'm sure it'll be fine. I'm okay to go on my own."

His voice fell to a whisper. "I know you can, but you don't have to. I'd like to help you when I can."

I let out a slow, silent breath. Poor Blaine. He was trying so hard, and I was maintaining the same distance that was in place when he'd first asked me out. The idea of actually steadily dating was still new to me, and I was unsure of what role to give him in my world. Bigger than that was the fact that I was still doubtful about wanting *any* guy to have a permanent role in my life. It still seemed to me like the journey would be easier alone.

Regardless, I wasn't a monster, and I felt a welling of guilt over his efforts. "You're sweet," I said. "It's nice to have someone try to look out for me. I'm truly okay, though. I promise to call you as soon as I'm done and fill you in."

"If that's what you want," he replied. His tone said he wasn't thrilled, but I appreciated him backing down. We chatted a bit more, making plans to get together soon.

After he hung up, I cleaned my brushes, changed my clothes, and tried to tame my hair. When I was as good as I could get, I retrieved my backpack, bundled up, and walked the half mile to Mainstreet Mechanic. The air had a bite to it and my cheeks felt a little wind-burned when I entered the lobby, which was once again empty. I peeked through the window into the work bays and saw two men standing over the open hood of a car, along with a pair of legs sticking out from under it. The legs obviously belonged to Connor, as he wasn't one of the standing men. My car was further down and no work was being done to it, which must have meant it was finished.

I waved and knocked lightly on the window. One of the men looked up and gave me a wave. He pointed down at Connor and flashed five fingers at me. I took that to mean I'd be waiting a minute. I glanced at the clock to see that I had about thirty minutes before I really needed to head to the grocery store and get back home to clean, so I gave the guy a thumbs up and went to sit on one of the lobby chairs.

In a moment of inspiration, I decided to access my physiology book online and do a little reading. Bonus points for actually studying today and making good on the lie I'd told Blaine. If no one appeared in the lobby in about ten minutes, I'd go back and really knock on the window.

I set my things on the chair next to me and got out my phone. I needed to finish two more chapters before the test on Monday. I crossed

my booted feet and settled in. For ten minutes I read with no interruptions I couldn't believe how far I got in that time. It seemed that I never had ten solid minutes to just read. Home was hectic and the diner was totally off limits. I sank back into the chair and kept reading after the ten-minute mark. I was making good headway and didn't want to give it up.

The sound of the door opening from the shop interrupted me five minutes later. I glanced up to see Connor, once again wiping his hands. Today his coveralls were gray, and he was wearing heavy black work boots. His hair stuck up in a way that reminded me of a troll doll, but I supposed being underneath a car wasn't good for keeping hair nicely coifed . . . and who was I to talk?

He nodded at the phone in my hand. "Find anything good?"

"A physiology textbook."

"Sure. Good choice for some light reading on a snowy weekend afternoon."

"I'm learning ways to cause the most pain with the least damage," I replied in a sugary sweet voice.

He nodded slowly as though I'd just told him I was knitting a doily. "Ah. That would probably come in handy sometimes."

"Indeed." I put my phone back in my bag and zipped it closed. "Is my car ready?"

"Yep. Everything went well. Total is the nine hundred I quoted you."

"Okay. What are your thoughts on a payment plan?"

"Are you going to school?" he asked.

"Yes. Online classes to prepare for nursing school." I waited for him to nod and then redirected. "About my car?"

"Why nursing school?" he asked instead of answering my question.

"It's a way out." I shrugged and shook my head. "Anyhow, I can't pay you more than fifty bucks a month. Is that going to be okay?

"A way out of what?"

I tilted my chin down and pinched my lips. I was not here to discuss my life, at all, with him. "Not answering that."

"Fair enough," he said casually. "I have an idea if you're open to discussing other options for payment."

My gut clenched and my face warmed. Here we go. He'd pulled the wool over Kelly's eyes, but things were about to get

real. "Depends on what 'other options for payment' you might have in mind."

His brows lowered. "What are you talking about?"

"I'm not going to pay off my debts by, like, kissing you and stuff." My face burned, but I kept eye contact with him, knowing it was important to not back down.

"Liv Phelps, does your mother know what kind of thoughts go through that head of yours?" he asked with wide eyes that seemed oddly surprised for someone who I'd long suspected of having underhanded dealings.

The only sound in the lobby was that of my pounding heartbeats. I wasn't sure what had just happened. I took a deep breath, playing the conversation back in my mind as I watched his expression turn stony. Maybe I'd jumped the gun here. This was his place of business, and regardless of what I thought, people seemed to think he ran a top-notch shop. Kelly said he was a cool guy. Oh man, I was an idiot.

My jaw tightened as pure humiliation poured over me from the top of my head to pool under my feet. I may not like him, but that foray back into childhood hadn't done either of us any favors.

"So," I cleared my throat and swallowed. "I may have jumped to conclusions."

"Yep."

"I'm not always like that."

"That's comforting," he stated with a little more sarcasm than I deemed necessary.

I scrunched up my nose and fidgeted a bit. "Okay. I'm ready to talk about payment options."

"I'm rethinking what I was going to offer," he replied.

I remained silent, knowing that opening my mouth wasn't going to help me. After a few more seconds of silence—where I accidentally got distracted by wondering what mix of orange, red, yellow, and brown I'd need to blend to get his exact hair color—he let out a big breath.

"Fine. Look, I've been needing to hire someone to come in once a week and clean the lobby and customer bathroom. That's it. Me and my guys take care of the rest of the shop. The lobby needs dusting, vacuuming, and windows washed. The bathroom, well, normal bathroom cleaning. It's probably a thirty-minute task, at most. When I priced it

out, a maid service would charge fifty dollars a week for a small job like that. If you're interested, you can take it and work until your debt is paid off."

Well, that wasn't what I'd expected. Pro: no money had to exchange hands, and I knew how to clean. Con: I would have to see Connor once a week after a lifetime of successful avoidance. Still . . .

"At once a week it would only take you about four and a half months to pay off, rather than the eighteen months if you paid me a monthly cash payment," he added.

A retort hovered on my lips, defending my ability to do the math myself, but I slapped my mouth shut before it could escape. "It sounds more than fair, to me," I said. "Too fair. Are you sure?"

"I'm sure that I'm tired of staying thirty minutes later on Saturdays to clean this space. It would be nice to have more weekend time free."

"Would it need to be done on Saturdays?" I asked.

"Not necessarily. Just once a week, after hours. Whatever day works best for you."

"My shift at the diner isn't set. Could it be a different day each week?"

"Sure."

I looked away from him to take in the lobby. Then I walked to the bathroom to check it out. It was a bare minimum one-seater and didn't look to be too awfully dirty. Heck, if I could clean my entire family home in two hours, I could do this rinky dink shop in under thirty minutes, no problem.

"Okay. Sounds like a deal."

"I'll pull your car out of the bay. Your new job starts next week."

He stepped behind the reception desk to snag my keys and then walked back into the shop where he pushed a button that got the big bay door sliding open. I exited the lobby and waited for him to pull my car around to where I was standing in the parking lot. Ice melt pellets crunched under my boots as I shifted my stance, still a little nervous about everything.

He pulled the car over to where I was standing and left the engine running as he got out. He held the driver's door for me while I climbed in. "You shouldn't have any more trouble getting it to start. If you do, let me know."

I closed the door and offered a slight wave as I pulled from the parking lot and headed in the direction of the grocery store. The grinding and knocking noises were gone. Things felt a lot more solid. The man really did work magic.

In the privacy of the car, relieved tears pricked at my eyes. I'd tried to play it off, but I'd been worried for weeks over the repairs I knew my car needed. I felt safe driving for the first time in a while, and it felt amazing.

CHAPTER SIX

"You thought Connor was trying to proposition you?" Kelly laughed, her shoulders shaking, tears of amusement pooling in her eyes. "I can't get over it."

"I noticed. You've mentioned it about eight thousand times today," I growled.

"I'm sorry, it's just . . . Connor? There's no way." Kelly handed me a stack of clean plates out of the dishwasher at Jake's Diner and leaned back to get her own.

I took the heavy stack from her and walked to the counter where we stored them. "What do you mean, no way? Connor is probably the only man in town I would worry about soiling my reputation."

"Because it's still 1850 and he ruffles your petticoats?" Kelly hip bumped me out of the way and stacked her plates next to mine. "Liv, listen to yourself. Has Connor ever done anything to you personally to make you distrust him?"

"He doesn't have to. I know all about him. I've lived here my whole life, remember?" Kelly pulled a face and walked back to the dishwasher with me following. "It's like you've forgotten that we had a front row seat to all the stuff he was doing, Kell. What happened?"

"I told you, he's my friend now. Besides, we've all been out of high school for years now, and people can change. Connor isn't going to chase a girl who's not interested in him, which you clearly aren't, so you have nothing to worry about."

"Thank goodness I'm not his type," I mumbled sarcastically and picked up another stack of plates. "Does that still include you?"

"It does. Now that we've spent some time hanging out, I'm willing to say he was right. We're good as friends."

"So, he's not your next potential husband?"

Kelly dimpled at me. "I didn't say that. If he changes his mind, I could still climb on the love train with him."

I couldn't help a little grin that peeked out. "Classy as always."

"How does Blaine feel about you working at the shop now?"

"He doesn't know. I just told him that I worked something out. It's my private business."

"You're the only girl I know who doesn't tell her boyfriend squat about her actual life." Kelly handed me a big bin of clean silverware and led the way out of the kitchen to a booth where we could sit and wrap the silverware into sets for the next day.

"I tell him things," I defended. The vinyl on the booth seat squeaked as I slid into place and reached for the bin.

Kelly sat across from me and shook her head. "Nothing real. Like, does he know anything about your family?"

"He doesn't need to worry about all the struggles in my life."

"Those struggles are what make up your life. Not telling him about those is the equivalent of not talking at all. He obviously wants to be a part of things."

"I know."

Kelly paused and caught my eye. "So why don't you let him? You've got a crazy cute boyfriend who is successful. What am I missing here?"

I shrugged. "Nothing. He's great, but . . . "

"But . . . "

"I'm still not sure I want a boyfriend, and I really wish everyone would stop calling him that."

To her credit she didn't remind me of her long-held belief that a man would solve everything. Instead she cocked her head to the side and asked, "Why?"

"I have plans."

"Your plans could have room for a companion."

"Maybe. But I need more time to see if that's true or not. I don't want to get sidetracked by a set of gorgeous blue eyes. I can't . . . "

She reached across the table and grabbed my hand. "I know. You can't do your mom's life." I nodded, appreciating that she understood my deep fears. We worked quietly for a few moments, before I blurted out, "Seriously, every time he says something about liking me or wanting to take care of me I feel like I want to run away or something."

Her eyebrows raised. "Sounds like it's safe to say you aren't getting warm flutters."

I shook my head. "I should be, though, right?"

"Listen, if I waited for warm flutters all the time, I wouldn't have nearly as much fun as I do. Blaine likes you. Good for him. I like you too. So does your family. It's not like being liked is new for you. Those words shouldn't make you want to run in fear." She steadily worked, keeping her eyes on her task. "Just let it play out. There are worse things than having a guy like Blaine fall in love with you."

"Fall in love with me? That's a huge step from 'let it play out.' My gosh, we're still getting to know each other."

"There's that whole love at first sight thing."

"I guess it's possible," I said thoughtfully. "Men are more visual than women and ten percent more likely to believe in love at first sight."

"This has nothing to do with science." Kelly groaned.

"Well, the type of love you're chasing is definitely not scientific," I teased. She tossed a fork at me, which I dodged while laughing. "What if I decide I don't want to be distracted by a boyfriend?"

"Then plant one last one on him and shut the door in his face."

I chuckled. "Good plan."

"I'm here anytime you need advice."

The conversation lulled after that, and I couldn't help but steal glances at the clock. My shift was over soon, and I was planning to go to Mainstreet Mechanic afterwards for my first cleaning shift. Connor had promised to come back and meet me there. He'd show me where the cleaning supplies were and give me a key so that I could come whenever I needed to after hours and lock up when I was done.

"Your eyes have that squingy look again," Kelly interrupted my musings.

"That's still not a word."

"Yet your eyes are still doing it. Worried about your first night cleaning the mechanic shop?"

I sighed. "A little. Do you want to come with me? Be a buffer between Connor and me?"

"You've never needed a buffer in your entire life. You'll be fine."

I wrinkled my nose. "How did he suddenly get sucked into our lives when it was our motto to avoid, avoid, avoid?"

"My fault. In my defense, though, he grew those muscles and let his hair get a little longer. Have you noticed that he has freckles? They're super dreamy . . . strictly from an observational friend type standpoint."

"My eyes are feeling squingy again," I replied.

She chuckled. "Seriously, Connor is just a normal guy. Be you. That will be enough to keep him away."

This time it was my turn to throw silverware at her. "You're probably the worst person I could have chosen as a best friend."

"The feeling is mutual."

"Stop yapping and get to work," Jake yelled from over the countertop as a last-minute customer came in.

"Aye-aye, Captain." Kelly saluted him and stood to go help the man waiting at the hostess stand. Before she walked away she turned to me and said, "You'll be fine. Everything really will be fine. Just breathe."

I nodded and gave her a small smile as I watched her flame-like hair bouncing back and forth while she sauntered up to the counter.

At exactly 9:07 I arrived at the mechanic shop and pulled warily into the dark parking lot. A single light was burning from the office behind the lobby, and Connor's truck was parked out front. The doors were locked, so I knocked softly. Connor appeared, out of his jumpsuit and back in his regular jeans and T-shirt look that I usually saw him in around town.

His hair was a bit disheveled, like he'd been running his fingers through it, and the office light caught it from behind, weaving bright highlights into it. It was a color I'd have to remember when painting something with fire.

"Hey, Liv," he greeted as he held the door for me.

I did my best to squeeze by him without making contact, but my hip brushed against him, causing a strange tingle in my fingertips. I balled them into fists, willing the feeling to go away. Why hadn't he moved and let me hold the door for myself?

"Come on through here and I'll show you where everything is," he said.

His voice was low and raspy, and he sounded tired. He'd probably been at work since early that morning. Having to come back had added time to his day. I hoped that meant he'd be quick in showing me what I needed and then taking himself out.

I followed him into the office, where he stopped next to a desk that took up the majority of the small space. "Here's your key." He handed me a key that was still warm from his hand. "Shop closes at 7:00 PM on weekdays and noon on Saturdays. We aren't open on Sundays. You're welcome to come anytime after business hours. Any questions?"

"Nope. I got it."

He turned and led me through a small door that opened up into a storage closet big enough to walk around in. It was cluttered with file boxes, random automotive parts and tools, and a shelf full of cleaning supplies

"How's your car running?" he asked over his shoulder.

I frowned, surprised by the sudden turn. "Better, thanks."

"I'm especially proud of freeing that kidnapped man from your trunk. I'm hoping for some kind of certificate of model citizenship or something."

My lips tugged in amusement. "I'm not going to ask what that knock was, or what you had to do to get rid of it. I'm just going to scrub toilets until the debt is paid."

"Well, I couldn't have made anything worse." He picked an empty bucket off the ground and started filling it with clean rags and some rubber gloves. "How's school going?"

"School?" Why was he asking me about my life? We'd lived in this same town for, well, forever, and he'd never once tried to talk to me. I liked it that way.

"Yeah, school."

"It's fine."

"You getting your studying done?"

Again, a strange question from someone I'd never spoken to until last week. I knew my expression oozed cynicism. "No offense, but what do you care?"

"I care about my community members," he replied.

I played a hunch. "Is this because you and my best friend have decided to be pals?" He stood up straight and raised his eyebrows but said nothing. I sighed. "If I tell you, will you let me start cleaning?" I asked. He nodded. "It's fine. I'm studying as much as I can."

"Great." He pushed off the shelves and gestured behind him. "Here are the supplies." Then he handed me the bucket and disappeared rather abruptly.

I turned to gather bathroom cleaners and went back through the office into the lobby. Connor was looking out the front window and making no move to leave.

"What are you doing?" I asked.

He turned slowly to face me. "Wondering how many classes you're taking."

"I think we need to set up some ground rules about me working here." I set the cleaning things on the reception desk and folded my arms across my chest.

His eyebrows raised. "Rules?"

"Yes, rules. Rule number one: we don't discuss my private life, and we certainly do not discuss yours."

"Afraid you'd be jealous of my exciting adventures?"

"No. Rule two: I'm dating someone."

"That doesn't seem like a rule as much as just information you're sharing with me. It's not really new info, though. I've met him, remember? Blaine. Nice guy. A little stiff, but he'd take good care of you if you'd let him."

My jaw dropped. "If I'd let him? I don't even—no, that goes back to rule one."

"Suit yourself. Just my observation. Why does your dating need to be a rule?"

"You flirt with everyone," I stated. He made a face. "You're the one with the reputation, not me."

"All malicious gossip. Are there any more of these rules?"

I nodded and held up my fingers, ticking off another. "Rule three: you should be gone when I come here to clean."

Now he sounded a tad incredulous, his chatty confidence slipping. "You're telling me when I'm allowed to be at my own shop?"

I sucked in a deep breath, knowing I sounded horrible, bossy, and rude. "Sorry. Can you please just go home and let me work?'"

"Fine. I'm going, but it's only because I'm tired and ready to call it a day. Lock the door behind me. Oh, and fair warning, next time I see you, I may have a few of my own rules to add to the list." He left through the front door, climbed into his truck, and drove out of the parking lot as I turned the deadbolt.

My estimation of how long it would take to clean proved correct. In twenty-five short minutes I had the lobby and bathroom sparkling. Even better, I owed fifty dollars less on my debt to the auto shop.

At home, things weren't quite as sparkly and clean. In fact, it looked like I hadn't cleaned in a week, when in reality I'd cleaned up that morning before my shift at Jake's. Blankets were strewn around the family room, plates and cups from mom's lunch and Sadie's dinner were piled on the coffee and end tables, the TV was still blaring although no one was there, and magazines lay open on every surface. I dreaded entering the kitchen.

When I did flip on the kitchen light my heart sank. Only three people lived in this house, yet it looked like ten people had come in and made themselves dinner before walking away from it without eating. I closed my eyes and took a few deep breaths.

My cell phone ringing split the silence and I answered quickly. "Hello?"

"Hey, babe," Blaine's cheerful voice replied. "How was your day?"

"Pretty busy." I thought about letting it go at that but remembered Kelly saying I didn't let Blaine in. "Just getting home and it looks like I'll need to clean the house. My mom and sister can be really messy." It was the most I'd ever complained to him about anything.

"That's too bad. That's why I stopped having roommates. Maybe they just had a busy day and they'll take care of it tomorrow."

"Yeah, probably."

No, they wouldn't. They never did. Mom worked two jobs herself. Sadie was on the high school dance team and was always off with friends in the evenings either for rehearsals or hanging out. I did the chores. All of them. The groceries, the cleaning, the meals. I couldn't remember how it started falling to me, but I knew why I let it continue.

I did it for Mom because she needed someone she could depend on, and I loved her.

I listened to Blaine tell me about his day while I stacked dishes in the sink. His voice was comforting and helped the chores go faster. For the first time I allowed the idea into my head of working as a team. During the good years of my parents' marriage they'd often worked together. The sounds of their chitchat and laughter had been the backdrop of my childhood. Maybe working with a partner—the right partner—would make things seem less like a burden. I'd have to give it some thought.

CHAPTER SEVEN

Music thumped through my bedroom floor hard enough that I could feel it on the soles of my feet as I jumped off my bed and stomped to the door. I walked far enough down the stairs to be able to see the living room. The smell of a lot of different fruity body sprays hit me, along with the sight of at least ten girls lounging around the room still wearing their athletic wear. They must have come straight from drill practice. The remnants of nachos were on plates laying here and there, the smell of the cheese adding another element to the situation. The girls were passing their phones around and laughing, although I had no idea how they could hear each other.

"Sadie, honestly, I have to study. Please, turn down the music," I called as loudly as I could.

She didn't even bother looking up at me as she yelled, "Stop being so old." A chorus of giggles followed.

I wanted to hurl angry words back at the group of teens below, but instead I went into my room and slammed the door, hard. I couldn't concentrate, which was a major problem seeing as I had a paper to write and needed to do some research first.

I'd worked the early shift that day, after which I'd cleaned the house and grocery shopped. I wondered if we had any food left after this spontaneous house party. My hands clenched in anger at my sides as a sense of dreaded helplessness boiled in my stomach. I hated it, hated feeling trapped by the impossible tasks of doing it all. I couldn't wait to be on my own, with only myself to worry about. It would be the sweetest feeling of freedom.

It was 7:15 PM and I hadn't seen Mom all day. I still needed to head to the mechanic shop to clean, and I didn't have time to be the adult right now. I'd been hoping to study for another hour and then go clean after I knew for sure that Connor would be long gone.

I stomped to my bed and flopped down on my stomach, pushing my face into my quilt and letting out a scream that I knew no one could hear. I needed a quiet place to study. I needed a place free of aggravations, bass notes, and interruptions. I needed so much more than I dared to voice aloud.

Then, the light bulb hit. The mechanic shop. I could take my books and study in the office before cleaning. I'd wanted to give him a wide berth, but the reality was that Connor should already be gone. He wouldn't have to know, and I wouldn't be bothering anyone. It's not like I'd be on the clock. They'd only pay me for actual time worked. It wasn't perfect, but it was a plan.

Newly energized, I frantically packed my backpack, bundled up in my coat and mittens, and raced out into the cold night. This was going to work. No one would have any idea I was at the shop, and they would never bother me there. I'd close the office door so that no one from the street could see the light on. It was perfect, perfect, perfect.

Light flakes of fluffy snow stuck to my eyelashes as I dashed from the loud warmth of my house out to my popsicle of a car. The quiet of the drive over to the shop allowed my tense shoulders to begin to unwind. This was going to work.

Sure enough, the shop was pitch black when I showed up. I let myself in and went straight to the office. I made sure to close the door before flipping on the light. The desk was messy, but there was a big, oversized chair behind the desk that I could sit in and read the chapters I needed to get done.

I slipped out of my coat and used it to cover over me like a blanket when I sat down with my feet tucked under me. The heat was turned down for the overnight hours, which didn't bother me while cleaning, but would catch up to me while sitting.

It was cozy and quiet in the office, wrapped in my coat and reading my textbook, and a welcome peace stole over me. The falling snow dampened outside noises as my breathing became deeper. I could hear the hum of the fluorescent lights above the desk. I hadn't felt this kind of stillness around me in ages. I sank into it, not wanting to break the spell.

"Liv?" A voice pulled me slowly from a dark place. It was a man's voice. "Wake up."

A large, warm hand landed on my shoulder and I jolted awake, blinking hard at the unfamiliar surroundings. A shadow in front of me caused me to scream.

"It's Connor. You fell asleep," the shadow said.

He gradually came into focus. His auburn hair, amber eyes, freckles that dotted his cheeks and nose. I'd love to paint those freckles. Wait . . .

"What?" I blinked some more.

He took a step back, giving me some breathing room. "You fell asleep. I drove past on my way out tonight and saw your car here. When I drove past on my way home and it was still here, I got worried. Thought I'd better check in."

"Well, bat's eyebrows." I stood up and heard the thud of my notebook falling to the floor.

"Bat's what?"

"You weren't supposed to catch me here." I bent to retrieve the book at the same time he did, and our fingers tangled. The heat of it climbed my arm, causing me to drop it again.

"Do you often sneak in here to sleep?" He handed me my notes.

I shook my head and pushed back my curls, avoiding his gaze. "Of course not. I was coming here to clean and thought I'd take advantage of a quiet place to study for a while first. I must have fallen asleep." I shoved past him to get to my bag and tuck the notebook inside. "I'll just clean now and be on my way."

"It's almost eleven."

My head snapped up to meet his eyes. They were liquid honey oozing amusement, and I understood, not for the first time, why girls liked him so much regardless of the risk he was. I licked my lips and blushed when his eyes moved to my mouth.

"Are you serious?" I couldn't believe I'd slept for that long.

"Totally."

Flustered, I went back to the storage closet. "I'll still clean and then be on my way."

"You can do it another night," he replied.

I shook my head. "This is the only free night I have this week."

"I can help you, then. We'll get it done twice as fast."

"No. No way." I hefted the bucket of supplies and came back out to where he was still standing. "You hired me and I'll do it alone."

"Is that rule number four in your life?" he asked "'I do it alone.'"

"It's a good rule. Statistically speaking, I'm twice as efficient working alone. Besides, I can't pay you back for fixing my car if you're helping me do the job. It's simple math," I replied without heat.

"Fair enough." He turned and walked out of the office. "But just so you know, it wasn't your statistics that convinced me. It was the math," he called over his shoulder. He reached the front door at the same time I stepped out of the office. "I don't like you being here alone cleaning this late, though. Make sure you lock the door behind me."

"It's okay. I have a foolproof plan to foil any attackers," I replied. He looked back at me with a question in his eyes. "If someone tries to carry me off into the woods, I'll just go limp, you know, like toddlers do when they don't want to do something. You've seen that, right?" He nodded. "Carrying dead weight is hard, even when it's only a thirty-pound toddler. When a full-grown woman's body plays dead, it's not going to be easy to spirit away."

"Your plan is to play dead?"

"Yep."

"How about, just as an extra precaution, you also lock the door behind me?" He was trying not to laugh, and for some reason it made a grin pop out on my own face.

"Fine. Scaredy-cat," I replied.

He said nothing more, just shook his head and left the building. I locked the door as promised and watched as his truck pulled out of the parking lot, fading into the darkness.

* * * * *

Two days later I was working the dinner shift. Blaine was sitting at the counter, and I'd been genuinely happy to see him enter the diner. He was wearing a navy blue suit and a pink tie. He was lean and the suit was tailored in a way that added to his allure. Unfortunately, he wasn't terribly happy with me at the moment. The feeling had become mutual, as I wasn't happy with him thinking he got a say in my choices. But I was trying really hard to play it cool. So, yeah, it wasn't going well.

"Wait, so to be clear, you're cleaning a mechanic shop after hours?" he asked for at least the third time when I walked past him. I nodded. "I thought you were working out a payment plan."

"This is the payment plan," I called over my shoulder as I walked back toward the kitchen.

His eyebrows furrowed. "I'm not sure I like it."

When I returned from handing in my orders I paused in front of him, still holding an order pad in my hands. "You wanted me to get my car fixed."

"Sure, but I didn't want you to end up slaved out to a sketchy mechanic."

A surprised laugh burst out. "When I told you he was sketchy, you told me he seemed like a great guy."

"Well, that was when I wanted you to trust him to fix your car."

"You got what you wanted," I reminded him. "He did a great job fixing my car. It runs better than it has in a long time."

"Just from new brakes and an alternator?"

I shrugged. "I guess. He'd have told me if he did anything else, and he didn't mention anything."

"What about that knocking sound?"

"Gone."

"Huh. Wonder what it was?"

"I have zero idea." I walked around the counter to the hostess station where a group of four was waiting to be seated. I could see Blaine tapping his fingers on the top of the bar while he waited for my return.

When I did come back, he was ready for me. "Are you safe there alone at night? Does he come back and bother you?"

"Come on, Blaine, that's not even worth asking."

"You said he had a bad reputation."

"I'm not his type at all," I shot back as I once more walked away.

"You're every guy's type, Olivia," he called after me.

His remark made a few of the regulars—old men drinking coffee and eating fries—clap and whistle. It was harmless, but it made me blush. I looked back to Blaine, who had an apologetic look on his face. He too seemed to have some extra color, and it made the light blue of his eyes pop behind his glasses.

I had to focus on orders and busing tables for a bit, but when I returned to where Blaine was finishing up his meal I was able to stop for a minute.

"I meant what I said." He jumped right back in like always. The man's mind was a steal trap. "How much do you really trust this guy? He's getting you to a dark building after hours with no one around to see."

"I have a plan." I smiled. I told him about playing dead like a toddler.

"Your plan is to play dead?" His voice was flat and staunchly unamused.

"You're not reacting the way Connor did," I replied.

"You told *him* your plan?"

Oops. Bad choice. "He wanted me to be safe."

"For the record, if you don't trust him you really shouldn't have told him your plan, even if it is ridiculous." Blaine's face took on a stubborn look.

I was taken aback by his reaction. Of course I wouldn't play dead if someone tried to kidnap me. I'd fight, kick, scream, claw, and hit them over the head repeatedly with my backpack. Connor had understood that. Blaine did not.

"If I'd been honestly worried about him, I wouldn't have agreed to clean the shop, or told him about playing dead. Besides, that's not my actual survival plan."

His lips were pinched. "Well, that's a relief."

The kitchen bell rang, saving me from any more of Blaine's remarks. I carried plates of food and took orders. All the while I watched Blaine out of the corner of my eye. He was so well put together, attractive, professional, successful, and as smooth as an ice-skating rink. Sometimes I felt like I had to be on my best behavior around him. Maybe that was why I held back with him. I was still trying to work out how we fit together.

"Liv, phone call for you," Kelly called over the noise of the diner.

I nodded at her, took food to the customers that were waiting, and headed back into the hallway where the phone hung on the wall.

"This is Liv."

"Liv, honey, it's Mom." My mom's perpetually sad voice came over the phone. "What time do you get off?"

"I'll be home around ten," I told her.

"It's just that I can't get home and Sadie needs dinner."

"Trust me, Sadie can make her own. I come home to evidence of that all over the kitchen every night."

"I don't need attitude from you." She sighed and I heard the weight she was feeling come through.

"Sorry."

I was. I was sorry that she had to work two jobs while Dad was off doing who knows what. I was sorry that I knew the oil workers made good money, but we hadn't shared in that. I was sorry that we all lived in a place somewhere between understanding we'd been abandoned and an ability to move forward.

"Is there any way you can take a break and run her some take-out?" Mom asked.

I hesitated, unsure of how to respond. I wouldn't have another break for a while, and even then it was only ten minutes. Then I thought of Blaine sitting out there, always wishing he could be more a part of my life. But, as usual, I couldn't bring myself to ask. Especially tonight, when he was already put out with me.

"I'll see what I can do," I said at last.

"Thanks, honey. I'll let her know it's coming."

I hung up and took a moment to suck in three breaths through my nose and let them out through my mouth. Mom babied Sadie, who didn't need babying at all. And I babied Mom, who didn't need it either. Only in my most secret place did I ever admit I'd like to be babied a little too. But we were in a cycle, with no apparent way out.

I popped into the kitchen and ordered a Cobb salad for Sadie before heading back to where Blaine was still sitting. His meal had been cleared, and he was sipping on water with a lemon wedge. Obviously he'd been waiting to say goodbye to me before he left, which brightened me up a bit.

I walked around the counter to stand next to him. He opened his arms and pulled me into his embrace, snuggling his face through my curls until his nose pressed in just above my ear.

"Sorry. I worry about you because I care so much," he said.

"I'll be totally fine. Oak Hills is a tiny town where we all know each other. I'm safe."

He pulled away and pressed a quick kiss on my lips, which had the whistling older men back at it. We both laughed.

"Who was on the phone?"

"My mom."

"Oh, yeah?" he rubbed his hands up my arms. "Everything okay?"

"Of course." The lie came easily, as all things do with practice.

"Good." His hands grabbed mine. "Can I see you again soon?"

"Sure."

He leaned forward and placed another quick peck on my lips before standing, gathering his beautiful wool coat, and heading for the door. I watched him go, wondering why I hadn't just asked him to drop a salad off to my sister a few blocks away. Especially because I had no idea how I was going to make it happen.

"I've been thinking . . . " Connor plopping down on the stool that Blaine had just vacated caused me to jump, and I squealed a bit. He had a toothpick in his mouth and a to-go bag in his hands. Everything about him broadcast a carefree feeling, and I felt resentment where none was warranted.

"A first I'm sure," I replied, taking a step back and putting my hand over my heart.

"Ignoring that. If you need a quiet place to study sometimes, you're welcome to use the office at the shop any time after hours," he said. I was too shocked to reply. "Just don't use it for making out with your boyfriend. I saw enough of that tonight."

He popped right back up without waiting for a response and headed out the door, his gait easy and confident. By the time I had a retort ready, the taillights of his truck were blinking goodbye.

"You lead an interesting life, Liv," Kelly said as she came to stand next to me.

"It's about to get even more interesting. I need to find a way to sneak out and deliver a salad to Sadie."

"How much time do you need?" she asked.

I smiled over at her and resisted the urge to give her a hug. Every time I started to feel alone, Kelly appeared and reminded me that I wasn't and never would be. She was my sister in all the ways that counted.

"Five to seven minutes."

"I've been meaning to throw a fit over something. I'll head back and distract Jake." She got a determined look on her face and headed behind the counter just as the Cobb salad was handed through the window.

I followed her, grabbing the salad and dashing for the door with a smirk on my face as I heard her loud voice carry through the diner. "Jake, you snake, I have a bone to pick with you . . . "

CHAPTER EIGHT

The next week, after banging my head against the wall to get some peace and quiet at home, I decided to go ahead and study at the mechanic shop. It wasn't because Connor had offered. It was because it was the logical solution to my problem. I wasn't planning to clean tonight but assumed he wouldn't mind if I used it whenever. The offer hadn't had any caveats.

The cool air felt good on my overheated skin when I lugged my backpack out the front door half an hour after the shop closed. Before trying to study I'd been mopping floors and vacuuming at my house, attempting to repair damage done by a serious lack of care from the others living there. As luck would have it, just as I'd finished, Sadie had banged through the door with her friends and I'd known it was all for naught.

My hair still felt sweaty, and I knew my curls would be extra frizzed out. I didn't care. I didn't bother to cover them or calm them. It was what it was. I grabbed my coat and carried it in my arms, enjoying the blast of ice when I left the house. My car door stuck a little when I tried to get in, so I delivered a swift kick to the lower panel and was rewarded.

The roads were dark and lonely this time of night, and the shop was blessedly black when I arrived after the short drive. I turned off the car and climbed out. Goosebumps covered my arms, and my head felt cold where the air blew across the sweat that had accumulated. My backpack slapped against my thigh while I crossed the parking lot to unlock the door and let myself in.

I let my backpack fall to a chair, then turned and locked the door behind me. The lobby smelled of grease and oil, with a slightly lemony scent underneath it all, a scent that was slowly becoming familiar to me. In the office I flipped on the light, but feeling no need to hide, I left the door open. Connor would know it was me and why I was there.

I cleared a small work space on the desk and sat in the big chair. Tonight's project was a math assignment. I detested math and the people who touted that it could be interesting. Mom insisted that I had a head for numbers, just not the heart for them. She was probably right. I understood it . . . when I tried to understand it. The rest of the time I just moped and moaned my way through it.

The room was cool, and the sweat my body had produced did its work, making the transition from overheated to chilled happen fairly quickly. I grabbed my coat and draped it over my shoulders. The chill was good. It would keep me awake. I lost track of the time as I labored over numbers that I had no interest in learning. Too bad that math would be an important part of nursing. I hoped that the computers would do most of the work for me. There was a chance I'd be disappointed by the truth.

The bang of a door opening startled me out of my seat. I was on my feet in an instant, my heart thumping as my eyes flew to the open office door. This was it, the thing that Blaine and Connor had both warned me about. I tried to think limp thoughts, but I was too nervous to relax all the muscles in my body.

"It's good that you're here." Kelly's red head popped around the door, but her body stayed out of sight. "Come see."

Wait, Kelly? "What are you . . . "

"Answers later, movement now."

Her head popped back out of sight about the same time I registered how sparkly her eyes had been. Whatever was going on, Kelly was happy about it. I pushed my arms into the sleeves of my coat and followed. Willing my heart to settle wasn't as easy as it should have been. This unexpected twist was making my skin itself jump.

I followed Kelly through the lobby and into the shop area where Connor's tow truck was backed up to one of the bays. On the bed was a greenish SUV of some sort. The rear end had two flat tires.

Kelly and Connor were standing next to the tow truck with their backs to me. I could feel the cool air blowing across the shop, and shivered a little. Kelly was wearing a big coat and had a bright purple scarf wrapped around her neck. She was listening as Connor said something I couldn't hear. He too was dressed in warm clothing, but where Kelly's coat was big and puffy, he was in a plain brown work coat.

Kelly turned as I walked up to stand next to her. "Isn't this a beauty?" she said happily. I wasn't seeing beauty, but I said nothing, understanding that my car wasn't going to win any contests either. "Connor helped me find it for a real great price."

"It's got two flats."

"Tires are an easy fix." Kelly shrugged. "Everything else seems to be in good working order."

"Good, you can do the driving from now on." I smiled. Kelly had never owned a car, and this would be a fun step for her. It would also be a fun step for me, as I'd no longer have to endure her whining about my driving.

"It'll be nice to not have to wear a helmet anymore." Kelly grinned, proving my inner monologue to be true.

Connor turned, and I noticed a smudge of dirt across his forehead. It made him look more human and less perfect. "Can one of you jump in the tow truck and move slowly forward until I tell you to stop? I need a little more room back here."

I shook my head. "Sounds like a job for Kelly."

"Come on, Liv, you can do anything." Kelly cheered and waved fake pompoms in the air. "Two, four, six, eight, who do we appreciate . . . "

I held up a hand as a corner of my mouth lifted. "Lies and peppy cheers won't help you."

"Get in the truck, Liv," Connor suddenly barked in an angry voice. I jumped, eyes wide, and he laughed. "I was trying a different technique."

Kelly giggled. "I'm not sure it got the result you were after. There's a little accident over there to mop up." Their eyes met and they shared a look that was surprisingly chummy, and annoyingly at my expense. Then Kelly turned to me, her eyes still big and bright. "Come on, I'll just die if I can't see the whole process in motion. Please? Bestie?"

"Fine." I pursed my lips and walked to the front of the big vehicle. "I expect a warm apple pie delivered directly to me."

"How about years of loyalty and devotion instead?" She pulled a face and I rolled my eyes, which was her signal to wrap me in a hug. "I love you the very best," she said. I hugged her back, briefly.

"When you two are done hugging it out, keys are in the ignition," Connor called. "Just start it up and close the door. You should be able to see my hand signals in the side mirror. Take it slow, like idle speed, until I tell you to stop."

I didn't feel like the right person for the job, but I climbed up the Mount Everest of trucks and positioned myself in the driver's seat. I couldn't reach the pedals, which made me wiggle with nerves. I was going to have to move the seat forward, and I hoped Connor wasn't one of those people who hated having their seat moved. Like me. I hated it. If someone else drove my car it took weeks of back and forth tweaking until I found the sweet spot again. This was one bonus to having a beater: no one asked to drive your car very often.

I let out a little squeak of surprise as I turned the key and the engine roared to life. I'd spent very little time around big rigs. Okay, none. I'd spent none. The way it jolted and rocked while sitting completely still surprised me. I hadn't known you could feel the vibrations that way.

"Ready?" Connor yelled. I slammed the giant door shut and angled my head to see him in the mirror. He was facing me, and I reached out a hand to wave. "Go ahead," he called.

I put the truck in drive and let off the brakes. It began to crawl forward inch by inch. I kept my eyes on Connor. He seemed okay with the speed, so I avoided pressing the gas pedal. He waved continually, only once signaling for me to stop before he disappeared around the back of the vehicle. Then he was back, waving at me to go again.

It felt like it took a long time, but really it was probably only sixty seconds or less before he signaled me to stop again. This time he yelled to cut the engine. I put the big guy in park, turned it off, and jumped down.

"Nailed it." I smiled as the three of us came to stand next to Kelly's new ride.

He grinned down at me. "What's happening with these curls of yours tonight? Did you have an incident with a light socket?" He reached out a hand, and before I could react, he was winding one of my spastic ringlets around his pointer finger.

"Oh, no, bad move. She hates people touching her hair," Kelly said before I had a chance to.

I shook my head, confused as a rush of unwelcome heat crawled up my back. His expression was unreadable, but he dropped his hand. "Rule number five: Leave my curls alone," I said, only it was missing the strength I'd meant to inject it with. Instead I sounded confused.

"I agree to nothing," he stated.

Kelly laughed. "She's setting rules already, huh?"

"Oh, so it's not just me?" Connor asked.

"I'm afraid not," Kelly replied.

"What kind of rules has she given you?" Connor's eyes filled with mirth.

Kelly held up her pointer finger and grinned. "Rule number one: no screaming in my car . . . " she began.

"Well, that's my cue to leave." I turned away.

"You don't want to stick around and watch us unload it?" Kelly asked while I crossed the shop floor.

I did, but I mostly didn't. I did not want to spend any more time wondering why Connor's way of talking jived so well with ours, or why he and Kelly were out car shopping together, or why he'd thought he could touch my hair.

I paused at the doorway into the lobby and called over my shoulder, "I've got math waiting for me back inside, but when you get tires on that thing, I get dibs on the first donut run." Despite my unsure emotions about Connor, Kelly was still my bestie, and I didn't want to hurt her feelings by bowing totally out.

"You'd never guess it, but she loves sprinkles," I heard Kelly say with a chuckle.

I didn't hear his reply, but their laughter told me they'd found it amusing. I retreated back to my study cave. What a strange night this had turned out to be. I saw firsthand what Kelly had been telling me. She and Connor were friends. Actual friends. She hadn't flirted with him at all. She'd been her true self, and I couldn't fathom what that meant . . . or why they weren't dating. I'd always thought friendship should come before love, and they seemed perfect for each other.

*****

The next night I was lacing up ice-skates and cursing Blaine's attractiveness. Only those sweet blue eyes could have talked me into this. I hated ice-skating. I was bad at it. I figured God had made a mistake when he gave me a curvaceous figure and tiny ankles that didn't offer the needed support. Plus, ice was slippery and wet. Two of my least favorite things.

However, it was a break, and it was with Blaine. I needed both. Ever since Kelly had planted the idea of letting Blaine in more, I'd been trying. I'd dared to express to him my stress over school, which was an opening. He'd been sympathetic and kind, remembering those days himself, and I'd been caught off guard by the sense of camaraderie I felt by sharing a little part of my life.

"You look really cute on skates," he said to me as he helped me rise to stand.

"I feel like a yeti." I glanced once more at him and wondered if he actually ordered fashion magazines and then matched his outfits to them.

He chuckled lightly. "You didn't have to wear that many layers. You'll warm up while skating."

I'd dug around Mom's closet until I'd found the puffiest marshmallow jacket in the world and layered it over my thinner winter coat. Add in a scarf and wool socks, and I was pretty set. "Yeah, well, I wanted the extra padding for when I fall."

He somehow performed the magic of walking backwards in his skates while keeping hold of my hands and helping me awkwardly balance-walk out to the ice. If I couldn't balance well on dry land, how was I going to balance on ice? The question didn't bear thinking about for long.

"It'll be romantic. We can hold hands the whole time." He pulled one of my hands up and kissed the back of it.

"My palms are going to sweat," I warned. They always got sweaty when I was uncomfortable.

"Doesn't bother me at all."

That's what everyone said, until they had someone else's palm sweat running down their hand. Infatuation only took you so far.

There was also self-respect and a sense of survival deeply embedded in every person.

We made it to the ice, and Blaine held me steady as I placed my feet onto the white death sheet one wobble at a time. I don't know who was more surprised when I didn't immediately tank it. Blaine amazingly continued facing backwards and holding my hands, for which I was grateful. I clung to him like a lifeline.

Up-tempo music played over the speaker system, competing with voices and the occasional happy—or terrified?—squeal. I could hear the sounds of skates slicing into the rink, and clung harder to his hands.

"What's that kid skating with over there?" I inclined my head.

Blaine turned to look. "Oh, those are walkers for learning to skate."

"That six-year-old is skating better than me thanks to that thing."

"Yes, but having a much less enjoyable time," he replied, swinging our hands back and forth playfully. "He doesn't get to hold hands with you."

I doubted that kid was jealous. It seemed like leaning on a walker and having some confidence was making this a pretty good experience for him. I also really doubted he was upset about not holding hands with someone at his age. I let it go.

"You're doing pretty great. Is this a hidden talent of yours?" I asked Blaine.

His eyes lit up, and I felt a little swoop. "Yes. I actually played hockey in high school."

"Really?" That's what I said, but what I really thought was, "Of course you did."

"I was pretty good."

"I believe that about you. Cool."

"What are your hidden talents?" he asked.

He spun to skate next to me and tucked my hand in his elbow. I didn't know what to do with the now free hand I had, so I let it flail in the air at my side. Seemed like it was helping. I hadn't fallen yet.

"Uh, nothing really. I clean house, cook, work at the diner, and do school. I'm a pretty boring book to read."

"I doubt that. I've been entertained for a couple of months now." He shot me a warm look, and I felt caught off guard by his genuine affection. "What do you do when you aren't cooking or cleaning?"

"Work or school."

"You're holding back on me," he nudged. "Your life can't really be that dull."

It was. Except for one thing. My painting. I wondered what his reaction would be if I opened my bedroom door and showed him the canvases stacked all around, filled with pictures from my head. I painted anything and everything. I wondered what he'd think of the piles of brushes, the smears of paint I'd spilled, or the underlying tang of paint thinner. I tried to open my mouth, but I couldn't make myself do it. I wasn't like so many other people, quick to open up and trust. I took time, even if it sometimes made me feel like something was wrong with me.

"I don't know what to tell you," I ended up saying.

"Fine. Then I'll just have to keep asking until you're ready to tell me."

He suddenly pulled us to a stop and leaned in to give me a kiss. He'd seriously underestimated my skills, because rather than enjoying a sweet moment, I toppled over backwards, pulling him with me. I slammed the ice flat on my back a heartbeat before he landed on top of me.

"Maybe we save the kissing for solid ground," I puffed out with a groan.

"Or, maybe I take advantage of this moment," he replied in a whisper.

He didn't linger over the kiss. We were, after all, in the middle of an ice rink surrounded by families. However, there was an intensity in it that I hadn't felt from him before. I shivered once more, but this time it was from the unspoken message: Blaine was ready to move to the next step, and it was time for me to buckle up for the ride.

CHAPTER NINE

I woke up a few days later and knew, before coming fully awake, that Dad was home. I could feel it in the way the house seemed full again. I could hear soft conversation coming from my parents' room down the hall, and the sound brought with it a comfort and security I missed. Then confusion had me sitting up straight in bed. Why was he here, and why was he in the bedroom? As far as I knew, nothing he needed remained in this house.

As a child I'd been a major daddy's girl. He'd tweak my curls and rub his whiskers on my cheeks, all the while telling anyone who would listen that his Liv was an angel. It had been that way even after Sadie, the mini female version of him, was born. The two of them were both tall and lean, dark and good-looking, with charismatic personalities. Maybe our connection came because I was so much like Mom, who was his comfortable opposite and, as Dad had insisted, his one true love.

When he'd changed jobs and essentially moved away a couple of years ago, it had felt like our house shrank in on itself, as though its life force had left it. We'd all relied on Dad's personality giving us a sun to revolve around. Mom was wonderful too, but she was more like me. Quieter, slower to warm up, slightly wary around others. She was the moon to his solar flares.

I sometimes thought of our home as a bounce house with a small leak. Over the weeks that he was gone the house would slowly collapse in on itself. Then he would come home, put some duct tape over the hole, pump it back up, and leave us in better shape. Only, his return visits grew sparse, and then when he would finally show up instead of duct tape he was using regular old gift wrapping tape that never quite attached firmly, and the house never got fully inflated. Finally, it had become my job to try to keep adding air, but it was getting harder, and it hurt to think about.

I heard his footsteps stop outside my door right before a knock sounded. "Olive, rise and shine," he called, using my silly childhood nickname, before pushing my door open. He was wearing regular street clothes and grinning as though he'd just slipped back into his old life.

"Dad?"

"I'm making breakfast for my three lovely ladies. Be downstairs in ten minutes." Too concerned to make a sound, I nodded before he moved down the hall to make the same announcement to Sadie. I couldn't hear Sadie's reply, but it was eight o'clock and I doubted she would be very happy about having Dad pop in without any warning either.

I'd struggled for a long time to figure out how one person leaving could tear things apart when the majority of us were still here. It was also hard for me to understand how I could continue to love him so much when I had a stone in the pit of my stomach, always suspecting he was holding things back from us, things that could have made life easier, truths that would set us all free.

I finger combed my hair, swished some mouthwash, and hurried downstairs, wanting some alone time before the others made their way down. I was happy to find him by himself, whipping up pancake batter and humming something along to the radio that sat in the window. It was the old kind with an antenna and circle-shaped dials that you had to rotate to find a station. It was only on when he was home.

"Hey, Olive, how'd you sleep?" he asked.

"When did you get here?"

He ignored that and leaned over to give me a light kiss on the head. "Mom says you've been a real help to her. Thanks, Liv. You know I depend on you to keep things going when I'm away."

With the compliment came the now familiar twist of wanting to please him, while knowing his words meant nothing.

"What's on your mind?" He read my expression, as he always did, before he turned to start cooking on the griddle. It irked me that he could still read me, as though he had any right to know what was going on in my mind.

I wasn't sure what I wanted to talk to him about. Anger, resentment, confusion, and a ball of hurt all lodged in my mind, making it impossible to know where to start. Did I hurl accusations, or was I grateful for any scrap of attention he threw our way? All those things I promised myself I'd say when I had the chance were frozen on my tongue. I hated myself in that moment for being too chicken to do anything other than stare at him.

He glanced at me while the spatula hovered over the sizzling pancakes. "Oh, that's right. I meant to give you some money to help with school. Don't let me forget, and we'll take care of it tonight." He smiled, flashing the one crooked tooth in the front that always gave him a boyish appearance, even though his hair had started to gray. "Tell me about this Blaine you're dating. Mom says he's a real 'upper crust' kind of guy."

Like a fool I sat at the table, unclenched my jaw, and spoke with all the emotion of a robot as I told him about Blaine, leaving out the parts about my mixed feelings. I already knew how my dad felt about love. He was firmly in the "love at first sight" camp, having sworn that's what had happened when he'd met Mom. Unfortunately for him, I now knew that love at first sight didn't mean it would last, and he was the last person I was going to take relationship advice from.

Mom and Sadie wandered in before I had decided where my emotions were. Relieved, I stopped talking. Mom was smiling indulgently at all of us, happy with her little family all together. Dad, as always, was the heart of it all. Laughing, teasing, and telling us stories. All the while I tried to tamp down on the fury over the fact that it was all a show, that nothing was actually normal anymore. I could hardly look at my mom, with her glowing eyes and her posture straight. How could she be eating this up?

As the week progressed, it became apparent that Dad hadn't just popped in for some random twenty-four hour visit. My worries about my family deepened. Rather than carrying on cheerfully like we had the first morning, Mom and Sadie fought and harped in a way they usually didn't. Sadie and Mom had always been close, and now it was me, desperately playing peacemaker for them. I vacillated between hoping this arguing and stress would open Mom's eyes, and an underlying fear that it would drive Dad away permanently—a situation I both dreaded and wished for. My chest was like a block of ice, but Dad pretended it wasn't happening. I was so entirely consumed with slapping Band-Aids on everything that I did the bare minimum on the jobs that I absolutely had to do and totally cut out studying.

The stress of it all finally wore me down so deeply that I got sick the day after Dad headed back to the oil fields, without giving me any of the promised college money, and without any real farewell. He wafted out of our lives the same way he'd drifted in. The money I could manage without, but the empty promise made my throat ache. It was painful to have such mixed emotions about someone the way I had about my father.

A cough settled deep in my chest, my head was on fire, and my throat felt like sandpaper. I snuggled on the couch, wrapped in the now-ratty pink and purple afghan my Grandma Phelps had given me for my eighth birthday, and flopped my head down on a pillow.

"I'm going to be really upset if I get that cold, Liv," Sadie said to me when she passed through the family room on her way to the kitchen. "I have a dance competition coming up, and I can't be sick."

Mom joined in from the doorway where she was putting on her coat to head to work. "Maybe you should quarantine yourself to your room for a couple of days."

I shot them both daggers. "When you two get sick you don't stay away in your rooms. You ask me to make you soup and you sit here and watch TV. Where's my soup?"

Mom's lips pinched. "I don't know what to tell you, Olivia. I have no more sick days, and Sadie is too busy to cook and clean." It wasn't like Mom to be callous, and the cut of her words was made harsher by the knowledge that they were coming from her own place of heartache.

"I manage to find the time," I murmured while misery tried to seep out of my eyes.

"Just stop whining and go upstairs." Sadie came from the kitchen with a box of crackers and a container of orange juice. "Here." She put them roughly down on the couch next to me.

I coughed hard, hunching into a ball. Sadie just pulled a face at me. I stood and gathered the items she'd brought into my arms. With one last look at them I stumbled up the stairs to my room. At least it was quiet up here. For now. I had no doubt that once Mom left, Sadie would invite some friends over.

I was going to have to call in sick. I never called in sick, but I couldn't serve people food like this. I was going to have to cancel my date with Blaine too. Luckily I'd cleaned the mechanic shop the day before, so I wouldn't be forced to also contact Connor.

I shot Blaine a text letting him know I was sick and we'd have to reschedule. I was thankful for that, for once, he didn't push but instead responded with a brief "okay."

Kelly was worried when I called her cell. "You're never sick."

"I know," I said in a scratchy voice.

"You sound awful."

"A dragon is alive in my chest right now."

She made a "poor you" sound. "You're pushing yourself too hard, Liv. You need to rest."

"Nature is forcing me to rest."

"Do you want to move in with me? Get away from everything?" Her voice was sincere, and it made me start to tear up again. Kelly was the only person who knew how my last week had gone and how deep my worries had become.

"I can't afford to right now. I'm working to pay for school, and every penny counts. I'm lucky that at my age I can still crash here and eat for free."

"You're not crashing for free, and they aren't doing you any favors. You're earning your keep, and they're scared to let you go." Her words were harsh, words that only a lifelong friend would ever dare say.

I closed my eyes against the headache that started at her truth bomb. I didn't want to think about it. Everything hurt too much. "I'm hoping to be back tomorrow. Can you cover my shift today?"

"Better plan on me covering tomorrow too." Her voice sounded resigned. "You're the only person in the entire world I'd pull a double for."

"The feeling is mutual."

In the end, she was right. I didn't make it back the next day. In fact, it was another two days of life in bed before I emerged, which had been upsetting to everyone in my life. Mom and Sadie acted like I'd personally disappointed them, Jake said my job was on the line—although who believed that?—and Blaine was getting downright whiny. I'd pushed him off while Dad had been in town, and now with being sick it had been almost two weeks since we'd seen each other in person. All I could do was continue to promise I'd make it up to him.

I still felt weak and woozy, but on the fourth day I decided I needed to get out for a change of scenery. The only logical choice was to head over to Mainstreet Mechanic for an after-hours study session. My schoolwork was falling drastically behind, and I wouldn't be around anyone else. Win-win.

I didn't bother taking a shower, knowing it would feel good but end up wearing me down, which I figured was fine because I'd soaked in the tub the day before. I put on a knit cap to handle my hair, sweat pants, and an old T-shirt that proclaimed "Science: It's like Magic, But Real." I covered it all with a coat, slung my backpack over my shoulder, told Sadie where I'd be, and braved the cold air with my mouth tucked into the warmth of my collar.

It was a relief to slip into the quiet, dark mechanic's office and soak in the peace after so many days of Mom and Sadie banging on my door and asking when I'd be better. I had all my notebooks, a phone charger, and a plan to do a lot of catch up. I was hoping to feel well enough to work the next day, so I'd avoid cleaning tonight but start exercising my brain.

After about two hours I needed to stretch, so I walked out of the office into the lobby. Darkness had fully fallen, and with the lights out in the building around me I was able to watch traffic roll by as light snowflakes fell. It made a dreamy scene, and I imagined how I'd paint it. I'd start with blacks and fade into sky blue at the top. Headlights and taillights would be slashes of yellows and reds. Trees would be a little green mixed into the black. My hands couldn't wait to hold a brush.

As I watched, a sedan pulled into the parking lot. It took me a moment, but I recognized it as Blaine's BMW. A smile lit my face when he stepped out and started walking toward the building. It was too dark to see much more than his outline as I unlocked the door and opened it for him.

"Hey, babe. I went to your house to bang down the door and insist on seeing my Valentine, but Sadie told me you were here." He bent to give me a hug, which I returned, but I turned my face away when he tried to kiss me.

"You don't want this, and I'm not sure I'm all better yet," I said in a voice still raspy from the illness combined with a little shock that he'd mentioned Valentine's Day. Was that happening already? I'd really lost track of time.

He released me quickly and stepped back. "Yeah. You didn't sound good at all when we talked on the phone." He looked around. "Do you think you'll be good enough to go on a date in a few days? I can't wait to spend our first Valentine's Day together."

A small smile curved my lips as I realized that this year I'd actually have someone to celebrate with. "I'll be better if it kills me."

He ran a finger down my cheek and looked at me with tender eyes. "I hope you're not already back to cleaning this place. Couldn't you have asked for a couple more days to rest?"

"Oh, yeah. The owner told me I could use the office to study after hours, so that's what I'm doing tonight. I have a ton to catch up on."

His tender expression frosted over with confusion. "You're using the shop to study?" His voice sounded a little ill at ease.

"Hey, I'm desperate."

"It's weird that he offered."

True. That had been my first reaction too, but I didn't say it. "It's a little different, but where else should I study? The diner and my house are both out. The library is closed this late at night. No one cares that I'm here, or comes to bother me." I shrugged.

As if to completely discredit what I was saying, another set of headlights shone briefly into the lobby as a truck pulled in. I groaned when I realized it was Connor. This wasn't going to look good to Blaine, or to him.

"Who's that?" Blaine said as he turned to look out.

I let out a heavy breath. "It's Connor. He probably saw your car in the lot and a man's shape inside with me, and wants to make sure everything is okay."

Blaine made a sound I couldn't interpret but said nothing as Connor came in. Connor's posture was stiff and wary until he saw who it was. He relaxed a bit, tucking his hands into the front of the green hoodie he was wearing. Between the green hoodie and his bright hair I immediately thought of a leprechaun but wisely kept it to myself.

"I thought I said you couldn't use this as a make-out spot," he said in a light tone, although his eyes remained cautious as he walked to stand near me and Blaine.

Surprised, I started to laugh at his remark, but it turned into a cough that had me doubling over. Blaine's warm hand settled between my shoulder blades and rubbed in soothing circles until the spasm was over and I could stand straight again. It felt amazing, and I was grateful for the compassion. Only . . . when I stood straight, Blaine was standing with his hands in his jacket pockets, and it was Connor's hand on my back. Blaine's eyes had taken on frosty disapproval. I didn't blame him. I wasn't sure I approved either.

"Do you need a drink?" Connor asked. He was either oblivious or unconcerned with Blaine's reaction. I was afraid it was the later. I nodded.

"Where's your water cooler?" Blaine interjected. Connor pointed and Blaine strode over stiffly to fill a paper cup, and hurried back to my side.

"Thanks," I rasped out as I took it from his hand. I took little sips until I felt my throat and lungs settle down. "We weren't making out. I was studying and he was looking for me. Sadie told him I was here."

"It sounds like you should be home in bed," Connor replied. I heard a crinkling sound in his pocket right before he shoved a hard candy in my direction. "Suck on this."

I awkwardly took the candy from his hand and popped it into my mouth. "I have been for days. I'm falling behind." The candy began its job of coating my throat, and I was able to breathe a little easier.

"Your school is online. It can't be so demanding that you aren't able to miss a few days without killing yourself to get back to it," Blaine said.

I shook my head. "I have deadlines just like any other school, and I really have to study tonight."

Blaine's lips formed a flat, straight line. "Fine. I'll sit here with you."

Connor scoffed. "She doesn't need to entertain someone. She needs quiet time to study; that's why she's here." His declaration surprised both me and Blaine.

"Do you often pop in while she studies?" Blaine asked.

I watched in horrified fascination as the two men turned their bodies away from me and angled them toward each other. It was like the nature channel had turned on right before my eyes.

Connor's jaw worked. "It's my shop."

"It's after hours."

"When I see a strange car in the parking lot and shadows inside, I stop."

"Does that happen often?" Blaine's stance shifted.

"Are you asking if Liv often has strange men visit her in my shop after hours? Because I doubt she'd like that accusation."

"I think I know better than you what my girlfriend would or would not appreciate." Blaine's eyes were shooting blue daggers.

"And I think you're wrong if you really think she wants you to babysit while she studies." Connor's amber eyes held their own strength as they met Blaine's.

I held up my hands, touching them each lightly on the chest as I stepped between them. I was surprised to feel two sets of fast heartbeats, two tensed bodies leaning in.

"Please," I soothed. They both looked down to me, and I felt overwhelmed by what I saw in their expressions. Anger, defiance, and protectiveness radiated off both of them. It had me baffled enough to make me clear my throat and swallow again. "I'm fine. I was just about to go home anyhow. Nothing to fight about here."

"We weren't fighting," Connor said. I felt his chest relax slightly under my touch, and I dropped my hand.

"We were just communicating," Blaine agreed, although he remained unyielding under my hand. "I think Connor and I understand each other perfectly."

"Well, understand this. I'm exhausted." I coughed again into my elbow and winced a little when it hurt in my ribs. I hugged my arms around my stomach.

This time two hands came to my back, but one lifted almost immediately. "I'll drive you home, babe. You can come back for your car tomorrow," Blaine said. The one hand remaining on my back now slipped around to encircle my shoulders.

All the energy I'd felt earlier in the evening began to drain, and my shoulders sagged under his arm. I nodded as Blaine said to wait there while he went to the office to gather my things. I appreciated his thoughtfulness, but I had no idea how I'd actually get my car if I left it at the shop.

"How long have you two been dating?" Connor asked as Blaine disappeared from view.

"A bit over three months."

"He must be a slow learner."

"I'm not interested in what you mean." I shivered a bit and rubbed my arms, fatigue beginning to take the heat out of me. Connor took a step closer as if he was going to . . . I don't know, but he didn't touch me and I was grateful.

"You don't sound good. You sure you're okay?" he asked. I nodded. "Did he bring you soup, or flowers?"

"Of course not."

"What do you mean, 'of course not'?"

"He's busy and I told him to stay away."

"Let me guess, he respects you enough to obey your wishes?" I could practically hear the eye roll in his tone.

"You say that like it's a bad thing."

"It's a terrible thing. Do you really want a guy who you can walk all over? If he cared that much, he'd have shown up, banged down your door, and poured the soup down your throat."

I coughed again. "You paint such a pretty picture. I've really been missing out."

"He's an idiot," he grumbled.

"He respects me enough to not bulldoze me. Besides, rule two, Connor. I'm dating someone, and you don't get a vote on who that person is or how he acts." I straightened as Blaine came out of the office with my backpack and coat in hand.

Blaine silently helped me put on my coat. He turned me to zip up the front. "You ready?" he asked.

"Yes." I turned back to face Connor. "I don't think I'll be studying here anymore. I'll be back to clean in a few days."

"Liv . . . " Connor started.

"Rule two, Connor," I replied.

I followed Blaine out the door and to his car, the entire time feeling like I didn't really understand, at all, what had just happened here.

CHAPTER TEN

I sat cross-legged on my bed with my physiology book open, willing my mind to focus. Across the room a white canvas with two sets of eyes was looking back at me. The day after the strange events at Connor's shop between him and Blaine, I'd had to paint out my confused emotion. What had come out of my mind and onto the paper had been their eyes. Two blue, two amber. One tender, one unyielding.

I closed the book with a groan of frustration and stood. My feet walked the familiar path to the corner where I kept my paint supplies. I found a sharpened sketch pencil laying nearby and went to the canvas to draw a quick outline of Blaine's face around the blue eyes. When I was satisfied, I returned to the supply table. The brushes were waiting for me like old friends. I pulled out the colors I always saw in Blaine's hair and mixed them slowly, steadily, mindlessly on the palette, all the while picturing him in my mind. As his face presented itself a smile stole to my lips. Blaine was interesting, accomplished, stylish, and kind.

My mind grew calm and clear as I painted him. His charm stood out in the gentle strokes I used, reminding me of all the reasons I'd encouraged our relationship to progress. I painted for over an hour, spending precious time I didn't have to work through my thoughts. As always, I felt rejuvenated and more at peace.

When the alarm on my phone went off, reminding me I had a shift at the diner, I was satisfied that I had the beginnings of a great portrait. I glanced to the set of amber eyes on the other half of the canvas. They had seemed tender when I'd been looking before, but now they felt mocking. I slashed a line across them, the blond of Blaine's hair color not quite fully hiding them. I looked back to Blaine's eyes. What had seemed unyielding, now seemed sure and steady.

With that in mind, I called Blaine on the way to work and invited him to have dinner at my house the following evening. It wasn't the romantic Valentine's date I'd originally thought of, but it was a new step and his surprise was evident. He'd been to my house a few times but had never come inside. He'd never met my mom or Sadie, because I'd never invited him to interact with my family at all. To be totally honest, he wasn't even aware that my parents were basically separated.

Of course, I hadn't met his family either, but there was time for that. Inviting him over would help one of my walls to crumble, which was a good thing, even though it made my hands shake as I hung up the phone.

The next afternoon when I got off work, I sped straight to the grocery store to buy all the fixings for a homemade lasagna, salad, breadsticks, and a pie from the bakery for dessert. I didn't cook full meals often, but I knew how and I wanted to impress Blaine. My first Valentine's date with him would not be frozen dinners.

When I arrived home, Sadie was sitting on the couch, a magazine in her lap and her feet propped on the coffee table. The nail polish was still open next to her, and the smell filled the air. I wondered for the hundredth time why she bothered giving herself pedicures in the middle of the winter when our mountain valley required shoes to be worn at all times. Homework papers were scattered around her, and the TV was on at full volume.

"Hey, did you get the kitchen tidied up a little? Blaine's coming over for dinner tonight, remember?" I said as I rushed through with arms full of plastic bags.

"Yeah, I had dance practice after school, and then a drill team Valentine party. Sorry."

She wasn't sorry, and we both knew it. My shoulders tightened in timeless reaction, but I held my tongue.

I entered the kitchen to find it a mess, which didn't surprise but did disappoint. I put the groceries on the table and took a few deep breaths while I decided how to handle it. First I'd make the lasagna. While that was baking, I could tackle the cleaning. Blaine would be here in a little over an hour. I could do it.

I heard my sister moving around in the family room and called out to her. "Can you please clean up the front room at least? I'll get dinner cooked and the kitchen ready."

"I'm just going to jump in the shower. I'm still sweaty from practice."

"But you just painted your toes," I called, but the only response I got was the slam of the bathroom door echoing through the house. I chewed on my lip and groaned in frustration. Why, why, why? And where should I hide her body?

Tamping down on my anger, knowing it would give me a headache that I couldn't afford, I got to work on the lasagna. Ten minutes later it was in the oven—a miracle thanks to no-boil noodles. I worked like a mad woman. I'd been hoping to have time to clean myself up after my work shift, but it wasn't looking good. A spritz bath was in my future.

With only ten minutes left until Blaine was supposed to arrive, I had everything ready to go in the kitchen, and the front room was as clean as could be. I ran up to my room and grabbed a cute skirt and top that I'd been saving, then hustled into the bathroom and stripped down. Using a washcloth I wiped down all the important parts before spritzing on fresh deodorant and body spray, and getting redressed. I washed my face, applied mascara and lip gloss, and corralled my hair into place with a few strategically placed bobby pins just as the doorbell rang.

"Honey, Blaine is here," Mom called up the stairs. The sound of her voice was at once startling and familiar. It had been a while since it had held that happier tone, and I was grateful she'd made it home, even if she hadn't been able to help prepare things.

I took a few deep breaths to calm myself before walking down the stairs as though I'd had everything under control. I was both nervous and relieved to find Mom and Sadie sitting on the couch together with smiles for Blaine, who was sitting on the chair nearby. He was holding three identical floral bouquets and wearing a truly remarkable navy blue suit. He looked like a million bucks. He stood when I entered the room and came to give me a kiss on the cheek.

"You look lovely, and it smells great in here," he said against my ear. "Happy Valentine's Day, babe." He handed me one of the bouquets and then did the same for Mom, who gushed appropriately, and Sadie, who remained silent although her face turned pink. My heart flipped a little over his thoughtfulness.

"I'm so glad you could come." I took his hand. "Have introductions been made?"

"Yes. We're so happy to finally meet this mystery man of yours," Mom replied with a smile of her own, which grew when she leaned in to smell the roses he'd just given her.

"Well, the food is ready. Let's go to the kitchen and take a seat," I said cheerily while my heart tried to beat out of my chest.

The three of them followed me into the kitchen and sat at our little four-seat corner table. I'd dug out Mom's place mats and nicer plates and cups. The table hadn't looked this good in a long time.

"Tell us about yourself," Mom said to Blaine after offering a prayer over our meal. She started passing the food around.

"I work and live in Springfield, I run a marketing firm with my father, and I'm an only child," he said in a perfectly polished tone.

"Sounds like this one is a provider," Sadie stated around a mouthful of food while wiggling her eyebrow at me.

"A provider?" he asked.

I shook my head, but Sadie persisted. "Yeah, you know, if Liv decides to marry you, she'll be well taken care of."

I tried to laugh, but it sounded strangled. "Sadie, stop teasing the poor guy. He just met you." She wasn't teasing, for the record.

"All I know is that I'm never going to marry someone who doesn't provide for me, or someone who's never around. I'm glad Liv found someone who isn't like that." Sadie took a swig of her drink.

It was kind of a sweetly cruel statement, but before I could decide how I felt about it, I saw Mom's face drain of color and knew how she'd taken it. My heart sank, even as I pasted on a smile.

"Marriage?" I meant it to come out with a light laugh, but it sounded strangled. "We're still getting to know each other. That's never even . . . "

Blaine's hand came to rest on my shoulder, causing my mouth to clamp shut as heat warmed my face. "We've never discussed marriage, but if it happened, I can provide for Olivia. And, I don't enjoy traveling, so I'd never be too far away." Blaine's eyes had become watchful, as though he realized he was in a minefield but didn't know which direction the explosion would come from. His smile, amazingly, remained polite.

I was momentarily distracted by the news that he didn't like to travel. It didn't seem to gel with the idea of him I had built in my head, or the idea of my own future. I wanted to travel someday, and he always presented himself as someone world-wise.

Sadie nodded and Mom remained mute.

Blaine cleared his throat and turned to me. "This lasagna is delicious, babe. I didn't know you cooked so well."

"She usually doesn't." Sadie shrugged.

Mom reappeared in the conversation at last. "Liv is so busy with work and school, but she does her best to help around here and keep us all in order." She patted me on the hand. "She's a wonderful cook."

"I wish someone had taught me how to cook." Sadie shrugged again. I was poisoning her next meal.

"I'm sorry about that, honey. I was able to be home more when Liv was your age," Mom replied.

"Yeah, before Daddy took off," Sadie mumbled.

Nope, poison was too good for her. The guillotine was sounding promising. "Dad didn't take off," I replied with stiff lips, the lie tasting terrible. I turned to Blaine. "He works in the North Dakota oil fields. We wish we saw him more."

Blaine nodded. "I'll bet his winters are awfully cold. He probably misses this warm house and his beautiful girls."

I pretty near cried over how nice his comment had been. He'd just outclassed my family by a thousand percent. I reached for his hand resting on the table and squeezed it. His expression warmed and relaxed.

"How did you and Liv meet?" Mom asked.

"I was in town meeting a client and they suggested the diner for a bite to eat before my drive back. As luck would have it, Olivia was working that night. I talked her into giving me her number."

"That's a nice story." Mom smiled. "How long have you been dating now?"

"Three months," I replied distractedly, wondering for the first time why he insisted on continuing to call me Olivia when no one else did.

I liked my name and had no problem with it, but it felt foreign to hear it somehow, like he was an acquaintance rather than someone in my circle. I'd have to mention it to him. Maybe he'd just assumed Liv was only a nickname.

"Well, I'm glad we can at last put a face to the name," Mom offered.

"I'm sure it took Liv so long to bring you around because she didn't want us to scare you off," Sadie cracked.

And so the next hour went—Blaine trying his hardest to be kind, Sadie trying her hardest to be the worst, and Mom trying her hardest to smooth it all over. For my part, I was trying my hardest to not commit murder and to chew my food slowly.

At last I was walking Blaine to the door. I grabbed a blanket off the back of the couch on my way out and draped it across my shoulders for warmth against the snowy night.

"In case you've been wondering why I haven't invited you over before," I said as I closed the door behind me, "Sadie was right about them scaring you off."

He laughed and reached for me, pulling me in to his embrace. "If you promise not to judge me by my parents when you meet them, I'll promise to not hold your family against you either."

I tilted my head back to look up at him. "It's a deal." I pushed up on my toes and pressed my lips to his. They still tasted sweet like the cherry pie we'd had for dessert. "I'm sorry for the most horrible Valentine's date in history."

"No apology necessary." One of his hands slid up my back and into my hair, weaving around in the curls and deepening the kiss. I responded warmly, trying to ignore the hands in my hair. It should have been cute and romantic, but it was a distraction.

I gently ended the kiss and tried to casually pull my head away, causing his hand to drop. I didn't want to offend him, so I snuggled up against him, resting my cheek on his shoulder and wrapping my arms around his waist.

"I don't deserve someone as nice as you," I said.

He squeezed me tight. "I wish we had more time together tonight, but the weatherman says there's a snow storm coming in, so I'd better head home. It's not fun driving through the pass in a blizzard."

I nodded. "Thanks for dinner."

I leaned back and kissed him again, this time trying to express how grateful I was for him without actually saying any words. I kept hoping the right words would come, but so far they'd stayed tucked away inside of me, and I couldn't find them anywhere.

* * * * *

The next morning when I told Kelly about Sadie's behavior at dinner, her reaction completely vindicated my anger. "I can't believe you didn't slap her across her sassy little mouth." She stood with her hands on her hips, her eyes flashing. Her voice carried over the sounds of cooking happening behind us through the kitchen window.

"Oh, she got an earful after Blaine left. She's not getting any meals out of me for a while," I responded. I knew the ire I still felt over my sister's behavior could be heard in my voice, so I tried to tamp it down around the customers even though we were standing out of the way. "I do everything for her. The least she could do is be nice to him."

Kelly pinched her lips together and wagged a finger in my face. "She's being a terrible sister, and that's the truth."

"She didn't used to be," I replied. "She used to be so sweet." I had been so excited when she was born. I was seven and I'd been wishing for a sibling for years. She'd been my little buddy for a really long time. "I don't know what changed."

"She became a teenager. A beautiful one at that."

"Beauty doesn't have to equal evil," I stated.

Kelly laughed and gave me an impromptu hug. "You're right. It's just that somewhere in the middle of being a teenager you should have to go through a dog ugly phase to keep you humble. It's against nature to be as flawless as your sister when you're that age. It's warped her mind."

"Well, having our father disappear didn't help either," I mumbled in a moment of insight. The teen years had been rough on me, but I'd had solid parents at home supporting me through it. Maybe I needed to cut Sadie some slack. It was worth pondering, at the very least.

I heard the bell above the diner door jangle before I had a chance to run my insight past Kelly. A customer had come in, and I was in charge of seating them. I zig-zagged around the drink station and stuttered to an awkward stop when Connor appeared before me. He was wearing a ball cap and a jacket, and he'd brought in with him the smell of cold morning air and a hint of something orange scented. His light eyes caught mine from under the brim and zoned in as though he was trying to read what I was thinking. I blinked and looked to the side where a woman was standing next to him. I'd never seen her before, but I doubted she'd ever had an ugly phase in her life. She was wearing tight jeans and a fitted top with high boots and hair that made girls all over the world jealous.

"Hi. Welcome to Jake's. Two today?" I said as I reached for menus.

"Just one," Connor replied.

I glanced up in time to see him look over at the lady as though he'd been surprised to find her standing there.

"If you're alone and I'm alone, maybe we could eat together," she said to him in an undertone that would have melted an ice sculpture.

My chin pulled back as though I'd physically felt the flirtation myself. Her eyes caressed him from head to toe, taking in all the things that had attracted women to him since his last pimple had faded. Tall, athletic, and colored so differently from most people, he was fascinating to look at, I had to admit. If I wasn't so against it, I'd love to figure out all those colors and transfer them to canvas.

I snapped back to attention and waved the menus. "So, two then?" I asked.

Connor's eyes swung back to me and he shook his head. "Just one."

The woman looked to me, and we shared an equally disbelieving glance. Neither of us could understand why he'd turned her down. If I could have picked out the type of woman Connor Hunt would go for, she would be it. She knew it, and I knew it, and it was like the world had tilted off its axis a bit.

I cleared my throat. "Okay. Ma'am, if you'll follow me?" My voice was sympathetic, and she offered me a kind look. I guided her to a small side booth and came back for Connor, careful to lead him to a booth in a different area.

"What was that all about?" Connor asked as he followed me. He was walking so close behind me that I was worried he'd step on my heel.

"You just shot that lady down cold." I gestured to a booth and he slid in.

"I've never seen her before in my life."

I handed him a menu. "She's very beautiful."

"I didn't notice," he said while looking down at the menu.

I scoffed. "Uh-huh, sure. Do you want me to get you a drink while you're looking over the menu?"

"Hot cocoa."

"Hot cocoa?"

He looked up at me. "This is the part where the waitress gets what the customer asks for." His tone was a little grumpy, which I found intriguing.

"I'm sorry, but I was caught off guard by your request. I wouldn't have guessed you were the type of guy who drinks hot cocoa. Do you want marshmallows with that?"

"What type am I, then?"

"The type who eats breakfast with the beautiful women who hit on him at the local diner."

"Proof you don't know me at all. I'll be ready to order when you get back with my cocoa. No marshmallows. Marshmallows are for wimps." He looked back to his menu, effectively dismissing me.

I walked back toward the front where another couple had entered. "Hot cocoa for your new smarty pants best friend in booth five," I called to Kelly as I passed the counter. "Extra marshmallows."

"Got it," she replied.

I picked up a menu and gestured for the couple to follow me. I got them situated with their menus, took their drink orders, and made my way back to the counter where Kelly had left a steaming mug of cocoa for me to take to Connor. There were at least fifteen marshmallows floating on the top, making a small mountain. It made me happy.

I put the mug down in front of him and waited with anticipation for him to see what I'd done. It had been childish, but I didn't really care. He'd made things tense between Blaine and me, and this was the payback moment. When he finally dropped the menu and looked down, it was all worth it. His face got slack before his eyes slit and he looked up at me.

"You're kidding with this, right?"

"Nothing's too special for our best customer," I chirped.

"When are you going to stop pouting and come back to the shop to study?" he asked.

I was caught off guard by the change of subject, still unused to the workings of his mind. He really *would* be at home with Kelly and me, not that I'd ever open that door. "I'm not pouting. Would someone who's pouting go to the effort of getting you fifteen of the puffiest marshmallows we have?"

"You're pouting."

I harrumphed. "I came and cleaned already this week. That's all the time I'll be spending at the shop."

"You'll fall behind in school."

"Rule number one, we don't discuss my private life."

He rolled his eyes. "But, really, when are you coming back?"

"The word I'm thinking of starts with N and ends with 'ever.'" I pulled out my order pad. "Are you ready to tell me what you want?"

"Are you going to sabotage my order?"

"Nope."

"I'll have eggs Benedict, a side of bacon, and a fruit bowl." He handed me the menu back.

"Excellent choice on this cold morning. Do you need extra napkins to wipe the marshmallow off your upper lip?"

"I wouldn't mind a new waitress."

"Sorry, that's not on the menu today." I smiled sweetly down at him and walked away.

After that the diner got slammed. It was always that way on snowy mornings. It seemed counterintuitive to me. If I'd been able to, I'd have chosen to stay home, but it's like the snow brought everyone out in search of warmth and camaraderie.

I distractedly waited Connor's booth until he left, but we didn't talk any more, which was more than fine with me. Before I knew it my shift was over and I couldn't wait to get off my feet.

"Oh, I almost forgot, Liv," Kelly called to me as I opened the front door. "There's a note for you." She was waving a napkin at me.

I walked back to the counter to get it from her. "From who?"

"Connor asked me to give it to you."

I unfolded it. *Stop pouting and come back*, it read. His handwriting was terrible, the words only half formed as though he couldn't be bothered to finish it properly. I actually laughed out loud. Kelly leaned across the counter to read it.

"What does that mean?" she asked.

"It means that Connor Hunt is living in a dream world," I replied.

CHAPTER ELEVEN

There comes a time in everyone's life when they can't stare at the pages of a book, or the booths of a diner, or the bathroom in a mechanic shop one more time without going insane. When that day arrives, some drastic, out-of-the-ordinary action must be taken.

For me, that was snow tubing with my sister. Even though lately I only liked her about 25 percent of the time. Sadie gave me other reasons this was a terrible idea, including but not limited to: We were too old, we didn't have decent snow clothes, what about her street cred, and my personal favorite, hat hair wasn't a good look for either of us.

After what an outsider would call a full brouhaha, Sadie and I stood with hats, coats, and mittens at the bottom of the local sledding hill. Because it was a weekend, the place was packed. Snow flew, voices squealed, and the line to take your ride was longer than I'd have hoped. Despite all that, I clung tightly to my pink tube. I wasn't going to be scared away. I hadn't done this in years, and I really needed something outside the box to reset my overloaded brain.

"We are the only people here over the age of ten," Sadie moaned as I plopped her tube on the snow in front of her.

"Not true. There's a whole group of older people over there." I pointed with my gloved hand as we headed to the line at the bottom of the hill, trying to pretend I wasn't a little embarrassed. I mean, it wasn't like I'd invited Kelly or Blaine to go tubing with me. I knew it was a kid activity.

"Those are the parents."

"Or, as I prefer to call them, sticks-in-the-mud." I grinned.

"This is a terrible idea. Why are you suddenly wanting sister bonding time?"

"To deepen our connection," I replied. I tried to keep a straight face but blew it at the end. Sadie's lips relaxed into a small smile as well, which made me happy.

"We can deepen our connection on the couch."

"We needed to see some sunshine and blue skies, and let the sun warm our faces," I defended. "We need to be somewhere where the scent of nail polish isn't clogging our lungs."

"There has to be a better way to do that."

"I'm sure there is." I nodded cheerfully.

"You owe me dinner for this," Sadie whined.

"I make you dinner every night."

"Dessert too, then."

"We could have a race down the hill to see who has to make dinner," I suggested. "Make things interesting."

"No thanks. I don't cook."

"I could teach you," I offered. I tried to be all cool and casual about it, fully prepared for her to scoff. Instead she looked at me with wide hazel eyes, and a small smile lifted one side of her mouth. It gave me the courage to press on. "I know Mom's busy and Dad's . . . " I waved my hands, unable to think of the right words. "But you've still got me. It could be fun."

She looked away but nodded. "Maybe."

I felt a little warmth in my chest. It hadn't been an angelic choir moment, but it was something. I joined her in watching with wide eyes as the kids now at the front of the line put their Radio Flyer sleds down on the snow and took off. From here, the hill looked much larger and steeper than it had when I was a younger. There was a chance I was about to sustain an adult-sized injury.

For a split second I was lost in the sounds of crunching snow, squealing laughter, and the feeling of the snow blinding me in the sunlight. Maybe this was a mistake.

"Do my eyes deceive me, or do I spy Liv and Sadie Phelps?" Kelly's chipper voice said from behind us.

Sadie and I both turned to find her standing near the curb, leaning on a truck that looked very familiar. She was dressed in jeans and a coat, with bright blue mittens and a scarf. A tall guy next to her was dressed similarly, minus the scarf. His back was to us as he spoke to the kids standing by the open tailgate, but I immediately recognized Connor.

Kelly took a step or two toward us, and we did the same, closing the distance. "What are you two doing here?" she asked.

"Bonding." I smiled.

"You're either very brave or very stupid."

"We're stupid." Sadie's voice was flat, which made Kelly and me share an amused look. "Who's that?" Sadie mouthed, pointing at the guy.

Kelly looked over her shoulder and smiled. "Oh, that's my friend Connor."

"So snow sledding is the next step after lunching and buying cars together?" I joked.

Sadie leaned close and quietly asked, "Who's Connor?"

"Nobody you need to know. Just ignore him."

At that moment he turned around, and Sadie's eyes grew at her first good look at him. "Um, he's kind of . . . "

"If you say attractive, I will ride you down the hill instead of my tube," I interrupted.

We exchanged a glance, and Sadie must have seen something in my expression that caused her face to relax. She uncharacteristically dropped the subject and looked around. "Oh, hey," she said and then walked away a few steps to talk to a boy I didn't recognize.

I decided to follow her and see who this kid was, and if he wanted to ride down the slope with us . . or, you know, with Sadie in my place. I could be cool like that.

"Liv!" I heard a voice call my name and looked up. I couldn't see anyone talking to me, so I went back to listening to Sadie, assuming there was another Olivia on the hill today.

"Watch out!" another voice called. This one sounded a lot like Kelly.

This time I looked up the sledding hill, but I didn't see anyone coming down it. Not a second later I felt something skim my leg as it passed me in a blur of black and white before slamming into the back of Sadie's legs. The impact caused her feet to fly into the air above her head. I watched in fascination as she all but did a back flip before landing hard on her side.

I gasped, dropping my tube and kneeling beside her. "Are you okay?"

She looked a little dazed but nodded. "What hit me?"

"All I know is it was big, round, black, and white. Must have been a rogue attack from a killer whale," I replied.

Sadie groaned. "You're such a dope." Then she sat up.

"Didn't you hear me calling to watch out?" Connor's voice joined the circle forming around us, and he held out a hand to Sadie to help her stand.

She took it and offered him a flirty little smile as she stood. "Thanks."

"Did you see what happened?" I asked Connor.

"Yeah, some guy bounced off the trail and came flying right at her. I tried to warn you."

"We didn't hear you. Sadie was too busy chatting, and I was too busy eavesdropping."

"You were eavesdropping?" Sadie asked. I nodded. Her eyes rolled.

"You looked around when I called your name," Connor replied.

"Oh, *you* called out? That explains it. Yeah, I've got your voice on mute."

His lips pinched and he looked back to Sadie. "Are you sure you're okay?" he asked.

She patted her legs and arms and wiggled around a bit. "I'll live. No thanks to Liv. This whole thing was her idea." She threw me one of her patented disgusted looks, and I sighed inwardly. What a bummer. We'd actually been getting along.

Kelly joined us in time to hear Sadie's last sentence. "I find that bad ideas stick to Liv like—"

I cut her off. "What brings you two here? You're not wearing snow gear," I said.

Kelly grinned. "Connor comes down on Saturdays after the shop closes at noon with extra tubes and an air compressor from his shop."

Embarrassment over my behavior made my cheeks warm. "That's kind of nice."

"I'm a nice guy," he replied.

"Hello, remember me over here?" Sadie's voice sounded shrill after listening to Connor's low, relaxed way of talking and Kelly's perpetually upbeat tones.

I turned to face her. "You know, your dance coach might be interested to know that you can do a pretty nice back flip," I said with as innocent an expression as I could manage.

"I could have been really hurt, Liv." Sadie's eyes grew stormy.

"Too soon," Connor whispered to me out of the corner of his mouth.

"Sorry, Sadie. I'm glad you're okay, really." I reached out to squeeze her hand, but she pulled away and folded her arms. That was another strike against me.

"You handled that like a pro," Connor said when Sadie gave her back to me.

"Nice one." Kelly smirked.

"I know, I know. I need to be nicer, but come on. Are you honestly telling me that I can't tease my sister for being ambushed by a tuber going a smooth sixty miles per hour?" I asked. They shook their heads. "I can't comment on the amazing tumbling move she accomplished thanks to his assist?" Lips twitched, but they shook their heads again. "Fine, I just have one question."

"What is it?" Connor asked.

"You saw everything, right?"

"Yes."

"Was it, or was it not, a killer whale having the time of his life in the snow?"

Kelly smirked and crossed her arms. "Here she goes," she said under her breath.

Connor, however, took the bait. "Whales live in water."

"Yes. If you'd spent more time in the classroom and less time under the bleachers you might remember that snow is frozen water." I nodded.

His eyes crinkled up. "The bleachers were comfy, and it was definitely not a killer whale."

"How sure are you? It could have been a killer whale on vacation. Snorkeling on dry land."

"I don't . . . what?" His eyes, always a warm honey, seemed to shift colors as he listened to me being totally absurd.

"It makes sense that if people use snorkels in the ocean, then underwater creatures would use them on land."

"I see."

"It's science."

"Mm-hmm. Does your science also tell you that your sister is leaving with that boy she was talking to?"

My head whipped around in time to see Sadie disappear over a rise. Her tube was still laying by mine. "That's rude."

"I don't think she cares about being rude to you right now," he stated.

"She rarely does."

"If this is how it goes when she's out with you, I can't blame her." Connor chuckled.

"So much for sister bonding time. I'll have to do something less outdoorsy next time." I started to bend down to pick up our tubes, but I paused and glanced back to Connor. "Really, though, wasn't that the most hysterical thing you've seen in a long time?" I asked.

He looked to the top of the hill, then back at me, and at last his face relaxed into an amused expression. "I haven't seen someone fly that high in a while."

"Right?" I felt a laugh bubble up and turn into full blown hysterics.

Connor joined me, both of us grinning wildly. It felt amazing to let go and laugh, holding nothing back. My face started to hurt, and I could feel tears of merriment gathering under my eyes. It really had been the funniest thing. I knew Sadie would hold it against me for a while, but even that didn't dim my enjoyment. I'd needed to laugh my head off.

I gradually remembered that Kelly was standing there too, and sheepishly looked to her, intent on including her in the funny moment, but her expression was serious as she glanced back and forth between Connor and me. Her face grew thoughtful, which terrified me. I quickly gathered up our tubes and said a friendly farewell before she could say anything. I had no interest in whatever it was that had made Kelly look at us that way.

* * * * *

I breathed in deeply the soft fragrances of lavender and vanilla as they floated around me. Gentle fingers scrubbed my palms and fingers, massaging and relaxing them. The nail salon was warm, soft music played from hidden speakers, and I curled my toes at the delicious feel of it.

"This is the nicest thing I've done for myself in a long time." I looked over at Sadie in the chair next to me with a silly grin. "Made even better by knowing I can't afford this. It makes me feel like I'm doing something illegal."

We were sitting side by side, our hands soaking in warm, bubbly water. While a few days earlier I'd teased her at the sledding hill, I hadn't forgotten my flash of insight over how much Sadie must be hurting. This was my way of trying to have a girl's day redo. I'd spent so much time feeling frustrated with my mom over how she hung on, waiting, stagnating, and forcing us all to live in limbo, rather than calling my dad out and making some decisions.

For a long time I'd done the same. For me, the first step to breaking out had been going back to school. I was ashamed to admit that I'd not given Sadie's situation much thought. So, my second step was going to be showing up for my baby sister and seeing how I could help her through things.

Sadie looked down at her hands, something intent in her expression that I hadn't seen for a while. The defensive, sour look was gone, and I knew she was churning over something. I waited patiently.

Finally, she spoke. "Why does Dad think he can just show up and make us breakfast and everything will be okay?" she asked. It was all I could do to keep my face passive.

I'd kind of hoped to eventually work up to some real conversations with her, but I'd totally assumed I'd have to drag it out of her like a magpie with a jewel. This was not how I'd seen our manicure afternoon going.

"I don't know," I replied honestly. "But it made me mad too."

"If he does it again, I'm going to change the locks." Sadie finally looked up at me. "He doesn't have the right to come and go as he pleases anymore."

Now it was my turn to look down at my hands while I thought quickly. She wasn't saying anything I hadn't thought. "I'll be honest, I wish we could too. It's still his house legally, though, and Mom doesn't seem to want to change that."

"Why does she hang on? Doesn't she realize how much of a loser that makes her?"

Two manicurists came and sat down across from us, taking our hands out of the water and wiping them on warm, soft towels. I was grateful for the moment to think before responding. Rather than getting defensive and angry over her trashing Mom that way, I heard the betrayal behind her words. After all, wasn't my reasoning for going to school as simple as not wanting to be trapped like my mother was?

We chose polish colors and settled in. I took a deep breath. "I've never been in love the way Mom and Dad were," I said. "They've been married for twenty-six years. It's not easy to just throw that away."

"Dad did," Sadie grumbled.

She wasn't wrong. It did feel that way. "I've been mad at Mom too."

Sadie's eyes grew round as she looked at me. Just as round as they'd been as a toddler, and my heart pinched. "Really?" she said.

"Yeah, really."

We fell into silence for a little while, lost in our own thoughts and distracted by the work being done to our hands. It was a nice silence. Not loaded with annoyance like it so often was between us lately. Maybe this would be a good first step to opening up with each other. I hoped so.

I heard Sadie take a deep breath and couldn't wait to hear what she was going to say. "So, that Connor guy from the tubing hill?"

Never mind, I could wait. "What about him?"

"You seemed to be having fun talking to him."

"You weren't even there. You'd left with that boy," I defended myself.

"No, I was still there. I saw you laughing together. I know it was about me and that accident. I'm not still mad."

"You're not?" I blinked.

"No. So, you were being really friendly with him."

I shot her a smile to hide my extreme discomfort. "I'm a friendly person. Most people would say that about me."

"You can be." She made a face.

I let my head fall forward and sighed. "Ouch. To answer your question, I barely know the guy."

"Do you think he likes you?"

My head shot back up, and I looked at her with a startled expression. My heart suddenly felt like it was slugging hard through mud as something about her suggesting Connor was into me made my breathing feel tight. "That's a definite no. Also, I'm dating someone."

She shrugged. "Who you don't actually love." I flinched a little as she went on. "Am I wrong?"

I looked away again. "I don't know, but I'm trying to figure that out."

She nodded and conversation drifted into other topics. Yet my mind felt off center and a little worried. Had I been flirting with Connor that day? Or even worse, was he flirting with me? I hoped not. The very thought caused my feet to sweat.

CHAPTER TWELVE

The snow fell so heavy and deep two days later that the power went out on my block. The house quickly became an ice box. I envied Mom and Sadie, who were warm at work and school, but it was my day off and I was alone and cold.

I bundled up on the couch in pajamas with blankets and a bright orange scarf wrapped around my head, covering my ears and neck. Knit gloves did their best to keep my hands warm while I flipped pages in my math textbook and wrote numbers in a lined notebook. I had to study. My mid-terms were coming up, and I was desperate to pass them. Not only did I not want to waste time by having to retake classes, I couldn't afford to pay twice for something I should have done right the first time. I had dreams. I had places to go. I wanted to be truly independent.

As the hours passed and the sun moved across the sky, I slid a chair over next to the window, hoping to catch some afternoon light, but the draft coming through was miserable. Daylight was running out, and my toes could have cooled down a kettle of hot tea. I needed somewhere warm and quiet to go. My car. I could sit in the car and turn it on for a few minutes here and there just to keep it warm inside. Of course, this wasn't going to help with the lack of light, but I didn't think that far ahead in the moment.

I gathered my things, including the blanket and scarf, and ran through the snow to my little car. I had to scrape off the door so that snow wouldn't fall in when I opened it, but soon I was inside.

Thanks to the recent repairs it started right up. It didn't take too long before delicious curls of heat began to blow over me. I sighed in happiness and set a timer on my phone to shut the car off after three minutes.

When the alarm beeped, I shut the engine off, but after only ten minutes of studying without the heater running I realized that the car was colder than the house had been, and it was getting dark. My solution was no solution at all. I couldn't use the lights inside when the car was off or I'd drain the battery, and I couldn't waste gas and kill the ozone by idling my car for hours. I took the blanket off, buckled up, and started Old Reliable. Time to find a place that had power where I could get my work done.

I hadn't shoveled the driveway yet, so the car slipped and slid out into the street. Thankfully it finally found traction in the roadway and I headed toward town. First stop was the diner. I pulled into the parking lot, and while it was clear Jake's had power, one glance inside told me it would be a bad choice. Another snowy day, especially one where many homes had lost power, meant every booth was packed. I could risk going in to the employee lounge, but Jake would take one look at me and put me to work, pajamas, orange scarf, and all.

I drove past the library, but there was a sign saying the power was out and they were closed. In desperation I tried a church. Locked and dark. My mind knew that Mainstreet Mechanic was my last choice. It was close to the diner and most likely on the same grid. I pulled to the side of the road and went over my options again, because I thought I'd possibly rather freeze to death and fail my mid-terms than see Connor. Especially after the conversation with Sadie that had left me feeling strangely achy.

Thinking of Connor led to thinking of Blaine, so I called him, wondering if his apartment would be an option. "The power is out, and I'm freezing, and I need to study," I said before he had a chance to say hello.

"Good evening to you too," he cracked.

"Sorry. Hi, how are you?" I tried to slow down my words.

"I'm good."

"Good. So, um, I don't suppose you're up for a visitor who will be very silent?"

It was an unusual request. I'd only been to Blaine's apartment building once, and I hadn't gone inside. He didn't reply for a moment, and I figured it was because I'd caught him by surprise.

"I'm sorry, babe. I guess you didn't hear that the pass is closed?" he replied.

Ugh. I hadn't heard. "Oh."

"Yeah. Is there nowhere else you can go?"

"I'll figure something out," I replied.

"Good luck and stay warm," he said.

"Thanks."

I hung up and dropped my head against the steering wheel. My hyperactive horn blared, startling me back up into a sitting position. Oops. I put the car back in drive and pulled onto Main Street. I'd just drive past the shop and see if they had power. If they did, then I'd think about possibly, maybe considering stopping there. If they didn't, I'd go back to my house.

It was with very mixed emotions that I glanced over at the shop and saw that they had power. Rats. I drove past once, circled around, and pulled into the parking lot. Despite my earlier thought process about the ozone, I idled for five full minutes before Connor opened a bay door and came stomping outside in his coveralls. He yanked my door open and bent down to eye level.

"Stop being dumb. I have power and it's warm inside."

I swallowed and nodded. His brusque manner had settled me in a way that kindness wouldn't have. "Okay. But all the rules are in effect."

"Fine. Rules, whatever. Just get out of the car. It's freezing."

I turned off the engine, grabbed my backpack, and followed him through the front doors into the lobby as he signaled an employee to shut the big bay door he'd left open. A wash of warm air rushed over my face and it felt wonderful.

It took me a moment to realize he was watching me but hadn't said anything. I blushed. "I need to study and I've been everywhere else. I even called Blaine about going to Springfield to study at his place."

"The pass is closed," he replied.

"Yeah." I shivered.

"The office is empty. Let's get you warmed up."

He led the way. In the smaller room I put my backpack on a chair and rubbed my hands together. Connor went back into the storage closet, where I could hear him moving things around before he reappeared with a space heater.

"This should do the trick," he said.

I immediately perked up. "I've never been so happy to see a space heater."

"You're welcome to study as long as you want. It's a slow day, so I was planning to send my guys home in a minute. It'll just be me in the shop. Make yourself at home."

I thanked him and he left as I settled in for some serious warm study time.

About two hours passed before I was interrupted by a middle-aged man coming into the office. I was startled enough to sit up straight. He seemed equally startled but recovered quicker than I and greeted me with a smile.

"I didn't expect to find a pretty girl curled up in the corner with a book."

By the time he'd finished I recognized him as Connor's father, Ken. His build was the same, and his smile was obviously something he'd passed down to his only son. His hair was more brown than Connor's auburn, with charming streaks of gray.

"Hi, Mr. Hunt. I'm Liv Phelps. I clean once a week and study here sometimes." I smiled up at him from my seat and tried to forget that my head was wrapped in a scarf and I was wearing a pajama set with snowflakes.

"I remember you. You were a lot smaller the last time I saw you, though. I know your parents. How are they?"

"Good," I replied out of habit.

"Good, good. I suppose Connor is out in the shop?"

"Yeah. I guess so. Haven't seen him for a while."

"I'm right here, Pops." Connor's voice entered the conversation a breath before he entered the room.

Ken turned to his son and smiled. "I see why you're so anxious to be at work all the time if this is what's waiting for you." He gestured to me.

I huffed, doing my best to play off words that suggested some sort of bond between Connor and me. "Trust me, he's not here because of me."

Ken grinned. "Is that so?" He looked to Connor.

Connor held up his hands. "Don't ask me to explain. She probably has a rule about that."

"A rule about that?" Ken looked curiously my way.

"Someone has to set rules for this one." I hooked a thumb at Connor. "Otherwise he's going to think he's the prince of everything."

"I like her," Ken said to his son.

"Don't be fooled by her fuzzy pajamas," Connor drawled sarcastically.

"I'm very pleasant to those I like." I tilted my head and gave Ken my most winning grin while I prayed that he wouldn't see my embarrassment over my pajamas being brought up.

"Lies, lies, lies." Connor turned to his father but not before I saw a glimmer of amusement that did funny things to my heart rate. "What brings you down?"

"I brought some soup and hot cocoa. Thought I'd see if you wanted to share dinner."

"Did you bring marshmallows too?" I inserted. "Because Connor really loves a nice pile of gooey marshmallows in his cocoa."

Ken's eyebrows furrowed. "You do?"

"I do not. Don't listen to anything she tells you." He shook his head. "I'd love to take a dinner break, thanks. Let me get washed up."

Connor left and Ken turned to me. "There's enough for three. I think it would be very entertaining for me if you joined us."

"Oh, no thanks." Dinner wasn't something I was going to do with Connor and his dad. I stood and closed my notebook as Kelly's voice echoed through my mind, telling me lunch was for friends and dinner was for dates. Time to scoot. "I should get out of your way."

"The roads are awful and the soup is warm." Ken disappeared into the storage closet and came back out with three paper bowls, three spoons, and three Styrofoam cups as I finished packing up my things. "Toss your bag into that corner and have a seat," he said.

"I really can't. I need to get home."

"Are you going to leave this lonely old man with only Connor for company?" Ken teased.

Well, when he put it that way . . . I shook my head and sat back down. I had not been raised to ignore lonely old men in their hour of need. It looked like I was staying. I'd think of it as having dinner with Mr. Hunt, which was totally non-threatening and meant I wouldn't have to scrounge up something cold at home.

Dinner with the Hunts was a far cry from what dinner with my family and Blaine had been like. I wasn't trying to impress anyone, and so I was able to relax into the corner chair and casually observe the way that the two men interacted. Conversation flowed easily, and Ken was kind and inclusive. The thirty minutes I spent with them was comfortable and nice. It made me a little jealous.

As we were finishing up, I realized that I'd felt more content eating soup in the office of the mechanic shop than I had eating at home with my family over the past several months. Which, of course, terrified me, so I needed to leave.

"Thank you so much, Mr. Hunt, for that dinner," I said as I stood abruptly.

Both men stood too. The considerate gesture made me feel somehow ungracious.

"You leaving so soon?" Ken asked.

I straightened the scarf around my head and nodded. "Yeah. I need to get home. My brain can't do any more math, and I should probably check on my mom and sister. Hopefully our power is back on."

I gathered my things while avoiding eye contact with them, afraid of what I might give away. The gathering had had an intimate quality to it that had shifted a barrier, and I was full on petrified by the whole situation.

"I hope to see you again soon," Ken said while he held my coat for me to slip my arms into. The fuzzy flannel of my pajamas didn't slide in easily, and I was grateful for the assist.

"Thanks again," I said.

"I'm going to head home too, Con. See you later." Ken gave his son a quick hug as Connor thanked him for the meal, and left as I was buttoning my coat up. I continued to avoid meeting Connor's eyes.

"Well, thanks for letting me study here again," I said when the silence started to feel heavy.

"I'm glad you decided to stop pouting," he replied.

At this I finally lifted my gaze and frowned. "I was not pouting."

"If you say so. You okay to get home? The roads are probably icy."

"I'll be fine." I slung my backpack over one shoulder and headed into the lobby.

"I'll walk you out."

I shook my head, but he ignored me and followed me out, holding the front door open for me against a gust of icy wind.

I tucked my head down and headed to my car, grateful that he stayed in the doorway. The parking lot was icy and my feet slipped a few times, but I managed to stay upright.

Until I didn't. One moment I was looking at my car, the next I was chewing pavement. I hit so hard and fast that I didn't have time to put my hands out or really register that I was going down.

The ice against my forehead burned, and my hands weren't getting traction as I tried to push up. My scarf had been knocked off and covered my eyes as I lifted my head.

"Liv!" Connor's voice was suddenly next to me. "Are you okay?"

He hooked his hands under my arms from behind and lifted me to my feet, which had me slipping again. I reached for my car to steady myself. He turned me to face him and pushed the scarf out of my eyes and back up onto my curls. He was back lit from the shop lights, so while he had a good view of my face, I couldn't see his in the darkness.

"You cut your cheek. Come on," he mumbled.

He picked up my fallen backpack and then put an arm around my shoulders as we walked slowly back into the light and warmth of the shop. He guided me straight back into the office we'd just left. It still smelled like soup and cocoa. I thought maybe I'd always remember that cozy dinner with Connor and his dad.

"You're not saying anything. How hard did you hit your head?" he interrupted my musings.

I blinked. "Me not talking is concerning?"

"Yes."

"I don't talk that much," I replied, but it had no sting, only weariness.

"You do."

I sat in one of the smaller chairs across from the desk. "This is karma, you know."

"For what?"

"Laughing so hard when Sadie got clipped by that tuber a few days ago." I tried to grin at the memory, but it tugged my cheek and

I winced. I looked up to meet his concerned eyes. "How bad is it? Do you think I'll need stitches?" I tugged a mitten off and felt my cheek. My hand came away with blood, and tears immediately pooled at the sight. "I'm bleeding."

His expression shifted to something tender, the same look I'd painted in his eyes all those days ago. It made my heart beat in my throat and my breathing feel shallow.

"Don't cry, Livy," he said in an oddly husky voice.

"Don't call me Livy," I whispered.

He said nothing, just went back into that storage room of wonders. *They must have everything imaginable back there*, I thought as I leaned into the chair. Sure enough, within a minute he was back with a first aid kit. He set it on the desk and opened it. After rifling around for a moment he came and knelt in front of me.

"I'm going to clean it up and get some bandaging on it," he said. I nodded. "It's going to sting." I nodded again and bit my lip. He opened an antiseptic wipe and took my hand to move it away from where I'd been holding it over my injury. "You have paint on your fingers." I nodded. "You have paint on your nails a lot. How come?"

He'd noticed? How? No one had ever mentioned it to me before. My mouth felt dry as I whispered, "Rule number one."

His eyes were amused as he dropped my hand to focus on cleaning my face. With his head so close to mine I finally had a chance to examine the facets of color in his hair. It reminded me a little of some pictures I'd seen of red desert sand, although it was darker in some places. It helped my mind focus when the stinging started. I winced, even though I was trying to hold still.

At my jerk he looked up and met my eyes. He was so much closer than I'd realized. Our gazes held, and I wondered what he was thinking. Suddenly I felt overly warm, and swallowing was difficult. Still our gazes held, his so rich in yellows and browns.

"How does it look?" I squeaked out.

"I don't think you'll need stitches," he said at last, tearing his gaze away.

My cheeks felt flushed, and new tears rose on the waves of unwanted emotion. I could not feel attracted to Connor Hunt. He was so wrong in so many ways. He just . . . no. I wasn't even going to go down that path. I had Blaine, I had school, I had a future. None of those things were in the room with me at that moment, and I had to remember that. I couldn't get sucked in to the false feelings prickling around me. I'd known Connor my whole life. I'd heard the stories, seen the swagger, and understood that no one got into his heart. It didn't matter at all that the Connor I was getting to know seemed to be the opposite of what I'd always believed.

Connor finished cleaning the wound and looked directly at me again. "All done." He must have noticed the tears, which wasn't really surprising as one had started rolling down my non-injured cheek. I caught it with my thumb. "Did it hurt that bad?"

I shook my head. "I'm okay."

"I'm not a big fan of crying," he mumbled as he turned to get some gauze.

"Rule number six?" I asked. "No crying."

One side of his mouth lifted as he nodded. He avoided eye contact with me as he applied the gauze and tape. His hands were warm and sure, callused against the soft planes of my face. They didn't shake at all, proof that he wasn't feeling those same strange zings I had. Proof that I needed to get away and breathe some cold air and call Blaine.

When he was done he stood and reached a hand down for me. I didn't want to take it, so I pretended I hadn't seen it and used the arms of the chair to push up to stand. I grabbed my backpack and slung it over my shoulder while Connor wordlessly led the way back out. This time he insisted on me holding his arm while we crossed the parking lot to my car. Thankfully we made it without further incident.

I got in and started the car, waiting a moment for the defroster to clear the windshield before backing out. Connor had gone back inside. No more words had been spoken. I was fine with that. I wasn't sure I could have spoken anyhow.

CHAPTER THIRTEEN

Within a couple of short days, life had slid back into its normal pattern. The snow slowed down, the power came back on, my face healed, and I took my mid-term exams. It was easy to push the dinner with Connor and Ken into the back of my mind as one of those strange and unexplained moments in time that would never happen again.

The first week of March had arrived, and with it came a pleasant surprise at work. Jake had called the staff back into the kitchen after closing and told us he was closing early Friday night to throw a staff dinner. We were all instructed to bring a date and dress fancy. It was being catered. Everyone seemed frozen in shock until Jake had yelled at us to get back to work.

"It's a girl," Kelly said as we carried our boxes of clean glasses to stack at the drink station. "No way would he be closed on a Friday night if it wasn't for some lady."

"Agreed. Weekends are always hopping around here. He'll lose the profits," I replied. "On top of all of that, can you believe he's having it catered? Do I actually know Jake anymore?"

She nodded. "I assume you're going to bring Blaine?"

"Yeah. I doubt this is what he had in mind for our weekend, knowing him, but it is nice to have someone to ask for a change."

I was extra happy about the dinner because Blaine and I had been missing each other quite a bit lately. We hadn't managed to see each other for a solid week, and I was worried about it. Was it a bad sign if we weren't able to make more time to be together? Was he backing off to see if I'd take some initiative?

"I have no idea who I'll ask," Kelly stated as she stacked the last cup in place. "I've got three days to find a date." We turned back to the kitchen to get enough for two more stacks.

We each picked up a stack of cups, and this time she held the door for me. "You know, the more I've seen you and Connor together, the more I think you two would be a good couple, actually," I dared to say.

Her head cocked to the side, but she kept her eyes on her glass tower. "I guess I can see why you say that, because I kind of feel like he's the first guy I've been truly comfortable with. Have you noticed how he just gets my jokes and stuff? And he's easy in his own skin? I think he's been a good influence on me, helping me settle down and see things more clearly. But, no, we aren't meant to be a couple."

I dropped it and finished putting my stack in place. One of the other waitresses turned on the house music and changed the channel to something upbeat. Before long we were all laughing and having a great time as we gossiped about what this employee dinner was really about. However, in the back of my mind I kept wondering what Connor had changed in Kelly, and why *he* was the one to finally help her see things clearly.

Three days later we found out that not only did Jake have a woman, but he hadn't been joking about dressing fancy. Jake was in a full tux. His date was none other than the bombshell Connor had turned down a couple of weeks ago. I almost laughed out loud but covered it with a cough into my elbow. I couldn't imagine how on earth that had come to be, but it was a fun shock and I hoped he'd found happiness. A person could do worse than Jake.

Blaine was in his element as suit and tie was his bread and butter. This time it was a sort of gray-blue that made his eyes really pop. His brown shoes were polished to a shine. I'd managed to find a red dress at a thrift shop with a sweetheart neckline, capped sleeves, and a skirt that billowed out from the waist down. I felt like a princess.

When we arrived, classical music played through the overhead speakers—a first—and candles were set up at every table. If it weren't for the fact that we were eating off the plates and silverware that I'd cleaned recently, the place would have been completely transformed.

I dragged Blaine straight back to a corner booth where Kelly was already seated with a handsome man I didn't recognize. I could not wait to hear this story.

"Liv, you made my eyes bug out when you walked in," Kelly greeted as I slid in across from her.

"Thanks. You're looking pretty nice yourself." I smiled at her. Her bright hair was pulled up in a mass of curls on top of her head, and she was wearing a deep purple dress that set off her beautiful coloring. Kelly was one of those girls who really knew how to dress up.

She turned to her date. "This is my date, Scott." Kelly leaned in closer and whispered across the table to me, "I met him this afternoon at the market. He showed me how to choose the best oranges, so I thought I'd keep him." I chuckled when Kelly leaned back and planted a kiss on Scott's cheek. Scott flushed.

"Funny how such a small choice to swing by the market today is turning into one heck of an adventure," he replied. He seemed a little bemused to find himself at a dress up dinner with spitfire Kelly, which made sense as they'd just met that day. He was older than us, probably mid-thirties, with brown hair and smiling brown eyes.

"What do you do, Scott?" Blaine asked after our food was served.

"I'm a fruit and vegetable wholesaler," Scott replied.

"Ah, thus the knowledge of oranges," Blaine said.

"Yep. What about you?" Scott asked him.

"I co-own a marketing firm in Springfield with my father."

Scott nodded and then looked to Kelly and me. "I already know you two ladies work here at the diner. Have you been here long?"

"I've been here for five years now, and Liv has been here for two."

"Olivia's going to college, though," Blaine inserted. "She's not going to be here forever. Isn't that right, babe?"

All eyes turned to me. "I, uh, yes. I'm still in the early part of the program, so I'll be here for a few more years, assuming Jake is willing to keep me around."

"Of course, he is. You're one of our best waitresses. The customers love Liv."

Kelly reached over to pat my hand.

"She's easy to love," Blaine said.

"I don't know what I'd do without her," Kelly added.

"If I have anything to say about it, you may find out sooner than later." Blaine turned to me with a secret smile.

Scott's smile broadened. "Sounds like congratulations will be in order soon."

I coughed and shook my head. "Oh, no. We've only been dating for a few months."

Blaine chuckled good-naturedly. "I meant that there are better employment options in Springfield that would better suit someone like Olivia. A side bonus is she'd be closer to me. Don't you agree?" he looked to me with shining eyes.

This time, the name bugged me, and I knew it was time to mention it. "Please, you should call me Liv." I patted his hand.

"Olivia is such a beautiful name, though," he said softly.

"It's just that no one calls me that, so, you know." I shrugged and when he didn't say anything else I pressed on. "I didn't know you wanted me to move to Springfield."

"It would make it a lot easier for us to see each other."

"Liv has dreams. She's driven and independent," Kelly said. Her eyes sparked in defense of me, which warmed my heart. "When she's ready to move, she will."

I hadn't felt attacked by Blaine's statement, but before I could say so, Blaine replied with, "I know all about Olivia doing things on her time." His tone was teasing, only it didn't feel playful and left me feeling strange. I hadn't heard that particular tone from him before.

I tried to redirect. "It would be nice to see each other more, but my family is here and . . . "

"Not much of a family, though, am I right?" Blaine interrupted, keeping his tone light, but the words cut. Granted, his dinner with my family had been pretty awful, but he didn't actually know them, and I spoke about them so infrequently that he couldn't possibly understand the dynamic.

I forced a light laugh even as my stomach dropped. "This is fun, hearing all about me, but maybe we could change the topic to something different."

It took a concerted effort from Kelly and Scott, but eventually conversation became less strained and we were able to enjoy ourselves. I liked Scott immediately. He was relaxed, witty, amiable, and had great manners. Kelly was beaming in a way I hadn't seen for a while. In that moment I decided to stop questioning what Connor had done to help Kelly and instead be grateful that he'd worked some magic with her. It left the door open for a guy like Scott. A new kind of guy. I crossed my fingers under the table, hoping Kelly was starting a good thing.

Blaine helped me put on my coat when it was time to go, and after hugging Kelly goodbye we ducked our heads against the cold and hurried to his car.

I thought about not bringing up the things he'd said at dinner, but then I thought about how we'd been dating for four months now and this was the first time I'd heard that he disapproved of my family or my employment. It seemed like something that needed to be discussed. Decided, I dove right in.

"I didn't know you thought my family was awful," I said as Blaine pulled out of the parking lot.

He sighed. "I'm sorry, babe, this isn't how I wanted the conversation to go. I've been wanting to discuss things with you, but the timing never seemed right. I shouldn't have brought it up at dinner with other people around."

"What have you been wanting to talk about?"

"I love you, Olivia." He looked over at me with an expression of pure tenderness.

It was the first time he'd said the words, and I wasn't sure how to reply. I mean, I still wasn't calling him my boyfriend. So, unfortunately what I said was, "That's so nice of you."

His face fell, because my response was horrid. "I want to support you and love you, but you hold me at arm's length. I've been driving back and forth for months, wanting more, but after dinner with your family I understand better why you're so inexperienced with warmth and love."

"My family loves me," I said, defensive again.

"Your family doesn't show that very well."

"What do you know about it?" I snapped.

"Nothing. Nothing at all, except for a short, tense dinner weeks ago. You never invite me in, we never interact with them. Getting you to talk about them is decidedly difficult. What am I supposed to think? You don't act like someone who's proud of her family."

I was humbled by his statement. I was also hurt by it, because he spoke truth. I had deliberately kept a space between him and my family. It was fear, and I knew it. Aside from my lifelong habit of not wanting to open up that way, I didn't think Blaine would understand the dynamic. I didn't think someone who'd been raised in a "perfect" environment could appreciate the intricacies in a relationship that at times felt based purely on mutual survival. I couldn't—or perhaps wouldn't—admit those things to him, so I moved on.

"What about me moving to Springfield? I didn't know you disapproved of me working at the diner."

"It's temporary, isn't it?"

"Well, yes, but not so temporary that I was planning to be gone anytime soon. It'll be a couple of years before I graduate."

"So, you're willing to do mediocre until then?"

Oh, wow. That stung. "I'm willing to do whatever it takes to support myself and pay for school," I stated.

"Why can't moving to Springfield and being near me be one of your options?"

"We aren't even engaged, much less married. I can't move to Springfield and let you fend for me," I replied. "I'm not counting on anyone but myself for survival."

"You don't believe in being part of a team?" Now his voice sounded incredulous.

"Of course, I can be a team player. What I can't be is someone who depends totally on another person for my welfare. I won't do it."

"I don't know much, but your sister made it sound like your father has run off." His lips pinched. "It's not always like that. My father has supported my mother for thirty-five years."

"You don't know enough about my parents' relationship to speak about it." My tone heated with a dreadful sense of betrayal on behalf of my parents who'd had a wonderful marriage until recently.

"In Springfield things are different. You could be part of that."

I'd said those same words to myself many times, so why did it sound so different coming from him?

We pulled up to my house, and I looked to the front window where the curtains were open and soft yellow light was streaming out. I knew what I'd find inside. Mom would still be at work, and Sadie would be watching TV. Things would need to be cleaned and Dad would be missing. I didn't want it to be my forever, but I knew for a fact that it was okay for now and I wasn't quite ready to move on.

"Look, Blaine." I turned to him with sad eyes.

"Nope. Don't say it. Tonight has been important. We finally aired some of our thoughts. It's clear to me that you're content here, and I won't push you to leave it behind. I do want to ask you for a favor, though."

"Okay."

"Can you try to open up to me, just a little more? I know there's so much in there that you're not sharing with me. What I do know about you, I love. Try to trust that I'd love the rest too."

He didn't let me say anything more but took my face in his hands and kissed me deeply. It should have been soothing and comforting, but I was too hurt to let it flow through me. When he ended the kiss with a soft smile I gave him one in return, all the while wondering what I thought I was smiling about.

* * * * *

Two days later when I showed up to work the diner was still dark, only bare minimum lighting on to allow the staff to set up for the day. Kelly, wearing a new shirt and more makeup than usual, was bouncing off the walls. I, however, was slugging around with a giant stone on my chest and the distinct feeling that I'd put on dirty jeans.

"Okay, squingy eyes, what's bugging you?" she said to me when I refused to dance with her to one of the juke box songs. "Spill it."

I'd been thinking a lot about the conversation I'd had with Blaine after the employee dinner. He'd made some good points about me being closed off. He'd also made some good points about my family. I knew it was true that there were better employment options in Springfield. Only, if I moved I had to suddenly pay rent and all my groceries on top of school. I'd have to find a large space for my painting—which he still had no idea about. I'd lose my friends and my support system. Blaine would become all I had. After only four months, I wasn't sure I wanted to put all my eggs in his basket just yet. Wouldn't you need to know you loved a person before you put it all on the line that way?

I told Kelly all of it. She listened quietly while we prepped menus and started setup, occasionally making noises of understanding, until it was time to flip on the open sign and get the day going.

"Do you think he's right, that I should move now?" I finally asked.

"First of all, he only knows the present, not the history. Your family wasn't always struggling. They're your people and you can't run away from them."

"True. He's right, though. I'm not planning on staying in Oak Hills forever."

"I know. You've been saying that for the past few years." Kelly smiled.

"I don't know why it sounded so terrible to hear him tell me to just move now. I mean, if it's inevitable?"

"Nothing in this life is inevitable. You've got to follow your gut, and your gut screamed at you that now is not the time to make the move. Who knows what will happen in the next couple of years while you go to school? Take it one day, week, or month at a time. Your path will open up soon enough."

"You sound very guru-ish this morning." I grinned.

"You can thank Scott. He's got me centered." She winked and did a little dance while walking to unlock the door.

"One last serious question, oh wise one. Do you think Blaine is my path?"

"I don't know. What I do know is that you've been dating the man for a while. It shouldn't take that long to figure out if he's worth continuing to see or not."

I pulled a face and leaned against the counter, watching an older couple make their way to the door. "He said he loves me."

"That's big. Do you feel the same?"

"It's just, he's my first actual boyfriend." I forced out the word, testing how it felt. "How do I know?"

"I'm pretty sure I'm going to be marrying Scott, and we just met." Kelly laughed and pushed the start button on the coffee.

I turned to her with big eyes. "Are you serious?"

"Totally. That man is so deep under my skin that I can hardly think about anything else. I'm counting down the hours until I get off work and we can be together again. He's like the sweetest chocolate bunny I've ever tasted."

Kelly left to seat the couple, and I smiled as I watched her walk away. I was happy for her, if Scott did turn out to be her true love. She'd spent a lot of time chasing that idea and had the scars on her heart to prove it.

I busied myself with an older single gentleman sitting at the counter and thought about what Kelly had said. I had been dating Blaine for a while, although I wouldn't describe him as the sweetest candy I'd ever tasted. I wouldn't describe anyone that way, even if I did understand the sentiment.

"Hey," Connor's voice interrupted my musings as he sat on a stool directly across from me. His eyes were bright and I smiled back without thinking about it as warmth started in my chest and heated my face. "I need food." He pulled off the ball cap he'd been wearing and ran his hands through his hair to tame it a little.

"You've come to the right place." I handed him a menu and looked down at my ordering pad, trying hard to hide the reaction as I scolded myself for it. "What do you want to drink?"

"Is there any way you can ruin orange juice?"

I glanced up. "Probably. Do you want me to try? I have some toothpaste in my purse that I could stir in."

He took a deep breath and shook his head while mumbling loudly enough for me to hear. "Sit at the counter, I said to myself, it'll be fine."

"You got cocky."

"Something I struggle with daily. I'll take an orange juice, hold the toothpaste."

"Coming right up." I turned away and filled a cup from the chilled carafe.

After putting it in front of Connor, I slid down the line to help two teenagers who were after a warm breakfast before school. I'd have chosen sleep over the breakfast, but to each their own. After taking their drink orders I made my way back to Connor.

"You ready?"

"Yeah. Pancakes, bacon, and some berries."

"Great." I jotted his order down and passed it through to the kitchen.

"You look a little tired this morning," he said to my back while I was filling coffee for someone.

"Cocky and a flatterer. It's my lucky day."

He chuckled. "It's what I do."

I gave him a nod as I passed by to deliver more drinks and take more orders. The morning was picking up steam, and I was glad. I needed the distraction after days of roller coaster emotions.

The next time I looked over, a woman I'd never seen before had taken the one empty stool left next to Connor. She was eating him with her eyes while he dug into his pancakes.

"Hi, can I get you started with a drink?" I asked her.

She looked up at me with a sunny expression. "Yes. I'd love a hot cocoa, extra marshmallows."

Connor lifted his eyes enough to share a glance with me, and I saw a glimmer of amusement in his eye, which made the corners of my mouth lift and my toes tingle.

"You've come to the right place," I said.

"Really? Wow, I'm extra glad I stopped in this morning," she chirped.

I turned away to get her drink, and when I came back I asked her, "What brings you to town?"

"I'm here shopping. I've heard your downtown is just too cute to be real."

"It is. Connor here works at the auto shop on Main Street. The façade is like a page from a storybook." Connor glanced up at me and I smiled winningly. "Will you be in town long?" I asked her.

"Maybe just overnight. It depends on what I find here." Her eyes slid to the side, and she gave Connor the coyest look I'd seen in a long time.

"Well, seems to me like you're in luck already. I mean, you got to share a nice breakfast with our handsome local mechanic." I smiled. "All the ladies think Connor's just about the sweetest thing around." I grinned at the look he sent my way.

Sunshine lady giggled. "It does look like things could be interesting around here." She stood from her stool and asked where the bathroom was. I pointed and had to stifle a laugh as she rubbed up against Connor on her way by.

"Sweetest thing around?" He arched an eyebrow.

"I could have called you a chocolate bunny, which is what Kelly is calling her new boyfriend, Scott. I thought it might be nice for you to be a sweet treat too. I'd hate for you to be lonely."

"I don't need you to try to set me up with some out-of-town lady."

I shrugged. "I just figured that an out-of-towner may have all the qualities you're looking for."

"I hate to ask, but what qualities are those?"

"Um, the out-of-town type. Love them and leave them. Two ships passing in the night, never to be heard from again."

"You have strange ideas about what I'm looking for," he said as he stood and pushed away from the bar.

"Tell me I'm wrong." I put my hands on my hips.

"Nope. Rule number one, no discussing personal lives." He shrugged into his coat, slapped on his cap, and turned away. "Money's on the counter."

"Where are you going?" I asked as I looked down to see the bills next to his empty plate.

"I'm getting out of here before she thinks she can take a bite out of this sweet chocolate bunny," he replied.

"I already told her where you work," I called after him.

"The shop is closed today."

"It's Saturday."

"I don't need the extra work." He waved his hand behind his head.

I laughed as he disappeared through the door. I was laughing a little less when I had to tell poor Sunshine that Connor had left and I had no idea where he'd gone. Yet another broken heart left in his wake.

CHAPTER FOURTEEN

A few days later I was driving down the canyon pass to Springfield for Blaine's attempts to make up with me. He'd called, apologized, and begged for me to come meet him in the city. I'd dressed carefully, unsure of what he had in mind and knowing that he held pretty tight standards himself.

The drive to Springfield normally took about thirty minutes, but it had decided to snow again. My little car wasn't the best in bad weather, so I took it slow and ended up arriving at Blaine's apartment ten minutes late. I knew he wouldn't like it. He probably had reservations somewhere that I'd just blown. Still, I pasted on a smile and entered the building.

Blaine said I kept up walls, but the truth was that I wasn't the only one. I'd never seen the inside of his apartment or met anyone from his life. In fairness, most of the time we were in Oak Hills. Tonight, however, I'd been invited to ride the elevator up. I hoped it meant good things because my heart was still a bit bruised after our last conversation.

He greeted me at the door in a T-shirt and jeans, and my mouth just about hit the floor. I'd expected to be going out, probably somewhere meant to impress, but we'd obviously be staying in. He looked good in the relaxed clothing, more approachable.

"Hi, you," he said as he opened the door wider.

I crossed the threshold and he closed the door before spinning me quickly up against it and kissing me. His arms snaked around my lower back, pressing me up against him. His mouth was warm and urgent, pressing kisses faster than I could return them. I put my own arms around his shoulders and leaned in, hoping to feel some of the same heat he seemed to be feeling. Instead I felt confused. How could he kiss me this way while hating so much about my life? Was that how love worked? You just blocked out the issues and kissed? Was this nothing more than simple biology, the desire to feel desire?

After a few moments he pulled away. "I've missed you so much and felt so bad about how things were left between us. I ordered in and thought we could have a nice relaxed evening."

"Sounds perfect." I smiled.

I wished he'd mentioned that casual thing to me, because I'd have loved to be wearing jeans myself rather than the same skirt and button down shirt I'd worn on Valentine's Day. It was much too dressy for takeout at home.

"I'm so sorry I'm late," I said as I shrugged my coat off and hung it over a chair. "The snow was starting back up and traffic was slow going."

"Not a problem at all. I hope you don't get snowed in at my place tonight." He wiggled his eyebrows playfully, letting me know he'd be totally fine with me being stuck here.

"Your apartment is gorgeous," I said in response as he guided me from the entrance area into a large open space.

Dinner was set beautifully on an all glass dining table. Candles were lit, and I was in awe as I took a moment to really look around. White everything with silver and glass highlights spoke of cold decadence. There were no personal touches, only steely perfection. His view of the city and its blinking night lights would be hard to top, and the apartment seemed designed to keep your attention on the view. It was such a contradiction to my own home that I momentarily wondered what he must think when he was with me. Was he as uncomfortable in my worn down comfort as I would be in this see-through fortress?

Blaine kept the conversation light while we ate a delicious meal. It was nice to do a general catch up. When we were done eating, I helped him clean, finding enjoyment in working together at such a mundane task.

When we were done we settled in on the couch facing a large widow. It practically felt like we were outside on a mountaintop. He slid an arm around me, tucking me cozily against his side.

"I know we've avoided it so far, but I do think we should talk a little more about the other night."

I swallowed and nodded. "Yeah, probably."

"I'm afraid I came off more intensely than I meant to."

"I didn't know you weren't happy with the way things were."

"I was, for a while. Relationships are supposed to grow and evolve, but sometimes I feel like we're in the same place we were when we met."

"It's my fault. It's just . . . we've been dating such a short amount of time. We're really still in a getting-to-know you phase and figuring out if we should keep seeing each other."

"No wonder you were so upset the other night. We're clearly on two separate planets. I'm telling you I love you and want you to consider moving closer to me, and you're still debating over if I'm someone you want to date or not." His voice was kind, but he sounded a little perplexed by the discovery that we were most definitely not on the same page.

I was equally baffled, but for totally different reasons. How on earth could he already know how he felt about me when there was still so much he didn't know? We saw each other about twice a week if it was a good week. That was by no means regular enough to have formed the kind of bond he said he felt—was it?

"I have a lot going on in my life," I said hesitantly. "I'm juggling a lot of things."

"Maybe it's too much," he replied, fingers softly stroking my neck. "Maybe if you took a breather from it all, and really focused on us, you could see where I'm coming from."

"You might be right, but I've thought about it many times, and there really isn't anything I can drop right now. I have to work to pay for school. I have to go to school to have a career and independence. My family is important to me, and they need my help. I'm cleaning the mechanic shop to pay off the repairs. What do I give up?" As I'd spoken, my voice had developed a desperation that I was sure he could hear.

He made soothing noises and snuggled me in closer. "I know how you value your independence, but if you can be open to it, I can make things easier. I'd be happy to pay for whatever you still owe Connor. Not a loan, a gift."

I started shaking my head before he was done speaking. "I don't want that between us."

"You've put it between us by making it into a point of argument. Just give in and it'll disappear," he coaxed. "I'd really love to seriously discuss our future. I think the first thing should be for you to start looking for work here. The opportunities are endless."

"Don't you think that we're moving a little too fast?"

He shook his head. "Not at all. I know what I like and I go after it. I like you."

"But that's a lot of pressure on our relationship. If I move here, you become my entire support network."

"For a time, but I'd introduce you around. With your fun personality you'd make new friends in a heartbeat."

I truly, truly doubted that. I made friends slowly and kept my circle small. "It's not just friends. It's housing and a job. How do I still pay for school? There's so much to consider."

Blaine turned to me and took my face in his hands. "Babe, you've got to breathe." He chuckled, but something about it struck me as the same way he'd said I was darling that night at the theater. I felt silly, naive, and inexperienced. He pressed a kiss to my lips before continuing. "All those things can be discussed. I have a lot of contacts here. It wouldn't be hard to get you situated."

"Situated?" My stomach clenched.

"Yes. A new apartment, new job, new car, new friends. It can all be done with very little effort." He pulled me close and planted yet another soft kiss on my lips. Another kiss I didn't return. "I've been saying it for weeks: Let me take care of you."

In my mind's eye I pictured an apartment just like his somewhere in the city. In the parking garage was a new sedan with a bow on it. Down the street was an empty cubicle with a name plate just waiting to be filled in. New friends were waiting in the apartment, ready for a welcome home surprise party. All Blaine needed was the girl to fit into the puzzle.

But I wasn't that girl. I couldn't live that life. My life was in a beat up house with worn out furniture where my sister flitted in and out, and my mom moped, and the dishes would never get done unless I did them. My car was a broken-down pile of rust, and my job was carrying trays of greasy food to the locals. When I did get my new life, I wanted it to be one I built myself, not one that I was plugged in to.

I pulled away and looked out to the city lights as his arm came around me again.

"Just look at that view," he said, oblivious to the struggle inside of me. "I've been wanting to share it with you for a while."

"You can see the entire valley," I agreed in a voice that only wobbled slightly.

"I can tell that you're still not sure. Will you think about it?" He squeezed my shoulders and I nodded. Words were impossible just then. "Great. I do love you, babe. We can build a great life together."

I swallowed and nodded like a robot.

"I have pie for dessert. Your favorite is cherry, right?"

It wasn't. My favorite pie was banana cream pie on account of the fact that my Dad had always taken me for a slice on my birthday. But he'd have no way of knowing that. So, I nodded yet again, and smiled and he served me cherry pie in his immaculate apartment while we watched the stars.

* * * * *

Like a chicken, I avoided Blaine and the discussion I knew we needed to have for an entire week. I felt a breakup was in my future and I wasn't excited. There had, after all, been an awful lot of songs written on the topic, and it sounded messy and emotional—two things I was doing my best to avoid.

He called and texted during the week. I answered and responded, but I was always too busy to chat for long and couldn't commit to a date night.

I'd admitted to Kelly what had happened, and she'd flatly told me I'd never really loved him, I'd be just fine, and that I needed to make the break in person. I'd appreciated the truth as only a best friend could deliver it, but I wasn't excited about anything she'd said.

I painted, studied, and generally threw myself into my life as a way to work through my emotions. The more I worked and thought, the more I realized that Kelly had been right. I wasn't in love with Blaine. I was sort of in love with the idea of Blaine and what he represented, but not the man himself. I liked him. Heck, I'd moved past like and had felt genuine affection for him. Yet true love, well, that was still banked in my heart waiting for the right person.

Finally I texted him and asked if he could drive up on a Saturday after my breakfast shift. He readily agreed, and the date was set. I felt a little sorry that Blaine didn't understand this was our official breakup meeting, but there was nothing I was willing to do to change that.

Friday night I snuck into the dark Mainstreet Mechanic shop to clean and then study for a bit. Having learned my lesson after accidentally falling asleep the first time, I always did my cleaning first. I took comfort in the routine of dusting and vacuuming. Even toilet scrubbing was welcome, as it allowed my mind to wander.

I planned out what I would say to Blaine the next day. I'd be sure to compliment him on what a stellar guy he was, thank him for all the good times we shared, and let him down gently. Maybe before I studied I'd even look online for dialogues to use when breaking up with a significant other. It seemed like the type of thing that would be posted somewhere.

I screamed when I turned away from changing the toilet paper roll to find Connor standing in the bathroom doorway. "You keep warning me to be careful when I'm alone here at night, and then you sneak in like that. Holy pretzels, Connor. Make some noise next time."

"Pretzels?" I simply nodded at him. "That's a first. I was surprised to see your car here."

"Why? I'm here every week." I picked up the cleaning bucket and moved past him on my way back toward the office to deposit the supplies. When I came out of the closet, he was standing in the office doorway, leaning up against the frame, his arms folded across his chest.

"Did you need something?" I asked.

"No. Nothing specific. Just checking in."

"Well, I'm here and I'm busy."

"And possibly a touch grumpy?"

I felt immediately humiliated, which only fanned the flames of frustration. "Well, you would be too if you were planning out a breakup dialogue while scrubbing toilets."

"Probably." His voice held a wary tone that caused me to glance his way. "What happened?"

"Blaine thinks I'm this . . . this . . . malleable piece of dough that he can form into something perfect. He has a whole life all prepared to simply plug me into. He's attempting to Stepford Wife me." My voice caught, and I stopped talking to take a few breaths.

"Huh."

I nodded. "The thing is that I've told him I won't be dependent on anyone. I'm not just waiting around for a man to show up. I'm in the driver's seat of my own life."

"Sure."

I took a few deep breaths and managed to admit something I wasn't proud of. "He says I don't know how to be a team player."

Connor's face remained passive. "I always thought being on a team meant everyone was equal."

"Well, he wants to be the captain, or the coach, or whoever bosses everyone around and tells them what position they'll be playing." I looked down at my hands, which were bunched into fists. "All I'd have to do is say yes and he'd hand me this perfect life on a silver platter." I shook my head. "I don't want to, though. I want to figure it all out myself. Can't I be independent and still be in a relationship?" I looked back up to where he was standing just a few steps away.

"I've always thought so. I wouldn't want someone trying to change me and calling it love."

His words resonated deep within me, and my legs felt weak enough that I sat down hard in the chair behind me. "Yes, exactly. Love isn't about changing someone to fit your mold."

The office was quiet as I looked toward the desk and thought over what he'd said. He was right, and it confirmed what I'd known to be true. Love wasn't about conforming so much that you lost who you were. It was about accepting each other and finding ways to fit your differences together.

"Have you talked to Blaine about all of this?"

"Sort of."

"Are you sure it wasn't just a fight?"

My lips pinched and I looked down at my feet. "Yes. I'm sure. He's set on creating a life for me that I'm not interested in. There's no way for us to meet in the middle."

"What are you going to do?"

I looked back up to where he was still standing nearby. "I'm going to use your office resources to look online for breakup dialogues even though I should be studying."

"You care if I stay and see what the internet has to say about breaking up?" His expression was one of amused hope and it made me grin.

I gestured to the seat behind the desk. His chair, even though I commandeered it sometimes. "Definitely. I'll pull a chair around. Let's fire this puppy up and see what the world's wisdom has to offer."

The world's wisdom, it turned out, was pretty basic. Do it face to face, give them your reasons, wish them the best in life, and avoid blaming them. Those, at least, were the proper steps to take. We drifted away from those after a time into the world of how not to break up and ended up laughing until our sides hurt.

During that hour together I sort of wished I could go back and tell fifteen-year-old me that someday Connor would stop dating anything that breathed and settle into a pretty decent human.

* * * * *

Blaine arrived on my front porch at just before one o'clock the next afternoon. The sky lit him from straight above, making his blond hair sparkle a bit. He was dressed handsomely in a royal blue suit and pressed shirt. No tie today, which was different.

The cold air bit at my skin, causing me to shiver as I rubbed my hands over my arms. "Hi," I said uneasily. "I thought we were going to meet at the restaurant."

He'd opened his mouth with a smile, but my words stopped whatever he was going to say and wiped the smile off his face. Silence dropped for a beat before he coughed slightly and said, "I, uh, well, I've missed you and hoped you wouldn't mind if we rode together."

I didn't immediately know how to respond, and my hesitation was obvious. I felt a little bruised and unsure, and didn't think the ride back home after my breakup speech would be a good one. Which meant I maybe fibbed, a tiny bit.

"Actually, I have other places to be after we eat, so I'm going to need to drive myself."

I watched as his expression transform the rest of the way from happy to wary and guarded. "Okay. Where did you want to eat again?"

I gave him directions, for the second time, to a Chinese restaurant on the edge of town. It was dumpy but good, and I didn't want to have this whole thing go down at my place of employment.

When I arrived Blaine was already there, waiting inside at a tiny table and looking comical in the shabby old place. The tinkling sound of silverware was comfortingly familiar, and the sing-song voices of servers going about their duties calmed my pounding heart. I could smell the sweet and tangy scents specific to Asian cuisine as I walked to where he sat. His expression was closed as he glanced around him.

"How have you been?" I asked as I shrugged out of my coat and joined him. I wasn't sure how else to open up conversation.

"Lonely," he replied. "I miss you." My doubtful thoughts must have crossed my face because he hurried to say, "We don't need to talk about anything. We can simply enjoy each other's company like we did before I opened my big mouth."

A softening began in the nostalgic places of my heart. We'd had some really good times. I wanted to go back too, but was there any point in that when we couldn't take back what we'd discovered about each other?

"I do miss the fun we had," I admitted.

"I should have kept quiet."

"No." I shook my head, causing one of my dark curls to fall in front of my right eye. I pushed it back into place and offered him a smile. "You should be honest with me. The problem isn't how you feel, it's that we don't agree on a lot of it."

"Couples argue. That was nothing more than our first fight, and it's behind us now," he persuaded.

"For me it was more than that," I replied quietly.

He reached over for my hand. His hands were smooth and warm against my cold fingers. "Let's just order and eat. No heavy topics."

"Blaine, I . . . "

"Food first. Then we can talk. Please?"

I caved and the next few minutes were taken up perusing the menu and ordering our food. Vegetable chow mein for me and orange pork for him.

"Do you want to hear the funniest thing?" he asked after our waiter walked away.

"Sure." I figured we may as well eat before the big talk. We both needed lunch. Plus, avoidance was comfortable for the moment.

He jumped into a tale about a customer who wanted to open a grooming store for exotic pets and the advertising nightmare they'd been fighting. It was amusing, light-hearted, and all the things I'd come to enjoy about Blaine. It helped my stomach unclench enough that by the time our food arrived I was able to get some down.

Until he said, "Sometimes I truly believe that if people would just listen to me, things would go a lot better."

My stomach constricted again. "This is your customer. Don't you want to make them happy?"

He gave me a quick look and his expression turned serious. "Yes, I do. However, I have more wisdom and experience. They need to listen and allow me to guide them along to a place where we'll both get what we're after."

I understood the concept that as a hired professional his knowledge should be respected. However, I also understood that we weren't only talking about business anymore. "True, but shouldn't it be about some compromise from both of you? They should also be allowed to follow their gut a little. This is their heart they've poured into something."

"Babe, the more I see, the more I think that people generally don't have any idea of what they really need. If I can look from the outside and see the best direction to take, don't you think I should express my thoughts and hope they listen?"

He looked at me with an intent expression, his hands gripping his chopsticks as he met my eyes. The steaming platters of food were forgotten, and it felt like the restaurant shrank to just our table.

I swallowed a sticky chunk of broccoli and cleared my throat as I set down my fork. Chopsticks had never worked for me. "It depends on the situation. People need to be allowed the freedom to make their own choices and suffer the consequences."

"Even if it proves disastrous?" he asked.

"What do you mean by disastrous?"

His voice dropped and he lowered his hand to the table. "Like a beautiful, talented, warm, and kind young woman who is throwing her life away in a backwards town with a—and I hate to say this—trashy family when she could break the cycle and be so much more."

I bit my lip as fury rose in my chest and a sharp and stinging retort begged for release. It took a few breaths, but I viciously clamped it down before saying, "Trash? Is that how you see me?"

"You? No. You're incredible. You have no idea how lovely you are. You have so much potential that you don't seem to see. You're not intentionally throwing your life away. You sincerely believe you're doing what's best, but from where I'm standing, you're making some big mistakes. I could elevate you from it all if you'd allow it."

I nodded. "I see. What would your wise and professional opinion be on how I fix that?"

He either didn't sense the sarcasm or chose to ignore it as he pushed on, blue eyes seeming to grow brighter. "You need to cut ties with your family and look out for yourself."

"Is that so easy to do?"

He leaned back and shrugged as he took a bite of his food. The sudden shift in his mannerisms was baffling. "Not always. I can take you under my wing until you learn to stand on your own two feet. Sometimes necessary things are the hardest."

I focused hard on my food, until I could count every noodle, wanting nothing more than to shove my chopstick up his nostril. "I am not beneath you. I do not need you to elevate me, or to break any cycles." I looked up to find him still chewing. My arms felt numbed by rage. "I can't help but wonder why you'd bother dating someone so in need of rescue."

"You're worth saving. I want to marry you someday, when you're ready. I think together we could do great things."

I had just taken a sip of my water and now I choked, covering my mouth with my napkin as I worked to recover. "Married?" I managed to wheeze.

"You're surprised by that?"

"Yes. The more we're learning about each other, the more we're appallingly different. Marriage doesn't seem like the next topic of conversation."

"Growing pains, babe. As relationships shift and change there's bound to be some irritation and bumping up against each other. We'll settle in to an even better normal once we scrape away the rough edges."

"Why do we have to scrape at each other?"

"In order to mold into one. That's what marriage is all about."

My mind flashed back to the discussion with Connor the night before, about how love shouldn't mean trying so hard to change the other person. My heartbeat felt heavy in my chest, and I knew my face was becoming flushed. "Can't two become one without reshaping each other? Can't we each be who we are, tethered together by mutual respect, affection, and genuine acceptance?"

"Are you honestly saying you'd change nothing about me if we were married?" He asked the question so matter-of-factly that I saw for the first time that he thought nothing of trying to change people, including himself.

"I'm honestly saying that when I do get married, I hope it's to someone who I don't want to change and who doesn't want to change me."

He scoffed. "Good luck with that. Everyone wants their partner to change, even if it's something small. Full acceptance is a myth."

"I don't agree. I fully accept my family, with all their faults and flaws, and still love them."

"Do you?" He was tense now, leaning forward to spear me with a glance.

"Yes."

"Well, could have fooled me. You've never said so."

The barb took my breath away, but I pushed on, hoping he couldn't see how it had affected me. "Then I have some work to do. But that work will not be going home and telling them how they have to behave in order to make me happy. That work will be in going home and learning to look for the good."

"That's pretty idealistic speech." He laughed, but it was without humor.

I tilted my head to the side and looked closely at him, peeling away the layers of who I'd wanted to see. "Interesting that it took so long for us to really see each other," I finally said. I folded my napkin over my uneaten food and prepared to stand.

His expression remained calm. "No, Olivia, I've seen you all along. My mistake was in thinking you'd ever be more than a poor girl from a hick town."

I took a deep breath and willed back a tide of tears as his words turned cruel. Not tears of sadness, but tears of indignation. Here he was telling me I was trash, when he was the one acting like it. It made it much easier to do what I'd come here to do and walk away without a backward glance.

"At lease we agree on one thing: We have no future together. Not only do you think I'm a joke, but you want me to uproot everything and follow the perfect path you've laid out. The only person who can choose my perfect path is me."

His face flushed a little, contrasting against his light skin, and I couldn't honestly tell if it was from anger or hurt. "I feel sorry for you, Olivia. You truly don't understand what it means to be a part of a team, and I shouldn't be surprised, because what's best for you is how it's always been."

I didn't rise to the bait. "I guess this is goodbye then."

He leaned sideways to tug out his wallet and threw a wad of cash on the table without counting it, before standing and slapping down his napkin next to the green bills. "It would appear so." He stood and put his napkin on the table.

The breakup websites had all said to end with a well-wish, and as my brain was mush I fell back on their advice, saying the first thing I could think of as he looked down at me. "Good luck with everything."

"Luck is something I have never needed." He spun in a tight circle and was out of the building in a flash.

The tears I'd expected didn't fall, but my spirit sank into the chair as I let the feelings hit me. He'd said horrible things, cruel things, and I'd had no idea he'd seen me as his rescue mission. It stung in a way I had never experienced, even as it also filled me with a new resolve to prove myself.

I was in no way less than he was. I *was* a team player. Who was he to say that the need inside of me to never become dependent on anyone else meant that I had no flexibility in my heart?

My thoughts spun in circles as I sat in that little restaurant, reflecting on the ending of my first relationship. I felt like I'd been so fooled by him. I felt like I'd let myself down as well, breaking my own promise to avoid anything that would distract me from my goals.

Yet, as his heated words sank further in I began to wonder what part I'd played in the disaster. Had I somehow morphed into a closed-off, distrustful, rabidly independent person? Had I stopped trusting in others? If so, what did I do now? Who did I really want to be?

CHAPTER FIFTEEN

I was sitting on hard, wobbly bleachers at the local recreation center a week later, watching a handful of men warm up to play basketball. Kelly's boyfriend, Scott, was one of them. "It smells like dirty socks," I grumbled to her.

"I think it's the scent of the floor varnish, because I've never been to a gymnasium that didn't smell bad."

"Do people still use the word *gymnasium*?" I tried to keep a straight face.

"I'm a person and I just used it." Kelly kicked my foot with the side of hers. "Focus less on the smell and more on those sweet calf muscles of my boyfriend's."

"I'm not comfortable ogling your man." This time I chuckled.

"He's man enough to handle us both ogling him," Kelly replied serenely.

"Remind me again why I'm spending my Saturday morning in a gym watching thirty-year-old men chase a ball back and forth." I leaned against the brick wall behind us and flinched as one of the men made a quick turn and the squeak of his shoes on the wood floor reverberated through the room.

"You've been grumpy this week."

"I'm getting that a lot lately, but I think it's my most endearing personality trait."

She made a face. "Maybe in the past, but you've been like Oscar the Grouch level, and it was time for you to leave your house and breathe some new air."

"Which explains why you brought me to the land of stale, stinky, sweaty air?"

"It was this or hot yoga at the retirement home."

I laughed, and it felt good. Kelly was right, I'd needed to get out. I wasn't broken-hearted, but I was grumpy and a little mopey after the breakup with Blaine and the self-esteem hit that had been. Obviously, it was disappointing to realize that he and I had been envisioning very different things—including the truth about each other. Plus, it was totally normal after a breakup to play the game of "poor me" and "I'm going to die alone." At least I'd heard that was normal. All the breakup websites I'd been visiting said it was.

Kelly's sigh pulled my attention back. "Be honest, don't you think my boyfriend is the best-looking guy on the court?"

"Out of the five men out there, yes, he is the best."

I grinned when Kelly pulled a face at me and said, "Count again. There are seven of them, and he's still the hottest."

I only smiled. Scott's dark hair was trimmed close, as was his equally dark beard. With his olive skin and lean build he was definitely attractive. I watched as he ran toward the hoop and hooked his arm to make a layup. The lines of his body were graceful, and I began sketching them in my mind. He'd be an interesting character to paint. Maybe, if the relationship lasted, I could do some kind of portrait for Kelly's summer birthday. I let my mind wander over colors and patterns while I stared unseeing at a wall across the way.

Another squeak of a shoe pulled me back. It had been a long time since I'd sat on bleachers and watched basketball. I wasn't a huge sports fan, but I had to admit that smells aside, it was nice to be looking at something besides my bedroom wall, or the diner booths. My social life had gotten very small lately.

We silently watched Scott's team continue to warm up. They were all men in the eighteen to thirty age range with a variety of skills and a lot of trash talk.

"Are you sure we aren't going to witness a group homicide here today?" I asked Kelly after I heard a man say something about the bodies never being found.

"Scott says that trash talking pumps them up. The worst I've ever seen happen is someone twisting an ankle."

"Was it a malicious twisting of the ankle?" I asked deadpan.

Kelly shrugged. "Nothing that could be proven in a court of law."

"Where is the other team?"

She shook her head. "I don't know."

"Whoever it is, they must hate them. I don't think this is normal trash talk."

"Nah, it's normal." Kelly waved a careless hand. "Don't let it bother you."

"Oh, I'm not bothered. I'm curious."

We both watched as Scott made a basket from the free throw line. Kelly whistled and cheered, which caused me to blush when the men looked toward us. Unlike Kelly, I'd never liked being the center of attention. Thankfully, the clunking sound of the side door opening drew the focus away as another small group of men jogged out onto the court. This group was wearing matching red and white sleeveless jerseys. They gave each other high-fives, and a few of them cheered.

"Things just got really interesting," I said. "These guys aren't messing around. They have actual team jerseys."

"Oh boy." Kelly's eyes grew round. "Now I know why the guys were talking such a big game. This team is their nemesis."

"Their nemesis?"

"Yeah. Scott was saying something the other day about a team who had jerseys made and always wins. Our guys are determined to take them down this season." Kelly grew silent, and I watched as her eyes grew rounder and a small smile lit her face. "Oh, this is great."

I looked but couldn't figure out what she was so happy about. "What's great?"

"They only have six guys. You have to have seven, or you forfeit. I mean, it isn't how Scott wants to win, but it's something, right?"

"Sure?"

She clapped her hands together and gave out a little squeal. "The universe approves of our love."

I looked over at her shining face and clasped hands and decided to let her think that the universe was speaking to the rightness of her relationship through a forfeited basketball game. I couldn't pop her bubble, even if science and common sense were dying a thousand deaths right now.

The referee came out of a different door and met the group of men in the middle of the court. He wasn't a very tall man, but the way he marched in, grasping his whistle with his chin held high, told me he took his weekend job very seriously. A forfeit was definitely happening.

Just then, that banging side door opened again and another man jogged in, sliding his arms into a red jersey and pulling it over his head as he hurried along. There was something very familiar about the way he moved and the lines of his arms and shoulders. When I saw a tuft of coppery hair peek out of the neck hole I gasped. Connor.

I turned to say something to Kelly, but she'd seen him herself. I watched as her jaw dropped open. "What is he doing here?"

I had a sudden flash of sitting in similar bleachers, cheering on our high school team and watching Connor make eyes at the cheerleaders as he ran up and down the court. "Didn't he play in high school?" I stuttered.

"Yeah, but still, what does he think he's doing?" Kelly surprised me by standing up and yelling in a loud voice, "Wipe the floor with them, Scott." She sounded bloodthirsty in a way that made me think in another era she could have been the official war crier of her people.

Scott and his team—along with the other team and Connor—all looked to where we were sitting. Well, Kelly was standing and slamming one fist into her other palm, making a smashing motion, but I was definitely sitting and trying my best to become invisible.

"You guys can take them. Show no mercy!" Kelly yelled in that same high-pitched, slightly crazed voice.

Scott's team cheered back at her, fists raised, while the opposing team shared confused glances. Connor's eyes were unreadable as they met mine. I raised my shoulders and shook my head.

"Ma'am." The referee's little body produced a big sound, which shut everything else into silence. "You'll abide by the rules of good sportsmanship or you'll leave the area."

Kelly immediately sat, and this time it was Connor's team who was smiling. "If Connor does anything to mess this up for Scott, then our friendship is over," she promised.

I stifled a sound of amusement. "I think Connor is here to play basketball, not to ruin friendships."

"Well, if he values my friendship he'll throw the game." Her jaw was set.

I reached over and pushed her lightly on the shoulder. "Reboot," I said. Her lips pinched but she looked over at me. "This is a recreational basketball league. Connor probably didn't realize he was entering a war zone."

"I'm being dumb."

"Yes."

The ref blew his whistle shrilly, and we fell silent as the game began. Scott was right in the thick of everything from the moment of tip off. He zigged and zagged, eyes focused, muscles bunched, and I realized how seriously he was taking this game. Connor, on the other hand, was on the team bench, and I had the feeling he was little more than a body needed to avoid forfeiting. The red jersey team moved like a well rehearsed, synchronized swimming team. In its own way, it was beautiful to watch.

My eyes caught the flashes of color, the way sweat darkened their hair and the backs of their shirts, the lines of their arms as they were raised or thrown quickly out to the side, the shape of a hand wrapped around the ball. The sounds of breath rushing out, groans of frustration, the men calling to each other, and always the squealing sound of shoes against the floor.

"The other team must practice a lot," I said to Kelly.

Her face was glum. "Yeah, they're really good."

"Scott's team is holding their own," I said cheerfully.

"Yeah. I guess. There's no way they'll win though."

"So what? They'll have had fun playing basketball on a weekend morning. That counts for something."

Kelly looked to me. Her blue eyes seemed to darken. "Remember when we were kids and they'd always say that it wasn't about who won or lost, but about having fun playing the game?" I nodded. "That was a dumb lie."

My mouth broke into a smile before I had any control over it. "Okay, then."

"Winning is important."

"I'm sorry I tried to be reasonable about it."

"You should be." Kelly turned back to the court. "Oh, fishhooks. They're putting Connor in."

"Is that guy limping?" I asked, watching one of the red jersey guys make his way back to the bench. "I missed who did it."

"The whistle didn't blow, so no one did it. He probably tripped over his own feet."

"Still, I would have liked to have seen it."

Connor jumped to his feet and wiggled his shoulders and arms a little. His face was stoic, but I could almost feel the energy radiating off of him. Connor typically held his body in a relaxed, unbothered way. That wasn't the case here. He'd come to play.

"He'd better remember where his loyalties lie," Kelly said darkly, and I felt a sort of peculiar amusement rise at the sight of her glaring at Connor as he jogged onto the court.

He was about the same height as the other men on the red team, but while they were all lean, he was a little stockier. Hours of lifting heavy car parts had given him definition in his arms that the other men were lacking. Not that I was noticing that kind of thing. It was simply my commitment to art that made me look.

What happened from there was nothing short of absurd. Grown men pushed, shoved, called names, pulled on each other's shirts, tripped each other, and generally behaved like a bunch of first graders. The ref's whistle blew more than it should have needed to. At one point I heard the distinct sound of something slapping against bare skin, but none of us could figure out who did it, or who the victim was.

"This is honestly the best thing you could have done for me," I said to Kelly as the clock was winding down. "It's really cheered me up." I'd been beaming for ten minutes straight.

"It's been a disaster," she replied. "We're losing by two points."

"Don't lose hope now. Scott's team has possession of the ball. I have faith in his great calf muscles."

A side of Kelly's mouth raised and she nodded. "He does have amazing muscles."

We leaned forward, intent on the final play as Scott's team dribbled, dodged, jumped, and passed their way to their basket. In one glorious final shot, the buzzer sounded and the ball ricocheted off the rim, and out of bounds. Scott's team lost.

"I'm saying lots of bad words in my head right now," Kelly said as she stood.

I did the same and followed her down the rickety steps to the gym floor. "That was seriously entertaining."

She turned to me, anger forgotten, eyes dancing, and said, "Did you see the guy who almost got pansted?"

My lips curved up to match her expression. "I did. I can't believe the ref missed it. This was better than a night at a comedy club." I started laughing and Kelly joined in.

"Well, I'm glad someone is laughing right now." Scott's voice behind us made us jump and squeal as we spun around. His cheeks were flushed from exertion, which made his dark eyes look even darker.

"I'm so sorry, honey." Kelly flung herself into his arms, unaware of the sweat that had soaked through his shirt. "How disappointing."

He wrapped his arms around her and tucked his head against hers, his mouth softening into a smile. "Yes, I can see how sorry you are."

"I've never seen anything like that game before," I teased.

Scott's eyes met mine and they weren't upset. "Pete almost got pantsed."

"It was epic."

His eyes moved from my face to slightly behind me, but his expression remained open and happy as he greeted Connor. "Hey, man. Good game."

Connor shook his hand and smiled back at him. He was flushed as well, which made his freckles seem to disappear. "I had no idea what I was signing up for when I agreed to sub in."

"I may need to start coming here more often. That was really entertaining," I said cheerily.

Connor's eyes moved to me, and something shifted in them as his expression seemed to soften. "It's nice to see you a little happier than you were last time we ran into each other."

I blushed. "Oh, yeah. The day before the breakup. I was grumpy."

Kelly, who had released her hold on Scott and was now holding his hand, pulled a face. "Don't let her fool you, she's still grumpy."

"Seems normal after a breakup," I stated matter-of-factly.

"I need ice cream," Kelly inserted before anything else was said.

"It's ten o'clock in the morning," I replied.

"Yes, that's true. I still want ice cream. Anyone else?"

Scott planted a kiss on her hair. "Count me in."

Connor looked to me, and I started to shake my head. As much as I had enjoyed the morning out, I needed to get back home to do some things before my work shift that night. As I opened my mouth to graciously decline the invite, Kelly grabbed my hand.

"We aren't taking no for an answer. Connor?"

"I'm more in the mood for pancakes," he said. Pancakes sounded tempting enough to make me hesitate. "Know anywhere we can get both?"

Kelly nodded. "Jake's."

"Are you two okay to eat there?" Scott asked.

"Sure. It's kind of fun to go in and play customer now and then," Kelly responded. They looked to me.

I nodded. "Pancakes are something I can get my mind around."

As Scott drove Kelly and me to Jake's, with Connor following behind, my mind flashed back to my freshman year in high school. It was the year that Kelly and I had discovered boys didn't actually have cooties, and that there was one in particular worth watching. His name was Connor Hunt and he'd been a senior.

He was the first boy I'd ever felt a hitch in my chest over. At first mine and Kelly's interest had been the same as the other girls. Connor was attractive and different; his coloring and natural athleticism set him apart. He'd seemed to have reached adulthood while the others were just boys. However, the more we'd covertly watched him, the more we'd come to realize that he was cocky, rebellious, and careless with the feelings of others.

A shift had happened in our thinking as the blinders came off. While other girls were chasing him, we began watching from our self-righteous seat in the stands. Many times Kelly and I had talked about what a terrible person he was—untrustworthy, full of himself.

I still couldn't quite figure how on earth he had found his way in with us. It felt surreal to be going for pancakes and ice cream together after a decade of judging him unworthy of my time.

Scott parked his car and cut the engine. "You ladies ready?" he said.

The three of us climbed out as Connor's truck rumbled in to park beside us. His truck was a newer model, shiny and clean, and I thought about him having bought the mechanic shop from the original owner a little while ago. Somewhere along the line, playboy Connor had made something of himself and settled in to adult life. I hadn't been paying enough attention to know when it had happened, but now that I was noticing, it seemed that a shift had occurred in my own world. How many more walls were going to crumble in my life?

Connor caught up with our trio as we reached the door, and he held it open for us. I avoided looking right at him but whispered a thanks as I walked through. His body was still warm from the exercise, and a hint of sweat masked by a minty soap smell reached me. It wasn't unpleasant.

Kelly and I waved to Jake as we chose our own booth and slid in—Kelly next to Scott and me next to Connor. I slid as far in as I could and got out a menu. It was nothing more than habit, as I knew everything there was to order here.

When fellow waitress Jenn came over, she gave us a big grin, her blue eyes sparkling in amusement at seeing us there. "I'm not sure I'd choose to eat here on my day off."

"It's worse than that," I replied. "It's not my day off. I'll be having dinner here too."

We all gave Jenn our orders. I shifted to hand her my menu afterwards and bumped my shoulder against Connor's. We were sitting close. Closer than I'd expected, and I tried to casually lean sideways against the wall without making it obvious. From here I could pick out all the laugh lines around his eyes and see how his eyelashes were actually a darker shade of brown, not the auburn color they appeared to be.

Conversation flowed into light topics as we waited for our food, but I was having a hard time relaxing into this new strange quartet. The rest of the group seemed to find no awkwardness in it, and I wondered if this wasn't the first time they'd all hung out. I knew Kelly had become good friends with Connor, so it made sense that Scott would have formed some sort of pal bond with him too. Scott showed no signs of jealousy as Connor and Kelly swapped inside jokes.

Another unexpected memory surfaced of Kelly and me sitting in the lunch room watching Connor at another table with his girlfriend. He'd leaned across the table and taken some of her hair in his hand, winding it around his fingers as they'd talked. The girl had beamed back at him the entire time. Kelly had said something about how smooth he was, and how it would be so easy to believe he meant it.

Our food arrived just as my phone rang. I reached into my purse to see who it was while Jenn set a plate in front of me. I mouthed my thanks to her as I saw *Mom* flash across the screen. Mom rarely called me, so I was quick to answer while the others resumed talking.

"Hey, Mom."

"I'm so glad you answered, honey." Mom sounded awful. Her voice was a croaking mess.

"Uh-oh. You sound sick." My heart dropped.

"Yes. Sadie too. I don't know what we have, but it's not good. Are you working?"

"Not until later today."

I could almost feel her relief through the phone. "Could you please stop by the store and get some things? I'll text you a list."

I nodded even though she couldn't see, and silently bid farewell to my plans to study that day. "You bet."

"Thank you, Liv. I'm sorry to be a bother."

"I'll be home as soon as I can."

We said our goodbyes, and I tucked my phone back into my pocket. The call had been like dropping a bucket of cold water over the morning. I took a couple of deep breaths and returned to the others.

"I'm so sorry. My mom and sister are really sick and they need me." I plastered a smile on, but even to me it felt fake.

"Are they actually sick?" Kelly asked. Her tone spoke more than her words did.

"Yeah. Mom sounded really awful on the phone."

"Okay, but don't let them run you ragged."

I wanted so much to give Kelly a hug. I loved that she was so protective of me and that she knew the little things about my life. Funny, how I hadn't wanted that same level of openness with Blaine. But thoughts of Blaine weren't welcome, so I shoved them down.

"I won't. I'll take my plate to the back and get it in a to-go box." I looked to Connor, who was already scooting out of the booth to let me and my plate by. "Thanks," I said to him. "Thanks for a fun morning, Kell. Nice game, guys. I'll see you all soon." I smiled at them as a whole and left as quickly as I could.

CHAPTER SIXTEEN

Mom and Sadie had not been faking. For the next seventy-two hours I was the on-call bucket brigade and Gatorade runner for my family. They managed to survive when I was at work, but school and cleaning the mechanic shop were pushed clear off my schedule. I washed my hands mercilessly, doing my best to avoid getting sick myself. I slept lightly, and some nights not at all as I held back hair, wiped down flushed faces, stripped sheets, and drew baths. Work became my retreat, and it was there that Kelly found me sitting in a booth with my head down on my arms during my lunch break.

"Still pretty rough at your place?" she asked. Light fingers settled on my back and patted gently while I nodded. "Any sign of improvement?"

"No one threw up this morning," I said into my arms.

"That's a good sign."

"Yeah. They seem to be coming out of the forest."

"How are you?" She slid into the booth across from me.

I raised my head to rest my chin on my hands. Tears I didn't want to shed immediately filled my eyes at the sympathetic look she wore. In so many ways, Kelly was my safe place. Her face was as well known to me as my own. I didn't have to be strong for my best friend.

"I'm exhausted." I sniffled. My throat became thick, changing my voice to something deeper. "The house is a total mess. I can't keep up with it all. I've done a million loads of laundry, and scrubbed the whole house every day to keep the germs from spreading. They're just lying on the couch, so how are they making a mess? I swear that it's evil dark magic. I don't know if I can do it another day without getting some more sleep."

"Three days is a long time to have no rest." She reached out and patted my head. "It's okay to be tired."

"It gets worse."

"How?"

"My dad called and he's coming home tomorrow, which is, like, I don't know why he would be, because he was just here a few weeks ago and . . . well, you know. But no matter what the reason is, he gets home tomorrow, and he's coming home to a disaster. I'm trying to be reasonable and understand that this is just life, but I can't bear the thought of it. Even though I'm mad at him, I still want him to come home to a place that will draw him back." New tears filled my eyes, and I blinked them away.

"That job isn't only up to you. Your mom and Sadie should help too."

"I honestly don't know if they can. They've been so sick."

"Listen, Liv, a few customers just came in, so I've got to run, but have a good hearty lunch, and things will be brighter soon. You'll probably go home to find everything is fine. They're feeling better and they'll want to get ready for your dad too." I sniffed one last time and nodded. "Can I have Jake make you something?"

"Vegetable soup and a roll?"

"Sure thing. I'll bring it right over."

I put my head back down on my arms and tried to empty my mind. I took deep breaths in and out, and I pictured the painting I had been working on last, with its sunny colors. I listened to the chatter of customers, the light instrumental music playing in the background, and the way the central heating was lifting the light hairs on the back of my neck. By the time the warm soup and fresh roll arrived I was feeling a little better. The meal did its work of renewing some of my energy, and I made it through the rest of my shift.

After work I did a quick grocery run and headed home around dinnertime with a carload of food. I bought extra knowing Dad would appreciate having food in the house, but as I carried it in I felt disgusted with myself for catering to him at all. Why couldn't I break that habit of wanting to make him happy?

I opened the front door and paused, wondering for a minute if I was in the right house. The living room was immaculate, and Mom and Sadie were sitting on the couch eating bowls of something that smelled delicious. They were eating! Eating was a great sign. They both looked as though they'd showered and cleaned up.

I made my way wordlessly into the kitchen, where I was completely bowled over to find the same situation. Sparkling clean with no signs of the sickness that had gone through the house. I wasn't sure who the angel of mercy had been, but I was swamped with gratitude.

"There's a bowl of homemade soup in the microwave for you," Mom called from the other room. "When you're done putting away the groceries you should come sit and eat with us." Her voice, while still a little raspy, sounded strong, and my knees actually felt weak with relief.

I wanted to cry tears of complete joy. I made quick work of putting things away and reheated the soup before joining them on the couch.

"The house looks amazing, and this soup is yummy, and I can't believe it." I was smiling so big that my mouth felt the stretch. Relief zigged down my back as my shoulders relaxed. "Thank you. Dad will be so happy when he gets here tomorrow."

Sadie turned big eyes on me. "Dad's coming tomorrow?" Her slender body was wrapped in a blanket, her hair still slightly damp, and her face free of makeup. She looked like the ten-year-old she'd once been.

"You forgot?" I asked. She nodded.

"Well, no matter the reason, I'm so grateful that you guys worked so hard to get the house in order. I could kiss you both."

"I'm not supposed to say anything, but we didn't do all of this." Mom turned to me. Her eyes, so like mine, looked more peaceful than they had in a long while. Her pale face had regained some color.

I couldn't imagine who it had been. I thought it over as I took a few bites, and then my heart pricked at an idea. "Was it Blaine? Did he hire a cleaning crew to come in?" Maybe he'd stopped by, wanting to try to get back together and had seen the state of things. Maybe he'd thought this would be a good way to get into my good graces. My happiness faded dramatically at the thought.

"No, dummy. Blaine had nothing to do with this," Sadie replied.

"Then who? Kelly was at work with me all day."

"It was Connor Hunt," Mom said. "He knocked on the door just after lunch and wouldn't take no for an answer. He cleaned up, brought dinner, and swore us to secrecy. I'll admit I was a bit shocked. Connor doesn't have the best reputation and doesn't seem the type to do something like this. I was really hesitant to let him in."

"C-Connor? Connor Hunt did all of this?" My bowl clattered to the coffee table, spilling speckles of broth on the shiny surface. All thoughts of Blaine washed out of my mind in a blast as honey brown eyes took his spot. A rush of heat crawled up my neck and into my cheeks. My heart seemed to slog to a stop.

"He made us shower too." Sadie nodded.

"Mm-hmm," I mumbled in a daze.

Sadie's eyes lit up. "He's yummy."

"Do not call him yummy," I said on autopilot as every emotion imaginable swirled in my chest. I knew how the house had probably looked when he'd arrived, and after what Blaine had said I felt vulnerable over it. "He came alone?"

"Yes. He was quiet, worked hard, and left just before you got here," Mom explained.

"But he has a mechanic shop to run, and it's a business day." My mind felt sluggish and my hands a little shaky.

Mom took another bite of her soup. "I didn't ask about that, but it was kind of him. Does this mean you and he are friends?"

"I, uh, guess so."

Mom's lips pursed. "I'm not sure I like the idea of you being friends with him. I haven't heard good things about him."

Irritation came on a sudden wave. "You're bad-mouthing the guy that just cleaned your house and brought you dinner?"

Mom's face reddened, which gratified me. "Well, when you put it that way . . . "

"How else is there to see it? He did a huge favor to this family today. You shouldn't believe everything you hear about people." I half expected a karma angel to fall out of the sky and tattoo a "hypocrite" sign on my forehead as the words left my mouth.

"There's always a little truth in every rumor, Liv. Be careful." Mom's voice was soft but firm.

"I barely know him," I defended.

"That's what you said last time we talked about him." Sadie's tone was warm and lightly teasing, which surprised me almost as much as everything else. "I'm starting to think you know him better than you're letting on because no guy I barely know would ever come clean my house for me."

I had no idea how to respond, so I grabbed my empty bowl and retreated to the sink. My hands were sweaty. I wasn't sure how to handle this news. Connor didn't know that I knew, but I did know. I had to thank him, even though he wouldn't be expecting my thanks. In fact, he'd probably hate having me thank him, which absurdly made me want to do it even more. Not tonight, though. Not while my emotions were high.

I rinsed and loaded my dishes in the dishwasher before heading up to my bedroom. With the house clean and the family fed, I could get back to the studying that I'd been needing to do. I had a feeling it would be harder than ever to keep my mind focused.

* * * * *

The next day Dad arrived home in the late afternoon and immediately called a family meeting. His dark hair had new streaks of gray, he was leaner than he'd been before, and worry lines dotted his forehead and created brackets around his mouth. The cheerful Dad of a few weeks back had disappeared.

Mom, Sadie, and I were silent as we sat down on the tired furniture. Dad didn't sit. He paced back and forth in front of the big window. His movements were jerky. Every few moments he'd turn to us and open his mouth as if he was going to say something, but then he'd start walking again.

The early spring sun coming through the window was lacking the same yellows as it would come summer, but it cast Dad's shadow across the carpeting, making it look as though two men were wearing a trail.

I glanced at Mom, but her hands were in her lap, grasping at each other, her face down. Her hair wasn't in its usual tidy style, and for a moment I was caught off guard at how beaten down she looked. Sadie, next to her, sharing her worry, was also looking anywhere but at Dad, although her expression said she was ready for battle.

In a flash of insight I realized that I was going to have to get the ball rolling. Dad had called the meeting but was flailing over where to begin. Mom, well, she was being herself—waiting as always for Dad to take the reins. Sadie was completely out of her depth here.

I'd worried and waited for my parents to handle things for too long. The fact that Dad had understood something needed to be discussed was a great thing, a good opening for us. But it appeared that all he was capable of doing was calling the meeting. So, I cleared my throat and got to adulting.

"I think it's time we stop pretending," I said. All eyes snapped to me. Mom and Sadie sat up straighter on the couch and Dad stopped pacing. "We're playing half-hearted family and it's killing all of us." I lanced each of them with a look until their eyes dropped into their laps. "Dad, you straight up abandoned us. We're all pretending it isn't true, but it's true."

His eyes leapt to mine. "Now, come on."

I held up a hand. "Until a few weeks ago we hadn't had any contact with you for six full months. That is, by definition, abandonment."

"Jane," he said, turning to my mom. "What have you told these girls?"

"Nothing. They know more than you give them credit for," Mom replied. At her defense of us, I felt more upset.

"She's right, Dad. She's said absolutely nothing to us, which is almost as bad as being abandoned has been." I glanced at Mom in time to see her mouth fall slack and hurt fill her eyes. Before I could say more, Sadie spoke.

"Are you making a decent wage or not, Daddy?" Her face was red. "Because things around here aren't good."

My heart broke at the look on my sister's young face. She'd been carrying more sadness than I'd realized. I'd only noticed her teenage petulance, and chosen not to dig deeper. I hadn't been the sister I should have been. I'd tried to take a few steps, but she needed more.

"I didn't come home and call this meeting for all my girls to gang up on me." Dad's voice sounded hard.

"Then why did you come home and call a meeting?" I dared to ask. "Because we've been living this way for a long time, and I kind of thought maybe you were ready to actually talk to us."

Dad's eyes scanned all of our faces, and his expression softened. "I've made some bad choices," he said at last. He couldn't seem to look at us, and he turned to look to the window. "I do make good money. I've been selfish. It's easy to forget about your responsibilities when you're away."

"Where's the money?" Mom asked in a soft voice that erased my frustration with her and caused tears to spring to my eyes.

A new insight—painful and raw—hit me as I watched her look to Dad. She was waiting because she loved him still. She didn't speak to us because she didn't want words out there that couldn't be retracted. She was harboring hope that I'd long left behind.

Dad turned back to Mom. "I've been living pretty high on the hog." His face was red with shame, and I was unapologetically glad for it.

"Oh, Paul." Mom's voice broke. "I've been slaving away here and been half a parent to these girls because of the worry and exhaustion. How could you do it?"

"There's one other thing," Dad said in a broken tone. Fear turned the rest of us silent with dread as we wondered what could be worse than what he'd already told us. "I don't work eight weeks on, one week off. I actually work four weeks on, one week off. I could be coming home double what I do now."

I saw Mom's throat working as she absorbed this information. Interestingly, her posture straightened and looked more like how she'd carried herself in the past. Sadie curled up into herself and tucked her knees against her eyes. For my part, I felt like I'd been punched in the gut. My eyes couldn't bear to look at him as he finally, and unequivocally, admitted that he was choosing to be away. Instead I absently noticed the light speckles of dust floating in the sunlight near him as my brain repeated over and over that he was withholding not only money but also himself. It felt like more of a betrayal than the rest of it put together.

"Why?" Mom voiced what we were all thinking.

"I guess that after twenty-six years of being a husband and father, feeling that weight of providing, it just felt good to have some freedom."

"Your freedom cost Mom and Liv theirs," Sadie said in an angry, muffled voice. My eyes focused on her, small and huddled in the corner of the couch. "Mom works really hard, and Liv has to take care of everything at home, and I hate watching it. I feel angry all the time." Her voice clogged, but she held up a hand before anyone else could talk. I wanted to beg her forgiveness for thinking she had no idea how hard my life had become, but I waited, watching her throat work. "I hate you, Dad, for what you did. I don't think you should be here anymore."

"Sadie . . . " Dad's voice was a hollow whisper. "You can't mean that."

"Are you asking us to forgive you? Asking to come home?" I interceded.

"I'm not sure," he replied.

"I think that's a lie. You've had years to think about it. I think you do know, but you don't want to come out and say it." I flung the words at him, not caring if they stung. I glanced at Mom, who was looking anywhere but at Dad, and felt something snap. "You and Mom need to start talking." I wanted to scream and shake them. "Talk, please. I'm begging you. Figure something out. We can't keep doing this." I waited until Mom and Dad were both looking at me before taking a deep breath and plunging further in. "I'm tired of being the slave to whatever is happening here. There aren't enough Band-Aids in the world, and I can't stop the bleeding all by myself."

"She's right," Mom said. I noticed that she was still avoiding looking at Dad, and it broke my heart.

"One more thing, Mom, you need to stop moping around here like you have no power to change anything."

Her mouth popped open into an O. "I don't mope. I'm just tired."

"You're mopey," Sadie inserted, which made me want to cheer.

Then I looked to Dad, and for once I saw him as nothing more than a man in his middle years. The sparkle was gone for me. "Dad, decide once and for all if you're in or out. If you're in, you have some serious kissing up to do. If you're out, then be out and free us from hanging on."

Now it was Dad's turn to have his mouth gape open. "Well, that wasn't pleasant to hear."

"None of this was," Mom replied.

"Leave it to Liv to bust things wide open," Sadie added, but she'd lifted her head and was smiling at me. It felt amazing to feel her support at last.

I stood. "I know that everything won't be fixed overnight, and that's okay. The important thing is that we're not going to hide behind the unsaid things anymore." When none of them did anything other than stare at me I said, "Is that clear? We're done hiding from the truth."

They all nodded at me. Satisfied, shaking, feeling like I was going to lose my breakfast, I hustled up the stairs to my room and fell against the closed door. I'd left nothing unsaid down there, regardless of cost. Now all I could do was wait.

Mom and Dad spent a full twenty-four hours sequestered away in their bedroom. Sadie and I heard fighting, crying, whispered conversations, and more fighting. We huddled together on my bed into the late hours that first night, relieved that they were actually communicating, and spending hours discussing what it all meant. If Dad decided to stay, was there any hope that he could undo the years of neglect? If he decided to go, would it be a relief or a new heartbreak? For the first time, however, we knew we had each other, and there was some comfort in that.

When they emerged from their room, both of their faces looked less worn than I'd seen them in a long time. They called us down to the living room, where Dad stood in front of that same window, only this time he was standing next to three suitcases. In that moment of understanding I hardly heard the words they were saying to Sadie and me. It didn't matter that Mom would be quitting her night job at the market and Dad would increase the amount he sent home monthly. All I saw was Dad making his final exit.

My hands shook as Dad made good on his promise to help me with schooling and handed me a wad of cash that would cover the next semester's tuition. He had to fold my hand around the envelope and tuck it close to my chest to keep me from dropping it.

Now I knew how it would feel to have him decide to go, and I grasped why Mom had put it off for so long. It wasn't as simple as either relief or sorrow. It was both. Agonized liberation left me numb, speechless, and empty. At least we knew; at least the guessing game was over. Now we could build from here.

Mom's face was deceptively calm, and I wondered if she was feeling the same way, only on a different level. Maybe it was good to finally know where she stood. Maybe hope had been cruel to her and reality was easier to bear.

The three of us Phelps girls stood at the window and watched Dad carry all of his suitcases out to his truck. Mom whispered that that was the last of his things, and Sadie's hand slipped into mine. We didn't say a word. What do you say when you're watching your world take its final fall?

* * * * *

I was still processing all that had happened when I entered the hardware store the next afternoon. I was cautiously optimistic that things were going to be okay, even if it hurt like the devil right now. It would take time, but we'd at least stepped onto a better path. Any path at all had to be better than floating aimlessly had been.

I made my way to the back counter where an order of paint supplies was waiting for me. I always chose to order them rather than drive through the pass to Springfield, even though I had to pay a small premium for shipping. It was a luxury I allowed myself. I couldn't wait to get home and have a chance to use the new set of brushes. I'd had a picture of two silver angels against a swirling black and white backdrop come into my head the other night, and I wanted to put it on canvas before it faded away.

I caught a flash of auburn hair and broad shoulders turning the corner of the aisle next to me as I finished paying and made my way to the front of the store to leave.

Connor. I still needed to thank him for the house cleaning, and now seemed as good a time as any.

I found him in the plumbing aisle and was grateful that he was alone. He didn't look up until I was standing right next to him. When he did, he seemed surprised to see me.

"I know, I know. You usually see me at the diner or your shop and never here, so it's made your head spin," I teased, knowing full well he'd seen me around town all our lives. He rolled his eyes, but they were smiling. "It's like when you run into your school teacher at the grocery store and get all tongue tied. I'll understand if you don't know what to say."

"I have no problem thinking of things to say to you."

"Oh, yeah? Like what?"

"Like, do you have a good showerhead at home that you'd recommend? Mine died this morning."

"I can see why you've dropped everything to hurry over here. You can't miss a shower. Have to stay fresh for the ladies." I leaned closer to the selection of showerheads and pretended to take it seriously. "Out of curiosity, how does a showerhead die? I mean, I've seen some pretty old heads in my lifetime. I thought you just kind of replaced them when you realized you deserve better."

"I went to adjust it and it cracked down the middle."

"Wow, bragging about your muscles, huh? Save it for your next date. I'm not interested." He chuckled, which made my toes curl inside my shoes. I hadn't realized before that I liked the sound of his low laugh.

"What brings you here?" he asked.

"Oh, mostly stalking you." I turned to face him.

"What?"

"You cleaned my house and fed my people."

He stood up straighter, sobering. "They were sworn to secrecy."

"You can't trust those two any more than you can trust your showerhead."

"Information that would have been helpful a few days ago."

"You were smart to avoid cleaning our toilets. You don't want to know what's been happening in those bathrooms this week." I pulled a face.

"I have a pretty good idea after hearing it in great detail from Sadie. In case you weren't aware, times have been hard on her."

I felt a smile tug at my lips. "You didn't have to do it."

"I know."

Then, the worst thing happened and my voice quivered when I went to say more. "I mean, it was kind of the best thing to happen to me in a while." I had to swallow hard over the truth. It had been a rough couple of months, especially the past two days, and his genuine service had been a bright spot.

"Don't get weird about it," he said lightly. "I helped out your family, no big deal."

"Is this something you do all the time? You just pop into random houses and go all Mary Poppins on the place?" The banter helped settle nerves that had been racing since I had walked up to him.

"We all have our secret side lives that no one knows about."

I laughed. His eyes took in my expression before growing warm. They seemed to pull me in, and before I was quite aware of what I was doing, I had crossed the distance between us, raised onto my toes, and wrapped my arms around his neck. His arms came around me with no hesitation, his warm hands resting on my back as he leaned forward a little so that it felt like he'd pulled me into a safe place and wrapped himself all around me.

I closed my eyes and pressed my cheek against him. "Why did you do it?" I asked.

"Unlike your mom and sister, I can keep a secret."

"It's a good quality," I whispered. "Thank you, Connor. I'll try to say fewer mean things about you to everyone." His shoulders shook under my hold, and I felt ridiculously happy that he found me amusing.

His arms tightened further, holding me close when we should have let go. His heartbeat against mine had a steadying rhythm. His breathing was slow and relaxed. He smelled of laundry detergent and the fast orange hand soap that mechanics use. My mind dazedly thought *I need this*, which was my cue that being held by him any longer would be a mistake, so I counted to three and released him. He was slow to let go.

I took a step back when I was flat on my feet and said, "See you around, Mary Poppins." I gave him a strange little wave before spinning around and hurrying out of the store.

I'd understood something during those moments, and it hadn't been a good realization. Turns out that for all my resolve, doubt, and cynicism, when it came down to it, I was just as bad as all the other ladies who were always chasing him. Worse even—because I had always known better. Yes, there was something fantastically potent about being held in Connor Hunt's arms, and I for one wasn't sticking around for more.

CHAPTER SEVENTEEN

April had officially arrived, and with it our little mountain town began to show its first efforts at digging out of winter. Down in Springfield the snow was melting and daffodils and crocuses were beginning to pop their colorful heads out of the frozen earth, but Oak Hills had a few more weeks before that would start happening.

Still, the weather had warmed enough that I'd packed away my winter coat and was enjoying running a few errands on foot before walking to the diner for my lunch shift. A light sweater and a colorful scarf around my neck kept me warm enough as I made my way downtown.

The last few days had been so relaxed and drama-free that I'd been waiting for something bad to happen. Mom had gone straight in and quit her night job with only two days' notice, so she was now home in the evenings and I had enjoyed the freedom of the home front being under control. She'd thrown herself into getting the house running again, and although I knew it was her way of working through her grief, I was grateful to have her back on the team.

My shoes scraped the curb as I stepped down from the sidewalk to cross from my neighborhood onto Main Street. A smile danced on my lips as I thought about something funny Sadie had said at dinner the night before. Something about finding out the hard way that she could do a handstand. The smile was still on my face when I arrived at the post office with bills to mail.

Some movement caught my eye from a few doors down and I turned to look, one hand on the door handle. Connor's profile was facing me, his auburn hair waving in the slight breeze. He was dressed casually in jeans and a long sleeve T-shirt, talking to a man whose back was to me. The other man was larger, rougher in dress, his stance threatening. Connor was holding his hands up in a peace-making gesture, palms out. However, I could tell by the way he was standing with his legs apart and shoulders tense that he was prepared for some sort of action.

It was interesting how now that I thought of Connor as a sort of friend, I seemed to see him around a lot more. It made me wonder how many people I saw regularly but didn't notice.

For a moment I pondered walking over to see what was going on, but it seemed like the kind of thing I didn't need to be involved in. Plus, when did Connor's conversations suddenly become something I was interested in? I was being crazy.

I entered the post office and mailed the bills. When I left I was somewhat surprised to see Connor and the man still in a heated debate of some sort. They had shifted a bit, and this time Connor noticed me. His face, which had been borderline angry, relaxed a bit and he tipped his head to me. The gesture made the other man look, and I recognized him as Levi Madsen. Ugh. Levi was trouble and always had been.

I gave Connor a small wave before crossing the street and going into the market, where I headed straight for the health and beauty section. I needed some deodorant and lotion. The fluorescent lighting flickered sadly, reminding me of how much I had been enjoying the sunlight outside. I didn't particularly love winter and always rejoiced when the weather warmed. I'd been feeling cooped up and desperate to be outside.

Deodorant and lotion purchased, I made my way back out of the store. My traitorous eyes looked back across the street to see Connor still chatting with Levi. I wondered if they were going to come to blows. The Connor I knew now seemed pretty even tempered, but I remembered his younger years when a few fights had needed to be broken up. Connor was big and strong, but Levi had straight up girth and a few inches on him. It would be an eye-catching contest, if I cared to stay and watch, which I did not. I needed to get to work, so when traffic cleared I hurried to cross the street.

Connor saw me again and waved, calling out, "Liv, I heard you were looking for me."

I almost laughed. What a sneak, using me as a reason to end a conversation. Levi turned to see who he was waving at. I didn't know if he was annoyed with the interruption, or with Connor, or just generally out of sorts, but I did know that he didn't appreciate being set aside.

I smiled winningly at them both, but didn't walk any closer. Connor's eyes narrowed on my face. I saw him shake his head very slightly, as though begging me not to hurry off. I wasn't planning to desert him, but I definitely couldn't resist watching him squirm a little. "Oh, hi, Connor. It looks like you're busy with Levi there," I called out, shrugging lightly. "No biggie. It can wait if you need to finish up what you're doing."

His smile turned as sweet as mine had been. "I feel bad that you've been waiting so long to catch me. I think Levi and I are done here."

I couldn't tell what Levi's reply was, but his grunt wasn't pleasant. This was kind of fun, a definite bright spot in my day.

"I'm on my way to work at the diner. Walk with me?" I asked in a carrying voice.

Connor said something else to Levi and then jogged to where I was standing a couple of yards away. "You're diabolical." His hand lightly brushed my lower back as he leaned close and spoke out of the side of his mouth. I staunchly ignored the shiver it caused. His tone was light, but it sounded forced and I could see something in his eyes that usually wasn't there. Levi had gotten under his skin.

I decided to keep things cheery. "Rule one is that we don't get involved in each other's personal lives. It looked like Levi had some personal things to say to you."

"I cleaned your house. Rule one doesn't exist anymore."

He was probably right about that. "Fine," I huffed. "You can pretend to talk to me while I walk to work, but then we're even."

"I *am* talking to you while you walk to work, so I think he'll fall for it," he responded, and I was strangely relieved to hear the amusement return in his voice.

"How's your showerhead?"

"Big."

"That's a strange answer."

"It's a strange question. Do you often ask people about their showers?"

My mouth gaped open at him. "You're a serious mental case. Like you can't remember that the last time we talked it was about showerheads?"

"All I remember about the last time we talked is that you hugged me."

We reached the diner and he stepped ahead to open the door for me. Our eyes caught and my hands got warm and tingly as I came to a stop near him, just outside the building.

"What, exactly, is the point of reminding me about that serious lapse in judgment?"

He leaned in until I could feel his breath tickle my ear. "It was a real nice hug, Livy."

My throat felt thick, and I knew he could hear the way my voice changed as I said, "My name is Liv." I leaned away and hurried through the door. "Find a seat, preferably in the section where I'm not working." I dodged behind the bar.

"Which section would that be?"

"Pick one, and I won't work there," I growled, hating how wonderful it had felt to have his cheek brush against my curls and his fingers tickle my spine.

I made my way straight back to the employee lounge to leave my things, wash up, and get my apron on. When I came back out Kelly brushed past me on her way to get an order.

"Can you believe this weather?" she said. "Scott says it's almost time to start planting a garden."

I frowned, unsure I'd heard her right. A garden? That sounded awfully domestic. "You must really love this guy if you're getting excited about gardening."

"It has been the best month of my life."

It was true that Kelly had a glow around her. While she remained true to her bubbly personality, there was a new peaceful confidence about her. Her eyes were lighter, her steps steadier, and the underlying desperation that had driven so much of what she did was gone. I was thrilled for her and told her so when I came to the bar to scan the dining room as part of my mission to avoid

Connor. Thankfully he was in a corner booth that I could easily steer clear of.

"Your eyes just got all beady. What's up?" Kelly leaned up against me and propped her head next to mine to try to see what I was looking at.

"I ran into Connor on the way in, and he's being a giant irritant. Do you mind waiting on him?" I replied in a quiet voice.

She straightened. "Sure, no problem."

"Thanks."

"Although, I'm having a hard time picturing Connor being irritating." She jokingly rubbed her chin as though thinking deeply over it.

"You were singing a different tune when he showed up at that basketball game the other day." I grabbed menus to take to some customers down the bar and threw her a look over my shoulder.

"True. What did he do?" she asked when I returned with two empty cups needing a refill.

The sound of ice clinking into glass kept me from answering right away, but I still pulled a face and motioned for her to come closer. "He was talking to Levi Madsen at the post office and used me to get away. Then he said inappropriate things to me on the way back. Typical."

Her voice was a whisper as she replied, "Levi? He's been after Connor about something for a while now."

"Connor probably dated his sister and broke her heart."

Kelly shook her head. "Really, Levi's sister? Isn't she in her forties?"

"I thought you said he dates anyone who's interested?" I turned away to finish refilling, hoping to hide the look on my face, because I knew I was being mean and lying all over the place. I didn't actually believe those things about Connor anymore. But still . . .

"I said he doesn't go after girls who aren't interested. He's looking for more than just a body sucking air," Kelly stated. "And what do you mean he said inappropriate things?"

"Use your imagination, Kelly."

"Do you really want me to use my imagination? Because I could probably come up with something much worse than he actually said." Kelly's eyes took on a faraway look.

I slapped her arm playfully as I walked away with the drinks. While I was in the dining area I took orders from two booths at the front and worked my way back to the kitchen to pick up some food that was ready. When I glanced toward the back booths, I saw Kelly taking Connor's order and chatting amiably with him. I was happy to let her have at it.

She made her way to me and pulled me off to the side with dancing eyes. "He says you're the inappropriate one. You threw yourself into his arms at the hardware store last week?"

"What!" I craned my neck around the corner to see Connor grinning at me. I pulled my head back and glared at Kelly. "I can't believe he'd say that."

"Well, you were calling him a heartbreaker. His honor was on the line."

"You told him that?"

"He's my friend."

"So am I, Kelly. Good nuggets. There'll be no peace for me now." I threw my hands in the air and walked back to my waiting customers.

It was a solid hour before I had a chance to talk with Kelly again. Thankfully Connor was long gone by then. I'd managed to avoid any more interactions, or eye contact, with him and had tried not to notice when he left.

We were clearing booths during a lull, and Kelly came to help me with mine. "So, care to explain what's happening between you and my friend Connor?" she asked.

"Nothing is going on. He's bothersome is all."

"You know, I've been thinking . . . "

"Nope."

"Oh, yes. I've been wondering for a while if maybe there's a reason Connor isn't dating right now." I averted my gaze and made a non-committal noise. "I think that reason might be you."

I couldn't stop the flush that rose as I remembered how much I'd loved being held close to him and had wanted to stay in his embrace. I cleared my throat. "Please, Kelly. You're way off."

"Am I?"

I looked her in the eye. "Yes. I'm the last person he'd be interested in."

"Plus, you hate him and would never be interested back." She raised an eyebrow.

"I don't hate him."

"You've repeatedly called him sketchy."

"In high school," I defended, even though we both knew it was a lie.

"As recently as last week."

I hoisted the slop bucket onto my hip and said, "Okay, busted. I gave him a chance because you said I had to, and I don't think he's as terrible as I used to think he was. That doesn't mean a dang thing. Connor makes a decent friend at best, and nothing more. I'm trying to put my family back together and graduate from college. I'm not interested in more distractions. Until I can find someone who can just jump into my life and asks no questions, it's not happening."

Kelly's eyes were dancing gleefully as I finished my speech. "Good luck with that. Most guys have a few questions before they jump."

I grinned humorlessly. "Alone it is."

"Don't bet on it, Liv. There's fresh meat coming in here every day." She wiggled in a little happy dance and followed me, carrying her full tray back to the kitchen. "You'll catch someone's eye before too long."

"Please, fairy godmother, I don't want much. Just a man who'll agree with all my decisions, think I'm charming, never talk to me in the mornings, and feed me chocolate cake every day."

"Your list is small and reasonable."

"I think so."

"I think I know a guy . . . " Kelly began to tease but stopped at the look on my face. "Fine, but when you're ready, just yell bibbity, bobbity, boo."

* * * * *

One week after my dad drove away found me almost as confused as ever. My thoughts on the finality of it all were a roller coaster. In some ways it had been a really great week as my mom, sister, and I worked to finding new footings. Things were cleaner, meals were prepared, and Sadie scowled less and less. Mom was working hard around the house and speaking to us more. Now that we had a definite understanding to go on, we were making the best of it.

And yet, I was cautiously waiting to see how things played out long term before I celebrated. I wondered how much of Mom's cheeriness was a front, her busyness a way to physically work through her heartache. I wasn't sure if I could trust Dad to hold up his end of the bargain as far as supporting us more financially, or that Mom would be strong enough to keep improving if he didn't. I was afraid that when legal proceedings started, Mom wouldn't have the guts to ask for what she was owed. Through it all, the days kept marching relentlessly forward.

For my part, when I wasn't at work, I loved the freedom to study hard, focusing in a way I hadn't done for a while. I'd dived back into my schoolwork without the usual guilt and was happy at how classes were coming along. I allowed myself to think that I might actually pass finals the next month if things continued down this path.

Best of all, I painted. The canvas became my therapy, soaking up my emotions and changing them into vibrant art as I worked through the aches and pains, doubts and fears. The first couple of paintings were pretty dark, but for the first time in a while there was hope blooming and I knew they would gradually become lighter and lighter.

I thought about all of this as I headed to the mechanic shop to do my weekly cleaning. It was dark and closed up tight when I arrived around 10:00 PM. I locked the door behind me and gathered up the cleaning supplies. I was hit by a sudden longing for something to tear me away from my own thoughts as I walked to the bathroom, so I stopped at the reception desk and turned on some music with the little radio they had sitting there. I didn't care what station it was. I just wanted something to focus on other than the questions that had been raging inside of me. The future would have to wait.

I found a jazz station and hummed along to the music while I scrubbed the toilet. I swayed my hips and danced along as I cleaned the mirror and sink. By the time I got to the lobby, the vacuum had become my dance partner. I couldn't really hear the music over the motor, but it didn't matter. I hummed a tune anyway as I circled the big beast around the lobby.

I put the vacuum away with a smile on my face and returned to the lobby to wash windows. The tune was upbeat and light, and my hands kept time as I wiped back and forth. I let my head bop along as I finished the last window.

When I turned around to go back to the office, the sight of a man standing outside the glass front door had me screaming bloody murder.

I knew it was a man based on the build and the facial hair, but his eyes were shadowed by a hat and I didn't recognize him.

"We're closed," I yelled. The spray grip of the window washing fluid dug into my palm.

"Open up," he called back. His voice was loud and deep.

"Go away or I'll call the cops," I returned, pointing my window washing rag in his direction.

"Take it easy. I just need to talk to Connor." He held up his hands, palms out, in a show of peace.

I didn't care about his hands; he wasn't getting in here. I shook my head. "It's really late. He isn't here."

"Fine, let me in and I'll call him." He knocked on the door and rattled the handle.

"No way." With trembling hands I reached into my back pocket and held up my phone. "I'm calling the cops if you aren't gone in five seconds."

His mouth opened into a growl, but he tugged off the hat so I could see his face. It was Levi Madsen, and he looked mad. All joking aside, I didn't honestly think Connor had wronged this man, and I doubted he'd actually planned to meet him here at this time of night. I had no idea what Levi wanted, but it wasn't a good news delivery. He banged on the door one more time, making me squeak.

"Get out of here, Levi," I yelled.

"Olivia, you've known me forever. Just open the door so I can call Connor."

"Call him from somewhere else." I inched closer to the office and waved the phone again. "I'm not bluffing."

He said something unintelligible, but he turned and stalked away to his car. I waited until he'd peeled out of the parking lot before I took myself into the office, where I closed the door and locked it before flopping down on the floor and crawling under the desk, out of sight. Only then did I pick up my phone. It took me several tries to make my shaking fingers press the correct buttons, but thankfully only two rings before he answered.

"Levi Madsen just came down here banging on the door and yelling. He scared me to death," I said before Connor had a chance to say hello. Fear made me sound angry, which I kind of was.

"Are you okay?" he asked. His voice sounded a little rough as though I'd woken him up, but his tone was concerned.

"I'll send you the mental therapy bill, but physically I'm fine."

"Sounds fair. What happened?"

I gave him a run down, after which I said, "He was mad, Connor. I don't know what happened between you, but you need to talk to him. I was here alone and I didn't like it."

"What about playing dead?" he kidded.

"It's not going to work. Turns out I'm more of a freeze-in-place-and-yell kind of girl."

"That doesn't sound like a good plan."

"Yeah, well, my only weapons were a rag and a bottle of window cleaner."

"Is he still hanging around?"

"No. He left. I think. I'm hiding under the desk, so I don't actually know."

"I'll be there in a minute." His voice became gentle, causing me to feel as if I would melt.

I tried to keep my voice firm. "No, really, I'm okay, but you'd better tell him not to come back and scare me again. I'll call the cops next time."

"I'll talk to him. Don't worry about it."

"Thanks."

"Sure. I'm sorry this happened."

"Yeah."

"You know, if you ever need a weapon, there are a million choices out in the shop."

"You're assuming I'd be able to run. My feet were frozen in place. He looked like a crazy person with his hat pulled down, banging on the door. Don't you have a wrench or something that we could keep in the desk, you know, close by?"

He chuckled, and the rest of the fear seemed to dissipate as a rush of goosebumps covered my skin. "Yeah. I'll get you a wrench."

"Get me some apology chocolate while you're at it."

"Done."

"One more thing before I sign off. Do you have a full understanding of the trauma I experienced tonight?"

"I do."

"Do you validate my feelings?"

He laughed and I could see his face in my mind's eye. Only a few short months ago it had been the face of a highly judged stranger. Now it was something different. I knew the colors of his hair and eyes, the way his mouth crooked up on one side when he was amused, the set of his shoulders when he was annoyed. It caused dual rushes of ice and heat to course through me. Connor both terrified and intrigued me.

"I do," he said.

"That's all I need then."

"Good night, Liv."

I had to swallow before I could reply. This conversation had started to feel close and cozy somehow. I found it all highly confusing. "Good night."

By the time I talked myself out of the office and into my car it was almost eleven. I was grateful for the warming temperatures as I hustled to my car. Before getting in I checked the back seats and even popped open the trunk. I didn't necessarily think Levi was a lunatic serial killer, but it was better to be safe than sorry.

When I arrived home, I was surprised to find Mom and Sadie sitting close on the couch and laughing at a show they were watching. The scene was just so darn relaxed and cheery it made my throat feel thick. A quick glance around showed that the living room was tidy. I felt a little off kilter.

Mom turned at the sound of the door closing behind me. "Hi, honey." She smiled. "Come sit down. I know it's late, but we're watching a movie."

Sadie's head popped around Mom. "I ate all the popcorn."

I grinned and set my purse on the stairs before joining them on the couch. "What are we watching?"

"*Clueless*," Mom replied. "It's a classic and Sadie said she'd never seen it."

"You've really never seen this?" I asked my sister. Her cheeks were full of munchies, so she shook her head and shrugged. "How does that happen?"

"I dunno," she mumbled.

"If we're doing movie catch up, I have a whole list." I snuggled in close to Mom like I'd done when I was younger. She patted me lightly on the leg.

"I'm not sure I trust your movie list," Sadie replied.

"You'll be eating those words faster than you ate that popcorn," I retorted.

Sadie snorted, Mom laughed, and my mind took a little picture as I focused on the screen.

CHAPTER EIGHTEEN

The text from Connor came two days later. *I have chocolate for you at the shop.* I texted back that I'd be off work at five and head straight over. When the time came, I happily walked out to my car and flung my purse into the back seat. For chocolate I was more than willing to pop by. I felt settled and light in a way I hadn't for a while. I was still feeling a little buzz from the homey movie night with Mom and Sadie. It had been the most pleasant, normal, boring evening at home that we'd had in a long time. I hoped we could do it again soon.

When I pulled up to Mainstreet Mechanic I could see Connor and a large man talking in the lobby. I grabbed my purse from the backseat and started in, but as I got close enough to pull open the glass door the man turned his head slightly and I realized it was Levi. He was back, and he seemed to still be angry. I was unsure about going in. Levi had scared me enough the night I was cleaning, and I didn't want to be in the same room with him. He was already large and loud when he wasn't angry.

I saw something flash just as I made my decision to wait in the car. Levi was holding a shiny silver object and waving it at Connor. A gun. Oh my gosh, Levi was pointing a gun at Connor. I wasn't sure what to do as my heart felt like it plummeted to my toes. I couldn't believe it. Was he robbing Connor? Was he mad about a car repair? What was going on?

I reached into my purse to grab my phone and call the police, but it was nowhere to be found. It had probably fallen out on the floor of my car when I'd chucked my purse into the back. I was about to run to my car and get it, but Levi took a step closer to Connor and icy alarm skittered up my back. There wasn't time to find my phone. I had to help Connor now. But how? I couldn't simply barge in if a weapon was being brandished around. What if I startled him and the gun went off accidentally?

I looked around and noticed that one of the bay doors was open. Thanks to slightly warmer temps, Connor could work with the doors open more often. Whatever the reason, I was grateful. Connor had said I could find a weapon of some sort in the shop, and that was my intention. I figured if I entered the lobby waving a large—I don't know—car part or something, I could distract Levi long enough for Connor to get away or make a move, or do whatever he needed to do. Now was not the time to freeze up.

"You are strong, you are brave, you can do this," I said to myself as I ducked down low in the doorway and searched the area for something I could use. "You laugh in the face of fear. You mock damsels in distress," I continued to whisper. "You will not run away. You will not hide." I was going to be there for a new friend who had cleaned my house and cooked my family food, and who had chocolate waiting for me inside.

I stumbled a bit over numb feet as I realized that I'd let my guard down enough to actually care about Connor as more than just a citizen in my community getting held up by a big jerk. With that caring came trembling. Whatever happened here today mattered to me.

My mind felt hazy as the fear and adrenaline coursed through my body. I entered the shop crouching down to avoid being seen through the windows that provided a view of the lobby. My gaze shot erratically from side to side until I spotted a tire iron hanging on the back wall. I glanced through the windows and was grateful to see that although Connor had to have noticed my car pulling into the parking lot, the men were still engaged in a heated discussion and he didn't seem to be looking for me. He probably wondered what I was up to. Would he be glad or angry when he found out? There was no time to debate the pros and cons. I'd have to deal with whatever happened.

I took the tire iron off its hook and tested its weight in my hands. It wasn't overly heavy, but still brawny and serious enough looking to get Levi's attention. With any luck the surprise of me entering the lobby with it would cause him to drop the gun to the floor. Then

Connor could kick it out of the way and hold Levi down while I called the police. I'd watched enough episodes of cop shows to have an idea of how it would go down. I gripped the iron tightly and took a deep breath. It was time to save a life.

Still bent down, I worked my way to the lobby door. I peeked up through the window. Yep, Levi was still flashing something silver and aiming it at Connor. I could hear their voices, loud and heated, but I was too focused on timing to listen to the words. I'd count myself down from five. No, from ten. When I got to one I was going to burst through the door, wave the tire iron, and yell for Levi to drop the gun. Then I'd run to the office and call 911 while Connor took it from there.

I counted with frozen lips and ice-cold hands until I reached one. Just as I did, Levi lifted his arm and I saw his face contort. It was now or never. I shoved the door open, raised the tire iron above my head, and started to yell at Levi in the loudest voice I could.

"Drop it, Levi!" I screamed as I rushed toward him.

Levi surprised me with his speed. Rather than ducking or dropping anything, he spun around and grabbed for the tire iron in my raised hand. I was holding on tightly enough that it yanked me off my feet for a second and pulled my body toward his much larger one. He was yelling at me, Connor was yelling, and I heard something clatter to the ground as Levi used his other arm to push me away from him. The tire iron was ripped out of my hand, and the shove at my chest caused me to fall back down to the floor. My feet hit and I stumbled backward, slamming hard into a wall of muscle. That impact hurtled me forward and I would have fallen to my knees, but Connor grabbed me by the waist.

He lifted me right back off my feet and swung me to the side as he moved in front of me in one fluid motion, causing me to stumble yet again as I found myself facing his back. I caught my balance using a nearby wall and stood still. Connor's shoulders were bunched and his breathing hard as he yelled at Levi, who yelled back, now waving my tire iron, until I could hardly distinguish who was yelling what.

I tried to step back into the fray and get them apart, but Connor stopped me with an outstretched arm as I came to stand next to him. "Stay out of this." His voice was the voice of a stranger.

Levi stepped toward me and Connor tensed further. The arm that had prevented me from moving forward now became a steel band blocking Levi's access to me.

"Your crazy cleaning lady just tried to kill me," Levi bellowed.

"He has a gun," I yelled back. "Call the police."

Both men turned to me, my statement causing a pause in the action.

"What is she talking about?" Levi boomed.

Connor's eyes were a mix of confusion and thunderous rage. "There's no gun."

I shook my head and pointed to Levi. "But . . . but he had a gun," I argued. "I saw him wave it at you."

"What did she say?" Levi wasn't yelling anymore, but he was still irate. "Never mind, save it for the cops." Levi threw the tire iron down and reached for his phone.

Connor dropped his arm, but stayed alert as he pierced me with hot, angry eyes. "What were you thinking?" he said in a furious tone I'd never heard from him before.

"I was saving your life," I stated.

"Levi wasn't trying to kill me. It wasn't a gun in his hand."

"How was I supposed to know that?" I asked.

His lips pursed and his face became even more cross, if that was possible. "You were supposed to walk in here like any normal person would and see for yourself."

"Well, would you walk into a place when it looked like a guy was waving a gun around, just to see if your eyes were lying to you? What if he did have a gun and I'd done that? Then we'd both be hostages right now," I defended.

Levi finished his phone call and reached toward me to point in my face. "You'll regret this."

Connor turned back to Levi and pushed his arm away. "Stay away from her," he growled.

I shut my eyes as more angry words flew. The fear of Connor being shot was replaced by the fear of them using their fists to kill each other while I helplessly watched. When I heard a siren pull into the parking lot I almost sank to the floor with relief.

"I can't believe you actually called the police." Connor's voice rose a notch.

"Of course I did. That little devil woman assaulted me," Levi announced.

"I never touched you," I cried as two officers streamed into the lobby and quickly took in the scene.

I had shrunk back out of arms' reach of both men, and stood with my hands clasped together while the two large and irate men were standing nearby. One of the officers yelled at them to back away from each other while the second came to me.

"Ma'am, are you okay?" he asked.

Levi went off like a rocket. "You're asking her? She's the one who did the assaulting. She came in here with this tire iron and tried to take my head off," he boomed. I looked up in time to see him pick it off the floor and wave it above his head.

"Sir, drop the weapon," the officer near him ordered briskly.

"This is the weapon that *she* tried to use on me," Levi insisted, but he dropped it to the floor.

"Was anyone injured?" the officer near me asked.

"She was pushed." Connor's voice was like ice.

The officer glanced at him and then turned back to me. "Who pushed you?"

"Um, it was more of a momentum thing, you know, in the heat of the moment." It was hard work shoving the words out over the rock in my throat. My hands trembled so hard that I tucked them into my jean pockets. The adrenaline let down was fierce.

Levi jumped in, his voice rising again. "She attacked me unarmed and unprovoked."

"I thought he had a gun," I returned, but for the first time it came out sounding unsure.

One of the officers—McGowen, according to his badge—looked to Connor. "Was there a gun involved?" Connor shook his head and McGowen looked back to me.

I sighed deeply. "I think we'd better start at the top. This is going to be a really great story for you to tell around the station."

"I'm pressing charges against her," Levi declared before I could say anything else.

I speared him with a glare. "You were yelling at Connor and waving something silver around. I thought it was a gun."

"It wasn't a gun." Connor entered the discussion. His voice hadn't relaxed at all, and his eyes were strained. "It was a part he bought for his truck that wasn't working."

"He was yelling at you," I stated. "And it wasn't the first time."

"What do you mean?" Officer McGowan asked.

"A week or so ago I saw Levi yelling at Connor downtown. Then the other night while I was cleaning here, he came and banged the door down, asking to see Connor. I sent him away. Now today he's in here waving something around and yelling again. I had every reason to believe Connor was in danger."

"So instead of calling for police help, or making sure her eyes aren't playing tricks on her, she picks up this"—Levi kicked the tire iron—"and decides to go vigilante."

"I couldn't let you hurt him." My voice rose, and my hands balled into fists in my pockets.

"It was a car part. He sold me a bad part," Levi retaliated. "He's a bum mechanic and a dirty cheat."

"I didn't sell you that part. I recommended a part and then you went home and ordered the wrong one online," Connor replied firmly.

"How is that Connor's fault?" I said.

Connor's amber eyes were as hard as flint when he glared at me. "You've done enough, Liv. Stay out of it."

"You're angry with me?" I lashed out, hurt and embarrassed. "For caring enough to try to save your life?"

"For the last time, his life wasn't in danger. Mine was, from this crazy . . . " Levi took a step back toward me and the police officers immediately got in his way.

"I'm not crazy. You're the one who came by late at night banging on the door and scaring me," I said. "You planted the idea in my head that you were going to do some harm to someone."

"You attacked me, and I'm pressing charges," Levi said.

"Go ahead, then. Press charges. They'll never hold up considering I never laid a finger on you." I stood firm, doing my best to ignore the flash of distress I felt over the situation.

"Liv, you have got to stop talking," Connor said in exasperation.

"This is the thanks I get . . . "

"Enough." His voice cracked like a whip through the confusion and we all froze. "Go home. I don't need you here," he said to me.

"She has to be here if I'm pressing charges. They'll take her down to the station," Levi argued.

"Miss Phelps, let's take you outside," McGowan said. "We'll get this sorted out in no time."

I started to shake my head, but Connor caught my eye. "Go."

I swallowed hard on the painful lump that rose in my throat. I'd royally screwed up, and rather than laughing about it with me, Connor wanted me out of his sight. I nodded and turned to the officer.

"I believe I dropped my purse in the shop somewhere. Can we go out that way?" I asked in a small, uncertain voice that I barely recognized as my own.

"You head on out, ma'am. I'll grab it and meet you by the cruiser."

I nodded and took a few stiff steps before my legs remembered how to walk. I didn't look back even once as I let myself outside. To think, just a few months ago I'd still thought the worst of Connor Hunt, and now I couldn't bear to have him thinking badly of me.

Officer McGowan and I stood next to his cruiser while he took his official statement from me. I again told him everything that had happened, starting from Levi and Connor talking outside the post office, to showing up late the other night, and the altercation just a few moments before. It was an exercise in extreme humiliation. My mind had created a scenario that never existed.

"Don't worry too much about it for now, Miss Phelps," he said when we were done.

"Easy for you to say. I just ticked off Connor, insulted Levi, embarrassed myself in front of law enforcement, and became town gossip in the process."

He smiled. "I'm sure Officer Campbell is doing his best to calm down the situation inside. For now, you're free to go home. If Mr. Madsen decides to press charges, we'll come get you there."

"I'd rather just be arrested here. My mom and sister don't need to see me taken away in handcuffs."

He nodded. "Fair enough. Wait here and I'll confer with the others."

I stood in the spring air that was still a little too chilly to be hanging out in and turned to face away from the shop to hide tears that finally escaped. How many times had I told myself to stay away, to not get involved, to keep my head down and focus on my own crazy life? This was the thanks I got for allowing myself to care.

It took another half hour and some smooth talking from Connor and the police officers, but Levi agreed not to press charges with the stipulation that I was to remain as far away from him as possible at all times from here on out. I wanted to tell the officers that the only person who'd actually been hurt was me, but I knew it was pointless.

I caught Connor's eye as he watched Officer McGowan deliver the verdict to me outside. He made no move to come out, and his stance told me he wouldn't appreciate me coming in. I drove home feeling beyond dejected.

* * * * *

Within a short twenty-four hours the whole town had heard about the mix-up at Mainstreet Mechanic, and everyone had an opinion. Some thought I was a hero for jumping right in, some thought I was an idiot for not assessing the situation better, and a couple thought I should be locked away. The worst were the handful of women I overheard saying I was just another one of Connor's crazy girls. I'd almost forgotten about his reputation at that point, but their gossip brought it all back. I'd been a fool ten times over. It had all started with accepting his offer to clean the shop, which had led to letting my guard down and starting to think of him as a friend. Then I'd hugged him and . . . sigh. That had been a fatal error.

The next day at the diner I begged Kelly to deliver a message to Connor for me. I wasn't going to keep cleaning the shop, and I'd get him the rest of the money I owed, which was only about $250 at this point.

Kelly was firm. "No way am I getting in the middle of this spat of yours," she stated. "You messed up, Liv, and you have to fix it."

"I know I messed up," I replied. For at least the hundredth time I felt a pinch in my chest. "But he wants no contact. He hasn't called, or texted, or popped by the diner in two days," I whined. "We aren't even in a spat. We're past that. You can't be in a spat with someone who has ghosted you."

"Part of ghosting suggests you're in a spat."

"No, ghosting is disappearing with no explanation."

"Then you haven't been ghosted, Liv. You know exactly why he's avoiding you." Kelly threw me a look as she gathered menus. Her usually laughter-filled eyes were serious and sad. It made me feel even worse.

"Well, what would you have me do? Send him a letter?" I paused in wiping down the booth that I'd just cleared, and nodded. "I could do that. A letter."

"No. Don't be a coward." Kelly shook her head. "You need to go down to the shop and talk to him face to face. Maybe he's not angry. Maybe he's worried that you're upset with him and he's waiting for you to make the first move."

"Nice try," I mumbled. I thought it over while we finished busing a table. "But do I really need to reach out to him?" I asked as I followed her back to the kitchen with my bucket of dirty plates. "I mean, we aren't really friends. It was more of a business thing."

"That's a lie, and I'm calling you on it. I understand you feeling confused and wanting to lick your wounds, but Connor has been good to you."

The bell dinged over the door, saving me from having to admit that Connor had become my friend. It was easier to push him back into his box.

Kelly was still on her high horse fifteen minutes later at the drink station. "If it really is just a business relationship, then you need to treat it as one. He's technically your employer. You owe him either money or labor. Go work it out." She walked through the swinging kitchen door and I thought she was done, but nope, she came back through only a moment later with her mouth already open. "And while you're at it, he deserves an apology."

"For what? For trying to save him from a mad man?"

Kelly's eyes closed briefly, and she took a deep breath before opening them again. "Look, I appreciate that you aren't a weak little petunia who needs to be rescued. For the record, if I ever find myself being threatened by someone, I'm glad to know I can count on you to be my backup. Still, the fact is that there was no weapon other than Levi's big mouth. You made a mistake. We've talked about it so much the past two days that I know every little detail, and I don't remember hearing you tell him you were sorry."

"Exactly what am I sorry about?"

Kelly made a face at me and walked away with her drinks, leaving me to ponder what she'd said. Did I owe him an apology? If so, what for? Had my actions hurt him somehow? Had I been so busy feeling hurt that I'd overlooked any fallout on his side?

A little while later, Kelly and I met at the dishwasher to start stacking dishes. The steam coming from the hot water I was using to rinse the dishes made my curls tight and heavy, which meant they were in my eyes. The bleachy smell of the sanitizing soap stung my nose.

I cleared my throat. "Kell, don't yell at me again, but I'm trying to understand what I did to hurt Connor."

"You barged into his shop, messed with his business, got the cops called down, and generally acted crazy." Wow. She answered pretty quickly, which meant she'd been thinking about it. Either that or she'd spoken to Connor.

"Fine. Although I was right about him too."

Kelly stacked her dirty dishes near the massive washer and turned to me with hands on hips. "How do you figure?"

I set down my own dishes and stood to face her. "I got close and I got burned."

"By your own fire."

I opened my mouth to retort, but there was nothing more to say. Kelly thought of Connor as a close friend these days. I understood the draw of that friendship. For the rest of the shift my mind darted over the scene at the mechanic shop and the words Kelly had said today until I started to understand the part I'd played in mine and Connor's falling out. Who wanted to be friends with a reckless she-wolf?

"Fine. I'll go talk to him," I said quietly when we had a breather toward the end of our shift.

"Good. A word of advice, though?" She tilted her head. I nodded once. "Don't go in there and get defensive, like he has something to prove to you, or that he has to earn your trust back or whatever it is you think. He'll forgive you if you're genuine about it."

"I'm not sure I want to be back on good terms. Things were fine when I steered clear of him. The hurt came from getting close."

"Contention will never win or give you closure."

Kelly was right. I hated that she was right. I hated how much it was going to stink to go down to the shop and settle things with Connor. And that was my plan, to settle things.

After work I went home and dug out the $250 from the cash my father had given me for schooling. I'd have to find another way to pay myself back. I'd apologize to Connor, give him the money, and we could part on friendly terms, going back to how we'd always been—nothing more than two people living in the same town.

My hands were shaking as I entered the lobby of Mainstreet Mechanic. I was surprised to see Steve, the founder and former owner of the shop, lounging at the reception desk. He greeted me cheerfully.

"Olivia Phelps. How nice to see you." He smiled. "I hear you're keeping things nice and clean around here. How can I help you today?"

"I was looking for Connor."

"Shoot. He's off this afternoon on a few personal errands. I'm watching the shop, keeping an eye on his crew. Is it something I can help you with?"

Relief flooded my body until my arms felt like rubber bands. I could handle this all without the need to have a face-to-face conversation. Cowardly? Yes. Didn't mean I wasn't grateful for the out. Steve would tell Connor I had come to the shop, which would give me bonus points. I'd not planned on talking to anyone but Connor himself, but in so many ways this was better. For a tiny blip of a second, I wondered what had taken Connor out of the shop for an afternoon. Maybe he was dating out of town now. The thought made my breath hitch until I pushed it away and focused on my good fortune.

"I need to settle my account." I opened my purse and pulled out the bills. "I believe this is what's left."

Steve sat up straight and tapped a few keys on the computer. "Yeah, looks like $250 is it. Does this mean Connor's going to need to start paying you for cleaning?"

"Oh, uh, no, actually this will be my resignation too." I stumbled over the words.

"Is this because of the kerfluffle that happened here the other day?" he asked. He reached out for the money and I handed it to him.

"I don't think I'd call it a kerfluffle." I bit my lip and wrinkled up my nose. "More like a complete disaster."

Steve laughed. "I'm sorry I missed it. Nothing that exciting ever happened to me."

"Well, it was bad."

"Nah. Every guy dreams of being rescued by a beautiful lady."

A small, unexpected bubble of amusement rose, causing me to grin. "I don't think Connor agrees."

"Does he know you're quitting?"

I wished I couldn't feel a blush coming on, nor the prick of guilt that came with it. "No, but trust me when I say he wants nothing to do with me after everything that's happened."

"It doesn't feel right that Connor doesn't know. This was his payment arrangement, after all. Let me just try to call him real quick." Steve picked up the reception phone and started to dial from memory.

My hands clasped together in panic as I waited, but Connor never picked up. It was all I could do to keep from clapping and instead paste on a disappointed face.

"Why don't I leave him a note in the office?" I suggested.

"I still think you should talk to him in person." Steve looked thoughtful.

"I'll leave the note and he can call me if there's anything more to discuss. How's that?" I gave him my best full-sized smile. He relented with a shake of his head. "Thanks, Mr. Anders. I know where everything is. I'll be right back."

Giddy feet carried me into the office, where I grabbed paper and pen and sat down to compose a note. Only, I wasn't sure what to say. Kelly had suggested I apologize, so maybe I'd start with that.

> *Connor,*
>
> *Sorry that I tried to rescue you and you were mad about it.*

Nope. Scratch that. It was about as passive aggressive as it could be. I chewed on the top of the pen and tore off that sheet, crumpling it up and shoving it in my purse so that he wouldn't discover it in his garbage can.

Step one: I needed to decide if I was actually sorry and what I'd be sorry for. Outside of the office I could hear the clanking sounds of automotive work. This was Connor's livelihood. Working hard to support yourself was something I could understand. If there was anything

I felt sorry for, it would be if I had caused problems with his business. It seemed like a good place to start.

Connor,

I never meant to do something that would hurt your shop in any way, and I hope that your business is okay.

Yeah, that was a better start. Next I just needed to get him the basic information so that we could both move on.

I've talked to Steve and paid off my account. Please consider this my resignation for the cleaning job. Thanks for your help with the payment plan.

Liv Phelps

I thought signing my last name added a little flourish to the statement. Like telling him without actually saying it, that we could go back to being virtual strangers.

I folded the note and wrote his name on the front. Then I dug into my purse and pulled out the shop key, setting it on top of the paper. Hopefully he'd find it on his desk. Before I stood up I looked around the small space. I was unprepared for the nostalgic feelings that came. It had been a study space when I needed it, an escape at times, and I'd even had a few laughs here and there. I let the feeling wash over me for a quick heartbeat and then tamped it back down when I stood. The last few months had been an interesting experience, nothing more.

CHAPTER NINETEEN

The ringing of my cell phone the next morning pulled me awake in a flash. My sleep had been fitful, with images of flame-like hair, brown freckles, and mocking honey eyes. I sat up straight, still in my bed, heart pounding as I reached for my phone. It had to be Connor. He'd gotten my note and he had something to say about it. Of course he did. Connor was one of the only men in my life who I expected to end up arguing with.

But it wasn't him. It was a telemarketer. I hung up and looked up at the ceiling, taking a few deep breaths. My mind caught in a vortex of thought as I stood and walked over to my paintings.

Glancing at the clock, I saw that I had some free time. I found my bib apron and tied it on. Then I began unconsciously grabbing colors and pencils from my stash and moving them to where I had propped a new, empty canvas. I picked up the pencils and sketched in an almost trance-like state. I didn't want to think too much about what I was doing. I preferred to let my mind transfer its thoughts out through my fingers. This worked for me in times of stress, as a way of sussing out what I was really struggling with.

A shape took place. It was a face. Square jaw line, strong cheekbones, heavy brow line. Next the eyes. Not big and round, but more teardrop-shaped, slanting down on the outer corners. The mouth was full and relaxed in a sort of half-smile. I knew before I set down my pencil that the paint colors would be warm: browns, oranges, reds, yellows, even a little black woven in here and there. I tried to pretend

I wasn't sketching Connor. I tried to ignore the rush I felt as I thought of hugging him in the aisle at the hardware store or laughing with him at the tubing hill. I didn't want to think about how much I'd grown to enjoy our sparring conversations, how he seemed perfectly capable of keeping up with anything I said or did, and giving it right back.

My hands began to shake as I put down the pencil and mixed the colors for his hair. I'd been studying it for months, and I knew exactly what colors it would require. I took a few deep breaths to settle my heartbeat as I positioned the brush where the first sweeping strokes of his hair would go. With the first swipe, I felt the tears come.

Why did I have to feel this way about Connor? Why did I have to like him so much? It was a huge mistake, one I'd done my very best to avoid for the entire decade that I'd known him. Once or twice I'd privately wondered why I was so against Connor and his antics, why when others laughed and rolled their eyes had I always been angry and disgusted. Why couldn't I just laugh too? His actions had no effect on my life.

Another sweeping curve, and more tears helped me to understand that it had been self-protection. I'd felt a pull to Connor that I'd resisted for years. I still remembered the heavy thunking of my heart when he had walked into my life at age fourteen. I'd never found another guy who'd made my heart crawl into my throat, or shivers crawl up my back the way he had. In fact, once I'd sworn off Connor and buried those reactions under a layer of self-righteousness, it had been easy to swear off all relationships as pointless. In that respect, he was also the only guy to ever break my heart.

Now, I'd allowed myself to get close and all the things I'd worried about were coming true. I thought of him constantly. I looked for him around town. I secretly loved the thrill of not having to hate him anymore, of him finally knowing who I was, and of becoming his friend. I'd covertly delighted in discovering his quick wit and easy-going personality. I found that I just flat out liked being around him, and that he still made my heart feel heavy in my chest.

These feelings, while finally acknowledged, weren't going to do me any good. Connor wasn't interested in me, which was what I'd known would happen all along, even as a young girl. I wasn't his type, and for every reason in the world, I couldn't risk letting him be mine.

On the canvas I moved on to his eyes, mixing in light browns and honey yellows. More tears fell as I painted them with their typical expression of amusement. This was what it felt like to want someone and know they didn't want you. It was the worst. Each freckle I painted was little a needle in my heart. I hated myself for crawling out from behind my careful wall of certitude and letting him get under my skin.

I painted in mindless abandon, allowing all the emotions to splotch down my face and be added onto the canvas. I let every feeling touch down, pushing none of them away, accepting that this was a one-sided breakup and I had no idea how I'd face him around town ever again.

* * * * *

For three days I lived like a hermit, going only to work and then straight back to my bedroom. Before and during each shift my stomach had been in knots, my eyes flying to the door every time the bell jingled. At home every time my phone rang my heart would speed up until I could check the caller ID. Connor never called or came into the diner on my shift. It was like he'd floated away, a figment of my imagination.

The silence from him had been longer than I could have imagined it would be, confirming that he'd been angry enough to cut me out. I couldn't eat, I couldn't sleep, I stayed awake all hours. I pulled the painting I'd done of Blaine and set it next to the new one of Connor. They stared back at me, stark reminders that I shouldn't be trusted with matters of the heart.

I was sitting on my bed in pajama pants and a tank top, studying on the afternoon of the fifth day after the Levi incident. I didn't have to work, and the knowledge that I could stay at home and hide away had made me grateful.

Mom knocked on my door mid-day. She had a food tray and a smile as she entered my room. I was surprised to see her in the middle of the day and raised my eyebrows at her.

"Lunch break," she answered my unvoiced question. "Care to tell me what's going on with you my little hermit crab?"

She put the tray down on the bed next to me and carefully sat next to it. It had a turkey sandwich, some carrots, and a big icy cola. My stomach growled more out of habit than actual hunger. My appetite had deserted me too.

"I'm going through second puberty?" I said with a half-grin.

She smiled at my attempt to be funny and looked around my room. Her eyes came to rest on the two portraits I'd been obsessing over. A quiet "oh" left her lips, and when her eyes returned to me they were a little sad and a lot sympathetic.

"It's bad, huh?" she said.

I nodded and shut the textbook I'd been reading. "Yeah."

"You know, I've known Connor Hunt since he was in grade school." Her eyes traveled back to the portraits. "He was a really good kid, actually. That all changed when his mom left."

"She left? I thought she'd died."

"Well, in some ways she did, I guess, and it was probably easier for Connor to let people think that. Ken and Connor never heard from her again. Suddenly this little red-headed boy who had been so happy became a problem child."

"I know. Kelly and I used to watch him in high school. We always swore we'd have nothing to do with him. So . . . I'm not sure what happened."

Mom reached out and put her cool hand on my bare shoulder. "I know what happened. The day he came to our house and cleaned up, I knew. He's very charming." I nodded. "I've been thinking about him a bit since that day, and I think I should have been more sympathetic toward him and less judgmental." I cocked my head to the side, willing her to continue. "A lot of people go through a wild phase as teenagers, but maybe his excessive dating was nothing more than a hurting boy looking for the connection he'd lost when his mother left."

Neither of us said anything as I processed that for a moment. It shaped his actions in a different light and tugged on my heartstrings. I was learning how it felt to be left by a parent, only I was an adult with more understanding. How would I have behaved differently if I had been a child living through this confusing time?

After a moment, Mom broke the silence. "He's the reason you're hiding away?"

I shrugged. "I realized a few days ago that I do like him. A lot. The feelings are like being hit by a bolt of lightning that does nothing but burn, made worse because I know he's upset with me."

She nodded, her eyes thoughtful. "I heard about the incident with Levi, and it's okay to hide out for a little bit, but you might be pushing it."

"Three days is too much?"

"I think so. Eat some lunch and take a shower. You'll feel a lot better." She stood and walked to the portraits. "I think you should probably put these away too. Blaine was a nice man, but he wasn't for you, and Connor breaks your heart a little every time you look over here." At my nod she picked up the canvases and took them to my closet, where she slid them in behind my hanging clothes. She moved back to my pile of art and selected a bright sunflower. "Here, this is better. A little sunshine is always in order."

"Thanks, Mom."

"I love you, Liv." She came over to kiss the top of my head before leaving my room. "I'm headed back to work. I'll see you at dinnertime."

"I love you too." Oh my gosh, it was amazing to have my mom working her way back to us.

An hour later I was towel drying my hair after a long, luxurious, wallowing bath when Kelly showed up outside my bathroom door. I screamed in surprise when I saw her face pop into my mirror, which made her snicker.

"My mom call you?" I asked.

"Oh, yeah. I know everything." She leaned against the doorway and crossed her arms. Her hair was pulled up into a messy bun on the top of her head, her makeup smudged under her eyes, and she smelled a little like roast beef. She must have come straight from work.

"What exactly is everything?" I asked, leaning against the bathroom counter in a similar pose.

"Staring at portraits, not eating, not showering."

"I've been better."

She gave me a sympathetic look. "You faked it pretty well at work. I thought you were just a little bummed out. I didn't realize you had fallen down into the dark abyss of heartbreak." I pushed away from the countertop and gestured for her to follow me into my room. As we crossed the threshold she said, "You ready to spill it?"

I nodded. "Maybe it would be better if I just showed you the pictures I painted."

She climbed up onto my bed as she had a thousand times before, taking her usual place leaning back against the foot board, legs outstretched. From the corner of my eye I saw her roll her shoulders and head, loosening muscles that always got tight while waitressing.

The paintings were easy to retrieve, and I brought them to the bed with me. Climbing up against the headboard, I laid them between us, face up. Kelly sat upright and looked them over. Her brows dropped as she studied them, lifting them up to see from a different angle. Her face was unreadable, but she chewed her lower lip, which told me she was deep in thought.

Finally, just when I thought I'd burst, she looked up at me. "I'd ask how long you've been in love with Connor, but I think I already know the answer."

Warmth filled my face. "First of all, love is a strong word. I'm not in love with him."

"The paintings say otherwise." She looked down at Connor's again and then back to Blaine's. "It's crazy to see my hunch spelled out so clearly like this. I mean, I knew you were holding back with Blaine, but no wonder you were. He looks cool and distant here, which is how your heart must have seen him. And Connor, I mean, wow. He looks like he'd start you on fire if you touched him." Her eyes came back up to meet mine. "Your face is telling me things you don't want to admit." Her voice was gentle, and I leaned back.

"I'm sorry."

"For what?" she asked as she set both paintings back down.

"You wanted to date Connor."

A laugh burst out and she slapped her hand over her mouth. "I did. I'd almost forgotten," she said through her fingers. "I don't anymore. He's not for me. My heart is full of Scott, and I have no regrets or doubts about him."

Tension I didn't realize I'd been holding released in a rush and my shoulders dropped. "Okay, good, because I really, really like Scott for you." She kicked out a foot and tapped my calf in acknowledgment. "I mean this seriously, though, Kell. I'm not actually in love with Connor." She kicked me again and raised her eyebrows. "I know it looks that way, but I'm not. I'm attracted to him and I like to be around him. I think it could become love if it was given a chance."

"Okay, I'll accept that answer if you'll admit that you've been crushing on him since we were fourteen years old and saw that amazing head of hair floating over the others in the high school cafeteria."

I leaned my head back and giggled. "I have not. He was nothing more than an interesting specimen to study, scientifically."

"Right. He was all you could talk about that entire year, and for a few years afterwards too. Sure, it was all negative, but you've always been interested."

I sat back up. "Fine, I admit it. What about you?"

"Eh, I only asked him out a few months ago because I was in a dry spell, and after all the years of talking about him and his bad boy ways I thought it might be fun to see what dating him was really like."

"You're such a schemer."

"True." She pulled a face and shifted directions. "Have you heard from him at all?" I shook my head. "Well, I haven't seen much of him either. I'm not sure what's going through his mind. I do know that you've been the focus of his attention these past couple of months. He may not be as indifferent to you as you think."

"Can we go back to spreading rumors and gossip about him and pretend none of this ever happened?" My hand swept out to point to both portraits. "Life was easier before this."

"Sure. If you'll pull yourself up and leave the house, I'll violently smear his name all over town."

We both busted up over that, leaning forward and clutching our bellies until our throats felt raw and I felt ready to stand tall again.

CHAPTER TWENTY

The next day I was sitting cross-legged on my bed again after working the morning shift. My headphones were in, classical music blocking out all the sounds of life from Sadie's dance team downstairs. I flipped through my anatomy book and tried like crazy to forget everything that had happened for, oh, I don't know, the last several weeks. I was doing a pretty good job of it too, which is why I didn't hear the knock on my bedroom door. In fact, I don't know how long he stood there before I caught him in my peripheral vision.

When I did turn, I was too shocked to react. Connor was standing as still as a statue, looking across the room at my paintings. My paintings! His eyes were wide and frozen, as though he couldn't quite believe what he was seeing. He was dressed in jeans and a T-shirt, and his hair was slightly damp, as if he'd just showered.

I tore the headphones out of my ears, my heart thundering in my chest as I watched him take it all in. So many thoughts were running through my head that they got caught and jumbled up. What was he doing here? Why was he in my room? What was going through his mind? How could I possibly accept that this was happening?

"Connor," I said his name as I clambered to my feet at last.

Instead of looking at me, he took more steps into my private world. One hand lifted, a finger pointing at the painting of a sunflower that Mom had put there to cheer me up. My stomach swooped as I checked to make sure the painting of him was out of sight. His fingers looked like they were trembling as they moved to gesture to the stack of canvases dotting the east wall of my bedroom.

"Liv," he said at last in an awed tone, "what is all this?"

"Connor, please . . . " Please what? I tried again. "You have to . . . " Only I didn't know what I wanted him to do, so I asked a question instead. "What are you doing here?"

"I came to talk with you because we have a lot to talk about, but we can get to all that in a minute. This—this is so much more important right now." He moved across the room and ran a light finger over the top edge of a canvas. "You painted these?"

My mouth felt horribly dry, and I had to swallow and lick my lips in order to make sound come out. "No one knows."

He finally looked at me and his eyes lit with understanding. "The paint I've seen on your fingers." Confusion was next to appear. "Why doesn't anyone know?"

I shook my head, helpless to try to put it into words, and reeling from the realization that my sanctuary had been shattered. "It's for me, alone."

He looked back at the paintings, and I watched helplessly as he soaked it all in. There were dozens of them, stacked up against each other, varying in size and theme. So much of my inner world was painted on those canvases. All of it was meant for my eyes only.

He turned back to face me and took a few steps to where my feet had frozen to the carpet. "Do you realize how talented you are?" It was a question he didn't expect me to answer. He stopped within a foot of me, causing my hands to shake and my knees to feel wobbly. I tilted my head back to meet his intense gaze. "Why aren't you sharing your work with others?"

I scrambled to think of a way to answer him without opening up a part of me that had stayed buried for most of my life. "I just, it's a hobby, I guess."

"This is more than just a hobby. I can practically feel the emotion you were experiencing when you painted each picture."

I pulled a face, astonished at his insight. It prompted me to take a risk. "These paintings are kind of like my journal." I breathed the words out on a shaky breath. His head cocked to the side and I pushed on, encouraged by the open curiosity in his expression. "It's how I process the world. Painting, for me, is like putting a piece of myself on the canvas." He nodded. "It would be like inviting people to read my diary, or to take a peek inside my heart."

"It would be taking a risk," he murmured.

"Yes."

"Why aren't you going to art school?"

That answer was easy. "Nursing is practical. I can support myself and it would be flexible if I had a family someday. Art is fickle. I can't do fickle. I need steady."

"Steady can't be all that matters in life, Livy." I felt weak in the knees over the way he breathed out his personal nickname for me as he turned to look at my work again. "How can you let these sit up here in your room and pretend you're okay with nothing more?"

"You're wrong. Steady *is* all that matters. I can't hang my future on a maybe."

He turned back to me, amber eyes drilling down into hazel. "Did Blaine know about this?"

"Of course not." My tone was sharper than I'd meant for it to be.

"Why is it crazy for me to assume your boyfriend would know about this?"

"I just told you, it's mine. I don't share it."

"Even with your boyfriend?" he pressed.

"With no one."

"Yet here I am."

My breathing felt like it had paused. "I kind of wish you weren't." My lips were tight, and my nostrils flared as I tried to get my lungs working again.

"Where'd you get the money?"

"What?" The question threw me even more off balance.

"Where did you get the money to pay off your bill at the shop?"

I shook my head, trying to reboot my brain, which felt like it was stuffed with cotton candy at the moment. "Oh, yeah, my dad gave me some money for school and I took it out of there."

"I hate for you to use your school money to pay me when we had a perfectly good arrangement."

"I think it's probably best if we just settle the account and, you know, move along. I've made things weird between us, and . . . " His expression was neutral, but I noticed some color on his cheeks that wasn't usually there, and an alertness in the way he was holding himself. "So, anyhow." I swallowed hard. "I hope that at some point you'll be able to forgive me, because I really am sorry, but for now I think we'd probably be better off going back to casual acquaintances."

"That's it, huh?"

"I guess. I don't know what else to do. We can't go back and undo everything."

"Hmm."

He took another step closer to where I was standing near my bed. His eyes chased over my face, watching my expressions and most likely reading me like an open book. I sucked in my lips and chewed on them for a moment while my mind spun, waiting for him to say what it was he'd come here to say.

The silence spun out, which allowed my mind to fret. What should *I* say? I was pretty sure I'd already apologized, but had I done a good job of it? Maybe I could get the ball rolling and he'd get out of here quickly if I apologized again. The most important thing was that he never know how I had come to feel about him.

I dove right in, the silence eating at me. "I'm truly sorry, Connor. I thought Levi was going to shoot you. I reacted without thinking. I caused you a lot of embarrassment and frustration, and I don't blame you for wanting nothing to do with me anymore."

"Why do you think I don't want anything to do with you anymore?"

At this my eyes grew large. "It's been almost a week, and nothing. You haven't been in the diner, or run into me around town, or tried to talk to me at all. I left you a note at the shop, and still you didn't bother to even shoot me a text."

His eyes softened. "I'll probably never forget how you looked bursting through that door swinging a tire iron above your head, curls flying, with a battle cry screaming out of you." His eyes crinkled and his teeth flashed.

I stared at him, my mouth falling open. "You think this is funny? I try to save your life, and you think it's funny? I almost get assault charges filed on me, and become the hot gossip topic of the year, and you think it's so funny that you give me the silent treatment for days?"

His amusement faded as my eyes shot daggers at him. Gone was the numbness and worry. Now I was angry. While I'd been agonizing over my part in everything and mourning my feelings for him, he'd been laughing about it behind my back. "I can't, I don't, I . . . " Hot, furious words all crowded in on each other, begging to release.

As I spoke, his expression became completely serious. "Actually, Liv, I've been trying to laugh about it because if I don't see the humor in it, then I feel like I'm going to lose my mind."

My mouth clamped shut and my eyes narrowed. "What do you mean?"

"I mean," he said as he took that last step toward me, "that I have never been so terrified and upset in my entire life. Yes, it's a little bit funny to think of you charging in the door, all five feet of you ready to do battle. Until I think of Levi, twice your size, lifting you in the air and shoving you away, and I just . . . " He bit off the flow of words and ran his hands roughly through his hair. It looked like flames coming out of the top of his head, and I was fascinated by the colors happening in his eyes and on his skin as he grew more agitated. "I wanted to kill him. Then I wanted to beat some sense into you. What on earth were you thinking?"

"I wasn't thinking about anything other than saving you," I whispered. I tried to take a step back to put distance between us, but my legs bumped up against my mattress.

He acted like he hadn't heard. "So, I stayed away from you for a few days. I was afraid of what would come out of my mouth if I did see you. Then I got back to my shop to find a note from you saying the friendship was over."

"I did not say that," I defended.

"You signed it 'Liv Phelps.' Don't think I didn't understand exactly what that meant."

His eyes took on a faraway look, and he reached out a hand to take one of my curls, much like I'd seen him do all those years ago in high school. His touch was soft as he wove it around his finger. I hated when people wanted to touch my hair, but his touch was exciting in a way I'd never experienced. His focus stayed on whatever it was he was doing with my hair as he said, "It took me another couple of days to decide how to handle that. As far as I could figure, there were only two options, and you'd like neither of them."

"What were the two options?" I asked as shivers started on the top of my head.

"I was going to yell at you, which I knew you really wouldn't like, or . . . " he seemed to falter as he looked down at me, eyes focusing on mine.

"Or?" I asked.

Rather than say anything, his other hand came to my chin, pressing softly under it until my head fell back even further, and my pulse leapt. He put that hand around the back of my neck and tugged my face to his, pressing his lips softly to mine.

The shock of it felt like diving head first into straight up lava. White hot electricity scorched me from where our lips pressed, down to the soles of my feet. Hands that had started to raise between us now grabbed his shirt and pulled him closer. I made a soft sound in the back of my throat, and he let go of my hair and chin, using his two callused thumbs, rough from his work, to stroke down the soft skin on the sides of my neck.

My heartbeat increased, and I pushed to my tiptoes, wanting more contact. It was like nothing I'd ever felt before. Swirls of color, white hot and then red, zinged around behind my closed eyes when he deepened the kiss. My hands left his shirt to tangle in his hair, and I was gratified to find it as silky as I'd thought it would be. Yellows and bright, brilliant greens sparked behind my eyes when his arms gathered me in, the palms of his hands pressed against my back to bring me flush with his body. He was so warm, and solid, and every particle of me wanted this moment. I was going to paint all of it, in swirls and curling patterns that had no beginning or end. This was chemistry and attraction in one hurtling mass of color.

"Livy," he whispered as his lips left mine, allowing both of us to take a deep breath before returning to the kiss. I didn't hate the nickname. I wanted to be Livy to him.

Something new and thrilling heated the air around us. Something I'd never felt before, with anyone, not even in my imagination. I wanted more. I craved the things he was making me feel. His hand came up to my head again, threading through my curls and making me want to arch like a cat under his attentions.

When he ended the kiss and slowly eased me back down to my flat feet, I knew I was in a world of trouble. His fingertips coasted down my back, and before I wanted him to he broke contact. I kept my eyes closed as he stepped away. The air around us felt charged and heavy with promise.

"Livy?" he said in a barely audible voice. I opened my eyes and met his questioning look. I watched him steadily, unsure of what to say. "Should I apologize?" he asked. "Because I wouldn't mean it."

My mouth pulled up at the corners. "No."

"Good." His smile was as warm as his eyes, and I was a little pleased to see the heartbeat in his neck beating as hard as mine was. "That was . . . " He didn't seem to have words to express what had happened, and I was grateful that he didn't try. His eyes darted around the room for a split second before returning to my face. "I don't think I'll ever stop being surprised by you." His hands reached for me and pulled me into an embrace. My arms wrapped around his waist as I gladly melted against him. "I wish I could sign you up for art school and drive you myself. I would love watching your dreams come true."

It was a sweet thought but one that had no basis in reality. "That dream will have to wait for a while. It's not part of my current life plan."

"Is there room for flexibility in the plan?" he asked and I shook my head. "I see."

He started tracing lazy circles on my back, and I leaned my head to the side to rest more fully against his shoulder. It felt wonderful to be cuddled and caressed. Peaceful, even.

"Do you miss Blaine?" he asked. Another curve ball, and an unwelcome one at that.

"I feel like a terrible person for admitting this, but I don't miss him as much as I thought I would."

He made a noise and resumed his lovely back scratching. "Why did you date him anyway? You two seemed so different from each other. Too different."

"Because he asked."

"That's it? It was as simple as that?" I nodded against him. "Then I'm asking you now. Can we please be friends again?"

"Friends?" The word poured buckets of ice on my butterflies and caused me to stiffen in his embrace. I was terribly glad he couldn't see my face as I worked through the new rush of emotion. "Um, friends, yes, for sure."

I released my hold on him and wiggled out of his embrace. I tucked a few stray curls behind my ears with nerveless fingers and stared at his chin blankly for a moment, registering that this was the Connor I'd long expected to show up. Connor, whose charm and good looks had roped me right in like a total sucker. There was no way I was the first girl to get a kiss from him as part of an apology.

"You okay?" he asked.

"Oh, totally." I bit my lip and slid around him, walking toward my door to put some much-needed space between us while I willed my heart to slump back into its regular pattern.

Friends. We were going to be friends. It didn't matter that his kiss had ignited a firestorm of response inside of me. We were buddies, pals, muchachos.

"I'm great." I smiled across the room at him. "I'm glad you came over and we could clear the air."

"You sure you won't reconsider taking your money back and cleaning the shop again?" he asked.

I looked out the window, not really seeing the view of the back yard. "I'll have to pass. I've really got plenty on my plate already."

He moved toward the doorway, and I felt the warmth return to my limbs as he drew close. My body was a traitor. "Livy, are you . . . "

I cut him off in a friendly way. "I'm great. Will I see you at the diner soon?" He nodded. "All right." I stepped through the doorway into the hall. "I'll walk you out."

He hurried to catch me in the hallway, his warm hand landing on my shoulder. I stopped walking and took a deep breath before turning to him with what I hoped was a bright expression.

"Yeah?"

"Are you sure we're okay?" He was trying to read my face again, and I almost felt bad, knowing I was confusing him. I couldn't help it, though. I had to maintain this for just a few more minutes.

"I'm good. Really. Good. This was a good talk." I sounded like an idiot.

The fact that the living room was empty as we passed through onto the front porch barely registered. Sadie's crew must have relocated. I was glad to avoid them and their curious eyes.

"Well . . . " I said when I came to a stop just outside the front door.

Connor stood next to me, shoulders nearly touching, and stared off in the same direction I was looking. He tucked his hands into his pockets, and I couldn't help but notice his jaw seemed tight. Being friends was going to be really hard.

"I'll see you soon?" he finally said.

"Yep."

He sighed and turned to me. "I don't know what I said wrong just now, but I know I did something because you've shut down on me."

I dared to meet his eyes and knew it was a mistake. The urge to kiss him again rose inside of me like wildfire. It had been so much better not knowing how being with him would feel. I shifted my bare feet. I wanted to tell him that I not only liked him, but I was attracted to him, and that the kiss we'd shared had been amazing. I wanted him to know that his arms around me felt like magic.

It didn't seem to matter, though. I couldn't do it. Images of him with so many other women floated icily along in my mind's eye. They taunted me, telling me I'd never have him either. I was too raw from all that had happened over the past half hour to combat any of that with logic, or to exercise faith in either Connor or myself. So, in an effort at protection, I lied.

"No, there's just so much going on and it was a shock . . . everything that just happened, you know?" I said. "I need a minute to sort it all out."

He turned to face me, leaned close, and pressed a kiss to my forehead. My eyes slid shut as a trickle of heat raced from that spot down to the tips of my fingers. His lips lingered longer than necessary, long enough to raise goosebumps on my arms. Then he was gone, down the steps, and into his truck before I'd opened my eyes.

CHAPTER TWENTY-ONE

I lay in bed the next morning staring at my ceiling for a few minutes after the alarm had gone off, reflecting on the crazy state of my life. In the pasts few months I'd dated, broken up, staged an intervention with my family, realized I was "in-like" with a sworn enemy, and just generally watched my life roller-coaster away from itself.

I had a choice to make. I could do another hermit session—but really, hadn't I already done enough of those over the past week—or I could get up, dust myself off, and be the fierce woman I knew I was. I was capable of getting things back on track. Even if my heart ached with every beat.

Admitting to myself, my mother, and Kelly how I felt about Connor had opened a door that I was going to need to weld shut again. Sadly, the only person I knew who owned a welder was Connor himself. It was a junky conundrum.

I got out of bed and padded to the shower, letting the hot spray work away the tightness in my shoulders and neck, along with the leftover feeling of Connor holding me close. I cried too, telling myself that I could have this moment to wallow and then I would face the world once more. I was done hiding. I needed to be able to respect myself at the end of the day.

I pulled into the employee parking area of the diner just in time to see Connor's truck pull out. He didn't notice me, and I was grateful for it. It was a good sign that he'd returned, but I was glad to have one more day before we came face to face.

Work was a welcome respite from my own traitorous mind, and for the next two days I dove so hard into my job that Jake complimented me, and Kelly expressed her concern for my mental health. At home I studied so hard that Mom had to beg me to get some fresh air. Sadie even offered to paint my nails, but I was a machine made of pure stone.

On the third day, Connor's schedule finally lined up with mine. As luck would have it, he seated himself at the counter area where I was working breakfast. My stomach lurched when I turned to see him, but his head was down and he hadn't noticed my eyes on him yet. I took in a deep breath and counted to five as I let it out slowly, trying to calm the butterflies in my chest. He appealed to me in ways I wasn't sure I'd ever be able to control.

"Well, hey stranger," I chirped as I came to stand across the countertop from him. "How you been?"

He looked up, his eyes smiling. "I'm good."

"Glad to hear it. What can I get you to drink?"

"I guess it's getting too warm for hot cocoa?" He smiled sheepishly, which was adorable, if you weren't trying to be immune to that kind of thing.

I shook my head. "Not if that's what sounds good to you," I replied.

"Okay. Hot cocoa and a Belgian waffle with blueberries."

"Coming right up." I tore his order off my pad and tucked the rest into my apron pocket. After hanging the order for Jake and the cooks to see, I filled a steaming mug with hot cocoa and placed it in front of Connor with a smile.

His face fell as he looked at the mug and back at me. "No marshmallows?" he asked.

I offered a stilted laugh in return. "Now that we're better friends, I thought I'd give you what you actually ordered."

"Right." He looked back down at the cocoa as though it had broken his heart.

I moved busily along, taking orders, filling drinks, wiping down the counter, and all the while I did my best to keep up a light stream of sunny chitchat with Connor. Hot topics of the morning were the weather, a little more about the weather, and lastly, the weather. It was torture for both of us. I missed the banter we'd so easily fallen into.

When he finally left it felt like all the muscles in my body were on fire. I told Jake I was taking a little break and ran back to the employee lounge to get a drink and do a few stretches. That had been nothing short of warfare in there, only I was alone in the battle.

True to his word, Connor kept coming back. He usually ate breakfast there, so I didn't see him every day with my varying shifts, but when I did see him I made sure to be unfailingly nice to him. He wanted to be friends, so I accommodated that. The more we interacted, the more I truly understood that I didn't want to be friends with him. It wasn't enough. My only hope became to slowly wean us into acquaintanceship in a way that he would one day wonder what had happened to that nice Liv Phelps.

"You're being weird," Kelly said as the breakfast rush was ending on our Saturday shift.

"I'm working. How is that being weird?" I asked her.

She handed me two menus that had been left in her booth and turned to pick up the plates. "Like, how you're treating Connor this week. You're being super nice."

"We're friends. I'm being friendly."

"No, you're being sugar with a side of maple syrup." She walked off with the plates and I followed her.

"I'm treating him nicer than I do the other customers, so what's the big deal?" I called as I tucked the two menus back in their place at the hostess stand.

Kelly reappeared from the kitchen and moved to clear another table. "Exactly. You're only that nice to people you don't like."

"That is not true."

"It's totally true. The more you actually like someone, the sassier you are to them. Why are you so mad at Connor? I thought you two worked it out."

"We did, it's just that . . . "

"Hey you two." Connor's voice interrupted from behind Kelly. We spun around, and I was sure guilt was written all over my face.

"Hi to you." Kelly smiled warmly at him. "Did you leave something?"

"No, I was just in the bathroom. Hey, Liv, I wanted to chat with you for a second."

I peeked my head around Kelly and gave him a wide smile. "Hi. I'm right here. What's up?'

"You free for lunch Monday?"

"Sure thing." I nodded my head. "I work at two, so as long as we're done by then."

"Great. I'll text you the details."

"Great."

"Okay. See you ladies later." Connor waved and I waved back at him with a cheery grin.

The second the door closed, Kelly spun around and blasted me with her gaze. "What happened?"

I shrugged. "Nothing. We're best buddies now, see. Lunch is for friends, remember?"

"Olivia Magdalena Phelps, spill it now."

"My middle name isn't Magdalena, which you know," I replied.

"You needed a middle name because I've never been more serious in my life. What happened?"

"He kissed my socks off is what happened." I slammed dirty silverware into the busing bucket and moved to another booth.

Kelly hurried to catch up. "What?"

My face heated at the memory and I kept my head turned away from her prying eyes. "He showed up at my house, saw all my paintings, and then he kissed me senseless."

"He saw your paintings?" When I chanced a look, her eyes were so wide I thought they'd pop right out of her skull. I was gratified by her dismay. "But, no one sees those. Blaine never even saw them."

"Exactly. Then, when we were done kissing, he said we could be friends again."

"No." Kelly's voice was a horrified whisper.

"Yes."

"How was the kiss?"

A flush rose from my chest to my cheeks. "Remember how you said the painting of him looked like he could set someone on fire?" She nodded. "Well, you were right. It was like nothing I've ever experienced. It was how you kiss someone you really . . . well, you know. It wasn't a kiss that said 'hey pal, I'm glad we could share this laugh together.' He made me feel things, things I did not want to feel."

"And he just asked you to lunch."

"Exactly. To lunch. How could he kiss me that way and then act like nothing had happened? It just proves everything we always thought about him. So now I have a great, super, totally fun lunch date with my new bestie on Monday. Which I'll be canceling because I already have the first signs of strep throat."

"Lunch is for friends." Kelly's voice still sounded shocked.

"That's what you told me."

"I can't believe he'd kiss you and then tell you he wanted to be friends with you. That doesn't seem like Connor."

"Um, correction, that's exactly the type of thing he does, which is what I'm trying to tell you. I was bamboozled just like all those other poor girls we watched him toy with." I finished filling my bucket and headed into the kitchen with Kelly hot on my tail.

"No, he doesn't do that anymore. I've been friends with him for a while now, and he's never tried anything on me. I've never seen him around town with another woman or anything. I was starting to think he was committed to a life of celibacy."

"A guy who looks and acts like him? No way."

"I'm serious. You two have your wires crossed somehow. He doesn't look at you like you're his buddy."

I handed Kelly a stack of plates to rinse and shook my head. "He made me feel things," I grumbled, repeating it so she'd really understand. "Big things. Things I hadn't felt with Blaine after months of dating."

"This is bad." Kelly's lips pursed as she rinsed. "Really bad. Does he know he's an idiot?"

"I doubt it."

"I mean, you *have* been really nice to him the past few days, so he has to know something's wrong."

I couldn't help but laugh at that. "Yet, still, I get invited to lunch."

"Liv, you have to talk to him."

"No. No way. Last time we talked I ended up with the most scorching kiss of my life, and a new pal. I'm not doing it."

"So what *are* you going to do?"

"I'm going to be his friend. I'm going to be such a friendly friend that he'll grow tired of me and we'll naturally move on from each other."

"But you're in love with him." Kelly's voice rose.

"I'm working my way out of that." I repeated the mantra I'd been telling myself. "I'm going to finish school, move away, and live a life full of happiness." I slammed the dishwasher door shut and wiped my hands on my apron. "And you aren't going to tell Connor one word about this conversation."

"Someone has to tell him."

"Not one word. Your loyalty is with me. Besides, this is a good thing. I wasn't looking for a man in my life, remember? Time to focus on good old number one here." I pointed at myself and left the kitchen with Kelly hot on my heels.

"But Liv, I'm friends with him. I could help . . . "

I turned to her and cut her off with a glance. "Not one word."

* * * * *

I watched as Connor's truck pulled into my driveway at noon on Monday. I'd tried several excuses to get out of lunch, even going so far as to tell him my cat had been hit by a car—a cat that did not exist. Desperate times and all that. In the end he'd been firm, and I wasn't willing to tell him the real reason I didn't want to spend time chumming with him.

I'd spent a full hour grooming myself and trying to pick out the perfect outfit that would say: I tried, but I only tried as a buddy would try, not as a girl who considers this a date. Normally my routine took about fifteen minutes, which mainly involved taming my curls. Makeup wasn't something I gave much thought to. Today the outfit and makeup had mattered, which was silly, because this was Connor, who had seen me looking pretty rough a few times. Connor, who I was trying to end a friendship with. Still, I had my pride. Plus, maybe I wanted him to see what he'd be missing out on once I was gone.

He opened the door and climbed down from his truck, looking amazing, and my heart gave an extra thump as I watched the way he walked toward the door. He'd always been athletic, but with adulthood had come a more relaxed confidence. I tugged at the hemline of my forest green sweater before I flung the door open and scampered out when he reached the porch steps.

"Hi," I greeted. "Beautiful afternoon, huh?" I was carrying a light windbreaker jacket over my arm just in case the mid-April weather decided it wanted to turn. I walked quickly to his truck and pulled open the door at the same time that he was reaching for the handle.

"It is. How are you?" he asked.

"I'm good. Hungry." I tugged the door shut and heard him chuckle as he walked around to his side.

"Is it still too cold to grab some sandwiches and eat in the park? We could sit inside the restaurant if you want to be warmer." He started up the engine and backed into the street.

"Outside is great."

Conversation flowed lightly—and really cheerfully if you ask me—on the drive to the sandwich shop where we ordered two subs, two bags of chips, and two drinks before driving to a local park. When he'd tried to pay for my lunch, I'd stopped him and insisted on covering my own. Lunch was for friends, after all.

We found an open bench at the top of a rise that overlooked the walking paths and basketball courts. The grass was still a yellow color, but the sky was blue and cloudless, and I enjoyed the fresh air and smells of new life around us.

"How's school going?" Connor asked.

"Good, good. I have finals coming up in a couple of weeks, so gearing up for that. I have a few papers to write, but holding steady. Mom quit her night job, so having her around to help with the house is taking some load off."

"I'm glad. I know you had a lot you were trying to balance."

"Yep. We're doing great. How about you? How's the shop?"

"Good. Busy. I've got those three part-time guys, but I'm thinking about bumping two of them up to full-time and expanding how much we can take on."

I nodded. "That's great. How's your dad?" I asked before taking a big bite.

"My dad asks about you all the time. You made quite the impression on him." Connor's chuckle made the back of my neck tingle.

"I'm pretty good at making an impression." I gave him a toothless smile around the bit of sandwich. "Good or bad doesn't seem to matter."

"It was good, I promise."

"I liked him." I took a sip of my drink. "Tell me about him."

"My dad?"

"Yeah."

Connor's eyes grew thoughtful, seeing something I wasn't privy to. While he thought, I savored the chance to watch his profile. He'd been good-looking the first time I'd seen him as a teen. Time had given him sharper features, all clean lines, a face I found even more fascinating now.

"He's a really good man, a good father. He's been alone for most of what I can really remember. Mom left when I was eight. I do remember before she left Dad was more . . . I don't know . . . tense, short-tempered. I think it must have been hard living with someone who was so determined to be unhappy. Now he's laid back and easygoing."

His candidness surprised me. I wanted to take the hand he was resting casually on his leg and offer him some sort of camaraderie. But I didn't.

"Why do you think she was so unhappy?" I asked.

"I wasn't old enough to understand then, but over the years Dad has said a few things and I've seen a little more of life. I think she wanted more and it never panned out."

"More what?"

"More of life, I guess. I think she had dreams, and being a small town wife wasn't how she'd pictured it going. She'd settled for less than she wanted."

Understanding blossomed in my mind as I remembered him so intensely telling me that I should go for my dreams and not settle for nursing school simply because it would offer security and stability. He'd seen the opposite side of that coin.

Without consciously thinking about it, my leg pressed against his. "How funny that we come at things from such different angles. I want to do nursing school because I've seen the way my dad's whims affected the stability of our family. I don't want to depend on, or need someone else, to provide for me. The idea of taking a risk, taking the fun path, leaves me feeling helpless. Nursing school makes me feel safe. In the same scenario you see the chance for regret in my future if I set aside a talent I have in order to do the 'smart thing.'"

"You have so much life inside of you, and your art speaks to it. It would be a shame to let fear put a lid on that."

I shifted, still looking forward and away from him. "Maybe."

"At the risk of this sounding wrong, there are men who believe there's room for a little dream chasing, and as your partner would be happy to help you."

I dared a glance at him and was surprised to find he'd turned toward me as well. His face was closer than I'd realized, his eyes intent, expressing that he truly believed what he'd said. I had never meant for this conversation to get so personal. I straightened my shoulders and did my best to put the casual friend façade back in place as I looked back out across the park, but it was so hard. He was here, he was warm against my side, and he was completely earnest in what he was saying. It was painful.

"Just like there are women out there who understand that family can also be an adventure, not just something you're saddled with." I shrugged. "Too bad neither of us can count on finding those people as a future plan. Possibly a hope, but not a plan." I stood abruptly, needing to move, to break this spell. "You up for a walk around the path?"

He stood too, but instead of starting to walk he put a hand on my shoulder and turned me so that we were facing each other. "I know where I went wrong."

I scrunched up my face. "What do you mean?"

"The other day, at your house. I figured it out." His hand ran from my shoulder, down my arm, and wrapped my cold fingers in his warm grip. "I said we should be friends again."

"Uh huh. So here we are, doing that."

"The problem is, I don't want to just be your friend." I started to shake my head, but he stopped me with a callused palm on my cheek. "I'm serious. I want there to be more than that between us."

My heart pounded. "I don't want to be on the list of girls you keep on a string."

Instead of being offended, his lips curved and his eyes crinkled. "I know you think I'm the local Casanova."

"I spent a lot of years watching you in action," I mumbled.

"That's been behind me for a long time. I know you aren't the type of woman that a man toys around with."

My toes curled inside my shoes. "I think friends would probably be the safest bet for us."

"I hate being your friend. You're the worst friend I've ever had. Friendship with you is like rubbing your face on a glacier and trying to tell yourself you had a good time." He raised the hand he was holding and kissed my fingers where they were joined with his. I felt a bubble of humor at the comparison to a glacier. He wasn't wrong. I'd practically killed us both with kindness. "I think it would be good to stop playing it safe, don't you?"

My bones felt melty at the look in his eyes. "How unsafe are we talking here?"

"Like, I hope you packed a parachute."

I wasn't surprised when he closed the space between us and pressed his mouth to mine. I'd felt the air around us vibrating, I knew it was coming, and I wanted it equally as much as it petrified me. I kissed him back, light and slow, but pulled away before it could go any further, just as the colors had started to swirl.

"Connor." I pressed a hand to his chest. "I'm not going to be okay if you . . . "

"I'm not. You have nothing to be afraid of."

"Nothing to fear but fear itself?" I cracked, the nerves making my head fuzzy.

"Something like that." He stole another quick kiss, a peck really, that made my toes tingle. "You took a risk on Blaine and told me that all he'd had to do was ask. So, this time I'm going to ask the right question and hope you can forget the wrong question I asked you a couple of days ago."

"I'll try, but it's not every day that a guy kisses me like that and then asks me to be his buddy. It's kind of unforgettable."

He laughed and pulled a face. "I was being a total idiot."

"Agreed."

He let go of my hand and slowly pulled me close to him, tucking my head under his chin and my ear against his chest. His voice vibrated against me as he spoke. "Liv, will you go on dates with me, let me kiss you, do strange things that I never expect, argue with me, and load up my hot cocoa with disgusting marshmallows?"

A smile filled my face. "What's the magic word?"

He squeezed me tight against him and dropped a kiss on my curls. "Please?"

"Okay."

"As easy as that?"

"As easy as that. And, seeing as you asked so nicely, I'll throw in a little bonus for you. I promise to ask before I jump in to rescue you from bad guys."

"Hmm. Actually, if you don't mind, I've always wanted my own personal superhero."

"Tire Iron Girl, weapons wizard, at your service."

"Man, the other guys are going to be so jealous."

CHAPTER TWENTY-TWO

Something inside of me shifted with the knowledge that Connor wanted to be with me. At first it was subtle: an easier time waking up, lighter steps around the diner, a smile that I couldn't contain.

I'd blushed hard when he'd walked into the diner for his breakfast the day after we'd decided to date. It didn't matter that I'd known he was coming, or that I'd seen him a million other times, or that I'd stayed up all night telling myself to get a grip. When I saw his half smile and the way his eyes crinkled as he caught sight of me, I'd felt the heat climb. It had been such a total head to toe reaction that I'd stood like a statue, holding a coffee pot and watching as he'd bypassed the hostess station and come straight to me. He'd stopped so close I was surprised our toes didn't touch. I'd tilted my head back to look at him, and his eyes had raked over my face.

"Morning, Livy," he'd said in a voice only the two of us could hear, and I swear it was the most butterfly-inducing moment of my life to date.

I'd done nothing more than nod. He'd leaned down and pressed a light kiss to my forehead, one hand coming up to tuck a stray curl behind my ear, making my eyes close as chills raced down my spine. He'd smelled fresh and his lips had been so soft.

"Hey," I'd breathed out, opening my eyes.

"I'll just find a seat, then?" His light honey brown eyes had been amused as he'd pulled away.

The diner had gone dead still, and I knew without looking that every eye in the place was on the Phelps girl and the Hunter boy. I knew many of them were shocked, wondering how this had taken place and how they hadn't noticed. I assumed several of the older women were thinking about how to tell my mother. The men, however, would be joking about it to Connor for weeks.

"I'm working the back booths today," I'd replied. "I think everyone's looking at us." I'd dared to glance around.

"Probably."

Without another word he'd slid around me and taken a seat in an open booth on the edge of my section. I hadn't been able to help watching him all but strut across the floor. Knowing he was doing it to make me laugh had been enough to unfreeze me from the spot.

However, I'd been flustered and hot all over the entire time he was there, as though I'd shifted back to a fourteen-year-old girl seeing him across the cafeteria for the first time. I couldn't get a handle on myself, and by the time he'd left the diner I'd been tempted to go stuff napkins in my armpits. It had been humiliating. I'd never fallen apart that way over a guy, and I wondered how I could feel so completely different than I'd ever felt before.

"It's because this is the real thing," Kelly had said when I mentioned it to her over the phone a couple of days later.

I'd leaned back against my pillowed headboard and looked across the room to see the stars shining through my window. "It takes time and shared experiences to know if it's real or not. Besides, I've liked someone before."

"Yes, you have crushed on someone before, but this is different."

"I don't know how. The same basic hormones are involved."

Kelly was thoughtful for a moment, and I'd waited, curious to hear her thoughts. "Maybe it's just that your soul . . . "

"Nope," I'd cut her off with a laugh. "I thought you were going to have something scientific to tell me and it was going to make sense and be interesting."

"The idea of souls finding each other doesn't interest you?"

"I'm a woman of science," I'd stated.

"Well, good luck figuring out the scientific reason that Connor's soul speaks to yours." Her voice had been light and teasing.

"Does Scott's soul speak to yours?" I'd teased back.

"No, silly." She paused briefly. "It sings to mine."

I'd made a sound of surprised amusement. "If you were in front of me, I'd be forced to smack you across the head with my pillow."

"Laugh all you want, Liv, but the heart knows what the heart wants, and your heart wants Connor Hunt."

Regardless of whether it was science or a spiritual connection, I'd floated through that first week on a cloud even higher than nine.

Now Connor and I were bouncing down the mountain pass between Oak Hills and Springfield, headed for the annual King Car Expo. I'd been excited when Connor had called to invite me along. He'd seen my painting, and now I'd get to share in something he enjoyed.

After opening the door for me to get into his truck, he entered on the driver side and looked over at me. His brows furrowed and his lips pinched. He shook his head and reached out his hand for mine. The second I'd put my hand in his he pulled me across the bench seat to sit next to him.

"That's better."

"This is not a seat where independent-minded women like to sit," I said with a soft smile.

"Even if I say please?" He squeezed my hand.

"You're sure throwing that word around a lot lately."

"So far it's working out for me."

I laughed, pulled a face, and buckled in, my thigh and shoulder pressing against his. I had to admit, now, that I kind of liked being close to him. Our entwined hands were resting lightly on my leg, and the typical palm sweat had miraculously stayed away.

"Are all trucks this bouncy?" I asked.

"Bouncy?" He kept his eyes on the road but raised an eyebrow.

"Yes, bouncy. Like the seatbelt is the only thing keeping me from hitting my head on the ceiling."

"You know, with all the things I've heard about you over the years, no one mentioned you were a princess."

My mouth dropped open. "We'll circle back to the princess thing in a second. What do you mean 'all the things you've heard about me'?"

"Things like, 'that Phelps girl has a solid head on her shoulders,' or 'that Phelps girl is sure a hard worker,' or 'that Phelps girl has the cutest little . . . " He playfully yelped when I pinched his hand before he could finish that train of thought.

"This is what people think of me? I'm a hard worker with my head on my shoulders?" I pulled a face, slightly disappointed even though I knew those were good things. "Nothing like, 'I bet that Phelps girl makes a lot of money in her secret life as a pirate'?"

"I'm sorry, but no. They must all think you just really like parrots."

"Hmph. Rude."

"Those are good things, you know. Better than what people have said about me," he stated lightly.

I felt a prick of shame at the things I'd thought about him in the past. "True," I said, matching his light tone. "But everyone thinks of you as so dangerous and exciting. It's kind of a bummer to find out everyone thinks I'm a total dud."

"Well, you didn't let me get to the good stuff."

I bumped my shoulder against his. "I am not a princess. I'm just confused because you probably spent a lot of money on this truck. You'd think it would float along like one of those Cadillac sedans. *My car* is more comfortable than this."

"I'm offended by everything you just said." He shot me a quick, horrified glance. "Your car is one pothole away from becoming a go-cart, and trucks are not meant to feel like you're driving a couch down the road."

"A go-cart? How dare you!" I shook my head slowly, even as a smile tickled at my mouth. I adored this banter. "I understand you've got an image to maintain as Mr. Tough Guy, but you didn't have to drag my poor car into it."

"Sorry, casualty of war."

"You'll notice I didn't say Mr. Totally Responsible Guy?" I sighed. "No one wants to hang around with him. No wonder I didn't date, like, ever."

He squeezed my hand. "Nah, all the guys were just intimidated by you."

I laughed. "Nice try. I can see how they'd be scared of the short girl sitting in the corner trying to tame her curls. I'm sure the acne that lasted way past adolescence lent me an unapproachable air."

"I can safely say you've grown out of your awkward teenage stage."

I tilted my head, thoughtful as I watched the dotted yellow lines on the road pass by. I was fairly certain he'd admitted that he found me attractive. . . but most girls aren't hoping to be complimented on their lack of acne. I'd like for him to find me as tempting as I found him. It was only fair.

"Thanks?" I replied after a moment.

He chuckled. "You need something better than that, huh? How's this then? I like your eyes, your smile, the way your hair curls all around your head and it's like an extension of you. I like your curves and the way you walk. I like how you hold yourself and how you aren't afraid to stand your ground. I like how soft your hands are. And kissing you is more than I thought . . . " He broke off as though he were suddenly embarrassed. What had started off as a joke now felt so real inside the tiny cab. Awareness sparked around us as my pulse leapt at the realization that he *was* attracted to me. Which should have been obvious, but still, it was quite lovely to hear.

My swallow sounded loud in the silent space. "Wow."

He immediately shook his head. "What do you say we just listen to some music and look at some cars?"

I leaned my head on his shoulder, relieved and amused. "Sounds like a deal."

He mumbled something under his breath that sounded a lot like, "Oh, thank goodness," before releasing my hand to turn up the music. But even the beat of the bass didn't overtake the beating of my own heart.

By the time Connor pulled into the parking lot of the event center, we had moved on to lighter topics. I smiled as we walked in, hand in hand. The event center was huge, with a promised three hundred and fifty cars on display. It was eye-opening.

"I didn't even know there were that many different kinds of cars!" I exclaimed to Connor while pointing at the sign. "It's like I've been dropped into another universe."

"It's a great universe to be dropped into."

I pulled up our linked hands to wave them in front of us. "I'm going to need you to keep a hold of this hand so that I can look around and not have to worry about steering."

"I'm your seeing-eye date?"

I turned to look at him with playful eyes. "You really get me."

As promised, he held on and I soaked it all in. For the next two hours I couldn't get enough. I'd never been that interested in cars before, but seeing Connor so in his element was eye candy. There were cars of every imaginable shape and color, many of them with signs saying not to touch and velvet ropes keeping the public at bay.

Those that weren't off limits became my personal playground. I ran my hands over their smooth lines, thought about the colors the factories had mixed for their paint, climbed in, and popped the trunks while Connor read the specs and occasionally spoke with the retailers.

"This is amazing," I said as I climbed out of a cherry red sedan. "I'll bet this one would feel like cruising on a recliner."

He'd reached out a hand to help me get out of the back seat and then used it to tug me close. His hands came to my waist, and he pulled me in so that my forehead was lightly touching his chin. "Are you always like this at expos?"

I lifted my shoulders. "This is my first one. I like it here."

"I'm glad. Are you ready for some dinner?" I tilted my head back and nodded. "There's a food court just through those doors if you wanted to stay here." He used his head to gesture to our left.

"Oh good, because I've only seen about two hundred of the promised cars."

"I think I accidentally unearthed a car junkie."

"Trust me, I'm as surprised as you are. Before this all I cared about was if it could get me somewhere. Now, well, now I'm daydreaming about cup holders and seat warmers. Hey, do you think they'd let us eat in that one car that had the massager in the back seat? That was amazing."

His lips curved upward. "I don't think even a pretty girl like you is going to be allowed to bring food inside here."

On a sudden whim I pushed up onto my toes and pressed a quick kiss to his chin. The growth of his stubble was prickly against my lips, making them tingle. His hands flexed on my waist.

"That was for calling me pretty," I said. "Don't worry, I'll get over the disappointment of eating at a plastic table." I kept my tone bright despite the butterflies the look in his eyes was bringing to life. It was the world's biggest rush to be free to touch him after so many years of being hands off. "They'd better have churros, though."

"Anything for the princess." He let go of my waist and took my hand in his, leading the way out a wall of doors and into the food court.

An hour later we were headed home, the truck bumping along underneath us, our shoulders and legs once again pressed together.

"Okay, so if you could have any car in the entire world, what would you drive?" I asked him.

"Any car?"

"Yeah. Money is no object. Any car at all." He shrugged. "Connor, you're a mechanic who just took me to a car expo. Obviously you've thought about this. What would it be?"

He grinned. "I'm sorry to disappoint you, but I really like my truck."

"Is this how I find out that you're not a dreamer?" I replied.

"I have dreams. I also have simple tastes in life, which makes it easy to be happy." He pressed his knee against mine.

"Ah, now I understand why we're dating. You're a man of simple tastes and I'm a simple girl."

"You are anything but simple." He stated it so firmly that my eyes grew large.

I turned in the seat to look directly at him. "I was joking around, but I do believe you're accusing me of being complicated."

He shook his head, and his eyes danced in the headlights of oncoming cars. "You're not simple, and you're not complicated."

"Difficult?"

"Eh." He shrugged again and I couldn't help but laugh.

"Well, for the record, you're much more difficult than I'll ever be."

"I'm about as easygoing as they come." He grinned.

"Whatever." I sat back in my seat, but a smile remained on my lips. "I still need to know what car you'd drive."

"What car would you drive?"

"Gasp, Connor, as if I'd ever give up Old Reliable," I replied.

He laughed out loud, something I'd come to realize didn't happen often. "My apologies."

"You're forgiven. When she dies, and we both know she will, I'd love to drive that purple one with the swivel seat on the passenger side.

I'd be the only person in Oak Hills with a purple car, and it would be so cool to have your seat face backwards so you can have, like, a dinner party while driving."

"The driver would be left out."

"That's fine."

"As long as the driver isn't you?"

"Obviously." I pulled a face.

"A woman of simple needs."

"Like I said before, you really get me."

His hand had been resting on my leg while we drove, but now he reached for my hand and wove my fingers through his before pulling our linked hands onto his leg. I liked the contact. I loved the way his larger hand, calloused and a little rough, enveloped mine completely. I liked the way he felt strong and steady next to me.

"I'm really glad you came out with me today."

"I wasn't sure if we could spend a whole evening together, but we did pretty good," I said. I leaned more heavily against his side and wiggled down in as close as I could so that my cheek lay against the top of his arm. "I'm proud of you for not pretending I was a stranger when I accidentally started the engine of that black truck. Who leaves keys in display models?"

"Honking the horn with your bum while you leaned over to see the backseat of the red truck was worse."

"Only because I was wedged for a minute, so it was the thirty-second honk." I blushed a little in the darkness, even as a sound of amusement bubbled out. "Thirty seconds feels like hours when it's echoing so loudly that thousands of voices stop talking and turn to look."

Another laugh burst out of him, loud and full, and it made my stomach try to rise into my throat as I felt his shoulder shake under my cheek. I liked it. "I believe that was the world's longest honk," he said.

I nodded. "It was so embarrassing. I'll try to behave better next time."

He turned his head enough to deliver a barely perceptible kiss to my curls. "You're well enough behaved for me."

I remained silent after he said that, and he didn't push for more conversation either. For my part, I was lulled into a sense of peace and comfort as the miles sped by. It was fully dark, with headlights and taillights flashing in front of us like beacons. The stars were brighter in the pass than they had been in Springfield.

The sound of Connor's even breathing, the soft music playing in the background, his hand in mine—it all wove a spell of contentment around me that I couldn't remember experiencing with anyone outside of my family. Even Kelly. Kelly and I rarely shared quiet moments. We were too busy laughing and talking when we were together.

The feeling seeped through me, and I sank into it. I didn't want to analyze it. I didn't want to try to figure out why Connor, and why now. I just wanted to ride that wave all the way.

CHAPTER TWENTY-THREE

I was walking past my mom's bedroom two days later and heard Mom talking softly on the phone. I glanced in and immediately knew Dad was on the other end of the line. Her profile faced me, and I could see the strain in her face while she spoke, which had me on edge. I wasn't sure what was happening. From what I'd seen, Mom had seemed more relaxed, more herself since the blowup a month or so ago. Sadie had made some good adjustments too, and I had felt as though some of the constant weight in our home was beginning to evaporate. I didn't want this conversation to take us backward, and I especially didn't want Mom to be hurt repeatedly.

I wasn't sure if I should broach the topic with her, but she was still on the phone when I had to leave. The image of her floated through my mind throughout the day, and as soon I arrived home that evening, I decided to find out what was going on. No more hiding things.

"Where's Mom?" I asked Sadie when I walked in the door.

She looked over her shoulder from her seat on the couch. "Cooking dinner."

"Great. I'm starving. Let's go see what she's got going."

Sadie seemed a little surprised at my request for her to join me but willingly stood and came along. Mom was standing by the stove, stirring a pot. Her hair, usually down these days, was pulled back with a rubber band to keep it out of our dinner. Her stance wasn't relaxed and her eyes closed slowly before she took a deep breath and finally noticed us. She pasted on the same sad smile we hadn't seen for weeks and my appetite plummeted.

"Dinner will be ready in about five minutes if you'd like a chance to wash up." Her voice sounded strange and tense. Her face was flushed, and she fidgeted with the apron she had tied around her waist.

"What's going on?" Sadie demanded abruptly.

Mom turned back to her stirring. "I'm making spaghetti."

"I know Dad called this morning," I said kindly. "Did something happen?"

She pulled the spoon out of the sauce and turned off the gas flame before lifting the pot and placing it on a hot pad on the table. "Nothing is wrong."

"Please don't go back to keeping secrets from us," Sadie pleaded in a soft voice.

That caused Mom to look up with alarm on her face. "Oh, sweetheart, I'm not keeping any secrets from you." She hurried to pull Sadie into a hug. "I promise."

"Then what's the problem?" I asked again.

"Relationships can be tricky, with speed bumps and adjustments. Dad and I are just, well, it's going to take time to figure everything out." Mom released Sadie and got the garlic bread out of the oven.

"Like what kinds of things?" I got a knife from the counter to cut the bread with.

"We were married for such a long time and there's a lot to work out. We had a little disagreement a few days ago about some of those issues, but we chatted this morning and I'm sure things will be fine." Sadie and I exchanged looks over Mom's head. We didn't entirely believe her. She read our expressions and hers softened. "Talking is better than not talking. We didn't talk for a long time. This is a good thing, even if it's painful."

My shoulders relaxed a bit as I felt the truth of her words. Talking was better than silence, yes. "Anything we can help with?"

Mom put the food on the table and turned to us. "I've asked a lot of you girls over the past years. You've had to be really patient with me. Do you think you can be patient a little longer until I feel stronger on my own two feet again?"

Sadie and I moved toward her without a word and wrapped her in a hug. We could be patient. We just had to be. It was the only way we'd be happy again.

*****

The next day I had a blueberry muffin on the drive to work, exhausted after a night of praying that my parents could find a way to separate without too much hurt. The truth was that I still didn't fully understand relationships. The ebb and flow, push and pull nature of them remained a mystery. All I really had was hope. Hope that the right things would fall into place.

After work I stepped out into the sunny world and took a deep breath. It was a gorgeous May afternoon. Flowers had finally decided to really bloom, and there was almost no real chill left in the breeze. It felt like a day for spontaneity, so I decided to drop in on Connor and see if he minded me studying for a while before I went home, even though the shop was still open. A zing of excitement tickled my spine as I jumped in my car and drove the block or so to his shop.

When I arrived the bay doors were open, letting air in. I could hear the sounds of rock music playing, but it wasn't loud enough for me to recognize exactly what the song was. I slung my backpack over my shoulder and, bypassing the lobby, headed to where I could see auburn hair sticking up over the raised hood of a car. That feeling of anticipation washed over me, making my feet move faster. Too fast, because I tripped over a wrench, and the clanging sound announced my presence.

Connor stepped to the side, and his face lit when he saw me. His coveralls were a dark navy blue today, which made his freckles and light eyes stand out even more than usual. He reached into his back pocket for that clean rag he always kept handy and wiped his hands.

"Hey there," he said as he started walking toward me. "Always entering with a bang." His voice was warm, and it was exactly the reception I'd been hoping for.

I met him in the middle of the shop, and rather than say anything I simply smiled up at him, taking it all in. I was so happy to be there and even happier to be wanted. His smile grew under my watch, and he tugged lightly on a curl next to my ear.

"What brings you my way?" he asked after a heartbeat.

I shook my head and blinked a few times. "I just got off work and was hoping you wouldn't mind me studying here for a while before I go home."

"You bet. Do you want to study out here or in the office?"

I was caught off guard by the question. "Is out here an option? Is there, like, an insurance law or something about that?"

"Probably. But I own the place, so . . . "

At that brilliant reasoning, I nodded, wanting suddenly to be wherever he was, which was the entire reason I'd come here in the first place even though I hadn't thought that much about it. "Out here sounds nice, actually."

"Let's get you a chair." He turned and strode into the lobby.

For the hundredth time I found myself watching the way he moved and being mesmerized. Everything about him spoke of a man confident and content within himself. Plus, he wasn't bad to look at. I knew not everyone would appreciate the color of his hair, or his freckles. In fact he'd probably been teased mercilessly about them as a child before his hair had darkened in adulthood, but I found myself constantly fascinated by it.

He came back with the over-sized desk chair from the office, and I grinned while shaking my head. His eyes caught mine and he smiled too. "Here's your throne, princess."

"I accept your offering, kind sir," I joked as he rolled it to the side of the car he'd been working on.

"I think this will work over here. You're a few feet away from the action, so you should be safe."

"Should be?" I moved to where he'd put the chair and hooked my backpack over it.

"I've met you. I don't think I can make any guarantees."

"Are you sure I shouldn't be bubble wrapped first?" I cracked.

"Do I have any grease on my face?" he asked.

I tilted my head to the side, confused by the question. "Um, nope."

"Oh, good."

He closed the space between us and leaned down, bringing his lips softly against mine. He didn't touch me anywhere else, aware that he was filthy from his work, but I reached forward and wrapped my hands around his wrists, wanting to touch him and have his steadiness sooth my worry. He'd intended it as a sweet greeting, and after a few seconds I felt him start to pull away, but I pushed up onto my toes to maintain contact, wanting to stretch it out for another moment, enjoying the sudden race of my heart and the way that bright yellow flared up behind my lids.

He pulled away, but gently. "Livy," he said "What . . . "

I kept my eyes closed and interrupted him. "I know, we're in public, and it's your business."

"I care more about what's got you upset." He was still close enough that I could feel his breath on my forehead. He smelled of cinnamon.

I opened my eyes, released his wrists, and looked up to him. "My dad called and my mom is acting strange and I thought things were getting better, but now I don't know what to think, and I'm not sure how I can hope to be happy while they aren't."

His nodded, his eyes concerned. "I see."

"So, I wanted a safe place to be and I thought of here, and I just drove straight over."

I saw his Adam's apple bob as he swallowed. His mouth worked a bit, as though he was sorting words before letting them out. "I'm really sorry that things with your parents are hard."

"Well, you know a little about that."

"Yeah. I like that you came here."

At that my heart felt immediately lighter. "Really?" He nodded, his face seeming to flush a bit, which I found fascinating. "Okay then."

He quirked a smile at me and turned back to the car he'd been working on. I pulled out my things and settled down into the chair to study. Today's topic was physiology, and I curled my feet up under me as I focused on the material. Time sped by and I found it somewhat ironic that the metallic banging, whirring of air compressors, and humming of engines didn't distract me. I took notes and flipped pages as though I was in a perfectly quiet library. I occasionally shifted position on the big chair, but otherwise I was a statue.

The sight of Connor's work boots coming to stand in front of me was the first indication I had that he was finishing for the day. I looked up to see him standing above me with an expression I couldn't quite read on his face.

"Pizza?" he asked.

"Obviously." I shoved down the thought that I should think about going home to check on everyone and gave him a smile.

"Okay. If you want to stand up I'll carry this chair back in and order."

I uncurled my legs and winced a bit. I'd been sitting that way for long enough to make them fall asleep, and pins and needles shot up my legs as I pushed to stand. I wiggled my limbs while packing up my backpack, and stomped on my feet to wake them up while I walked to the lobby where he was on the phone, ordering the Combo Five, whatever that was.

I set my bag on a lobby chair and turned off the "open" sign before going around and closing the blinds. When he got off the phone, he thanked me and told me he was going to go clean up in the shop bathroom where there was a small shower stall.

I moved into the office and got paper plates and cups from the storage room. I filled the cups with water at the drink station in the lobby and grabbed a few paper towels from the inside bathroom to use as napkins. When Connor reappeared about five minutes later in a T-shirt and jeans, hair wet and hands scrubbed clean, everything was set up.

"I could get used to this," he said as he took it all in.

"Careful, I wouldn't want you to start expecting these kinds of things and become spoiled."

"I'll try to play it cool."

We chatted idly about what I'd been studying that night while we waited for the pizza to come. Thankfully, Connor was considered a priority customer, so it only took about ten more minutes. He suggested I wouldn't want to know why he was a VIP, so I left it alone, although when the teen girl arrived to deliver it, I had a pretty good idea of what was going on and it made me grin.

Connor filled my plate and passed it to me before serving himself.

"Okay," he said as he leaned back in his chair, "I left you alone for hours while you studied, even though you looked seriously tempting sitting in that big chair out there. Now I've filled your stomach. It's time to tell me what's going on with your parents."

"First, this Combo Five is amazing, and thank you for changing my life." I dimpled.

"Liv."

I sank back into the chair. "What? I don't like to talk about this stuff."

"Do you want this to be a real relationship?"

"Probably," I grumbled.

"Then we talk about this stuff."

"I never talked to Blaine about things," I replied stubbornly. He raised an eyebrow, the message loud and clear that things hadn't worked out there. "Fine. You first. What's something going on with you, that's real?"

He took a bite of pizza and chewed thoughtfully while he looked at the ceiling. I could practically see his mind sifting through possible options to share. "I'm tired of being the guy that everyone likes to talk dirt about. I haven't had a girlfriend in a few years. I own a business and a home. I help out in the community. I'd like to be taken seriously and seen as who I am now."

He looked back at me, his gaze direct and open, and in the openness of it I could see the hurt and frustration. I wanted to curl away, knowing how much I'd contributed to that talk over the years.

"I'm sorry for the things I added to that conversation," I whispered.

He didn't let me off the hook easily. He quietly watched me for more seconds than I dared to count. Finally he blinked and dipped his chin once. "Thanks. Your turn, and don't try to sugarcoat it or make a joke of it."

"This seems a little heavy for, what, like our second date?"

"Is this a date? Because if you think it is, well, life just got easier for me." He wiggled his eyebrows and I rolled my eyes. "Come on, tell me."

"My dad lied to our family . . . " I began, and then I told him everything. It felt as though I'd finally uncorked the bottle and was tipping all the spoiled liquid out. I told him about my mom working her two jobs, my dad living his high life, Sadie and her suffering, me trying to hold it all together. I totally unburdened myself. When it was all done, I slumped forward in my chair and laid my head on the desk. It was strange to have someone besides Kelly know everything. It was both freeing and terrifying. I wondered if he understood just how much this moment meant.

Connor, who had been silent the whole time, sat up in his chair across the desk and leaned forward to place his hand on my head. "That sounds like a lot."

"Yeah."

"I don't know if this makes it better or not, but I would have never guessed all that was happening."

I turned my head to the side and looked at him with one eye. "Really? You didn't look at me and think I seemed to be barely keeping it together?"

"No. Not at all. You blaze around town like you haven't got a care in the world. That must have been really lonely."

That insight had me spellbound, and the words slipped out unexpectedly. Words I'd thought often but had never said aloud. "People assume that strong people don't need any help."

He nodded slowly, chewing his lip and running his hand through my hair. I closed my eyes at the gentle gesture, surprised at how much I was loving it.

"Thanks for telling me," he said quietly.

"Thanks for not going deer in the headlights," I replied.

"You talk a big game, Livy, but nothing you've said or done has scared me off. I'm not going anywhere."

"Good."

CHAPTER TWENTY-FOUR

When I entered the kitchen the next morning Mom was already gone and Sadie was standing around looking a little lost. I had a thought that I kicked myself for never having before.

"Want to grab breakfast at the diner? My treat?"

She startled a bit, having not heard me come in, but a smile gradually bloomed and she nodded. "Yeah, I do."

We gathered our things and got in my car before I asked, "Did you see Mom this morning?"

She shook her head. "It's just so weird. It's hard to keep track of how Mom and Dad feel about each other. I don't like it."

My heart went out to my sister, once again. I'd had the first eighteen years of my life with parents who acted like, well, parents. She must be really confused all the time.

"Yeah, it's strange," I replied. "The good news is that they are still talking and they're figuring it out, even if it's . . . "

"Totally dysfunctional."

"Yes. That."

It was still early enough that the diner wasn't in full swing, and I waved at Kelly as we entered, signaling that we'd take a seat at the open counter area. She nodded and went back to taking orders at a booth. We climbed onto two red vinyl stools, the material squeaking as we got settled.

"What are you going to have?" I asked Sadie, who was perusing the menu.

"Oatmeal and apple juice."

"You might be the only kid I know who orders oatmeal," I teased. She bopped her head back and forth once and shrugged. "Do you want anything in it?"

"Like what?"

"Like raisins or . . . "

"Pass."

I stood from the stools and walked back to the kitchen to give Jake and the cooks our order, hoping to save Kelly some effort seeing as we had an unspoken rule that we didn't tip each other. I filled our drinks and went back to where we were sitting.

"Can you just do that when you're not working?" Sadie asked. I nodded. "What was your first job?"

My mind blanked for a second over the fact that my sister didn't know what my first job had been. Quickly doing the math I realized she'd only have been eight or nine when I started working. "I worked at that old drive-up car hop place that closed down. I had to wear roller skates and deliver food."

Sadie surprised me by chuckling. "Sounds dangerous."

"It was. Are you thinking about getting a job?"

"Maybe. I only have one more year of high school left. I should probably be thinking about my future. I guess I'll need some money." She ran her finger around the rim of her juice glass, never taking her eyes off the liquid.

"What do you think you'll do after graduation?" I tried to keep my voice as casual and uninterested as possible, afraid of not playing it cool enough and her closing up.

"I'm thinking about doing, like, dental hygiene or something."

I leaned my chin in my hands to keep my jaw from hitting the countertop. What? I had no idea she'd actually thought about it.

"I hear you can make a good living doing that," I said.

"Yeah. I'd have to move somewhere else to go to school, though."

"True."

She finally looked up at me, and I was taken aback by how worried she looked. "It's just, I don't really want to leave you alone to handle everything. I'd feel like I was running away."

This time I allowed my natural reaction to show, relaxing my lips into a smile as my heart swelled. Here was something I could understand. I'd made many of my decisions based on not wanting to desert my family. It was a struggle I didn't want her to go through as well.

"Don't take this the wrong way, sis, but please feel free to run away."

One side of her mouth lifted up, and she returned to staring at her apple juice. "Okay. I'll think about it."

"You don't need to worry about us. Chase your life."

"Is that why you're going to nursing school?"

I nodded and kicked my feet back and forth under the stool. "Do you really want to know why I'm so set on getting a degree?" She again turned to look at me. "Because I want to make sure that no matter what happens in my life, I'm taken care of."

She looked away and picked up her cup, taking a big sip and letting it swish around in her mouth before swallowing. "Same. I hate feeling helpless, which is all I usually feel."

"I know. I realized I had to stop feeling that way and do something."

"Yeah."

Jake himself popped out of the kitchen, carrying our orders. Sadie's oatmeal was steaming and looked surprisingly tempting, but I still would have chosen my omelet. We thanked Jake and dug in, aware that Sadie needed to get to school.

"What brings you two fine looking ladies here today?" Kelly's chipper voice greeted us as she came around the end of the counter.

"Sister date," I replied with a smile of my own.

Kelly nodded. "I'm super glad you're here. I need a Connor update."

At this Sadie's head popped up and she looked at me. "Connor?"

Kelly's expression became mischievous. "Oh, you didn't know?" she said with faked innocence. "I guess I thought Liv would have told you that she's dating the freakishly good-looking town mechanic now."

Sadie's eyes grew mischievous. "I kind of figured it was coming after he cleaned our house."

Kelly's eyes bulged. "He cleaned your house?" Her voice rose on the word *house*, which caused a few people to glance our way.

Flustered, I shook my head and looked back and forth between them. "No, I mean, he did, but, it's not, well . . . "

Kelly beamed and held up a hand. "Allow me to translate, Sadie. Yes, he did clean your house. And no, she's not going to admit anything to either of us. Even if we ask her how his big, strong, hunky arms feel when he . . . "

"Stop." I put my face in my hands. "Oh my gosh, Kelly. One day you will be my cause of death."

"Unless drowning in Connor's eyes gets you first," she retorted. Sadie chuckled and I rubbed my face back and forth in my hands. "We're dying for details here."

I sat up and took a deep breath. "Okay, I've gone out with Connor. We've been on like one and a half dates, so I wouldn't really say we're official yet."

Kelly playfully leaned forward and whispered, "Does Connor know that you aren't officially dating? Because he's been telling everyone that you're his GF." On the "GF" part she really lowered her voice and mouthed the letters.

"What?"

"Yep. It's the truth. If you don't believe me, ask around." She opened her mouth like she was going to pose the question to the entire diner, which forced me to launch forward on my stool and cover her mouth with my hand.

"Don't you dare."

"Fine." She shook my hand off. "Tell me about him cleaning your house."

"Sadie can tell you. I wasn't there."

"Wait, it really happened?" Kelly's eyes grew larger with delight, if that was actually possible at this point.

Sadie jumped in. "Remember a little while ago when Mom and I were so sick? One day he just showed up at our house all bossy and gruff, and he cleaned the whole first floor. Then he brought some soup for us to eat."

Kelly kept her gaze locked on Sadie. "And Liv had no idea?"

Sadie shook her head. "None. He swore us to secrecy. But he must not understand girl code, because we told her the second she asked who'd done it."

Kelly laughed and clapped her hands together in front of her chest. "This is probably—no, yes, definitely—the best thing I've heard all week."

"He was being friendly," I defended.

"Yeah, because Connor is known as the cleaning fairy around town. Liv, he's obviously been falling for you for a long time," Kelly chirped. A bell dinged behind us, which brought her back to quick attention. "Oh, yeah, work. I've got to run. But, man, you've really made my morning." She skirted off with a little cheer.

"So, you're dating Connor now?" Sadie's eyes, amused and interested, swerved to me.

"Kind of, yes."

"Nice. What is that, two guys in the last few months? Things are heating up for you," she teased. I tossed her a look and dug into my omelet.

* * * * *

For three days straight I kept catching my mom in clandestine phone conversations with Dad. Things seemed to be going okay with their discussions, because Mom wasn't quite as mopey afterwards, but she still told us very little. Sadie was quiet about it, so I didn't know how she felt, but she continued to be more pleasant to be around, which I figured was a good sign.

For those same three days, even though I spoke to Connor on the phone or saw him when he came into the diner to eat, I avoided asking him if he was telling people we were a couple. Enough had shifted for me lately, and I didn't necessarily want to have a DTR (define the relationship talk) at this point. It was too soon for that. I was content knowing he liked me and wanted to spend time with me. Other things could wait.

I was excited when he arranged to pick me up on Saturday evening, after his shop closed and I was done working. When I answered the door, however, I was caught off guard by seeing an unfamiliar silver four-door truck parked in the driveway. Before I could ask about it, he leaned down and gave me a peck on the cheek.

"You're a sight for sore eyes," he whispered against my ear, and distracting chills raced up my spine. "You ready? Did you grab a jacket?" I nodded and held up the jacket in my clenched hand.

He took my free hand and walked me to the waiting vehicle. As we neared I could see Kelly cheerily waving at me from the passenger seat and Scott smiling behind the steering wheel.

I turned to Connor. "Kelly and Scott?"

"Yeah, I mentioned an idea for a date to Kelly. She helped me work it out and then begged to come along. I thought a double date sounded good, especially considering they helped with everything." He opened the rear passenger door for me and I climbed in.

"Hey, Liv. You ready for a wild night in nature?" Kelly chirped as she craned her head to see me.

"Come again?"

Her hand flew over her mouth, and her eyes grew round as she looked to where Scott was shaking his head. "Oopsies. I think Connor wanted it to be a surprise. Act surprised, okay?" she said back to me.

"Won't be hard," I mumbled under my breath. I had no idea where we were going or what we were up to. All Connor had said was to wear good shoes and bring a jacket.

Connor slid in next to me and nodded to Scott, who put the car in reverse and backed out onto my quiet neighborhood street. I looked over to Connor, and his smile faded a little at whatever my expression was telling him. My guess is that it is was screaming, "What the devil is happening here?"

"Trust me, I think you're going to really like this."

"Did you bring a treat for later?" I asked, trying to squash down my nerves. I wasn't big on surprises or feeling at someone else's mercy.

"Obviously. And before you ask, yes, it's chocolate based."

I nodded and did my best to relax into a smile. "Okay then."

He took my hand and, noticing how cold my fingers felt, rubbed it between his own for a moment while he and Scott talked directions. The conversation was light on the way up the mountain. We headed the opposite way of Springfield, and as the road turned to a simple two-lane surrounded by forest, I relaxed and enjoyed the pleasure of being with Connor and our two friends.

After about thirty minutes Scott pulled onto a dirt road, and we began climbing higher into the trees. It was beautiful up there, and it had been a long time since I'd spent any time off the beaten path. My parents, back in better times, had often brought Sadie and me up for Saturday picnics. Nostalgia flowed over me like gooey caramel, sweet and sugary, and I appreciated the sweetness of those happier memories.

After another ten minutes we crested a small ridge and found ourselves in an open meadow. Trees ringed the circular opening, with a few jagged rocks here and there that would offer a great view of the valleys around us if we climbed on top of them.

"Okay, we're here." Connor squeezed my hand before releasing it and getting out. I followed suit, opening my side and getting out too. He was waiting behind the vehicle, where he'd reached over the truck bed and was pulling out a duffel bag.

"Here, man, why don't you take this one," Scott said, trading the bag Connor was holding for another. "Kell, honey, can you grab the blanket? Liv, if you'll snag the picnic basket that would be great."

We all followed directions and then walked in a line to the middle point of the meadow. Kelly and I spread the blanket out, and we all sat our things down on top of it. Connor took a deep breath and offered me a smile.

"I know how much you like to paint nature scenes. I thought maybe it would be fun to come up here in the late afternoon, when the light is so perfect, and take a ton of pictures. Trees, flowers, rocks, people. I'll get them printed for you and you can use them to paint from."

"Scott has great cameras that will really capture all the little details of everything," Kelly inserted. "I came along for a romantic picnic dinner."

I looked around the meadow and chewed my lip for a minute while I tried to hide the swirling emotions that had risen at the knowledge that he'd planned something so focused on my personal interests. Had anyone ever done that for me? The answer was no, and the reason was simple. No one else had ever been let into that secret part of my life.

My silence must have worried him, because he moved closer to me and ran a hand down my arm to take my hand. "Is this okay? I know you said that painting is your private thing, but you also know that I'm really supportive of that, so . . . "

"She's trying not to get all mushy weird over it," Kelly suddenly stated. "Give her a minute to breathe. She's happy."

Kelly's outburst made the three of us laugh. Connor's eyes asked if I was really okay and I nodded. "This is great."

"Good. Scott will show us what he brought and give us a few pointers first, and then we can hike around and take some pictures. We can take a break for dinner and get some more pictures at twilight if you want."

"Yeah, I want." I grinned.

Scott really did have fancy camera equipment, and I paid close attention while he explained how everything worked. I knew I wouldn't be able to afford to replace any of this if I messed something up. At the end of the tutorial, all four of us slung cameras over our necks. While the guys finished up some last-minute stuff, Kelly came to stand next to me.

"When I found out what Connor wanted to do I almost melted into a puddle. He's kind of the greatest."

"Yeah." I flushed and her eyes danced. "I just have one question."

"Shoot," she said.

"How many strange and unexplainable pictures has Scott taken of you with these fancy cameras of his?"

"If you mean tasteful and inspiring, a lot."

"Have you become his muse?"

"From the first moment he laid eyes on me at that grocery store. Now, if you'll excuse us, he's coming toward me with that artistic look on his face. I think we have some rocks to photograph." She gave her hips a little wiggle as she walked to meet him. He bent to whisper something to her and her whole face lit up.

Connor came to stand next to me. "Those two are . . . "

"Peculiar?"

"I was going to say nice together, but I think your word is the better choice."

"Smart man. Shall we go find a tree that wants to be painted?" I held up my camera and looked through the viewfinder. "I see some interesting things over there." I pointed and we started walking.

"How are things going at home?" he asked, falling into step beside me.

"Odd, but good."

"Odd how?"

"Odd, like, how do you really feel about your parents having secret conversations?"

"Well, that sounds like an improvement over the last time we talked."

"Yeah. It probably is." I stopped walking, having spied a small, purple-pink wildflower blooming. Connor was quiet while I took a few pictures from different angles. It was going to look really amazing all blown up on canvas. When I stood and started walking again, I picked up the conversation. "You know, they've been married for twenty-six years, or something close to that. That's a long time. Longer than I've even been alive. It's hard to imagine sometimes."

"It can't be easy to take all that apart."

"I know. Even more interesting is that there are people who manage to stay together." I paused again, intrigued by a view of the tree line with oranges of afternoon light streaming through the branches. "The science behind that would be fascinating," I said as I lined up the shot.

"The science?" The tone of his voice caught my attention, and I looked over my shoulder to see his eyes traveling over my face. "Hold still," he said, and lifted his own camera to snap a shot of me.

"I wasn't ready, or smiling, or anything."

"You were perfect." He let the camera hang from the lanyard around his neck. "Now, you were saying something about science?"

"Right." I turned and walked closer to the tree line, interested in photographing the branch and trunk detail up close. "All those laws of attraction and chemistry—they must fade over time, so what keeps people together?"

"There are things science can't explain, you know."

I gave him a look. "Of course I know that." I lifted a branch out of my way and held it for Connor to pass by as well. "People stay together for a lot of different reasons."

"Now I'm curious what you think those reasons are."

"Things like common interests, commitment to promises made, mutual affection, comfort, tax breaks, and companionship." I listed them off, all the while scanning through the camera to find exactly what I was looking for.

"What an encouraging list. No wonder you think chemistry fades." He leaned back against a tree and folded his arms across his chest. "At the risk of starting a fight with you, I think you're full of it."

I let the camera fall from my hands, the tug on the lanyard telling me it was secure, and put my hands on my hips. "Well, I hate to break it to you, but those are fighting words."

"Have you ever simply looked at someone, without knowing anything about their personality or character, and found them attractive?" he asked.

I flashed back to sitting with Kelly, her showing me her new braces, and both of us seeing Connor for the first time. He'd entered the cafeteria with a girl, holding her hand and laughing at something she'd said. I could still remember how it had felt to have the heat of a first crush crawl up my skin and cover my face. Then I thought of the day Blaine walked in to the diner and gave me a smile. Both times, I'd felt instantly attracted.

"Honestly? Yes."

"What happened to end that feeling?"

I pulled the camera up to my eye and snapped a picture of the tree I was standing next to as I thought about it. "I guess it was when I got to know them."

"Right. So, you realized that you aren't going to get along with this person and the chemistry fades, never turning into love."

"I guess so."

"I know so. There's no way you can predict any of that with a checklist. It's about a feeling in your gut. I don't think you've ever actually been in love with someone, which is why you think it all comes down to science."

My teeth clenched with hurt. It didn't feel good to have that fact brought to my attention in such an emotionless way. To be told that just because I hadn't experienced a certain thing meant I had no right to discuss it was, well, irking.

"Please, do go on," I said to him. I turned my back and pretended to be engrossed in a root sticking up out of the earth.

"If we flip that same idea around, it stands to reason that if you first feel attracted, and then find out your personalities are compatible, there's no reason for chemistry to die. That, I believe, is what being in love is. Friendship combined with chemistry."

"Uh-huh." I snapped a few more pictures, entirely focused on avoiding his perceptive gaze, even though his arguments were racing through my mind on a wave of irritation.

"Liv?" His voice was close to my ear, which startled me into almost dropping the camera.

"Yeah?" I dared to glance up at him, knowing he'd see what I was feeling.

"You're mad now."

"No, I'm not. I'm open to hearing other points of view," I defended. Weakly.

"You want to use that camera to take a picture of my insides, using my throat to get there." His eyes crinkled at the corners, which helped some tension ease.

I made a face. "No, no, I really enjoyed hearing about how I've never experienced love and have no idea what chemistry is."

"I was only trying to point out that there are some things that can't be explained but are very real. It's okay to lean into the mystifying things in life."

"Like dating you?" I cracked.

"Exactly. I can't imagine any scientist on earth would put us together." He took me by the shoulders and turned me so we were face to face. "Yet here we are."

"I sure never saw it coming."

"Me either. You're different from anyone else I've dated."

I pulled another face, feeling a little of the hurt return, even though I'd insulted him many times. "Thanks?"

"Before you get mad at me, the truth is"—he swallowed and looked away—"I don't think I've ever really been in love either." His face did that cute flushed thing that I'd only seen a couple of times, and I was entranced. "The initial chemistry and attraction faded with everyone else because they weren't right for me. But with you, well, it's like it just keeps growing and I can't get enough."

My throat suddenly felt like I was trying to swallow my own tongue. My fingers were nerveless, and my toes curled in my sensible shoes. His eyes were bright and open, and from this close I could see that the stubble coming in on his cheeks was at least two shades darker than his hair, the color of the cocoa he loved. The sunlight glinted off of it, making him look glittery.

"I hear you've been telling people around town that we're a couple," I stated, feeling at loose ends. How could he be so open? Where did he get the courage to say things like that? I was courageous in a lot of ways, but sharing my heart wasn't one of them.

He placed his hands on the sides of my neck, which caused a stutter to race straight down to my stomach. "I've been calling you my girlfriend."

I ran my tongue over my lips. "That's pretty bold of you."

"I'm a bold guy." One side of his mouth quirked up.

"But you can't know yet, about us. We haven't been dating for long enough to claim a real relationship."

"It's sad that I have to spell this out for you, but we are, in fact, right in the middle of an actual, factual relationship."

I shook my head. "No. We're just getting to know each other and having fun while we decide if we want to keep seeing each other."

"I could start telling everyone we're pals who feel a lot of chemistry for each other instead."

My mouth softened as a smile bloomed, but he leaned down and pressed his own smiling mouth to mine before I could reply. This time it wasn't the yellows and reds that burst into my mind, but cool blues and deep greens, the whites and browns of tree bark, the pink of the flower I'd captured before.

My hands climbed his arms and clung to his shoulders as his hands left my neck to float lightly down my back, all the while inching me a little closer to him. As the kiss went on my legs felt shaky and my head dizzy. The cool mountain air against my cheeks was in direct contrast to the warmth surrounding me. I had to pull away and catch my breath.

"Connor." I turned my face to the side and gulped down some air.

He pressed his warm lips against my temple. I could feel puffs of breath pushing at my curls. "I was trying to make a point." He breathed on a chuckle. "But I've forgotten what it was."

I smiled even though he wouldn't see it and wrapped my arms around his waist. I tucked my head in under his chin and listened to his heartbeat. "I think your point was that you're hopelessly attracted to me," I said.

"Yes, well, point proven then, eh?" His arms wrapped me tightly against him. "There's nothing scientific about what's happening here." He whispered it so softly I barely heard the words.

But I did hear them. And they were words that I both craved and feared. The Connor who I had watched from a distance for a long time was only a shadow of the real Connor I had gotten to know. Fourteen-year-old me was cheering with pom-poms. Twenty-four-year-old me knew there were certain things—and people—the heart would never get over.

CHAPTER TWENTY-FIVE

The next Monday was the official start of finals week. I had warned Connor during our nature day Saturday that we probably wouldn't see each other until it was all over. He was disappointed, but understanding, which was one heck of a guilt-inducing combination, especially considering I felt the same way. In a shockingly short amount of time, I'd become more attached to him than I was comfortable with.

The week became a steady flow of study, eat, work, study, sleep. The tests started on Wednesday, and I had two that day and two on Thursday. The past couple of months had been hectic, but I felt like I'd given it my best. Still, I clamped down on anything social and put my nose to the grindstone.

Mom and Sadie surprised me by becoming my biggest cheerleaders. They had meals ready for me, and even the occasional shoulder rub or chocolate bar made an appearance. I almost bawled each time one of them reached out to me. This was family, and I had missed it so much.

In the interest of honesty, I did talk to Connor every night before I conked out. Our conversations were brief, maybe fifteen minutes at the most, but they became a highlight of the day for me.

Monday night we talked about nothing important, just laughing about a customer at the diner who was eerily similar to a customer he'd had the week before. Tuesday night we talked about pets we'd had and agreed that pets belonged in childhood, as neither of us were interested in caring for an animal now. I wanted freedom to travel and see things. He just worked too many hours. Wednesday night he called to see how my finals that day had gone. They'd been intense, and I'd shocked myself by breaking down in tears, telling him I was sure I'd failed. When he'd said he was coming over I'd firmly told him not to. I needed to go to bed, and if he was there I'd want to stay snuggled up on the couch all night long. Instead I'd asked him to tell me the three most embarrassing moments of his life, which had resulted in me laughing so hard that Mom had come in to see what was going on. Thursday night was a repeat of Wednesday's tears and my worries, which meant it was my turn to tell him my three most embarrassing moments.

Friday finally came and I was dead on my feet at work. Exhausted after my shift, I drove over to Mainstreet Mechanic, intent on seeing the one person I wanted to see the most. The week of nothing but short conversations had somehow forged a deeper connection to him. It was like without other distractions, all we had was our words and our voices, and somehow it felt more open and honest.

Driving straight there without calling first was a gamble, seeing as it was already seven thirty and he might have headed home, but the light was on in the office and my heart tripped at the sight of it. The front door was locked, so I shot him a text telling him to come let me in. His smiling face appearing at the glass door made my knees weak.

"Hey, you." He held the door for me to walk through, turned and locked it, and then turned back to me. He opened his arms and I walked right in, nearly shivering with delight as I leaned against him. "I'm glad you dropped by. I'm working on a few things in the office, but I'm almost done. Come take a load off. You look tired." His warm hand on the small of my back soothed some of the aches that had gathered there.

We walked into the office and he went behind his desk, sitting in the big chair. I glanced at the other chairs, hard and cold, and then back to where he was sitting. In a moment of exhausted boldness I walked around the desk and climbed into his lap. I could feel his startled reaction in the way his body tensed for a moment before his arms came around me. I swung my legs so that they were hanging over one of the arm rests and leaned my head onto his shoulder, tucking my own shoulder under his arm, and sighed.

"That's better," I said as my eyes closed. "I think I'll just live here from now on."

"I can think of worse places."

"Feel free to finish what you were working on. I'm just going to sit here and dream about the beach and a masseuse named Eduardo."

He scooted closer to the desk until I could feel the edge of it against my hip. I didn't mind. The desk took over the job of holding me in place as he released me and started typing on the computer. I didn't mind that either. This might be the happiest I'd felt all week, and as long as he let me stay here, I was fine.

"Liv?" His breath tickled my cheek and I realized I must have dozed. When I opened my eyes the computer screen was off and he'd pushed back away from the desk. His arms were deliciously warm around me.

"Mmm?"

"Does this mean you're free tonight?"

"Yes. I'm hoping you'll let me make you dinner at my place. Sadie is out with friends, but my mom will be there if that's okay."

"*You* are offering to make *me* dinner?"

"Mm-hmm." I snuggled in deeper, pressing my nose against his neck, my eyes closing again.

"After the week you've had? I'd feel like a jerk. Besides, I'm already cooking for my dad at my place. It's our monthly guy night. It would be great to have you come."

"What do you cook for guy night?"

"Meat."

"I eat meat," I replied and he chuckled. "But you work long hours and are tired too. I can make dinner."

"I'd have to take a rain check unless you're coming to my place. My dad is probably headed there now."

At the thought of missing another night with him, I caved, promising myself I'd return the kindness soon. "I'm in. If you're sure I won't get in the way."

One of his hands lightly ran up and down my forearm. "You don't seem to be in a difficult mood, so I'll take the risk." I poked at his chest with one finger. "Come on, sleepy one, I'll drive. We'll come back for your car later."

I climbed clumsily off his lap and took his outstretched hand when he stood. We gathered our things and got into his truck. This time he didn't need to ask for me to slide over by him. I just did it and then let my head flop onto his shoulder. He turned on some soothing music and put a hand on my knee.

"I have no idea where you live," I suddenly realized.

"Unless you've been stalking me, you'd have no reason to."

"Don't you think that's strange, though? You know where I live."

"You've lived in that house your whole life. I'll bet you know where my dad lives, right?" I nodded. "See. I bought a house a few blocks away from him, just outside of town last year."

I grinned and bumped his shoulder. "You're such a grown-up."

"I think a lot of people are relieved that it actually happened."

I laughed. "Nah, they're all disappointed that you're not giving them things to gossip about anymore."

"Like you and Kelly used to? I almost feel bad that you have no one to giggle about behind your hands anymore."

"Uh . . . " I sat up straight, instantly on alert.

"Kelly has told me a little bit about how you and her used to have a great time talking about me in high school, and afterwards."

"Why would she tell you that?"

"So it's true, then?"

"I feel awful about it, truly. But in our defense, you were making time with all the girls, breaking hearts, playing sports. It made for interesting conversation."

"I put on quite a show," he said after a brief pause. His voice was light, but now I knew him well enough to hear the effort behind keeping it that way. "No wonder you wanted nothing to do with me."

"I . . . what? No. . ." I stuttered.

He laughed. "You've steered clear of me for as long as I can remember. You never said one word to me until a few months ago. Then when you did finally talk to me it was to give me rules and say how little you trusted me."

I let my head plop back onto the seat and groaned. "This is a terrible conversation. What do I have to say to make myself stop looking like a monster?"

He took my hand. "You can't save yourself now."

"Well, it isn't like you were trying to be my friend and prove my assumptions wrong."

He nodded. "It's hard to be friends with a girl who clearly wants nothing to do with me. Only a complete fool would try to scale that wall."

"It's not like you ever noticed me before Kelly volunteered you to look at my car," I defended. "I wasn't breaking your heart by keeping away."

His thumb lightly caressed my hand, but he said nothing for a moment. Finally, he whispered, "Another assumption."

Caught off guard I turned to look at him. His profile was serious, his gaze focused on the road. No eye crinkled or lips lifted in a smile. "What are you saying?"

"I'm saying that I noticed you a long time ago."

The cab suddenly felt like it was a thousand degrees, and I was no longer sleepy at all. "Well, how was I supposed to know that?" I threw my free hand up in the air. "You never acted interested or tried to talk to me or gave me any signs."

"You weren't ready, and neither was I."

"What does that mean?" My voice raised. "That kind of philosophical talk hurts my brain."

He chuckled and gave my hand a squeeze. "I'm not sure you're ready for this conversation either."

"Oh, my grandma's pants, you don't just drop something like that out there and not follow up. These little teasers will drive me completely bonkers." While I was ranting, he pulled into the driveway of a bungalow-style home. It distracted me for a moment as I took it in. It was baby blue with a red front door, white trim, and a porch with a swing hanging from the roof. "Well, this house is just darling," I said as I gestured to it. The words came out hot and angry, which startled me into silence.

He put the truck in park and killed the engine. "Thanks. I like it too." He turned to face me. "You're either surprised or annoyed to find out I've been interested for a while."

I slid away from him enough to be able to turn and face him better. "I'm confused. A little nervous, not sure what to think."

He nodded. "I'm not sure why I said anything, really."

"Sometimes stuff slips out." I shrugged. It was true. I said things all the time that were a shocker to me.

"Look, I'm not trying to blow you off or mess with you at all, but my dad's car is here, so we don't have long before we need to go inside." He pointed to a small red pickup parked at the curb that I hadn't noticed. I nodded. "Let me just say this. I've been aware of you, and curious, and interested, but the timing was never right. Either you were putting out the 'stay clear' vibe, or I was trying to build my business and get my life settled. Then Blaine happened, and that was fun to watch." He reached out and took a curl that had drooped down into my eye, his fingers brushing my forehead as he twirled it back up onto my head. "You're beautiful, you're funny, you're determined, independent, never predictable, and yes, I noticed."

My heartbeat filled my ears as I watched the truth flicker in his eyes. I wasn't sure how to respond. I'd realized a little while ago that I had been into Connor for years, but how did I become brave enough to follow his lead and tell him that after only three weeks of dating?

Honesty, and a little cowardice, won out. "I don't know what to say."

"You don't need to say anything. I'm just happy that you're giving me a chance. Come on then, let's get inside."

He opened his door and slid out onto the ground, reaching for my hands and pulling me out the driver's side door too. He kept hold of one hand as he guided me around the door and closed it, but I tugged him to stop him before he could drag me to the front door of his house.

"Connor?" I used our linked hand to pull him back toward me. "I'll never be as good with words as you are. I'm sorry about that. But what you just said, I, uh, I'd noticed you too. I fought it for a long time, um, and I'm really happy that this is happening."

I placed my free hand on the back of his neck and drew his face down to mine, wanting to show him without words how I felt. His lips were formed in a smile as his eyes closed, but a cheery voice interrupted, causing us to break apart without making contact.

"Oh, good, you brought Liv." We looked up at the porch to see Connor's dad, Ken, standing there, a broad smile on his face. "You two must be starving, the way you were . . . "

"Thanks, Pop." Connor waved at him. "We're coming."

Ken turned and walked back into the house. Connor shot me a sheepish grin.

I groaned. "Good thing I was hoping to humiliate myself tonight."

Connor laughed as he released my hand and swung me up into his arms. I squealed loudly and grabbed onto his neck to steady myself. "Welcome to my house, where humiliation is always on the menu."

I laughed, my mind and heart racing as he carried me across the grass. He put me down in front of the door that Ken had left ajar and gestured for me to enter ahead of him. I did with curious eyes and a smile still lingering on my face. It was a cute, cozy, cottage-like home, and I immediately felt comfortable. Everything was in order, not at all how I would have pictured a bachelor pad, and nothing like how I'd imagined that Connor Hunt would live. Further proof about making assumptions.

Ken came out of an archway that opened into a small kitchen. "Hey, Liv, officially." He was holding a glass of cola, and the ice cubes tinkled on the side as he raised it to me in greeting. "What's for dinner, Connor?"

"Steaks and salads. Maybe potatoes if someone wants to cut them up and get them broiling?" Connor replied.

"I can do that," I said quickly, wanting to be helpful.

"You're our guest," Ken replied with shake of his head.

"I can't let you two just take care of me like that. I'm perfectly capable of pitching in," I defended.

Ken and Connor exchanged looks. Then, as though they had actually communicated, they shrugged in identical gestures. Ken looked back at me.

"Suit yourself," he said. "I'll chop veggies for a salad."

"Thanks." My brows furrowed as I followed Connor into the kitchen.

"Why the face?" Connor asked. He reached for a cutting board and handed it to me.

"I'm not helpless, and you don't have to act weird about letting me join in," I mumbled as I took the cutting board out of his hands. "Knife, please."

"We don't think you're helpless. We're just confused about why anyone would want to help when they have the chance to bum around on a chair and watch," Ken teased.

"If I'd come to your house tonight for dinner, would you have wanted me to pitch in cooking, or would you have wanted to serve me as a way of showing that you like me?" Connor asked as he handed me a knife.

I pulled a face. "I'd have probably made you watch while I did all the work."

"Hypocrite," he said lightly. He opened a cupboard and grabbed some potatoes, which he handed to me.

"Well, I don't like other people to take care of me. You know that."

"I very definitely know that about you. Independence is a great quality. So is the ability to be gracious when accepting service from people who care about you," Connor responded.

My stomach muscles tightened. "It would be the best if we could move onto topics about other things. I think I've hit my quota of self-realization today. Gossiping, lack of graciousness, unapproachability. I don't know why you bother with me." I started cutting the potatoes into chunks, feeling mildly disappointed in myself.

"I heard that sloths move so slowly that algae grows in their fur, which can make them look green. They can also turn their heads 270 degrees." Ken's head popped out of the fridge, where he'd been bending over gathering lettuce and vegetables.

I stopped chopping. First I looked to Connor, who was looking to me, and then we both looked at Ken, who was grinning.

"That's really something, Pop." Connor chuckled and Ken winked at me.

"I was born in the Chinese year of the pig. It means I'm responsible, independent, and optimistic, but I can sometimes be lazy and short-tempered," I added. Both men's eyes swung to me.

Connor said casually, "Did you know that a camel can carry about four to six hundred pounds on their backs and can completely shut their nostrils during a sand storm?"

Silence dropped for a few seconds, and then we all started laughing hard. I wiped at my eyes and shared a look with Connor. He said nothing, but I felt suddenly as though I'd never need to explain myself with him because he already knew me and accepted who I was. I could lay down my porcupine quills and allow him to get close. My shoulders relaxed, and we moved on to light chatter while we prepared the meal. The food, and the company, were delicious. And when Connor took me back to my car later that night with a fully belly, I felt as light as air.

CHAPTER TWENTY-SIX

I hummed to myself while mixing paint colors a few days later. Propped on the corner of my easel was the picture of the bright purple-pink flower that I'd taken when we'd gone on our nature double-date with Kelly and Scott. The flower itself was going to take up the entire canvas, and I was excited to get started. I'd spent a long time on the computer and finally found that it was called the rosy paintbrush, which I thought was a good omen.

A soft knock at my door came seconds before Mom's voice greeted me. "I haven't heard you humming for a while," she said. She crossed to where I was standing and took a closer look at the picture of the flower. "That's really pretty."

"I'll give it to you for your birthday."

Mom's laugh tinkled lightly, a sound I'd sorely missed. "Which painting should I take down to make room?"

"I appreciate your enthusiastic support of my art." I smiled.

"I didn't get to hear much about how finals week went."

She moved to sit on the side of my bed and twisted her torso to rest her arms on my foot board. There were still some shadows under her eyes, but they didn't concern me the way they had before. I knew time would help, along with the freedom that came from having answers—even if they were harsh. Limbo had worn her down far more than heartbreak seemed to be doing.

"I won't hear my results for another week or so, but I feel pretty good now that it's all over. I have to say, I'm really looking forward to a couple weeks of sweet freedom."

"I'm proud of you. One year under your belt. That's more than I ever did."

I looked over my shoulder at her as my paintbrush stirred some colors. "Do you regret not going to college?"

She pinched her lips and shook her head. "No, not really. I never felt that pull. You, however, you're meant for more."

I turned fully away from the canvas as her words struck me. "It's not that I'm trying to be more than you were." I paused, unsure of how to express my thoughts without insulting her. In the end, I didn't have to. She was my mom, and moms everywhere want more for their children than they have.

"It's okay to admit that things have been rough around here and that was a catalyst for you taking more control of your future." Her look was tender. "I do want more for you than what I'm living through." Her voice sounded detached, as though she were seeing long ago images in her mind. I could practically hear it when she snapped back to the present. "I have no regrets, though. The choices I made were right for me, and I look forward to seeing where your path takes you."

"I'm glad you're doing better." I felt hesitant about saying anything. I wasn't sure if we were talking about that yet or not.

She sighed. "Me too, honey. I have to be honest, I've been worried that watching me and Dad would make you steer clear of finding love."

"Oh yeah?"

"Yes. Just because we didn't work out doesn't mean that love is a lie."

I turned back to the canvas and lifted my brush to make the first stroke that would eventually turn into one of the petals of the flower, and thought about what she'd said.

"Connor seems like a man who would pull his weight and be happy doing it." Surprised, I turned with my paintbrush still in the air. She grinned. "I know the two of you are dating. Sadie is a chatterbox. Do your future plans include him?"

I shook my head. "It's only been a couple of weeks. It's too early to know how he'd play into my future plans." Lies, lies, lies. I'd done my fair share of daydreaming.

"Then your plans haven't changed as far as schooling and moving to a larger city for work?"

My brows dropped and I shook my head. "Why should they? I don't see a reason to change them." The sternness in my voice was out of proportion to the question, and I knew it, but I wasn't ready to really say any of this out loud.

"Oh, sorry, I must have misunderstood. I thought you really liked him."

"I do."

She unfolded her arms and held up her hands. "It's a natural question, honey, but one with no right answer. If you and Connor are happy with how things are, then there is plenty of time to figure it all out."

"Exactly."

She stood and came to stand next to me. She put a hand on my shoulder and squeezed. "For what it's worth, I've decided I like Connor."

I looked over at her. "Why?"

"You aren't an easy person to impress, or to get close to. He's done both. Plus, he makes your cheeks turn pink."

"My cheeks aren't pink."

"As pink as cotton candy." Mom laughed as she left the room, leaving the sound of it lingering behind her.

During my dinner shift that night I kept thinking about what Mom had asked about my future plans and Connor. The fact was that I'd thought quite a bit about it, even though I tried to stop myself. I was going to school to be a nurse and I was dating Connor—they were two different tracks in my head that I'd tried to keep separate. However, the lines were blurring and it was overwhelming. My mind worked over the issue while I took orders, cleared tables, filled drinks, and chatted with customers.

What did I want? I wanted the same things I always had. I wanted to be financially independent and secure, and find happiness in knowing I would be in charge of my own destiny.

How would I make that happen? By going to school and establishing myself in a good career.

Where did I want that to happen? I used to be totally committed to seeking out the new in Springfield, but as that thought rolled through my mind, I felt a tug in my gut that made me question it. The truth was that I was no longer sure I needed to leave Oak Hills to make that happen. Oak Hills had a health clinic and a few doctor's offices. There was also a retirement home in a neighboring town that always seemed to be advertising for nursing staff.

I'd always associated the life I was trying to create with the need to leave my sleepy little town. But now I wondered if the one thing I was trying to escape was the fear of being dependent. If that was the case, I'd fear that wherever I lived. If I found purpose and a career here, then I could find financial freedom here while still being with the people I loved. Where was I trying to run to?

The clearing of my thoughts brought me to a standstill as it solidified in my mind. Oak Hills wasn't the problem. I could have a good, stable life anywhere I chose to build one. I'd been so busy looking for happiness outside of the familiar that I'd discounted my own strength and the ability I had to make my life whatever I wanted it to be. I'd been putting myself in a box and never understood that. All my judgments and prejudices had only hurt me.

"Liv, I'm going to send you home early and call someone else in if you don't put your head into the game," Jake growled at me.

I unfroze, suddenly aware that I'd been staring into the kitchen through the window. I cringed, deserving the set down. "Sorry, Jake. I think I just had an epiphany."

"Well, if you need a doctor go see one. Otherwise get back to work." He slammed a plate down into the window with the practice of someone who knew exactly how to get attention without breaking anything.

I shook my head, a smile warming my face. "No, I'm great, actually." I picked up the plate and got back to work.

The next couple of hours flew while I cast away old thoughts in favor of new ones. The truly amazing thing was that these new thoughts were more empowering than the protective, shielded thoughts I'd been surrounding myself with. Staying skeptical of love and wary of partnership was only feeding into itself by keeping me alone and scared.

I felt almost giddy with emotion when my shift ended. I needed to tell Connor everything. It was late, but I decided to drive past his house anyhow. I appreciated the clever way his mind worked and knew that together we could cut through all the smoke to settle on something new. I trusted him with my future, and the realization had my hands trembling on the steering wheel.

His porch light wasn't on, but his screen door was open, emitting a soft glow that showed his shadowy form in the swing when I pulled into the driveway behind his truck. I was glad he was still up. I knew he went to bed early, having to open shop at 7:00 AM. I'd served him enough 6:30 breakfasts to know.

He stood and walked down the porch steps, reaching my door by the time I'd parked and killed the engine. I got out and walked straight into a hug, one of his arms coming around me while the other shut my car door.

"Livy," he said softly, bending close so that his lips were near my ear, "this is a nice surprise."

The greeting made my scalp tingle. I did my best to return the embrace, but I was nearly dancing with the enormity of what I'd discovered today. My hands felt like they had live wires shooting out of my fingertips, and I wiggled out of his embrace without exactly meaning to. He looked down at me with a curious smile.

Words rushed out. "I'm sorry it's so late, but I really had to talk to you." I belatedly noticed that he was wearing flannel pajama pants and a white T-shirt, and his feet were bare. He'd been relaxing for a minute before going to bed. "I should have called first."

"You're welcome here anytime." He ruined the effect by yawning widely and covering it with a hand.

I deflated a little, wanting so badly to talk to him, but equally wanting to let him have his rest. I rocked from one foot to another as I tried to decide what to do. "I feel silly now, but I wanted to chat with you. It's nothing big. I can wait until tomorrow."

I took a step back, intending to leave, but he cut me off and wrapped his hands lightly around the tops of my arms. "Nice try. I know you better than that. You've got something on your mind. Come sit down and tell me what it is."

"It really can wait, Connor. You need your rest." Only, I didn't want to wait. I wanted to share everything with him so much that my chest felt tight.

"Nah," he replied with a light nudge toward his porch. "I'll rest another time. Besides, the night is perfect for sitting outside."

I took his hand and walked to the swing, where I sat down on one side and tucked myself back into a corner so that I could face him where he was sitting on the other end. Connor pulled my feet onto his lap and pushed the swing into a rocking motion, gazing toward the yard. It felt like we'd done this a thousand times, as though we'd always been meant to swing together on this porch with peace surrounding us. For the first time in forever, I felt like I'd stepped into my real life. This was real. Connor was real.

I spent a few seconds simply taking him in. I felt humbled and extremely lucky that he'd seen something in me worth waiting on. Emotion, sudden and hot, rose in my throat when he gazed back at me. I could feel that heat rise to my face, and I tried to take a few breaths to ward off the sudden moisture in my eyes. I loved him.

Connor, of course, saw it and his eyes grew worried. "What's wrong?"

I licked my lips and cleared my throat. Where to start? I supposed that the beginning was good, so I said, "My mom asked me today what my future plans are."

"Oh, yeah?"

"Yeah. I told her that they're pretty much the same they've always been. To be financially independent and secure in a good career."

Connor nodded, but I could feel the way the swing stuttered for a moment before resuming its steady motion. "You've told me that a few times too."

I chuckled. "Yeah, I think I've told it to anyone who I've talked to at all in this past year."

He attempted a grin, but it didn't reach his eyes. "It's a good goal."

"It is. I think it's really smart for people to take as much control of their destiny as they can, you know?" He nodded. "I guess what I'm saying is, that, um, nothing has really changed in that respect. I still want a degree and all that."

"Sure."

"So, then my mom asked if my future plans include you."

At this the swing stopped and he sat up straight in his corner. "Oh?"

"Yeah. I was kind of surprised she'd ask. It's only been a few weeks, right?" He nodded slowly and clasped his hands in front of him. "What can you really know in a month?" I shook my head and then realized I was making him think I didn't obsess over him constantly. I was botching this badly. "I'm making a mess of this."

"No, I think I understand what you're saying," he said in a soft voice.

I sighed loudly. "Thank goodness." I pulled a face. "It's kind of strange to already be thinking about our future together when everything is still so new."

"Yeah."

"For a long time all I've thought about is getting out of Oak Hills and making something of my life, and then my mom asked me about my future, and it was like all these thoughts just came crashing down on me. It took me all night at the diner to process everything. But I think I figured it out, and that's why I had to talk to you tonight."

His eyes had dropped to his lap while I'd been talking, hiding his expression from me as his shoulders tensed. "So being independent and getting away from Oak Hills are what you need to be happy," he stated.

My eyes scrunched up. "Well, not exactly . . . "

"Oh, right, and money," he interrupted. "A lot of money, and being secure and in charge of your own destiny."

I shook my head, my expression falling further. "No. That's not what I'm trying to say."

He finally looked up, and the way his eyes shot at me caused my heart to skip a beat. I pulled my feet off his lap and let them fall to the porch while I sat up.

His voice was cool when he said, "Sorry. You just want to have enough money that you'll never be stuck depending on anyone. That's what you've been saying ever since you finally started talking to me. Money, security, and running from this junk pile of a town." He stood suddenly, making the swing bump hard enough to almost topple me. My eyes darted up to follow his movement.

I stood too, my mouth opening and closing while I shook my head. "No, Connor, no. You're misunderstanding me. Please let me finish." I'd always been bad with expressing myself, and now my mind was frozen with worry.

"Okay. Finish." His eyes were like granite as he folded his arms over his chest.

This was a Connor I'd never seen. I'd seen angry before, but this was different. This was angry with a layer of hurt and disappointment, and all of those emotions were directed at me. Before I could work out what to say, he jumped back in.

"Actually, don't finish. I'm smart enough to recognize a breakup speech when I hear one."

It was like a punch to the gut. "What? You've been expecting me to break up with you?" He was supposed to understand me. He was supposed to trust me like I trusted him. But he obviously didn't, and the way my stomach dropped told me I'd never eat again.

"And here you are, fulfilling that prophecy." His voice was hard.

In confusion I matched his hard tone. "I don't understand you. Just the other night you told me you'd been waiting for a chance to be together. Why would you date me at all if you expected me to end it?"

"I could ask you the same question. Why would you date me, knowing you never intended to stick around? You just told me you were shocked when your mom asked if there was a place for me in your future, like you'd never thought about it at all. Do you know how that feels to hear when all I do is think about you and our future? You say it's too soon, but it's not for me. I have been waiting for a chance to be with you. I'm a fool for believing it would go anywhere when you're . . . " He cut off what he was going to say, but before I could speak he almost shouted, "I'm not a risk, Liv. I have a steady job, I have a home, and I'm not a bad guy. What else do you have to have from someone? Are you really that difficult to please?"

His words ignited an insulted fire in me. "Just because you're a good guy who has a steady job doesn't mean that I should suddenly give up my personal goals and rewrite my entire future. That kind of stuff takes time and thought. It's not all emotion."

"It's not all science either. It's chemistry, and going with your gut, and just knowing things without overthinking them."

Now I was ticked, which was good because it masked the gaping hole that was growing in my heart. "I've seen what happens when people dive in with no plan or no foresight, and I'm not living my life that way."

His eyes shuttered. "I'm not spending my life trying to convince someone that I'm worth sticking around for."

My stomach heaved once more in agony. "Is this how you do it?" I asked in horror. "You reel the girls in and then when they fall for you, you pick a fight with them so they'll handle the breakup for you?"

I tried to stalk around him, but he stepped in front of me. "You're blaming me for this?"

"That's what you do, right? Break girls' hearts?" I hissed.

"No, Liv. You're the heartbreaker. You're the one unwilling to see any version of the future if it isn't the one you create. You're the one walking out on me." He leaned in close, and I almost shriveled on the spot at the look of utter, bleak disappointment that he was trying so hard to mask.

I struck back, my own hurt making me just as vicious. "I didn't come here to break up with you, Connor. Far from it. I actually *have* thought about our future together, but one hint of misunderstanding, and you're shutting down and bowing out. Guess neither of us can escape our assumptions about each other." I spoke cruelly. "We're both meant to be alone." The last words came out on a broken wobble. How could he not see past my words to how I was feeling? Did he truly not understand that he held my heart in his hands and I'd never get it back if he let me go?

His face shifted and his eyes froze. "Looks that way." We stood like blocks of ice, staring, hearts pounding for several seconds before he took a step away from me. "Goodbye, Liv."

Red hot fire flared up in my chest. "Just remember when you wake up tomorrow and you think over what happened tonight, that *you* broke *my* heart," I stuttered out on a voice thin with despair as my mind screamed, *Please don't do this, Connor. Please don't let me go.*

He said nothing as he walked into the house, slamming the door behind him. I fled down the porch steps and to my car. The sound of the engine starting shattered the awful silence around me, and I sobbed the entire way home, barely seeing the road, and praying for the night to swallow me whole.

CHAPTER TWENTY-SEVEN

The facts were in. My track record with love was complete trash. In the past five months I'd had two boyfriends and two break-ups. One had left me feeling melancholy. One was ripping my heart out piece by piece, each breath painful.

The day after the horrifying misunderstanding with Connor I had the lunch shift at the diner, but I couldn't sleep and by six o'clock in the morning I was rage-cleaning the entire house. When Mom and Sadie questioned me about it, I crashed onto the couch in a pile of tear-soaked blankets while they did their best to comfort me.

I showed up to work with the same enthusiasm as a kid going out-side to scoop dog poop. Thankfully Kelly had the same shift. I texted her something dramatic, and she quickly agreed to show up fifteen minutes early so that I could fill her in on the entire debacle. We sat down next to each other at a table where she appropriately expressed her undying need for vengeance and offered to bust his kneecaps.

"The thing is, I went over there to tell him that I realized I didn't need to move or break up or any of those things to be happy. Instead I made a total mess by bumbling through it and he purposefully misun-derstood. He dropped me without letting me finish or try to explain. I don't understand. I thought we had a good thing. I know it had only been about a month, but he'd become such a part of my life that I actually thought he might be my . . . "

"Soul mate?" Kelly finished when I couldn't. I shrugged. "Would you be more comfortable calling him your best bet for evolutionary coupling? The one with the highest probability of success?"

This made me laugh, and I leaned over to hug her with one arm. "No. Science has nothing to do with how I'm feeling. If science were everything, I'd be dead right now because my heart literally stopped beating last night."

"What are you going to do?" she asked as I released her.

"I don't know what to do. This isn't the first time he's gotten mad at me, if you'll remember. After the tire iron incident he froze me out for a week. Maybe I don't want to be in a relationship with someone who reacts this way when they're upset with me."

Kelly nodded. "You'd be at risk of hypothermia daily."

"I'm serious. I need someone who can take the lumps with me and keep communicating."

"I agree with you, so don't shoot me a dirty look when I say this, but I don't think Connor knows what to do with all the emotions you bring alive in him."

"That was super cheesy."

"Deal with it." She pursed her lips. "I'm saying that the tire iron thing scared him really bad, but you hadn't exactly admitted you liked each other, and he didn't know how to react or what to do."

"Fine. What about the other night? I really messed up what I was trying to say, and believe me, I have replayed that conversation in my head a million times, but the fact still remains that he reacted before hearing me out. Then the ice man showed up."

"Didn't he say something about not spending his life proving he's worth sticking around for?" I nodded. "His mom left him, Liv. His mother. Now he loves this new woman, maybe for the first time in his life, and he hears her saying something that sounds like he isn't going to be enough to keep her here, and he overreacts to that. Didn't you do the same thing to Blaine when he tried to make you into his plastic Barbie doll wife?"

"Yes, but I went home and thought about it first. I didn't break up with him on the spot." I bowed my head over the table and closed my eyes as I processed what she was saying. There was a lot of truth there, and my heart ached even more at the thought of Connor feeling like he was expendable to me.

"I have to talk to him again," I said. "Try to say the things I wanted to say the other night. I can't just let him walk away from me."

She put a hand on my forearm and squeezed. "Good. I'll bet he's feeling as mopey as you are. So, after the shift today, go to the grocery store and buy him some apology meat. Then, take it to the shop and lock him in that office until he agrees to eat your meat, and only your meat, for the rest of your lives."

"Great idea." I sat up straight and nodded my head. "I can do this."

"Do you want to practice on me so that you don't choke again?"

"How's this: Connor, you stupid oaf, I was trying to tell you the other night that I want to adjust my future plans and create something new with you."

"Sounds good. Just make sure you throw in something about how temperamental and unreasonable he was being. People really like to hear that."

"Smart. I'll lead with an insult."

"Definitely do, because making up is the best part of any argument." Kelly stood and shot me an exaggerated wink as she went to tie on her apron and pull up her hair. "You going to make it through this shift, or am I going to be doing double duty?"

I stood and went to my locker to retrieve my own apron and change into my work shoes. "I think I can manage."

"Good."

In the end I only got yelled at once by Jake and twice by a customer. Pretty good for a woman with her head buried firmly in the automotive shop down the street. I made it through my shift and hustled out as quickly as possible when four o'clock came around. My stomach was in knots as I pulled out of the diner and came to a stop at the one light in town. As predicted, I hadn't been able to eat all day. The grocery store was the opposite direction of Mainstreet Mechanic, but I liked Kelly's idea of showing up with some steaks. It would hopefully make him laugh and break the ice . . . and I desperately wanted the ice to be broken.

The light turned green and I proceeded forward, visions of Connor's amber eyes smiling at me and his low voice quietly telling me he was sorry too. I was so distracted thinking about a blazing hot makeup kiss that I didn't notice the car running the red light on my right side.

The car slammed into me, and I slammed into the door with enough force to make my head spin in time with my car. When the rotation was complete, I was facing back in the direction of the diner. My head was pounding, small white lights twinkling in my vision while I blinked slowly to try to get rid of the blurriness. I heard voices yelling, and then a man poked his head inside the passenger window that had been broken upon impact.

"Liv? Is that you?" It was Mr. Matthews, a neighbor of mine. He was wearing his trademark ball cap, and his white mustache moved up and down when he talked.

"Yeah," I groaned.

"You okay? Can you move?"

"I . . . " I wiggled my toes and fingers, but a shooting pain raced up my left arm when I attempted to move it, making the stars reappear and my head swim while my stomach dipped. "My left arm. I think something's wrong."

"Hold still. We've called 911. Help is on the way."

"What happened?"

"Some kid ran the red light just as you were getting into the intersection. Didn't even slow down. Must have been doing thirty at least."

Nausea burned up my throat and I closed my eyes, wishing it back down. I would not humiliate myself by throwing up all over the place. I took a few deep breaths, my lips quivering from the pain and adrenaline. I could feel a little trickle of warm fluid running down my face and reached up with my right hand to find that I'd cut the left side of my forehead as well. It didn't seem to be a large cut, but head wounds are bleeders.

"Mr. Matthews?" I called when I felt like I had a handle on things.

"Still here."

"Please call my mom."

"Sure thing."

I heard sirens, and everything became a blur as the police and paramedics showed up. They asked me a few questions before they removed me from the car and put me in the ambulance. I rode quietly in the rig while they did their work of bandaging my head and getting some pain meds started in an IV to help with the arm situation.

When we reached the hospital, they wheeled me straight into the ER. I kept my eyes closed the entire time, only opening them when the door to my exam room closed behind the EMTs. A nurse was standing at the computer next to the exam table, typing some things in that the rescue workers had told her about my situation.

"How bad is my arm?" I asked her.

She glanced over and smiled. "I've seen worse."

"Not the most comforting answer."

"Yes, welcome to the hospital."

It made me chuckle, which was probably her intention, and I decided to remember the technique for when I became a nurse myself.

A doctor came in and sent me directly to X-ray, which made me want to scream in agony as I had to hold a clearly very broken arm in a few different positions. It was then that I got my first glance at the damage. No skin was broken, but my arm was bent between the wrist and elbow at a very incorrect angle. I found it fascinating rather than disgusting, which was a good thing, considering my career aspirations.

I was wheeled back to my room and helped back up to rest on the bed, my arm still resting tightly at my side. I dozed a little, trying to breathe through the aches and pains that the medicine was barely dulling, when I heard the door open and Mom came in followed by a disheveled Sadie.

"Oh, thank goodness you're okay." Mom came straight to my side and brushed back my curls to kiss the right side of my head. "You can't imagine what that phone call did to me."

One side of my lip curled up. "I *can* imagine, actually." I looked to Sadie, who was standing near Mom with a worried expression. "You look a little less put together than usual."

"I was in the middle of dance rehearsal when Mom came and dragged me out. I think I'm actually the most traumatized of the group. She comes in waving her hands and calling my name and yelling something about an accident and Liv being taken by ambulance." She shook her head. "I'm going to need therapy."

"We can split the cost of the couch," I replied. She grinned and tapped a finger against my knee. It was her way of telling me she was glad I was okay.

Mom fussed around with my blankets and pillows for a while before settling down next to Sadie, who had immediately flopped into a chair when she realized I'd live. I told them my version of events, and then they slipped into light chatter while I closed my eyes.

Eventually a doctor came in and introduced himself as Dr. Wilson. He was older and looked friendly, which put me at ease. "How is your pain?"

"It's not great, but I'm surviving," I replied.

"I thought that might be the case. I'm going to increase your dose a little. You'll probably start to feel sleepier, so let's get to this information before I do that."

He put my X-rays up to a light and began explaining what had happened to my arm and what would need to happen to fix it. Before he'd said more than a few sentences, the door to my exam room flew open and a harried looking Connor burst into the scene. He was holding a very worn-out looking bouquet of flowers and was wearing his gray work coveralls and a ball cap. His eyes looked wildly around the room before landing on me. He took a step closer, but the doctor suddenly blocked his way.

"Who are you and why are you in this room?" he said to Connor.

Connor's eyes took in every detail from the bandage on my head to the way I was cradling my arm. He didn't bother looking at the doctor when he replied, "I'm with Liv."

The doctor turned to me. "Is this true, Miss Phelps?" I felt my face heat as I nodded, loving those three simple words: *I'm with Liv.* Man, I hoped that was true. "Fine then, but we can't have this many people in here, so someone will need to leave." Sadie immediately jumped up and headed out the door without saying a word.

Dr. Wilson gestured to the empty chair, and Connor sat down next to Mom. I studiously avoided his eyes while the doctor continued to explain what the X-rays were telling us. I couldn't listen to any of it. All I could hear was the tapping of Connor's nervous foot on the floor and the crinkling sound of him messing with those poor flowers. I got little out of what the doctor said other than my arm was broken and they would need to reset something and I'd be put under anesthesia for the procedure. When the doctor finished he looked to me and asked if I had any questions. I did, actually. I needed him to repeat the entire thing with Connor out of the room, but I shook my head.

Dr. Wilson came to stand near my IV and pressed a few buttons, increasing the medicine as promised before he left. "A nurse will be in soon to take you up to surgery."

Mom turned to me. "Are you okay with everything?" I nodded. She cleared her throat. I knew she was wondering what to do. Just that morning she'd cradled me while I'd sobbed out my heartbreak over the man who was currently sitting next to her. "Well, I could use a drink and I'll check on Sadie. Connor, are you okay to sit with Liv for a bit?" He nodded and Mom left the room.

The silence became unbearable as I continued to look anywhere but at him. I found a favorite place on the ceiling and counted tiles. He didn't make a peep. It was like he was a wax figure of himself. What was he doing here? I hadn't had a chance to buy my apology steak.

"What?" he said.

Oops. Maybe I'd said that out loud. I looked to him for the first time. "What?"

"You said you were buying an apology steak?"

I looked back up at the ceiling. "I was on my way to talk to you when the accident happened."

"You were going the opposite direction."

"I was going to buy meat as a peace offering."

"Really?"

I nodded and silence descended again. I hated it. Connor and I had never had trouble talking, even when we weren't supposed to be friends. I closed my eyes and let out a heavy breath.

"Are you in pain?" he asked.

I ignored his question. "How did you know I was hurt?"

"I'm the one they called to tow your car."

"Of course."

"It wasn't a very professional tow. I was in a hurry to get to you, and I'm not sure I bothered to hook all the chains up correctly."

"Oh, yeah?" I felt amusement tug at my lips.

The sound of a zipper was loud in the room, and I chanced a quick slit-eyed glance in his direction. He'd set the poor droopy flowers down and was unzipping the top of his coveralls and pulling his arms out. He wore a blue T-shirt underneath with the Snap-On Tools logo printed on the front. He tied the arms of his coveralls around his waist, keeping the pants on. When he looked back in my direction I quickly closed my eyes again.

"I lost my head a little when I showed up and it was your car and everyone was talking about how you'd been taken by ambulance."

I nodded. "This town really likes to tell stories."

A screeching sound started as he slid his chair across the floor to the right side of the bed, which sank a little where he leaned on it. A fission of familiar awareness rushed through me when his voice spoke nearby. "Why were you buying steaks?"

"I was going to come talk to you, and they were my 'get in the door' offering."

"Ah. Smart move. What were you coming to talk to me about?"

"I was going to open with insulting your intelligence."

"Understandably." One of his hands came up to play comfortingly with my curls, the backs of his fingers brushing against my cheek. I loved it.

"Then I was going to ask you what your problem was, and if your father raised a complete moron."

"Seems redundant, as you'd already have insulted my intellect, and unfair to my father who has nothing to do with my issues." I pinched my lips and he cleared his throat. "Sorry, please go on."

"Then I was going to ask where you get off breaking up with me, and not listening to what I was trying to say."

"Yeah. Sounds like you're headed in the right direction."

"Next I was going to suggest you stop freezing me out when you don't like something I've done." I opened my eyes and turned my head slightly to meet his gaze. He'd taken off his ball cap, and his face was so close, his eyes so familiar that I wanted to sob, but I forced the emotion away.

"Livy . . . " He opened his mouth but I shook my head.

"Not done. I'm not perfect. I overreact, say things wrong, make mistakes, get grumpy, and will annoy you day in and day out. But what I actually came over to tell you the other night is that when my mom asked me those questions it made me think, a lot, and I've realized I don't need to search for happiness somewhere else when I have it right here. I can reach for my dreams without walking away."

I could see his throat work as his eyes scanned my face. "I thought you didn't want me."

"Please refer back to the part about being an interrupting dummy."

"During my lunch break today I bought you flowers."

I raised my eyebrows as my eyes grew large. "Really?"

"Yes. I was going to come over after work and beg you to ignore everything I'd said last night, because I couldn't let you go."

I felt a sudden sadness for this man who wanted nothing more than to have a companion who chose to stay with him, but who had been willing to chase me down and beg. I smiled softly at him and reached out to hold his hand. "Just so you know, I would have let you beg for a while first, but I would have stayed. I never meant to leave anyhow."

"I almost ruined everything."

"You had a little help from this bumbling idiot." I pulled a face.

"I hardly slept at all last night," he admitted quietly. "I've been practicing what I was going to say to you when I got off work."

"What were you going to say?" I asked.

"You want me to tell you now?"

"We're alone and I'm on high doses of pain medication. Seems like a good time."

"I was going to tell you that I don't want to control your life. I don't want you to give things up to be with me. I only want to be your partner and work together and . . . "

"Okay."

"Okay? But I'm not done yet."

I grinned. "You already said the really important things, and I don't want you to make me too many promises because I'll hold you to them."

His face lightened and he dropped his head to lay on my shoulder. "I won't ask you to change who you are, because then you wouldn't be you anymore. I knew who you were when we started dating. Nothing about your hopes and dreams is a surprise to me."

"I like who you are too."

"I'll probably lose my temper, get bossy, tease you too much, and all sorts of other tiring things."

I leaned my cheek down to rest against his hair. "Probably."

"I hope I won't ever make you feel like I know what's best for your life, because I don't. I hope you'll trust me enough to be a sounding board when you're making decisions, and that you'll believe that all I want is for you to be happy."

I shook my head. "Stop, stop, stop." I laughed. "You don't have to say all these things."

He ignored me and pushed on. "I've watched you for a long time, and I think you're the most beautiful girl I've ever known, Liv." My stomach dropped like I was on a roller coaster. Connor Hunt thought I was beautiful? And he was still talking. "I want you to paint. I want you to find a place for that in your life. I want you to travel and see new things. I can't stand the thought of you feeling like I was trying to clip your wings."

"Do you know what I really want from you?" I asked in a soft voice as I began to feel sleepy.

"What?"

"I just want you to try to forgive me when I make a mud pie out of life, and to keep me from accidentally killing myself."

"That's a pretty big job for one man."

"You're up to it." My head felt heavier and my eyes closed. "And, Connor, I want you to be happy too. You don't have to give everything up for me either. Partners fifty-fifty, okay?"

"I'm sorry about last night."

"Me too. I should have sat on your head until you listened."

"I'd like to request an addition to our pact: No physical violence."

My laugh turned into a yawn, and I nodded. "You have a deal."

"You do realize that this little conversation means two things."

"Oh yeah?"

He grinned. "First, I get to call you my girlfriend, officially."

"Fair enough, but only because you're pretty good-looking and it gives me street cred to be seen with you."

"Second, you owe me some meat." He leaned forward and kissed me softly. I wanted it to last forever, but I could feel things beginning to go fuzzy. "I'm falling in love with you, Miss Olivia Phelps," he whispered as things went from fuzzy to black.

"You lose this round, Hunt. I fell for you a long time ago."

EPILOGUE

Livy, can you hand me that socket wrench?" Connor's voice interrupted my studying, and I flicked him an annoyed look. "Where is it?"

"That one right there. It's silver."

"They're all silver."

"It's the one that makes the ratcheting sounds you love so much." He grunted as he pushed at something under the hood of the car he was working on.

"Fine." I stood up from the big office chair that he'd rolled out and I'd officially claimed as my study zone. "You've sure gotten lazy these past few months."

"I tried to warn you about spoiling me rotten."

"What do you do when I'm not here and a tool is out of reach?" I reached into the toolbox and held up a wrench with a questioning look. He nodded that it was the correct one.

"I spend all my time moping around and get hardly any work done."

I walked to where he was standing with his hands deep in machinery. The Jeep he was working on was lifted and bright yellow. I'd told him at least ten times that he shouldn't ask me any questions if it disappeared as soon as the repairs were done.

"Obviously." I nodded and grinned, happy to hear he was lost without me, and headed back to the chair. Before I could reach it, he had turned with more speed than I could imagine and had me wrapped in his arms, my back pressed along his front. "Connor, you're going to get grease all over my clothes." I pretended to be annoyed, but we both knew I loved being close to him.

"What? These sweats of yours?" He used a hand to pull at my sleeve. "You used to at least try to dress nice for me."

I laughed and leaned my head back to rest on his shoulder. "Don't fool yourself. I've never dressed nice for you. I've dressed nice for myself here and there." He tickled my waist and I squealed. "Fine, it was all for you," I said. "I dress like this because I can't afford to ruin any more clothes in this grease warehouse."

"This place isn't the problem. It's your accidents that cover you in grease."

"I'll never admit that. It's about warmth and nothing more. It's the middle of winter."

His lips pressed along the side of my neck, and I felt the same tingles run straight down my spine as I had for the past nine months. "You can't blame me for wanting to keep you close."

I couldn't. Sometimes I felt so sad when I thought about the years I thought he was the devil. We could have had so many more memories together than we had now. I close my eyes against the regret, and as always, he sensed the shift in me. His arms tightened, and his cheek pressed against mine.

"No regrets, love. Just gratitude for where we are now."

He was right. I turned in his arms and, oblivious to the grease and grime, stood on tiptoes to put my arms around his neck. "I love you."

I really did. I'd tried too many times to tell him how he'd changed my life, but words failed me. With Connor I had a rock-steady foundation. He remained unchanged from day to day, as reliable as a watch, dedicated, and principled. My needs were met before I knew I had them. He was my best friend, my study partner, my art critic, my travel agent, and the one who made me laugh the hardest. Our banter brought so much light, and his love brought that completely unscientific chemistry rushing through my days. His stability gave me freedom that I'd never understood when I thought I had to be at the helm of everything. He'd taught me the value of a partner in helping me reach for the stars.

In return I hoped I'd brought the same sense of partnership to his life. I tried to look out for him, as I finally understood the difference between being served and being pitied. I was forgiving of his long work hours and as protective of our time together as he was. I was his sounding board, his cheerleader, and I did my best to make sure there was time for fun. We had formed a team of two, and it was the most precious thing in the world to me.

"What's not to love?" he joked. I playfully pretended to swat at him, but he caught my wrist and straightened the diamond ring he had placed on my hand last month before leaning in to kiss me.

I fell happily into the familiar rhythm of it. The colors swirled differently now. Fewer bright flashes and more blissful whirls that still made my heart pound even as they pulled me in and centered me, always offering exactly what I'm looking for.

When Connor had proposed he had also given me a small gift, a quote by Mother Teresa that he'd framed: "The greatest science in the world; in heaven and on earth; is love."

I treasure that quote, but between you and me, I've come to believe that there are some things that have nothing whatsoever to do with science.

ABOUT THE AUTHOR

Aspen Hadley loves nothing more than a great story. She has devoted herself to storytelling for the majority of her life, writing her first novel at her kitchen table in the eighth grade with pen and paper. The tools have improved, but her love of stories remains the same.

Outside of writing, Aspen's number-one hobby is reading. Number two is sneaking chocolate into and out of her private stash without being caught. Other favorite things include playing the piano, eating ice cream, traveling, a good case of the giggles, monthly dinners with her friends, and riding ATVs over the red rock and mountains of Utah.

Aspen shares her life with her patient husband, four hilarious children, and one grumpy dog in a quiet Utah suburb next to her beloved mountains. *Suits and Spark Plugs* is her third published novel, and she hopes there will be many more to come. You can follow along and share some laughs by finding her on Facebook at facebook.com/aspenthewriter/ and Instagram @aspenhadley_author.

Scan to visit

aspenmariehadley.com